DARK GOLD

GEOFF LYNN

Neil & Vicci

I hope you enjoy reading this book as much as I did writing it.

Geoff Lynn.

Dark Gold © 2017
Geoff Lynn

ISBN: 978-1-925732-18-4 (paperback)

This is a work of fiction. Names, character, places and incidents either are the product of the author's imagination or are used fictitiously, and any resemblance to any actual person, living or dead, events, or locales is entirely coincidental.

Cataloguing-in-Publication information for this title is listed with the National Library of Australia.

Published by **Geoff Lynn** and InHouse Publishing
www.inhousepublishing.com.au

IN HOUSE PTY LTD PUBLISHING

Dedicated to my three children,
Jenni, Saphron and Jamie, my three best friends

300BC

The Phoenician Bireme weltered precariously as it navigated through the immense swells. The vessel, built for the calmer seas of the Mediterranean, was no match for the vast, unpredictability of the unknown waters.

Master of the Bireme, The High Priest, stood at the helm, resplendent in the traditional red brocade gallabiyah, inlaid with precious gems; draped around his neck was a solid gold chain with a medallion, the status symbol bearing the crest of his reign and from the region from which he hailed.

Although remarkable seafaring people, The Phoenicians had not ventured so far from home. The Kings and High Priest Council of the Elders had ordered their ships to explore the seas to find new trading partners. With only the planets and stars of the solar systems to guide them, they sailed from the comfort of the calm Mediterranean into the vast unchartered oceans; their cargo filled with casks of wines, fine linens, rich embroidered fabrics and purple dye. Hidden in the bowels of the ship, concealed under a secret trapdoor lay an ornate bronze casket filled with gold coins for the purchase of woven cloth and suchlike for textile manufacturing.

One hundred oarsmen, their muscular bodies glistening with rivulets of sweat as they moved in synchronisation to the well-timed beat from the man who stood before them; striking his goatskin drum with monotonous regularity. With each pulsating strike, the men skimmed their oars through the water in circular motions. The propulsive power controlling the speed in which they travelled

The Priest ordered the drummer to beat faster, deciding there was a need for haste. Striking his drum and quickening his pace with a rhythmic thump… thump… thump the oarsmen moved in harmony through the escalating swells, increasing to an unbelievable seven knots. Having voyaged for many weeks without sighting land it was imperative they reached terra firma soon as provisions were dwindling. Now surviving on meagre rations, the men were weakening and losing heart.

The thirty metre Phoenician Bireme built from Lebanese Cedar had a curved post at the stern, bent in the shape of a Scorpion tail, while the decorative carving at the bow, resembled a face; embodying the spirit of the ship to placate the Gods. The tall timber mast just off centre, strained with the weight of the large rectangular cloth sail, strengthened by leather straps that now billowed in the strong winds.

Dramatic black clouds filled the sky and without warning a jagged bolt of lightning illuminated the heavens followed by an ear piercing clash of thunder; spreading the fear of God throughout the Bireme. Heavy rain fell, drenching the men who struggled to hold on to the wet oars in the fulcrums. A loud crashing sound vibrated through the vessel as the large waves lifted it high in the air, before dropping it down into a concave water bowl, threatening to turn them over. The High Priest fell to his knees and gazed upwards, being of the belief the Gods must be angry with him for daring to venture into their oceans without an offering. He prayed for their forgiveness.

The ferocity of the wind proved too much for the sail, causing it to stretch to capacity. There was a sudden loud cracking sound as the mast snapped in half. Falling to the deck, it shattered the amphora that stored the last dregs of their fresh water; and landed across two unsuspecting oarsmen, crushing them without mercy. Copious amounts of blood mixed with rainwater spread over the timber decking. The two men stared with vacant eyes into the heavens before closing them forever. Ripped from its fixings, the sail blew away with the wind, disappearing into the storm.

At the sight of his dead men, The Priest was in a dilemma. The Phoenicians were free men, and entitled to a ceremonial burial. However, this was neither the time nor the place for such a ritual, as their lives were in danger. With a heavy heart, he ordered six crewmen to release the dead oarsmen and together with the mast, throw them overboard.

Lowering the broken bodies into the sea, the men showed great sadness. The Priest knelt and prayed for their souls, then ordered the drummer to resume beating his drum. Before long the remaining oarsmen, picked up their pace, continuing on their journey.

The man holding the rudder suddenly gave out a loud cry making everyone look towards him. He had spotted a mountainous land mass in the distance and was pointing hysterically. The

Priest rose to his feet craning his neck to take a look, relieved The Gods must have heard his prayers at last and had forgiven him. He believed the ship and its cargo would be guided to safety.

In stubborn abandon, The Priest ignored the drummer's pleas, he was too weak, ordering him to beat his drum even faster and hasten them toward the land. On his Master's command, the drummer obeyed his orders and with all the strength he could muster, quickened his beat. With tenacity and determination, the oarsmen kept in perfect time, increasing the speed of the vessel, placing it in a dangerous and vulnerable position.

Battered once more by the huge waves, the Bireme was carried high on the crest before crashing down, causing several cedar planks to split, and within seconds a huge gush of water shot several metres into the air. The oarsmen stopped rowing and leapt from their seats to take cover.

Realising they were sinking, The Priest descended into the hold so he could retrieve the bronze casket containing the precious coins. Opening the lid, he stared at the glistening contents. Taking several coins, he thrust them deep into the pocket of his gown. In his haste, several coins fell to the floor and rolled out of sight. He gave out a sound of hopelessness realising it wasn't worth his while retrieving them. Closing the lid of the box, he held it against his chest. Lying down, he curled himself into a ball and whispered to himself. *"As a rich man, the Gods will favour me in the afterlife."*

As the ship broke in two, the men were tossed into the sea, crying in fear through the blustery winds, sadly there was no-one to hear them. The Bireme sank to the depths of the briny deep a short distance from the safety of the unknown land mass.

Chapter 1

Roused from a deep sleep by the buzzing sound of a mobile phone, Ray Ellis, narrowed his eyes and peered through the semi-darkness at his unfamiliar surroundings. Recognizing the ring tone, jolted him into life. Feeling for his jeans on the floor, he rummaged in the pocket and pulled out his phone, lighting up the immediate vicinity. The blonde, lying next to him stirred, reminding him where he was. Reading the name on the screen he pressed the green button and yawned loudly.

"Sir?"

"Raymond… did I wake you?"

"It's six o'clock in the morning, what were the chances?"

Without an apology, Dunn continued. "I need you to pick me up, we have to be in Balmain as soon as possible. We have a body."

Ellis scrunched his nose in annoyance before replying. "No worries, Sir," he said, as a long bare leg wrapped around his. He glanced at the blonde. "Give me about an hour," he mumbled.

Nuzzling into his neck, the woman purred. "I hope you're not thinking of leaving."

Hearing the sound of a female voice, Dunn's tone changed.

"Make that half an hour, Raymond. Doctor Webb is waiting for us." he snapped.

"Okay, Sir, I'll be there in half an hour," he replied, mouthing an obscenity at the phone as he hung up.

"Sadly, I have no choice," he whispered, slipping out of her grip and throwing the quilt back, forgetting he was stark naked. Scooping up the pile of clothes from the floor, discarded in haste the previous evening, he padded to the bathroom. "You don't mind if I take a shower, do you?" he called back without waiting for a reply.

Ten minutes later, showered and dressed, he bent over the sleeping blonde to kiss her forehead. Blinking her eyes open she stretched her hands above her head, bringing them down, behind Ray's neck, pulling his face towards hers.

"Hmm, pity you're leaving so early, I was hoping we'd carry on where we left off last night," she said, in a breathy voice.

Freeing himself from her strong grip, Ray straightened up, still holding her hands. "Sadly, duty calls. I'll ring you later so we can arrange a time to meet up again, there's few positions we didn't get round to last night," he teased, as his eyes swept over her body, half covered by the white bed sheet. With a loud sigh, he gave her a cheeky wink as he grabbed his car keys and mobile phone, from the bedside table. "Nice place you have, by the way."

Rolling onto her side, the young woman propped herself up on one arm, minus the sheet. "What'd you mean," she called back. "I thought this was your place," she said watching Ellis' eyes widen as he stared at her in disbelief.

"You should see your face!" she said with a giggle.

Pulling the pillow from under her he dropped it on her head before disappearing through the bedroom door. Standing on the pavement for a few seconds, taking in deep breaths of cool early morning air, Ray cast his eyes up and down the street, looking for his car. Spotting it, a few hundred metres away, parked at a strange angle, he smiled. *Geez, I must've been in a hurry last night… now I just have to work out where the fuck I am!*

Arriving a little late outside the home of Detective Inspector Stephen Dunn, Ray gave out a long, drawn out groan at the sight of his boss, standing on the doorstep with an angry expression, holding up his arm and tapping his wristwatch. Leaning back in his seat, he watched as his boss strode towards the car. Even at this ridiculous hour, the man was dressed immaculately, making sure everything he wore matched. *What I wouldn't give to see that old bugger in a pair of jeans and t-shirt. One with an old sixties band emblazoned across the front. Probably make him look ten years younger.* Breaking into a smile at the thought.

"What kept you, or need I ask?" Dunn bleated as he waited for Ellis to remove an empty take-away coffee cup and a pile of chocolate bar wrappers from the passenger seat.

"Sorry Sir, you know what these women are like, they can be very demanding."

"Actually… I don't," he replied, tersely, wiping the seat with the palm of his hand before climbing in. "I don't know where you get the stamina, Raymond."

Ellis winked as he threw the gears into reverse and backed out of the driveway. "Balmain right?"

"Yes, I'll guide you as we get closer, and make it snappy, we're already late."

"So, what we got this time, Sir?"

"It's a jumper, female, found at the foot of a fifteen story building. Although we don't know from what floor yet."

"No witnesses?"

"I know nothing, we'll soon find out when we get there."

Dunn casually picked up a pile of CDs from the centre console and began flicking through them. "So… Raymond… who was the lucky lady this time?" He asked, pretending to read the labels, trying to sound casual as though not really interested, but really was.

"I don't ask their name, Sir, it complicates things," he said, grinning. "Only joking... her name is Erica, she's a Swedish masseuse and likes to practice her skills on me," he laughed again. "I should get her to give you one… a massage that is, I meant a massage!"

"Yeah, I know exactly how they work, Raymond, I know all about the 'happy endings' and no thanks"

"I've no idea what you mean, Sir," he said, having a flashback to the previous evening.

"Wipe the stupid look off your face and put one of these things on. Maybe you can educate me as to what music I should be listening to."

Ray switched on the radio. "I think it best you listen to FM radio at this time of the morning, Sir," he said, taking the CDs and tossing them on the back seat. "Believe me, I know you too well and that music is not for you."

Dunn turned and looked out the window, feeling a little miffed. Ray had a way of making him feel old, although only a ten year age gap, there were times he felt more like a father figure. Allowing himself to drift back to when they'd first met, over five years ago, a smile stretched across his face, recalling how they'd got off to a shaky start. When Ray joined Homicide after being promoted to Detective Sergeant, his Jack-the-lad attitude to life was alien to Dunn's serious, no-nonsense nature. However, within a short time, he'd more than proved himself to be a competent young Detective, winning Dunn over and accepting his larrikin behaviour; even finding him a source of entertainment. They'd settled into a good working relationship.

The sound of Ray talking interrupted his thoughts, realising he was confiding in him a humorous, but raunchy anecdote from the previous evening with the sexy Erica. Making Dunn change his mind about being more a father figure to him. No one would tell their dad that story. Dunn smiled.

Raymond Ellis was tall and athletic with a permanent five-o'clock shadow that boarder-lined being a well-trimmed beard at times. His mid-length dark hair fell in a centre parting, and had an annoying habit of combing his fingers through it at every opportunity. Being fanatical about sport and having a wicked sense of humour, he was, without a doubt, the whole package.

"Left at the next set of lights," said Dunn, directing Ellis to the luxury apartment block in Balmain East. Ellis swung the car into the curb, next to where a crowd had gathered. "The sicko's are already here I see," he said as he yanked the brake on.

Inspector Dunn climbed from the car with a feeling of dread, having considered the body lying on the pavement, could be one of the missing women from his earlier case and wasn't looking forward to seeing the body. Pushing through the crowd of morbid bystander's that had already gathered, Ellis lifted the blue and white police tape, allowing Dunn to duck underneath and make their way towards the decontamination tent covering the macabre sight of the crushed body.

Dunn addressed the Officer standing at the entrance. "Is Forensics here?"

"Doctor Webb is waiting for you inside, Inspector Dunn."

At the sound of familiar voices entering the tent, the silver haired man, kneeling over the dead woman, turned and held out his hand. "Stephen, Ray, you're here at last. Give me a hand up one of you."

Dunn shot Ellis a sour look, letting him know, under no uncertain terms, it was his fault they were late.

Responding with a shrug of his shoulders, Ellis grabbed Doctor Webb's arm and helped him struggle to his feet.

As Webb moved away from the body, Dunn's heart almost leapt from his chest as he looked down at the woman's bloodied body. Fighting to hide his alarm at seeing the main of dark hair, matted with blood covering the woman's face. *No... it can't be,* he thought as he bent down and brushed the hair to one side. With sheer relief, the dead woman was unfamiliar to him.

Seeing the stunned expression on Inspector Dunn's face, Ellis guessed what was going through his head and changed the subject. "So... Dr. Webb... nothing like a body covered in blood to start your day, eh?" He chirped.

"I can think of nicer things that's for sure," Doctor Webb replied.

"What've you found so far?" Dunn asked

"Well, as you can both see, it has all the markings of a body falling from a high balcony," Dr. Webb offered, stating the obvious. "Not much to tell you really at this point in time." He said, sounding mystified.

"Are you able to say how far she fell? Maybe give us a hint which floor she fell from," Ellis asked.

"Well… looking at the injuries sustained, I'd say eight stories upwards."

"Who found the body?" Dunn asked,

"I've no idea, you must ask the officer standing outside, he should be able to tell you," Webb offered, stabbing the air with his index finger.

"Sorry to interrupt Sir," said the Officer, leaning his head into the tent. "I overheard you asking who found the body." He pointed towards a man of Asian appearance dressed in an orange, high visibility jacket standing next to a cleaning cart, looking distressed. "The man over there, the street cleaner, says he found the body, Sir."

"I'll head over there, Sir," said Ellis. "And find out what he has to say."

Dunn leaned over the body for a closer look, while continuing to question Doctor Webb.

"Any ideas what age, Richard? Would you say around forty, perhaps?"

"Yep, I'd say she's around forty to forty five and a good looking woman. I'll never get used to seeing this. It saddens me to think someone can be driven to take their own life in such a violent way."

"It's about time you left all this behind Richard, you should be taking your lovely wife on a relaxing world cruise, a man of your age."

"Cheeky bugger… I'm only seventy three, just a mere lad, plenty time for world cruises when I'm old." He chuckled.

"So, what d'you reckon, a clear case of suicide, eh?"

"Hmm… from the way she has landed, I'd say she's gone backwards over he rails."

"So, you're thinking she was pushed?"

"No, I'm keeping an open mind at his early stage. You know yourself, Stephen, it's difficult to assume anything at this stage. From my experience, people who commit suicide, more often than not, fall backwards. This is common if the person is afraid of heights."

"So now you're thinking it could be suicide?"

Webb shook his head in annoyance. "No, I'm not saying that either, that's something you will have to find out, you know what I always say Stephen, I find the cause of death, it's up to you and your men to find out *how and why*." Doctor Webb added, giving Dunn a sideways glance.

Webb slipped his finger under a gold pendant hanging from a thin chain around the woman's neck. "This is the letter L. So there's every chance her name begins with L."

"Or it could be the initial of her partner," Dunn suggested. "And that's quite a flimsy nightdress she's wearing."

"I think you mean, negligee," Webb corrected him.

"Okay," said Dunn, "Makes you wonder if she's wearing it to

sleep in, or was it for another reason? Perhaps there's a lover in the picture. They might have had a row, and he's pushed her?"

"Or maybe she was just sleepwalking. Either way, it's tragic." Webb sighed. "We could go on speculating all day."

Inspector Dunn leaned closer to the victim. "Can you smell alcohol?"

"Not much and if you're wondering if there are drugs involved, you must wait till I've got the toxicology report."

The sheet of material covering the entrance to the tent flipped back and without waiting for a gap in their conversation, an officer, dressed in blue coveralls spoke to the Doctor, ignoring Dunn. "How long before we can remove the body, Doctor Webb?" He said in a harsh tone.

Angered by the insubordinate manner of the man, Inspector Dunn replied, without giving Webb a chance to speak. "Can't you wait another twenty minutes? I've only just got here."

Still showing no respect, the officer turned to Inspector Dunn. "Sorry Sir, I'm only relaying a message. One of your traffic officers suggested we should try to remove the body before the morning rush hour. In this neck of the woods, it could cause pandemonium," the officer added.

"We will be at least another half hour," Webb snapped. "You should know, these things take time to sort out."

"Okay, we'll be back in half an hour. And just giving you the heads-up, the reporters are here, so prepare yourselves," he said. "Give me a shout when you're finished, Sir."

"Thanks for the warning," Dunn said.

On conclusion of his examination of the dead body, Doctor

Webb took out a neatly folded handkerchief and wiped his forehead. Snapping the clasps shut on his medical box, he gave Inspector Dunn a questioning look. "You okay Stephen, is there something bothering you?"

Dunn waited for a few seconds before replying. "If you must know… there is.

"Do you want to talk about it?"

Hunching his shoulders and giving Webb a faint smile, Dunn opened up. "After my last case with two major players still missing, I feel rather touchy when hearing anything to do with women dying in a violent way."

"You don't think she may be one of your missing ladies do you?"

"I have to admit I had my suspicions after the call to say a woman had fallen from a balcony. However, even though her face is very battered, I'm pleased to see, she's *not* one of the missing women."

"You're *pleased* to see? That's a strange thing to say…"

Annoyed at himself for saying that, Dunn tried to think of something to back step but nothing came to mind. Fortunately, Webb didn't pick up on his bumbling's.

"You're getting a little paranoid Stephen and overworked. You need to put that case to rest and move on, young man. Well, I'm done here, there's no more I can do until I've made further tests back at the lab," Doctor Webb said as he picked up his silver box.

Dunn agreed with Doctor Webb, and liked being described as 'young man'. He dragged back the flap of the tent, allowing

Doctor Webb to leave, following close behind. Tilting his head back, Dunn looked towards the top of the building before turning to Webb. “Right then, we need to find out the apartment she fell from. I’ll see you later Richard.”

“You’ll have the autopsy results in a day or two Stephen.”

Dunn slowly walked to where Ellis was talking to the cleaner and took in a deep breath, releasing it slowly through pursed lips. He knew nothing else other than police work, having spent all his working life in the police force. He’d started at the bottom as a young police constable and worked his way up the ranks to Detective Inspector by sheer hard work and dedication. The job had toughened him and he did not suffer fools easily. He’d surprised many of his fellow officers when he shunned promotion to Superintendent. He was comfortable with his role as Detective Inspector and although a hard taskmaster, he showed his appreciation when he felt it worthy, gaining admiration from his dedicated team.

Wrapping up his interview with the cleaner, Ellis allowed the man to be taken away by an officer as Dunn reached him. “Sir, the man’s suffering from shock at the moment, so is a little incoherent. He said he was on his regular cleaning round when he noticed, what looked like a pile of clothes on the pavement. After taking a look, he realised it was the body of a woman and phoned the police straight away.”

“In that case, it’s time we talk to the building manager and see what he can tell us.”

Chapter 2

Eight, self-assured male swimming competitor's, in the same, blue, rubber hats and black goggles, balanced on the starting blocks of the fifty-metre Olympic-sized swimming pool. On block five, Peter Buckton flexed his muscles, preparing for the race while his best friend, Peter Ashcott jiggled his arms two lanes across, on block seven. As the competitors positioned themselves for the pending race, the two friends sneaked a knowing smile to one another. As champion swimmers and this being the stroke, they excelled, the boys were in no doubt they could win this race with ease. The referee, judges, and official starter were ready and in position next to the pool.

This was the final heat of the comp and was also Peter Ashcott's best swimming style. He'd qualified in all his heats and decided he was ready to end on a high note. The row of competitors bent forward and reached down to their toes, poised at the ready. The voice of the official starter rang out with his command. "*On your marks.*" Followed by a loud gunshot, resonating through the building as he fired the starting pistol into the air. With perfect swallow dives, all eight swimmers hit the pool in unison, disappearing below the clear blue surface, before appearing again with arms rotating, cutting through the water like windmill blades.

A thought flashed through Peter Ashcott's mind, grateful it hadn't been a false start, something he always dreaded. Using every ounce of strength he soon gained a full stroke ahead of his rivals putting him in a comfortable lead. After the first turn, he checked his advantage over the other swimmers and to see what position his friend held.

He could see Peter Buckton was running a close second. Not wanting to slip back, he mustered all the strength he could to push on with even greater speed. The school coach watched on feeling extremely proud; he had earmarked Ashcott and Buckton for the next Olympic tryouts and was certain that his two prodigies would represent the Queens College, making everyone proud.

Taking the next flip turn in an effortless movement, Peter Ashcott could see he had now gained at least a metre on his friend. However, Peter Buckton had other ideas, he'd reserved some of his strength for a final spurt, sending him home the victor of the day. He too made a swift turn and taking a deep breath, he pushed hard against the wall of the pool with both feet. *This is it… It's now my turn to be the winner.* An unexpected feeling swept through his body. Strange pains shot through his chest, sending a tight feeling up into his throat making it difficult to breathe.

The coach trained his swimmers to push through the pain barrier, but this was no ordinary pain. Gasping a mouthful of air, he thrust forward, trying to ignore the discomfort that had now turned into a hot, burning sensation, deep in his chest. His heart rate increased, making him feel lightheaded and nauseous.

Struggling on, he watched as the other competitors overtook. As he tried hard to breathe, Buckton could feel himself weakening, making it difficult to stay afloat, and gulping a mouthful of chlorinated pool water as he sank below the surface. The unbearable pain ravaged through his internal organs, causing him to go into panic mode. With every ounce of strength he had left, he splashed to no avail. As his limp body sank to the bottom of the pool, a feeling of darkness surged up through his body till everything went black.

Peter Ashcott was Feeling pleased with himself, knowing he was a full body length ahead, he glanced back to see how close his mate was. Unable to see him at first glance, he realised straight away that something must be wrong. Peter Ashcott slowed his pace, trying to keep a watchful eye on his competitors while checking out where his friend was. A feeling of horror swept over him as he witnessed Peter Buckton thrashing about, then disappear beneath the surface of the water.

All of a sudden, the race held no importance as he turned midway through the last lap and crossed over two lanes in front of the oncoming swimmers, he swam back to where he'd witnessed his friend flailing about in the water. Spotting Buckton under the water, Ashcott swam towards him and grabbed at his body, pulling him back to the surface.

Everyone looked on in horror not believing what was transpiring in front of them, the coach instantly kicked off his footwear and dived straight into the water and swam in the direction of the two boys. The officials made their way to the edge of the pool and quickly helped pull Buckton's limp body up and out of the water. A first aid officer pushed through the small gathering of onlookers and without any hesitation, began CPR.

The head teacher informed everyone an ambulance was on its way while the first aid officer continued applying CPR to Buckton, not daring to hesitate for a moment.

After what seemed like a lifetime, Buckton coughed and spluttered as chlorinated water expelled from his mouth. His breathing was more like a wheeze and came in a rapid abrupt rhythm. His eyes blinked open with a look of distress. Kneeling at his side Ashcott gave out a nervous laugh.

"You frightened the shit out of me, you dopey sod, what happened out there?" Ashcott said as he shook his arm gently.

"I thought I'd let you win," He garbled as his breathing improved. "I dunno what happened… I got the most excruciating pain in my chest and I couldn't breathe… it was horrible… I thought I would die," He stammered.

The loud wailing sound of the ambulance siren stopped abruptly as it reached the building. Two paramedics, pushed their way through the crowd, calling out for everyone to clear the area to give the patient room. A clear, plastic oxygen mask was placed over Buckton's mouth.

"Looks like you've had an asthma attack, Buddy, do you have your puffer with you?" the paramedic asked.

Not understanding why the officer should ask that, Buckton shook his head as the thought went through his head, he didn't have a puffer and what's more, he didn't suffer from asthma. Why should he be having an attack now? Noticing his heart rate was excessive, one of the paramedics took out a syringe and proficiently, injected Buckton's arm. They then lifted him carefully onto a stretcher ready to convey him to the ambulance.

The swimming coach patted Peter Ashcott on the back as he congratulated him. "Well done Ashcott… Buckton could've drowned out there without your quick thinking. They've postponed the race and rescheduled the start so you could still win the race for the school if you want to."

"No thanks coach, I'm going to the hospital with Peter."

Looking up from the stretcher, Buckton lifted the mask away from his mouth,

"No you're bloody not, go win the race you idiot! I'll be okay, you can come and see me at the hospital when it's all over. And bring the trophy with you," Buckton forced a smile as he placed the mask back over his mouth.

The school female swimming champion, Jenni Sherwood stood close to Peter Ashcott and placed her hand on his shoulder.

"I've finished all my events, I'll go with Peter," She offered. "You go win your race."

Ashcott gave his friend a cheeky smile as the ambulance officers wheeled him away.

"Okay, I'll win this one for you and will see you later."

Peter Ashcott climbed onto his starting block alongside the other competitors. At the sound of the starting pistol, he dived into the water. Fifteen minutes later the large silver cup was retained by Queens College for the sixth year in succession.

On arrival at the North Shore Hospital, the specialist doctor examined Peter Buckton and explained to him, he'd suffered a mild cardiac arrest brought on by an asthma attack. Hearing what the Doctor had to say shocked Peter. He had no idea he had asthma and that he'd had a weakness in the airways, since birth. Both attacks were brought on by the excessive exercise and the stress of the race. When the Doctor advised Peter he was only to swim for exercise and not for racing, he was devastated. This would put an end to his hopes and dreams of becoming an Olympic athlete. It was the worst news he'd ever heard in his life.

Chapter 3

The two Peters had met four years previously when on the first day of term, at the prestigious Queens Grammar School, Peter Ashton and Peter Buckton had clashed head on in a corridor. After picking himself up and finding he had suffered no ill effects from the collision, the older boy Ashton went into panic mode seeing the younger one looked in pain. And if the Masters found out he'd injured a first year boy, he'd be in big trouble. Believing humour was the best cure, Ashton set about making him laugh. Learning they both had the same name, Peter, also helped. Several weeks later, while trying out for the school swimming gala, the two Peter's met again, discovering they had another coincidence besides being called Peter. They both excelled at swimming.

Peter Ashcott had won a scholarship to attend the prestigious Queens Grammar School. This had thrilled him, knowing his parents could never have afforded the fees, and meant he could follow his dream of becoming an Olympic Gold medallist in swimming.

Peter Buckton, the son of The Right Honourable Clifford Buckton, Chief Prosecutor for the Crown, had no such problem. Clifford Buckton selected Queens Grammar for his son to attend because of its high achievements in swimming and had produced several Olympic gold medal winners. He himself had a cabinet full of swimming trophy and medals.

Not long into their friendship, Asho decided to give his new best friend a nickname, being both called Peter would always be a problem. He thought the name Fish was appropriate for two reasons. First, because of his aquatic performances and second, it was too confusing them both being called Peter. The name Fish stuck.

The school swimming team considered them as kingpins, having won many trophies and medals for the school. By Coincidence, they both favoured the same swimming styles and had same speeds. They shared a secret agreement where they would play paper, rock, scissor's deciding who would win the race that day.

When Asho learned the devastating results of Fish's attack and that the Doctor had advised him against ever competing in swimming again, he made the ultimate sacrifice and decided to quit competing too. To his way of thinking, without Fish by his side, taking part, the fun and excitement had gone. They were a team, with an invisible bond. They would need to rethink their plans for the future. Something they could both do and definitely something to do with water sports.

An idea came to Asho sooner than expected. While scanning the morning newspaper, an advert caught his eye. '*Dive courses from beginners to instructors*'. Without hesitation, he phoned the number hoping to find as much information he could so that he could run it past Fish. He needed cheering up and this would certainly do that.

Armed with the newspaper and a wad of notepaper filled with facts and figures on everything about diving, Asho rushed to the hospital. Arriving, breathless at Fish's bedside, he dropped the folded newspaper, with the advert highlighted, on his bed. Without stopping for breath, Asho yakked none-stop, referring to his notes, relaying everything the dive school had told him; knowing in his mind Fish would approve. "And the best part is, there's a need for scuba diving instructors due to the huge demand in the tourist industry," he added, hoping to strengthen his case.

Fish' face lit up as he listened, nodded in agreement to everything Asho was saying. Then, his mood changed, his mouth drooped. "You've forgotten one thing, my asthmas, I'm not sure I'd be a suitable candidate for scuba diving," said Fish.

"No worries there, you're swimming achievements impressed them and because they wanted us to sign up as soon as possible… I've done it."

"I'm impressed and I have to say, you've cheered me up. When do we start?"

"Just as soon as you get out of this place."

"I'm ready now, I feel great, my breathing has improved, and the Doctor assures me there's no permanent damage. He said there's no cure for Asthma, but most people can lead a full and active life with the right management, and that's what I intend to do."

"Good… I knew I could count on you, so talk to your Doctor and see if you can get out of this place today. And I'll talk to Jenni."

"Talk to Jenni? Why?" Fish asked, sounding annoyed. "What's she got to do with all this?"

"Because she's part of the plan. Trust me. I'll tell you all about later when you're out of here. Phone me when you're ready to come out and I'll pick you up and run you home."

"Let's hope it will be sometime today."

"Okay, I'm off, there's lots to sort out."

Fish watched as Asho hurried from the ward. *If only I had half his energy!*

◆◆◆

Asho wound down the window of his battered old car, outside Jenni's house and watched her walk down the garden path towards him. "Looks like you're off somewhere," he called out.

She bent down level with his window. "Hi, Asho! What brings you here?"

"Fish might be out of hospital today and wants me to pick him up."

"That's good to hear he's coming out, but what does his mum have to say about you picking him up? I thought they were still attached by the umbilical cord!"

Asho gave her a sideways glance. "Meow!"

"Come on, Ash, it's what we both think. Her Ladyship would drive me bonkers if she was my mum, keeping tabs on my every move like she does with Fish."

"Don't be mean, it's something to do with her having trouble having him."

"Point taken," she smirked as he straightened up and hurried round the car. Stumbling into the passenger seat, she leaned towards Asho and plonked an unexpected kiss on his cheek.

"What was that for," he asked, taken completely by surprise by her out of character show of affection.

Asho had had a thing for Jenni for some time, but wasn't sure how she felt in order to take their friendship to the next level. They'd been friends for a long time and neither of them showed any sign of affection to one another. That is until lately, when he'd picked up on small gestures she was making. A kiss on the cheek was one big gesture.

"Because hearing Fish is coming out of hospital, is great news and I'm happy. That's all," she said with a coy smile.

The three were inseparable since meeting at a sixteenth birthday party three years previous. Their friendship got off to a shaky start when Asho, clowning around, pushed Jenni into the swimming pool. She was wearing a silk top she'd bought that day and thought she looked fabulous, hoping to attract his attention. Being pushed in a chlorinated pool was not what she meant and refused to speak to him for a while. However, Asho's sheer persistence to win her round, paid off when Jenni caved and started talking and sharing the same passion for the swimming.

Being a keen sports person with a youthful confidence, Jenni was quite capable of keeping up with the two boys. Her angular shaped figure and long slender legs made her a perfect contender for swimming.

"Where were you off to?" Asho asked.

"I was bored, being on my own, so I thought I'd head over to the mall and have a wander around, that's all, nothing exciting," she said, scrunching her nose.

"Lucky I caught you then… I've just saved you from spending all your money." He laughed, starting the engine, ready to pull away just as his cell phone rang. Picking it up, he handed it to Jenni to answer. After a short conversation, she hung up.

"That was Fish, he's ready to leave the hospital, so I said we are on our way." She smiled.

They drove in silence for a while as Asho mentally prepared the best way to explain to Jen his plans about the dive school.

"You're quiet, something bothering you?" Jenni asked.

"No… well… yes…." He stammered.

"So what is it? Spit it out"

"Jen… there is something I need to run past you." He began.

She looked at him with a concerned expression. "Oh, oh, this sound serious. Are you worried about Fish?"

"No, no, on the contrary, he's looking better than ever, it's amazing what a few days in hospital can do for you. I've been talking to Fish and we've agreed to take a two-year sabbatical before we go to Uni."

"That's not a bad idea, after Fish's near death experience, he could do with a holiday. Where are you thinking of going?"

"We're not *going* anywhere," he said, tilting his head to one side and frowning. "What we discussed was, if Fish isn't allowed to race any longer, why not pursue our diving? As you know, we've both been diving since we were kids. So I suggested to him why not set up our own dive school? I've convinced him to join a scuba diving course with me and train to be instructors."
"Is that wise, I thought the Doctor told him to give up swimming, what makes you so sure he'd be safe going deep sea diving after what happened to him?"

"Diving is so much more relaxing than swimming in races so there's no problem there. Fish is dead keen, he loved the idea. The only problem is his parents," Asho grimaced. "He said they'll freak out. So the only stipulation is that we keep it all a huge secret from them."

Jenni frowned, without speaking.

Asho saw the look on her face. "I know what you're thinking. I wasn't happy about that either, but I knew it wasn't worth arguing with him. Under the circumstances, it's for the best. Anyway, I've already signed us up to start the course." He paused for a second before continuing. "I'm looking out for an empty shop, somewhere close to a beach. Then, as soon as we have our licences we can start our own business.

What I wanted to talk to you about is, we will need someone to look after our shop and take bookings while we're out on the boat."

"You mean someone to keep you on the straight and narrow," she giggled.

"Well, yes, that's another way of putting it. We hoped you would like to join us. The only trouble is, you will have to take a sabbatical, too.

I know it's a lot to ask, if you need more time to think, I'll..." Jenni held her hand up to his mouth, interrupting him.

"Would you stop talking for a minute and let me talk, you're right, it is a lot to ask, I'm not sure what my parents will say. But if it is okay with them, I'm in," Jenni announced. In the excitement, she reached over and plonked a kiss on his the cheek.

"It sounds fun, but where are you going to get the money to rent this shop, buy a boat and all the equipment you will need?"

"I'm working on that little problem." He grinned. "But it's whether she will come to the party."

Jenni looked curious. "She?"

Don't ask," he grinned.

Asho changed the subject. "Jen, d'you want to come out with me tonight? I thought we could go for a pizza or something."

"You asking me on a date?"

"Yes, yes, I am," He grinned.

"Will you be bringing Fish along?"

"No, why? D'you want me too?" he asked with a frown, disappointed she was asking.

Jenni slapped his knee. "No stupid, I was being sarcastic, I often think you two are joined at the hip. Yes, I'd like that, I'd like that very much," she smiled.

◆◆◆

"This isn't as easy as I thought," Said Fish, sprawled across the sofa in Jenni's lounge room and tossing a real estate brochure aside with disgust. "I don't know about you two, but I'm having no luck finding something suitable for our dive school."

Sitting in the chair opposite, Asho threw him a newspaper. "Try this one, it has a boating section, you never know, just keep going," he offered.

"And I thought the PADI course was going to be the hardest part!" Fish said, downheartedly.

With sheer determination to gain their diving instructor credentials, the boys wasted no time in signing up and spent months of intense training, classroom lectures and exams; even finding time to log up the one hundred and fifty dives needed to qualify to be instructors. Now they needed to find suitable premises to run their business from was the next step.

Jenni swung round from her laptop to face Fish. "Stop your whining, ye of little faith," she scolded, holding a sheet of notepaper with scribbled writing. "I suggest we go for a drive," she said, scooping up a bunch of car keys from the table and tossing them at Asho. "I won't make any promises, but I think I might have found us a place."

"You… how come *you've* found a place and we're having no luck?" Asho groaned.

"Hey, I take offence to that. And if this works out… you owe me big time for that remark." Jenni pouted.

"If this works out, you have my word," said Asho, giving her a cheeky wink.

"I'll make a phone call and arrange an inspection," she said coyly.

After a twenty minute drive, the GPS announced they were at the Congwong Bay address Jenni had found. Asho stopped the car next to the water's edge and all three stumbled from the car. "This is gorgeous," said Jenni, placing the flat of her hand across her brow as a sun-visa and gazed out over a huge expanse of water. She turned to look across the street where a sad, derelict shop stood; the paintwork sun-bleached and peeling. "That's the building, over there. Oh my God! How good is that, right across from the water!" She squealed with excitement.

"And a marina," Asho added, pointing further along the water's edge. "This is too good to be true!"

The three dashed across the road to the building. "I hope the guy I spoke to comes soon," said Jenni as they sneaked a peek between the sheets of browned newspaper covering the display window.

"Are you the Sheila I spoke to a few minutes ago," said a voice behind them with a strong antipodean twang.

Startled, Jenni turned to see a tall Adonis standing in front of her with hair bleached almost white by the sun and a deep bronze coloured skin.

Jenni offered the man her hand. "You must be Cory?" she said.

"That's me," he said, accepted her hand and bobbing it up and down, holding on to it a little longer than necessary; his eyes sweeping up her long legs towards her face, making her cheeks turn pink.

Asho slipped between them. "Hi, I'm Asho, and this here, is Fish," he said, grabbing Fish's arm and pulling him forward.

"Fish?" the man said, giving Fish a puzzled look.

Asho rolled his eyes. "Long story," he broke in, not wanting Fish to start explaining his name for the trillionth time.

"So, Cory, I take it this is your place?" asked Fish

"Sure is, and you're lucky you caught me, I'm only here for a few more days and its back to Fuerteventura, where I live. That's in the Canary's, before you ask. Best surfing in the world. And I should know, I've surfed in every god damn country in the world!" He bragged.

"Well, you've certainly got the tan to prove it," Jenni said, with a schoolgirl giggle.

"Hey, why don't I show around the place, see what you think," said Cory, It's not much, but as they say, it has location, location, location," he smiled, crinkling his vivid blue eyes and flashing perfect white teeth. "The shop overlooks Congwong Bay and you have the marina with its brand new, shiny aluminium walkways and security gate; *and,* your own private berth," he said, without taking a breath and pointing to the row of boats opposite.

After struggling with the lock, the door burst open. The smell of musty old wood greeted them as they spilled into the main room, once used for the shop. While taking them on a tour of the premises, both inside and out, the young man gave a running commentary, ending up back in the shop.

"I don't know what you guys are wanting this place for, and that's your own business. But it has potential. And I'm not asking that much, I just want to be rid of the place. Now I live on the other side of the world."

"We have an idea up our sleeve and just need to check a few things out first. Do our sums and all that," said Asho, not wanting to reveal too much.

"We're opening a dive school, we're diving instructors," Fish blurted out.

Asho threw him daggers. "Well, it's a thought, but as I said, we need to do our figures first."

"I understand, but this place would be the ideal premises, with easy access to the South Pacific Ocean," he said with a grin. "There's a lot of diving went on around these parts a few years back. You should check out the history of Congwong. You might find there's a sunken treasure out in those waters," he said, throwing his head back and laughing.

"I don't know about these two, but I think it's perfect," Jenni gushed, overcome with eagerness about the premises; making suggestions about the fit out. "This will be perfect for our booking office where I can set up a reception desk. And a customer waiting area over there," she said, jabbing her finger around the shop. "The smaller room, at the back, would make an ideal workshop for you boys." She placed her hands on her cheeks. "It's perfect," she repeated.

Fired up by her enthusiasm, the young man joined in. "And an added bonus is that ginormous, freestanding garage at the rear of this building. That could be where you store your boat and diving paraphernalia."

"I know, and I've already got a name for it, 'The Boathouse,'" said Jenni, continuing to be carried away with excitement.

"Well, you two seem to have it all sussed," said Asho. "I have to say, it's ticking all my boxes. What d'you think, Fish."

"I love it. And when we eventually buy our boat, how convenient to have it moored right there, across the street.

As they stood on the pavement outside the shop, Cory opened the back of his 4X4 and like a true blue Ozzie, pulled out an eski filled with cold drinks. "So, guys, let's talk business."

On the drive home, Fish sat in the back passenger seat, thinking about what Cory had said about Congwong Bay. While Jenni and Asho sat in the front, talking incessantly about plans for the surf shop, he opened his smart phone and clicked on Safari, immersing himself in finding something on Congwong Bay.

"Listen to this," said Fish, interrupting Asho and Jenni's enthusiastic bantering. "I've found an interesting web page," he announced, turning his phone sideways to read the text more clearly. "According to the Australian Marine Society of Historic Relics, in the early sixties, a diver, working for an oil company, surveying the ocean floor near Congwong Bay, discovered the remains of an ancient ship. The old relic society, examined the ship and concluded that it was an ancient Phoenician trading boat. The phenomena attracted scuba divers from all over the world. There was a concern that the divers were showing disrespect for the historic ship and so a six metre protected area was set up around the vessel making it a no-go zone."

"That's good news and bad," said Asho. "Now what do we do?"

"If you wait, I'll tell you," said Fish, skimming through the remaining text by reading it to himself. "Blah blah blah, okay, what they're saying is, to be able to swim in the enclosed area you need to obtain a special licence. These are issued rarely and under strict conditions and if you fail to comply with the strict instructions set out by the old fart society, the licence is revoked immediately."

Asho made a loud tutting sound. "Well, if they're that difficult to get, that's us out."

Fish laid his phone down and went into thinking mode. *Surely having a Judge for a father must have some clout. If we can obtain one of these licences, it would give us a huge advantage over any other diving schools in this area.* A broad smile stretched across his face. "Leave it with me guys.

◆◆◆

"For God's sake Fish, what's all the secrecy, where are you taking me?" Asho asked for the umpteenth time as they drove through an unfamiliar suburb of Sydney.

"Just wait and all will be revealed," said Fish, as he turned off the main road and drove at a snail's pace along a quiet street that ended in a cul-de-sac at the edge of a waterway. Leaving the car, Fish led Asho to the top of a grassy bank and pointed to where an old, wooden marina jutted out, with five boats either side, all shapes and sizes, swaying to and fro on the water.

"Come on then, let's go, what you waiting for," Fish said as he leapt down from the bank and hurried towards the marina with Asho following close behind; not daring to guess what he was up to. As they reached halfway along the creaky walkway, Fish stopped suddenly and spread his arms open wide. "Ta-dah!" he exclaimed, standing in front in front of a gleaming, navy and white, thirty-five-foot boat.

Asho stood next to him gawking, his jaw dropped. "Shit! Is… this… what I think it is?"

"Depends on what you think it is."

"Don't tell me you've bought a boat?"

"Okay, I won't"

"Stop messing about, have you really bought this? It must have cost a fortune?"

"Best not to ask. Let's just say, I had a bit of money left to me, so why not use it?"

"I know you've never heard me say this before… but I'm speechless."

"Good… that means I don't have to listen to your whining voice?"

Everything was falling into place. They'd found the perfect premises to run their business and now they had their dive boat. As a result of placing an advertisement in as many publications as they could and set up a web page, the bookings flooded in thick and fast. Most of them from overseas visitors and backpackers.

Asho devised a cunning plan. When they arrived at the dive site, before taking their groups of students for their dive, he would make an excuse to go down first and place a large Conch shell, some colourful Star fish and a replica of an old coin in specific locations. They'd watch the expression on the student's faces thinking they were the first to find them; making their dive more interesting. This would encourage them to tell their friends and, in turn, more people will book to see all the underwater treasures and the remains of the Phoenician ship.

At the end of their day's dive, Asho would return to the seabed and remove the items, making sure they didn't lose them. A perfect plan.

Chapter 4

Ellis trailed his finger down the panel of names on the intercom system of the apartments. “Manager, that’ll do,” he said as he pressed the bell. “Let’s hope he’s in,”

“Yes?” A half-hearted sounding voice echoed through the speaker within seconds.

“It’s the Police, we need to speak to you,” said Ellis. “I take it you’re the Manager of the building?”

“Yes. Yes, that’s me, I’m on my way.” Said the voice as the entry door lock released with a loud clicking sound, at the same time the apartment door at the far end of the lobby opened and a stout man, appeared pulling on a jacket. “I’ve been expecting you,” said the man, leading them towards a reception area across from the lift and assumed his official position behind the desk. “Frank Farrow, the Manager, or to give my correct title, Commissionaire,” he added. “But that sounds so pretentious for the like of me,” he waffled. “Manager suits me fine.”

Dunn waved his ID in front of the Manager, Dunn. “I’m Detective Inspector Dunn and this is Detective Sergeant, Ellis. You appear unaware there’s a body of a woman lying on the pavement outside, we believe she fell from a balcony in this building. Mr Farrow.”

The man cast his eyes down and waited for a moment before replying. "I am aware, Inspector," he croaked.

"And the reason we're here is to find the apartment she may have fallen, which will prove her identity." Dunn continued.

Returning his ID back in his wallet, Ellis stepped forward. "I take it you're familiar with all the residents?"

"Yes, I know everyone who lives here, well, I have worked as the Manager for over ten years now."

"We will need the names and in particular, those who have apartments on the west side of the building, five floors upwards," Ellis added.

Farrow glanced out through the glass entrance doors where the blue tent was only just visible. "I hate to ask, Inspector but I have to. Are you able to describe the person who fell, it's possible I could identify her from your description?"

"Understand, Mr Farrow, for obvious reasons, it's not that easy," Dunn began. "All I can say is the lady is average size, her age would be around forty and she has dark hair. I realise it's not much to go on. One thing, though, if it helps, the woman has a distinctive pendant around her neck. I say distinctive because it's a simple gold letter L. Does that sound familiar to you?"

Farrow's hands shot to his mouth. As a low groan emanated from his lips, he slumped into the chair behind him.

"Are you okay, Mr Farrow? You've gone white." Said Ellis.

"I... I... know who the woman is. I'm sorry, I feel sick," he gasped as he leaned forward on the desk and cupped his head in his hands.

"When you're ready Mr Farrow, take your time," Ellis said.

"But I spoke to her yesterday evening, she always lets me know when she's going on one of her trips." Recalling the conversation he'd had with her, appeared to lift his mood a little. "We talked about the trip she's going on today and gave me my usual instructions while she'd away."

"Can you give us her name Mr Farrow?"

"Her name is Laura… Laura Verwood, she lives on the eleventh floor, she's such a lovely lady. But private. She keeps herself to herself, I never know when she's there half the time." The realisation struck him making him speak out loud. "She fell eleven floors!"

"Looks like it," said Ellis, taking out his notebook, and scribbling in it.

"I've known that woman for more than five years and I never, imagined something like this would happen to her," Farrow said, his head flopping forward.

Ellis stuffed his notebook into his pocket. "Sorry to rush you, Mr Farrow but we need you to take us to her apartment," he said tapping his wrist watch.

Farrow gave Ellis a blank stare, not liking the idea of being asked to do something unpleasant. "You better follow me," he said, striding towards the elevator and hitting the up button with more force than neccessary. Once in the elevator, he pulled out a master swipe card attached to a chain, allowing him to operate the console. The smell of fresh paint filled the air as they stepped from the elevator into the plush, carpeted hallway that led to the apartment. Retrieving a small bunch of keys from his pocket, the Manager unlocked the door and stepped aside, allowing the two detectives to enter in front him.

As Farrow was about to follow, Dunn raised his hand, stopping him. “This is as far as you go, Mr Farrow. I don’t want you in the apartment.”

“I’m sorry, Inspector, but as Manager, I have to accompany you into the apartments in this building. It’s my duty.” Dunn butted in. “Let me stop you there. We’re investigating a death. At this stage we have no idea if its suicide or something more serious and we do not want the apartment contaminated in any way. A young woman has died and we need to investigate all possible scenarios before we make any conclusions. Stay right where you are, while Sergeant Ellis and I take a look inside.”

Farrow held both hands up in front him. I’m sure I can make an exception on this occasion,” he agreed, stepping back.

“Somehow this is not what I imagined,” Dunn said, glancing around the room. “Didn’t Farrow say she lived alone?”

“So?”

Dunn slipped on a pair of latex gloves and stood in front of a white dresser, displaying colourful dinner plates, combined with an assortment of framed photographs. Choosing a picture he studied it for a moment. “Take a look at this, Ellis. It’s a family portrait, showing a blonde woman, I’m assuming is the mother. The lady lying on the pavement eleven floors below is brunette.”

“You can’t assume anything, they could be relations!” said Ellis.

“Just look around… this is a *family* home. Check out the bedrooms, see if ones a children’s room.”

Ellis poked his head around the door of the smaller bedroom where two white single beds, neatly made with pink bedspreads;

both displaying a neat row of dolls placed in size order. "No doubt about it," Ellis called out. "Kids live here, the female variety by the décor in here." He grinned.

"We should be checking the balcony anyway, there's nothing to say the woman didn't fall from here, she could've been visiting," said Ellis making his way towards the French doors that led out onto the balcony.

The doors were locked with the key protruding. Turning the key, Ellis pulled the doors open and stepped outside. The only furniture on the narrow balcony was a solid wooden table and matching chair butted up against the wall of the apartment; and one, brightly coloured, decorative pot, against the chrome and glass railings, tied securely with a cord.

Holding onto the top of the railing, Ellis leaned over to check the view to below. "Hang on, that's not right," he called out. "That's not the view we should be seeing. We're on the wrong side of the building."

Inspector Dunn joined Ellis on the balcony and leaned over the railing. "What the? It's deserted down there!" Dunn swung round and stormed back into the apartment. "What the hell is he playing at? This is the wrong bloody apartment!" Dunn fumed, throwing the entrance door open wide and stomping into the hallway. Farrow stood up straight, faced with Dunn's wrath. He appeared out of breath with a guilty expression. Dunn yanked off his latex gloves and stuffed them in his pocket.

"This is *not* the west side of the building and this is *not* the Verwood apartment, *is it*?" Dunn roared, pushing his face inches from Farrow's. "You deliberately took us to the wrong apartment *didn't you*?" He continued, reaching for the Manager's lapel.

Stepping in, Ellis pushed an arm between the two men, grabbing Farrow by the shoulders and pushing him backwards, while pressing his back against Dunn, separating the two men. "I think you need to take us to the right apartment, Mr Farrow. Before Inspector Dunn gets really annoyed,"

Looking distraught, the Manager smoothed his collar and stammered an explanation.

"I… I'm sorry… but… as I said… I've known Laura Verwood since she moved into these apartments five years ago, I needed to check to see for myself if it was her. I just don't see why she would have wanted to commit suicide. She's a beautiful, successful woman, always so pleasant and happy," he said, his voice trembling. You need to understand, I'm devastated about Laura, I can't think straight."

The scowl on Dunn's face softened slightly. "I've never heard anything so bloody ridiculous in all my life, but I'll try to keep that in mind. Now, the Verwood apartment, otherwise I'll have you arrested here and now for obstructing our investigations."

"Okay, okay… I understand! Follow me."

The Manager walked ahead, leading the Detectives in the opposite direction. The three slipped into a single file to allow a tradesman, carrying a battered metal toolbox and a small step ladder, to pass.

The Manager bobbed his head to the man. "I hope you've fixed the lock to Mrs Emerton's door?" The Manager called out.

"Keep your hair on… I'm on my way there now." The tradesman snapped without turning his head.

"This is it, this is Laura Verwood's apartment, Inspector, I can assure you," said Farrow, unlocking the door without opening it and taking a long step back wanting to distance himself from Dunn. "I do have things to attend to downstairs, but I'll be back" he added.

Dunn turned to face him, making him recoil. "Do you know if anyone has been in or out of this apartment since last night… other than the lady herself?"

"That I wouldn't know Inspector, I have no idea what visitors the residents have."

"I didn't mean visitors, I meant tradesmen, cleaners, yourself?"

"In that case, no. No one was scheduled to do any work this morning," turning on his heels, he scuttled back towards the elevator.

Watching till he was gone, and slipping his gloves back on, Dunn pushed open the door, with more strength than necessary; and heard a loud crashing sound followed by small thumps, from the apartment.

"Fuck, there's someone in there!" Ellis said under his breath. "I'll go first."

Moving with caution through a small lobby, Ellis peered around the dividing wall into a spacious, open plan living area and stood up straight. "Panic over," he said with a relieved grin. "There's the culprit." Pointing to the glass doors leading onto the balcony. One door had blown open and was knocking against the frame; the white net curtains, billowing towards the ceiling. Ellis pulled on his gloves and using a dining chair to hold it open, stepped out onto the balcony. "Whoa! Is that a view or is that a view?" He called back. "The apartments on this side must be a helluva lot more expensive with that outlook," he mumbled to himself, checking out the view over Parramatta River, before reaching over the rails and looking to the ground below.

"That's more like it, Sir," he called back to Inspector Dunn. "I can see the blue tent and the crowd of morbid onlookers has now grown to twice the size."

Joining Ellis on the balcony, Dunn took a step towards the rail. "We're on the right side, but until we've given the place a quick search, we can only assume we're in the right apartment, after that last debacle that still has me reeling," he said, shaking his head as he ran his hand along the top of the rail, studying the surface before a quick mooch around the general area. "Hmm, I can't see anything out the ordinary, there doesn't appear to be any sign of a struggle out here."

"As I said, she didn't *have* to fall from her own apartment," Ellis offered.

"Forensics need to get up here right away, they'll have all the answers. I'll call Doctor Webb and his team while you go find Mr Farrow and talk to him about Laura Verwood. Make sure he tells you as much as he can. Does she have a husband, boyfriends, were there any visitors who called? He's put me in a bad mood, so tell him if he lies again, I will lock him up myself, and throw away the key."

"Don't worry Sir, I think he got the hint." Ellis smiled.

Left alone, Dunn studied the balcony, he leaned over the railings to work out the trajectory of the fall. The fence was the standard height for a balcony and there was no outdoor furniture that could be used as leverage. Dunn turned his back to the railings and pressed his back against it as though someone was pushing him backwards; deciding it wasn't probable but not impossible. Perhaps by force, a person could go over with ease.

Stepping back into the lounge he hadn't really noticed much when he first walked through the apartment, being more interested in checking the balcony. Glancing around the room, he could see the lady was indeed a keen collector of antiques. The apartment was piled high with boxes of fine china ornaments; he surmised were valuable. Having an eye for antiques himself, Dunn recognised the Lladro and Royal Dalton figurines.

Gently opening the lid of a large velvet jewellery box, he stared at the contents, an elegant antique brooch and matching earrings, encrusted with exotic gemstone.

Idly picking up a magazine that lay on the floor, he pondered over it for a moment, before placing it on the coffee table next to a pile of antique reference books. Deciding to check out the bedroom, Dunn peered through the door to find it in much the same state as the rest of the apartment. Boxes were piled everywhere. Laying the middle was an open suitcase, half packed with neatly folded clothes and a large toiletry bag. Next to the suitcase was a matching handbag. Dunn pulled the bag towards him and released the clasp making the lid spring open; revealing a travel wallet and a purse containing a large sum of American dollars.

Flicking through the travel wallet, he removed a folded document. Opening the sheet of paper he could see it was an itinerary for return flights to New York, departing at ten forty-five that day. Placing everything back into the handbag he snapped the clasp shut and returned to the lounge to find Ellis flicking through a magazine.

"I don't think you'll find anything of interest in those magazines Raymond. They're not Playboy."

"So I've just discovered," he said, tossing it back on the pile and eyeing the room. "Not exactly house proud or even the homely type," Ellis observed as he wandered around aimlessly. Opening the lid of a solid wooden writing bureau, he found several small, leather bound boxes containing old fashioned necklaces. "If this is all genuine stuff, she must have been loaded," he remarked.

"That's what I was thinking. There's no sign of a husband or boyfriend, no photos and although the bed in the master bedroom is slightly ruffled, it hasn't been slept in. I think we better give Julie Miller a call and have robbery check this lot out, for all we know, it could be stolen goods.

"Maybe it was a robbery gone wrong," Ellis suggested. "The only thing with that theory is, what was taken, there's stuff all over the place and if these things are genuine antiques, there must be a million dollars' worth of items still here."

Changing the subject, Dunn asked. "So what did our interfering manager have to say?"

"Repeated what he'd already told us. He said she wasn't married, lived alone and spent all her time chasing antiques, mostly jewellery and coins. Because of her lifestyle, he believed she was very rich. Seemingly she was very generous with her tips and she drove a top of the range black Mercedes, which apparently is still parked in the basement car park and hasn't moved for at least six months."

"Did he mention anything about a family? Does he know of any friends visited her?" Dunn pressed on with his questioning. "He must've observed people coming and going. He strikes me as the sort of person who would know everyone's business."

"Nope, he said she lived alone and as far as he knew, hardly ever entertained and the only family he knows of, is her son, a lad in his late teens, early twenties called Peter."

"Well, I hate to say it, but this is beginning to look more and more like a suicide and not an accident or a homicide. Except for just one thing. Come with me and check this out."

Ellis followed Dunn out onto the balcony, his jackets whipped up by a sudden gust of wind. "Whoa! It's a bit blustery out here," Ellis remarked. Someone of a slight build, could easily be swept over these railings, they're not exactly high are they, Sir."

"Or... let me demonstrate, now that you mentioned the height of the railings. Neither of us are overly tall, but if I lean backwards like so," he said, resting his back against the rails. "And you were to come at me with force," he continued holding both hands in the air, flicking his fingers, beckoning Ellis to come towards him.

Ellis stood still for a second, not understanding.

"Come on... come at me, make out we're in a scuffle."

With a smirk on his face, Ellis stepped forward and placed his hands on Dunn's shoulders and pressed firmly. "We've got to stop meeting like this, Sir," he laughed.

"Be serious Raymond… you can see what I mean, can't you, with the height of this railing, you could easily push me over. There's something else I want to show you."

Dunn steered Ellis into the bedroom and pointed to the packed suitcase on the bed, he opened the handbag and showed him the travel wallet and the purse, stuffed with American dollars. "Clearly, she was about to leave on a trip."

"I see your point, Sir, why top yourself if you're off on a trip to New York? Unless of course she didn't want to go, not everyone is enamoured by the Big Apple, and it's a helluva a journey to get there." he said, trying to think of a reason why anyone would not want to go to New York.

"Something's not right." Ignoring his ramblings. "And it's time to leave, Raymond," he snapped, leaving the room.

"*And…* there's no suicide note," Ellis continued, following him.

The curtains had tangled from the gusts of wind that were blowing through the door they'd propped open. "Close those doors, before that wind causes any more damage. We'll head back to the office and see what Lindsay can find on his computer. And I want robbery to check this place out. For all we know, this could all be stolen. It certainly looks odd, boxes of valuables strewn far and wide."

Removing the chair he'd used to prop the door open, Ellis closed the door and turned the key in the lock. Finding it loose, he rattled the handles. "Looks like the lock's not working properly, Sir, the doors won't stay closed without turning the key but the lock's not engaging. Look," he said, giving a demonstration.

"Find something heavy to hold it closed, we'll mention it to the manager on our way out."

Ellis dragged a chair towards the doors and wedged it under the handles.

"I think that should do it." He said, rolling his latex gloves off his hands.

Surprised to see Farrow back at his post outside the apartment, Dunn gave him final instructions as they walked towards the elevator. "Forensics are on their way, you'll need to let them in. After that, no one is to be allowed through that door, is that understood?"

"Yes, Inspector Dunn, I understand."

"Talking about Mr Farrow," Ellis interjected. "The lock on the doors leading onto the balcony appear to be broken, they refuse to stay locked, and the one on the right had burst open when we entered. I've wedged it closed for the time being. But it's an issue that needs fixing… but not until our forensic team has finished in there."

The elevator doors opened. "Speak of the devil, here's Doctor Webb and his team now, you better let them in, and remember what I said."

◆◆◆

"For heaven's sake Ellis, try to make one trip without the language, you've got my nerves all in a jangle," said Dunn, as they inched their way through the traffic.

Pulling into his designated space in the Command Centre car park, Ellis yanked on the break throwing them both forward.

“I could’ve bloody walked the time it’s taken us to drive from Balmain to here,” he whined.

Leaving Ellis in the car, Dunn went on ahead, feeling he needed space from his voice. Slumping into his office chair he stared at the pile of messages and letters neatly piled on his desk. His attention was drawn to a large blue envelope sitting on the top of the pile; the address written in copperplate. Using a pen, he tore it open and read the card. It was an invitation to Stephen and Sarah to attend the ninetieth birthday of his elderly aunt. Staring at the names written on the card, Stephen inhaled a mouthful of air and exhaled slowly. It was over two years since his marriage to Sarah had crumbled. He hadn’t bothered to tell his family because, truth be known, he didn’t feel up to telling anyone. And as he hardly kept in touch with his family, it hadn’t seemed a problem. Until now, seeing their names together struck a nerve. Stephen spun his chair around so he was facing the window and stared expressionless out over the harbour.

After only three years of marriage, the cracks began to appear. Sarah complained over and over again about feeling neglected. He’d tried his hardest to keep the marriage together but his commitment to his work was too strong. Stephen winced as he recalled the day she left after the worst row. The saddest thing being, her parting words, as she walked out the door, in floods of tears, that the force was more important to him than her, was true.

The split had remained amicable, until Sarah began a relationship with his best friend, Fortis Green. This not only caused a rift between him and Sarah but ended a long friendship with Fortis. Thankfully, Fortis and Sarah moved to Western Australia, making life easier, not having to bump into them at every turn. Stephen pushed that memory out of his mind, not wanting to go back to those dark days of feeling bitter and angry. With things now resolved since he'd travelled to Western Australia on a case and forced into meeting with Fortis.

Old wounds were fixed and a reconciliation was put in place; prompting Fortis to take the position of Superintendent at Sydney's Command Centre, he'd been considering. With his friend back in the fold and a better relationship with his ex-wife, Dunn was now happier.

Pushing the card back in its envelope, he made a mental note to contact his family and let them know he was no longer with Sarah.

Chapter 5

Taking time out from the others, Asho sat, legs outstretched, on the dive platform at the rear of the boat soaking up the warm rays from the early morning sun. He glanced over his shoulder at their new acquisition with an uplifting smile; thinking it was more than he'd hoped for. And although eternally grateful, Fish had insisted on buying the boat himself, he felt humbled. A feeling he hated, even though he knew it was no big deal for him to spend huge amounts of money, borne with a silver spoon in his mouth.

Asho could see Fish at the stern in the wheelhouse on the upper level of the three tier boat, smugness written all over his face. It was times like this he hated him. He had everything, lifestyle, wealth, and doting parents. That was the thing he hated most. Fish had real parents, he wasn't adopted. But then Asho would feel guilty, knowing the feeling was only jealousy. Fish hadn't asked to be born into the perfect family. What's more, he would do anything for Asho. The boat was proof of that.

After purchasing the smart, navy blue and white boat, they'd needed to make a few modifications to suit their own personal requirements. The boys had fitted two bench seats back to back to accommodate twelve passengers. In the open space at the rear, they'd erected a custom-built stainless steel cage, designed by Asho to store the 10.5 litre scuba tanks; and next to the cage they'd fixed a long box containing all the flippers, masks, goggles and regulators. And covering half the rear deck, a white fibre-glass sunroof gave protection from both sun and rain.

The galley on the lower deck was Jenni's domain where she was busy unpacking. And on this level was a changing room, shower and toilet.

Fish shut down the 350hp Cummings engine, bringing them to a slow stop. "We're here if my reckoning is correct," he shouted down.

Jenni gave Asho a beaming smile. "We've done it!" she cheered.

Fish stumbled down the steps to join them. "We'll anchor up and then have a little celebration to commemorate our first day out," said Fish, handing Asho a long pole with a hook attached. Asho reached over the side rail and snared a buoy, floating on the surface close by. Tugging it closer, he hitched it to a cleat at the rear of the boat. "That should do the trick. Now let's celebrate," he said, throwing his arm roughly around Fish's neck and hugging his head. While Jenni dragged out a blue and white plastic eski with cold sodas.

Without the roar of the engine, the only sound to be heard was the waves, gently lapping against the hull as it rocked from side to side. Unfolding a blue and white flag, Fish attached it to the ropes of the flagpole and raised it above the sunroof where the light gusty winds, opened it out; revealing the international warning sign to other vessels, that a dive was in progress.

Handing Fish and Asho a coke each, and after a short, meaningful speech, from Fish, held high, he concluded. "To our boat… and all who sail in her,"

Jenni raised her drink. "And may we never have a mutiny on the bounty or a pirate attack."

"In these waters?" Asho chided.

"I just wanted to say something nautical," she chuckled.

Fish aimed his empty can towards the waste bin and missed, starting a chain reaction with others wanting to have a go. Jenni lifted her arm and pointed at her watch. "Okay, you guys, we're wasting time," she said, "We better start getting ready for our dive before the best part of the day's gone. As they stood on the stainless steel diving platform fully kitted out in their diving suits, air tanks in place, Asho stopped and faced Jenni and Fish. "I have to say, you two, this has to be the best day of my life, it's a perfect day for our first, official dive, with my two most favourite people in the whole wide world. Let's hope we have many successful dives and our equipment never lets us down and that goes for my state of the art underwater camera…" he rambled.

Jenni and Fish gave each other a sideways glance. "I think we've heard enough," Jenni whispered.

"After two," Fish replied.

After counting they ran at Asho and all three flew through the air, landing together in the water.

One by one they surfaced. "Not funny!" Asho shouted."

"We had to do something to stop you prattling on and wasting time," said Fish.

Fixing their mouthpieces in position, they disappeared beneath the surface, leaving a mass of air bubbles, bursting into millions of crystal-like balls in the glare of the early morning sun.

Visibility was perfect as they descended through the vibrant blue water towards the seabed. And to Jenni's delight, a school of bright yellow and black striped fish swam past, totally oblivious of the three divers as they darted into a clump of swaying sea grass. As they sunk lower, the water turned to a light green colour. Finally, they reached a wide gravel patch on the seabed and could see through the hazy water, what looked like a large rocky mound covered in sea vegetation. They faced each other and signaled that they were all okay.

Pointing towards the mound, Asho nodded sideways, indicating to the other two he wanted them to follow him. As they approached the mound, they could see a protective barrier had been erected around the area. With the realisation that this was the sunken ship the three turned and high-fived each other.

The thought raced through Asho's mind that the last remaining remnants of the sunken vessel looked ghostly. Unhooking his underwater camera from his utility belt, he began snapping away merrily. He wondered how many men died when this ship had sunk, how many skeletons were laying right underneath where they were. If only the ship could talk.

Fish was slightly disappointed at the sight of the shipwreck, thinking it was going to be much larger and not so disintegrated. To him, it just resembled a long sand castle with large pots sitting mid-ship with even larger broken pot at the rear, covered in algae. It was still fascinating, even ghoulish.

Jenni could see by his demeanour, Fish was disappointed. She had to agree with him, it wasn't impressing her in the least. Shards of sunlight passing through the dark green water made eerie shadows fall over the relic. Asho noticed a narrow winding crack making its way behind the ship. Swimming closer for a better view, he knelt on the soft powdery surface, causing a white cloud of sand to billow around him. He could see the crack widened to almost six inches as it disappeared into the distance.

Moving further along to a small coral reef half covered in plankton, he was stunned by the natural beauty that surrounded him. Determined to capture the sights in their entirety, he clicked his camera many times. Raising his hand and making a circle with his thumb and forefinger, Asho indicated to Jenni and Fish, following close behind, that everything was okay. They both responded with the same sign. He pointed the camera at them and clicked the shutter, thinking to himself, what a good photo it would make for the family album.

Exploring slightly further along, Asho noticed the seabed darkened dramatically. Swimming closer for a better look, he soon realised he was at the edge of the continental shelf which he knew could descend for miles. This was an area that definitely required the correct equipment to explore; something they didn't have. Moving away from the edge, he began tentatively heading back to where he'd discovered the winding fracture on the sea floor. Inching along slowly, he reached a two metre high, basalt volcanic lava rock formation, surrounded by rock debris where the crack appeared to stop.

Asho was puzzled and for the first time, felt uneasy. Changing direction, he followed the winding fracture in the opposite direction, where he could see the gap widened to half a metre. Lying on his belly, Asho pushed his arm into the crack as far as it would go. He felt nervous realising he was unable to make contact with a hard surface. This made him shudder at the thought of how deep it could be.

He turned to his two companions who had continued to follow close behind and gave the thumbs up sign indicating it was time to go. Shoals of tiny fish darted in every direction as they made a beeline for their dive boat.

Feeling exhausted, each one climbed the stainless steel ladders, back onto the diving platform. After removing their diving gear, Jenni left the boys and made her way to the galley. Asho waited till he knew she was out of earshot before speaking with a concerned expression.

"Did you see that fracture on the sea floor? It went right across the shelf. I'm no seismologist, but if I didn't know any better, I'd say the whole shelf could break off at any time."

"I did… and that thought crossed my mind too," Fish replied

"I'm not saying it's going to happen today, but we shouldn't rule out the likelihood of a submarine earthquake occurring at any time."

"*Yikes*! That means the ship could be lost forever?"

"Quite possibly, you can see where the fault, marks out the boundary, passing right behind the shipwreck."

"That's a bugger, just when we thought we had something good, showing our divers a bona fide shipwreck. So what's going to happen to our diving school?"

"Look, it may not break for years, we just have to make the most of it while we have the chance."

Jenni appeared with a tray of sandwiches and cold drinks. She could see the unsettled expressions on Fish and Asho's faces.

"What's with the serious faces… who's died?"

"No one, we were just discussing the wreck, we were just saying, it's not as big as we hoped," Asho said, quickly changing the subject, not wanting to worry her with his discovery.

"*Yeah,* not much to see was there. I thought the shape of the wreck was quite hard to work out. After centuries of being on the seafloor, the wood is very decayed, but the jugs and pots look intact. Still, on a positive note, there *is* a real shipwreck down there and we can show it off for many years to come," Jenni said innocently, having no idea what the boys had just discussed.

Fish gave Asho a sideways glance, trying to think of something to say. Holding his drink in the air, he called out loud. "This deserves a toast."

The other two raised their drinks and joined Fish, chanting together. "Here's to us."

Asho jumped to his feet. "Okay, time to untie the boat and get back to the Bay, we have a lot to do and prepare before we take out our first group of divers," Asho advised.

Jenni lowered the blue and white flag as Fish started up the engine and headed in the direction of Congwong Bay.

Chapter 6

Having been instructed by Inspector Dunn to find as much information as possible on Laura Verwood, Detectives Lindsay and Jones were determined to come up with something to impress their boss. Especially in front of Superintendent Green on one of his impromptu visits to the office putting everyone on edge. Sergeant Ellis placed a tray with three coffees on Inspector Dunn's desk. "Hope you like flat white, Sir," he said, handing a large takeaway cup to Superintendent Green.

"Suits me fine, thanks, Ray," said Green, turning to Dunn. "So, Stephen, what makes you think there's a possibility the woman's fall was *not* suicide?"

"Let's just say it's a hunch, there's one or two inconsistencies I'm working on."

"You and your bloody hunches, Stephen. I hope you realise we can't afford to waste time on this case. What did Doctor Webb have to say?"

"Not much, yet. And we're still waiting for his report. I'll admit, his comments at the scene were that in his opinion, it's just an unfortunate accident or suicide. And before you say anything, when he said that, it had only just happened. Those comments mean diddly-squat."

Lindsay appeared through the open door to Dunn's office, interrupting their conversation. "Sir, you might want to hear what I've found on Laura Verwood. It's quite interesting."

Dunn, Green and Ellis positioned themselves near Lindsay's desk, ready to listen to what he had to say. Lindsay held up a sheet of A4 copy paper. "It wasn't easy," he began, pushing a thick lock of dull blond hair out of his eyes. "I couldn't find a thing at first when I searched through the usual channels, so I decided to check Medicare records. This led me to The Department of Health and Community Services. I was able to find out information from her health records. Her full name is Laura Marie Verwood.

"According to her records, she gave birth to a baby boy, registered with the name, Peter Verwood. As that's her maiden name and the father's name is not mentioned on the birth certificate, I assume she's a single woman. Lindsay stopped referring to his notes and raised his head. "This is where it gets more interesting," he went on. The records show, she was admitted to hospital after attempting suicide, an overdose of sleeping pills. After leaving the hospital, she was admitted to the exclusive Hillcrest, a private psychiatric clinic."

Inspector Dunn butted in. "There was obviously a partner somewhere in the picture if she had a baby."

"Not necessarily a partner, Sir," Ellis pitched in. "Could've been a one night stand. She could've been a rape victim, hence the depression and attempt at suicide. I have to question the exclusive psychiatric clinic; was she wealthy? These places aren't cheap."

Lindsay shrugged his shoulders. "That I don't know."

"So who took care of the child when she was out of action?" Ellis asked.

"For the safety of the infant, Community Services, and child-welfare arranged for him to be looked after by Foster parents. Then after she left the clinic, Laura Verwood decided to have the baby adopted making it official. The baby left his Foster parents and went straight to his adoptive parents.

"I can imagine *that* would have caused issues… mental issues that is," Superintendent Fortis said sympathetically.

Lindsay waved his sheet of paper to get everyone's attention. "You reckon? Well, that's only half of it. Listen to this. A year later, Laura Verwood returned to the same maternity hospital where she gave birth to a second baby. Another boy. This time she left the hospital without the baby who was taken by his adopted parents. Shortly after leaving the hospital, she took an overdose of an antidepressant. Once again, she was saved. Hence being sent back for another stint at the same private clinic," Lindsay stopped talking to take a swig of coke from a can sitting on his desk, giving Detective Jones the opportunity to jump in with his information.

"She must have sorted herself out, Sir," Jones began. "I checked her business records and it turns out Laura Verwood was quite an intelligent lady. She attended The Sturt University here in Sydney, graduating with honours in Mathematics. Her employment records show she worked for a multinational bank in the city for many years and resigned from the bank five years ago. I'm not able to find out when her interest in antiques came about.

Although her tax records show her as being self-employed for the past four years."

"Were you able to find out the names of the people who adopted the babies?" Ellis asked, sticking to the baby line of enquiries.

"For the first baby, yes, that was easy. The names the adoption agency gave me are." He glanced at his notepad. "Graeme and Frances Ashcott."

Jones directed his next statement at Inspector Dunn. "As for the second child, Sir, I'm still waiting to hear from the agency who seemed cagey saying they had no information. It appears that baby is a mystery. " He leant towards Inspector Dunn and handed him a torn-out page from his notebook. "Here is the Ashcott's address, Sir."

Taking the piece of paper, Dunn folded it neatly in half before pushing it into the breast pocket of his jacket. Pressing his chin into the v made by his thumb and index finger, he reflected for a moment.

Green watched the change in Dunn's demeanour after listening to the two Detectives. *He must realise, from their information, the woman's death was nothing other than suicide?* He thought as they moved back into Dunn's office.

"So, Stephen, what's your thoughts now after hearing what they both had to say? Still of the same opinion. Or do you agree, it's a classic case of suicide. The woman had a history of depression brought on by losing babies. One of the worst things a woman can endure, so I have learned."

Green knew Stephen Dunn well enough to know he'd be finding it difficult to swallow having his opinion compromised. What's more, it was impossible for him to change his mind once he had one of his hunches. And worse, being told he was wrong.

"I'm not changing my mind, this proves nothing," said Dunn. "There's much more information I need. And sorry to send you on your way, Fortis, but I think it's time I paid a visit Doctor Webb, followed by a visit to Mr and Mrs Ashcott at the address I have here," he said, patting his pocket.

"The Ashcott's?" Green burst out. "Why involve them?"

"Someone has to break the news to them about Peter's biological mother."

"Fair enough."

"Then I want Lindsay to find out what he can on Laura Verwood's antique business. She must have associates, friends or even enemies that could reveal something about her we don't know. See if he can dig up something on ex-partners about the time of the pregnancies, who might be the fathers."

Superintendent Green got to his feet. "I hope you know what you're doing, Stephen. It seems to me your opening a can of worms," he said, shaking his head. "I'm giving you forty-eight hours, then let's put it to rest and move on." Without waiting for a response, he turned and left the room.

Watching in silence, Dunn waited until he'd disappeared out of sight. *There's times when I could punch that man right in the jaw. It's good having him back in my life, but he certainly knows how to rattle my cage.*

Stephen Dunn and Fortis Green met at the Police Academy in their early twenties. After discovering they hailed from the same suburb of Sydney and had a mutual interest, became friends and then partners. And although similar in looks and build, their personalities were different in every way. Which is why their friendship worked. Even as a young Police Officer, Green was confident, bordering on arrogant. He charged through life making sure he got what he wanted and no one dared step in his way. Whereas Stephen had a quiet, serious nature, with a reputation of rarely smiling and laughed even less. He chose friends carefully, wary of people he could trust. His good qualities were that he made people feel important and safe in his company and was well respected by his team. Although only in his early fifties, Stephen preferred a sedentary lifestyle, preferring to spend his evenings with a good book and a glass or two of his favourite whisky.

Standing in the doorway of his office Dunn gazed around the main office. "Is anyone interviewing the occupants of the apartments in Balmain?" He asked.

"Yes, Sir, You sent Detective's Hunter and Lloyd, they're there now," Lindsay replied.

"Good, I'm off to see Doctor Webb, Lindsay, where's Ellis?"

"Take a guess?" He said, pointing to the far corner of the office where Ellis and a female Officer appeared to be sharing an intimate conversation and laughing. Dunn watched with a tight lipped grin, shaking his head. Ray Ellis was a well-liked young man, and in particular woman, with his affable personality and good looks; he was also popular with his male counterparts. Although there were times when Dunn found his casual attitude to life, irritating, deep down he had nothing but admiration for his Sergeant who helped him through his marriage break up with sound advice and relentless humour.

"Sergeant! Let's go!

◆◆◆

Outside the lab of Doctor Webb, Dunn and Ellis slipped on the disposable blue gowns and shoe covers before entering. Doctor Webb gazed over the top of his glasses. "Ah, good timing gentlemen, I've just finished my report on your Miss Verwood," he announced getting up from his seat and rubbing the base of his spine with a groan.

"Follow me," he said, as he walked with a pronounced limp towards a stainless steel trolley where a body lay under a green sheet. "I've estimated the time of death between midnight and four o'clock in the morning," he declared, pulling the sheet downwards, exposing only Laura Verwood's head and shoulders.

"Sorry, Stephen, not a pretty sight, as you can expect from such a high fall. There is extensive damage to the head, face, and torso, with a mass of broken bones, all consistent with a fall from a great height. Although difficult to detect, there are no defensible wounds on her body that would show a struggle before the fall." Picking up her hand, he continued. "As you can see, her hands are in remarkably good condition, no broken nails, marks or bruising.

The toxicology report revealed a quantity of red wine, maybe a glass or two, and traces of a drug called benzodiazepine. In laymen's terms, a sleeping tablet." He grinned.

"Sleeping tablets? She's tried that before, overdosing on sleeping tablets," Ellis remarked.

"This was the recommended dosage, not an overdose, Raymond."

"We know she'd had unprotected sexual intercourse before her death."

"So, we now know she had someone with her that evening. She kept that well-hidden, with no evidence whatsoever. According to Frank Farrow, the building manager, she had few visitors and as far as he knew, she was single," Ellis said, before adding. "What you're saying, there's evidence she had someone with her that night. And you now have the DNA to prove it. That must mean something."

"You're correct, Sergeant Ellis. But having DNA is one thing, finding who it belongs to is another. And even though we now know she had a visitor, you have no idea if they were there at the time of the fall."

Dunn pressed the palm of his hand against his forehead. "It opens a multitude of questions. Did they argue and she was pushed during a scuffle, the man running away in fear. Or did he leave and she's accidently fallen. After all, we've discovered that it's quite blustery on that balcony. And she's quite petite."

"Or Miss Verwood," said Ellis, speaking to the body. "Did your boyfriend end the relationship and you've thrown yourself off the balcony, in despair," he mocked.

Moving him out the way, Webb replaced the sheet. "Sorry I can't help any further and it will be hard for you to answer those questions. This, to me, has the classic characteristics of a suicide. Or misadventure."

"Well, if that's what you've concluded, it's time for us to leave and pay a visit to her son and his parents, Mr and Mrs Ashcott, to tell them the sad news," Dunn said sounding deflated.

Turning on his heels Dunn left without looking back, his mind racing. With a mutual understanding of Dunn's moods, Ellis shrugged his shoulders and flashed Webb a flat grin before going after him.

Reaching the passenger side of the car, Dunn took out the piece of paper from his pocket with the scribbled address of the Ashcott's.

"You drive Ellis… I'm not in the mood… Let's hope someone's home, this is not going to be pleasant," he snapped.

"You do realise Sir, that this young lad Peter may have no idea he has a biological mother," Ellis offered as he climbed into the driver's seat. "How do we know it's not a delicate subject in the Ashcott's household? Have you thought of that?"

"I had, as it happens. But we need to find someone that's related or just close to the dead woman. Otherwise, she'll be just another Jane Doe and her life would have all been for nothing. How many times do you hear, people as young as thirteen, taking their own lives due to depression? Sadly, they have no idea how devastating it is for the friends and family left behind, wondering if they could've prevented it?"

"It really is a major issue, this depression problem," Ellis added. "I remember as a young Police constable, I had to go to a hospital on a case. I watched a nurse handing out prescription drugs to a line of patients. When I asked the doctor standing next to me, what they were being prescribed, they seemed healthy to me, his reply was that they all suffered from depression and had the potential to self-harm."

"So why were you at the hospital?" Dunn asked sounding curious.

"It was a case where a single mother of three small children, registered at that hospital, had jumped in front of a truck. Allegedly, she walked out of the hospital's main entrance while the nurses were busy and didn't notice her leave. No one would've batted an eye as she walked along the street; she looked like any other pedestrian. Sadly, she just jumped. Ironically, it was mother's day." Ellis' voice trailed off as the memory flooded back.

"This job's not for the faint-hearted that's for sure. We've all been there, Raymond."

Neither of them said another word till they reached the Ashcott's.

"Nice house," said Ellis, while executing a tight opening between the gateposts. "And there's no way we can turn up in secret on one of these driveways," he added, as he drove down a gravel driveway to one side of a well-manicured lawn flanked with neat flower beds and pulled up in front of the large, detached weatherboard cottage.

Striking the ornate brass door-knocker twice, Dunn stepped back to wait for a response. The door opened almost at once by a pleasant faced woman. Although slightly older than Dunn had expected, he guessed late fifties, the woman standing in the doorway was attractive with brown hair, streaked with blonde, swirled into a loose topknot, dressed in a flattering multi-coloured jumper with pale blue jeans, accessorised with lots of silver jewellery on both wrists and round her neck.

Dunn apologised for their visit and made their introductions. "Sorry to call unexpected like this, I'm Inspector Dunn and this is Sergeant Ellis." The two detectives held up their ID cards.

"Would you be Mrs Ashcott?" Dunn asked.

"Yes, I'm Mrs Ashcott…what's this about? Is it Peter? Has he had an accident?" Her voice changing to anxious.

"No, Mrs Ashcott, he hasn't had an accident, but we do need to talk to you about something that concerns Peter. Would we be able to step inside?"

"Of course," she said, stepping aside, allowing them into the lobby. "Please follow me."

Mrs Ashcott led them into a large, well-appointed lounge where a man, sitting in an armchair with a tartan rug over his legs resting his hand on an open book, looked at them confused.

"This is my husband, Graeme and by the way, I'm Frances,"

As Mrs Ashcott fussed over her husband, explaining to him, in a raised, pronounced voice, who the two visitors were, Dunn scanned the room, overwhelmed by the décor. And in particular, he liked a large, antique, oak cabinet dominating one wall displaying a large collection of his favourite Lladro figurines. A wide selection of books that took up the rest of the shelves made him smile inwardly, at the way they were neatly placed in size order. Something he had a habit of doing. On another wall stood a large display cabinet, with an impressive collection of swimming trophies and medals. And dotted around the room, in no particular order were Fine paintings of landscapes, and a selection of framed photographs of the many stages of a boy growing up.

"I must apologise for my husband, he's a little hard of hearing," she explained, with a weak smile. "He's also a little unwell today."

Mrs Ashcott sat on the arm of her husband's chair and rested her hand on his shoulder.

"What's this about Inspector?" Asked Mr Ashcott.

Dunn sat on a sofa close to the Ashcott's. "It's about Miss Laura Verwood. You're familiar with Laura Verwood I take it?"

"Laura? Yes, of course, she's our son Peter's biological mother." Mrs Ashcott said, without hesitation. "We have a good relationship with Laura, as does Peter. We have never kept her a secret from him."

Dunn was relieved the subject was not taboo and the Ashcott's were comfortable hearing the name Verwood.

Dunn stood up and walked towards the photos of the boy. "I take it this is Peter?" He asked, pointing to the most recent photo of a good looking boy, flashing perfect teeth.

Mr Ashcott got up from his chair and stumbled shakily to the display of pictures and proceeded to explain them one by one, starting from the baby photo.

Dunn tried hard to appear interested. "You both must be very proud of your son Peter," Dunn remarked.

"It goes without saying, he's been a joy to us since the moment we clapped eyes on him," Mr Ashcott said proudly as he sat back in his chair.

"He certainly *looks* like a nice young man," Dunn said, being polite.

Please, take a seat," Mrs Ashcott said, pointing to a sofa as she sat on a chair next to her husband.

Dunn and Ellis sat together on a large dark brown leather sofa.

"Will your son be home soon?" Ellis asked. Hoping they'd say yes; then they could meet the lad, and be on their way.

"Unfortunately, Peter is at work right now and won't be home for ages," Mrs Ashcott said.

"We couldn't have children. We tried everything but nothing worked and the years were passing us by. So we contacted the adoption agency. It wasn't an easy process, there were many rules and regulations, a lot of red tape, not to mention a long waiting list. However, patience is a virtue, as they say." She smiled. "We were overjoyed when we were given our precious Peter."

"So you were happy to keep the name Peter?" Ellis asked, sounding surprised.

"Yes, we were told he was called Peter, and we liked the name. We thought he looked like a Peter, didn't we Graeme?" Mrs Ashcott said, glancing at her husband for reassurance.

"Whatever you say, dear," He replied as he rolled his eyes with a smile at the two detectives.

Ignoring her husband's comment, Mrs Ashcott continued.

"We were aware of Laura Verwood's health problems. It's an awful thing to suffer from depression. At the beginning, we always thought she might come looking for Peter when her health improved, and we'd welcome her with open arms. But she didn't. Not until he was much older."

"How old was Peter when you adopted him?" Dunn asked

"He was eight weeks old and the most beautiful baby you have ever seen, we felt we were the luckiest people in the world."

"So Peter must be aware he was adopted?" Ellis asked.

"Of course!" We were always very open about his adoption. We talked to Peter openly on the subject as soon as he was old enough to understand. We were always prepared for him to meet his mother when the time came. However, that didn't happen until Peter was fourteen. Laura contacted us regarding his education, she wanted him to attend the prestigious Queens College. We couldn't argue as Peter was really keen.

"As luck would have it, Laura and Peter hit it off straight away, you know the old saying, blood being thicker than water," she smiled. "But then she is such a lovely lady, you can't help liking her. We're very happy with the connection we now have with Peter's biological mum, and he was overjoyed at the prospect of going to Queens College, with its long line of Olympic swimming champions. It's Peter's ambition, Inspector, to become an Olympic swimmer. Laura insisted we tell Peter he'd won a scholarship so as not to know she was paying for his education."

Dunn thought it was time to break the bad news about Laura before they said any more. The way they were talking, the news would hit them hard. "I'm afraid we have bad news, Mr and Mrs Ashcott."

"What bad news, you said Peter hadn't had an accident!" said Mrs Ashcott.

"It's not about Peter, it's about Laura Verwood. She passed away yesterday."

"No, she didn't! She couldn't have, you're wrong!" Mrs Ashcott babbled.

"I'm not wrong, Laura Verwood died as a result of a heart

attack," he announced, not wanting to reveal the truth about her death at this stage. Seeing the baffled expression on the Ellis' face, he shot him an icy stare, hoping he'd realize why he said it. Ellis gave him a wink letting him know he understood.

Mr Ashcott reached over and gripped his wife's hand as she continued to babble.

"A heart attack? That's ridiculous, she looked perfectly fine the other day and she's far too young to have a heart attack!" said Mrs Ashcott, pulling her hand from her husband's grip and reaching into her handbag for a tissue.

Mr Ashcott patted her knee. "Why don't you go make us all a cup of tea Frances?"

Mrs Ashcott stood up. "A heart attack?" She muttered as she left the room.

Mr Ashcott turned to the two Detectives. "Is there anything we can do? We feel we're related, with Peter being her son. My wife does a spot of cleaning for Laura every now and again. Laura's into antiques. Frances tells me her place is always in such a mess, with stuff everywhere," he sighed. "Not for money, you understand, we certainly do not need money. No, Frances likes being in contact with Laura, makes her feel like we're family."

"We've visited her place Mr Ashcott, I know exactly what Mrs Ashcott means," Ellis said, smiling, hoping to lighten the mood. "Her place is a bit of an Aladdin's cave."

Inspector Dunn took out his wallet and removed a business card. "We won't stay any longer, I think your wife needs privacy and time alone. We will leave you to break the news to your son,

I'm sure it will be best coming from you two. But, I will need to speak to Peter at some time. Please give this to your son and ask him to call me so we can arrange a meeting. I have a few things I need to discuss with him," Dunn said, handing his card to Mr Ashcott. "One more thing, do you have a photo of Peter that you can give me?"

Mr Ashcott gave out a small laugh. "We have thousands Inspector, I'm sure we can spare one," he offered, getting up and leaving the room.

"Phew! The plot thickens," said Ellis. "That's quite a bit of info on this elusive woman."

Mr Ashcott returned holding a photo. "This was taken only last week, so it's the most recent."

Dunn held the photo to the light. "Nice looking boy, just another question, do you have any idea when Peter last saw Laura Verwood by any chance?"

"Hmm, I think he met up with her a couple of weeks ago, at her apartment. But I'm really not sure, you will need to ask him."

Ellis started the engine, it was late and he hoped he wasn't expected to be driving anywhere else, having arranged a date for that evening. "So, why the lie about Laura having a heart attack, Sir?"

"Until we talk to the boy Peter, I thought it best to keep the cause of her death a secret. He could be the last person to have seen her alive at this stage. I'm keen to speak to him now."

Ellis looked at his watch. "If it's okay with you, can I drop you off somewhere?"

"Why, what's the hurry?" He said, seeing the stupid grin on

his face. “Need I ask?” giving a loud tut.

Chapter 7

Although Fish had set the alarm clock for six o'clock, deciding he'd beat Jenni and Asho to the dive shop; he was already wide awake. Without waiting any longer, he leapt out of bed, showered and dressed as fast as he could. Finding it hard to contain himself with excitement that today was the day, after weeks of planning, their first day taking a group of novice divers out on the boat and showing them what they'd learned themselves. It was nerve wracking, but something Asho and he had become passionate about.

As he hurried down the stairs to the kitchen at the rear of the mansion, the smell of fried bacon wafted towards him. He barged through the door to see is mother standing next to the large stove, stirring a large frying pan filled with bacon and eggs. With a broad smile, she pointed with her spatula to the table, set with fine china dinner plates and Peter's personalized mug, filled to the brim with frothy hot chocolate. "I know you're competent in all water sports, my Darling, but I hope you won't take risks today. Promise me all you're doing is pottering around in the water with your friends. Remember what the Doctor advised."

"I promise I won't do anything stupid, mum. I'm only mucking around today with Jen and Ash. Please don't fuss," he said as he sidled up to her and wrapped his arms around her shoulder with an affectionate bear hug.

One thing's for sure, my Darling, you're not leaving this house without a good breakfast inside you." She stressed.

Peter ate his breakfast listening to his mother chatting non-stop and hating how he was lying to her as to his real plans for that day. Having told her he would only watch his friend's scuba dive, knowing how much she worried about him. Peter and his mum were close, being an only child. He'd learned at an early age how she'd found it difficult to have babies and that he would never have siblings, which meant she mollycoddled him. He knew she would never give her seal of approval with the diving school venture. Keeping it a secret was, without a doubt, in both their best interest.

Finishing his breakfast, he pushed his plate away and grabbed the corner of his mother's floral printed apron, pretending to wipe his mouth; to which she responded by reaching out to give him a playful slap. Pulling his hand back, she missed.

"Ah-ha! Too slow, you have to be quicker than to catch me," he joked, leaping from his seat.

He slipped on his hooded jacket. "I've places to be, people to see." Leaning forward, he kissed the top of her head. "Thanks for breakfast, mum,"

"Don't be late back," Mrs Buckton, urged. "I'm making a special dinner tonight, your father needs cheering up, he's been down these past few days. He's been overworking lately, he reckons," she added with a frown.

"You're too good to him, mum, I don't think he appreciates what a good cook you are," he called over his shoulder as he bounded along the expansive hallway and out through the front door. Aiming the remote towards the wrought iron gates, he stood next to his four wheel drive Jeep while they opened. He cursed they were taking too long and wasting time being determined to reach the dive shop before Jenni and Asho got there. He knew Asho had volunteered to give Jenni a lift, making them late. It hadn't gone unnoticed to him that over the past weeks Asho was giving Jenni a lot of lifts. The sound of Mrs Buckton, interrupted his thoughts.

"Be careful my darling. Remember what your father told you last night, when you're in the water, you're no longer the top of the food chain," she laughed.

Peter shook his head and smiled. "Thanks, mum, see you later," he shouted back, giving her a mock salute. Driving through the gates at the end of the driveway, he turned onto the main road and sped off toward Congwong Bay. Blaspheming most of the way as almost every traffic light, he approached, turned red.

Glancing at his watch, pleased to see he was still in good time he turned into the road to see Asho's car parked in front of the shop. "I don't bloody believe it! They've beaten me. They're already here." He cursed.

Parking next to Asho, he leapt from his car and sprinted to the front of the shop. Thinking Asho would have already unlocked the door, he tried the handle to find it wouldn't open. Using his key and giving it a push, it still wouldn't open. "It's still bolted, what's going on?" He cursed.

Now agitated, he made his way to the rear of the building to try the back door. Cupping his hands and peering through the small workshop window, he snapped his head back; seeing Jenni and Asho, in an affectionate embrace. His first thoughts were to burst through the door and make a joke of it, then changed his mind, deciding not to embarrass them. He held back for a few discrete moments before making loud noises with his keys and door handle. Pushing the door open he stomped into the workshop where Jenni had scuttled to the small kitchenette, arranging and rearranging kitchen utensils, her cheeks pink. Asho looked hard at work wiping diving equipment with an old towel.

Fish cleared his throat. "How come you're both here so early?" He asked, giving no hint he knew all about their clandestine activities, but wanting to say something. "I thought I'd have everything organised by the time you reared your ugly head," he said with scorn, before digging Asho in the ribs.

"*Huh!* Funny that, I thought the same thing, I thought you'd be still snoring your head off in bed," Asho responded, flicking the towel across his back. Fish reacted by grabbing Asho in a headlock. They both plummeted to the floor yelling obscenities until till Jenni stepped in to intervene. Holding a tin box filled, she let it fall to the ground with a clatter.

"That's enough, you two," She yelled, trying hard to grab either one of them, but failing. "You're both acting like a couple of kids."

Have you forgotten we have people arriving this morning? Supposing they walk in when you two are acting like a couple of school boys… how professional would that look?" She chided.

The boys pulled away from each other's grip and straightened their clothes.

"She's right, sorry mate, hope I didn't hurt you," Asho said, ruffling Fish's hair.

"Phff… as if?" Fish replied, yanking his head back and giving one last jab to Asho's arm.

"*That's enough!*" Jenni boomed. "We've got a lot to do

"Okay, okay, what d'you want me to do?" said Fish, smoothing down his hair.

"The tanks and equipment need sorting, for one thing," Asho said, sounding in charge. "I'll take care of that while you get over to the boat and check everything's in order. You must check the Sonar equipment so we know if there's been any movement on the seabed. And check the fuel, we don't want to run out in the middle of the ocean," he joked. "We'll leave Jenni here to pack the lunches and sort out the paperwork for our divers when they get here."

"Aye, aye, Cap'n," Fish replied with a mock salute, spinning around and marching from the workshop.

◆◆◆

By ten o'clock the preparations for their first dive as instructors, were complete. Fastened to the stainless steel jetty opposite the dive shop, the thirty-five-foot dive boat sat idling. Fish and Asho were on board, waiting for their first group of novice divers.

"That's everything sorted," Asho called out over the engine noise. "I've checked the tanks, the wet suits are hanging up and are in order of size. I only hope we have one for every shape," he chuckled.

"We're about to find out, a minibus has pulled up in front of the shop," said Fish, pointing across at the dive shop.

Jenni skipped from the shop and out onto the pavement to meet the minibus driver from the nearby backpackers. They'd met days earlier when Jenni had had an idea that the backpackers would have a constant turnover of young, enthusiastic tourists from all over the world. Perfect candidates for a diving adventure? The proprietor, Adrian, had thought it a brilliant idea. And already, here he was delivering a bus load.

"I have eight, excited eighteen-year-olds to join you on your diving adventure. Four of the male species, four of the female all the way from Hamburg in Germany," He announced with proficiency, as he shepherded them from the bus. With the help of the driver's interpreting skills, Jenni struggled through the administration part. "I hope the boys will be okay communicating out on the open water," Jenni said to the driver with concern. "None of us thought about language barriers. But I guess it's an international language, under water," she giggled.

Jenni escorted the noisy group to the Marina and introduced them to the two boys. Asho launched into his inaugural speech to welcome their first group, who appeared to understand every word. Quashing any fears Jenni had the boys might have trouble with a foreign speaking group.

The faces of the four boys had lit up at first sight of the boat. So the instant Asho stopped talking his talk, they clambered on board. And in broken English, bombarded Fish with questions. The girls stayed with Asho, giggling and hanging on his every word.

The boat slid from the mooring and out into the open expanse of water where Fish cranked up the engine. With the power from the 350hp Cummings engine, the boat sat high on the water and cut through the waves with ease. Fish radioed the coast guards to inform them their destination. The time needed and the reason for their trip.

Reaching the dive site in record time, Fish slowed the boat to a stop and switched off the engine. The only sound was the gentle sound of water against the hull of the boat as it rocked on the calm waters. Asho reached over the rails with his special hooked pole and snared the buoy and attached the rope tied to the cleats on the boat. There was an eerie silence except for the sound of water, lapping against the side of the boat.

Fish gathered the students around him on the open deck and cleared his throat ready to begin his demonstration. "It's important to relax and remember to breathe through your mouth. With every inhalation, you will see a flurry of bubbles purging around your cheeks. This is perfectly normal. The best feeling you will experience, is the total weightlessness… bit like you're floating in a different universe," he grinned.

Asho announced his big little lie that regulation, demand he makes a quick dive making sure everything is as it should be. He slipped backwards into the crystal, blue water, disappearing below the surface and swimming to the sea bed. Scrutinising the sandy surface, he could see two protruding rocks and removing the large Conch shell from the bag attached to his belt, he placed it between the rocks. Moving further along the ridge, he found a perfect spot for the starfish, on a low flat coral reef, covered in plankton. *Now for my genuine plastic coin, I think that deserves a place close to the volcanic lava rock.* Swimming a few metres further, he found the perfect spot under a small lip at the foot of the rock, laying it on the soft white sand. *Whoa! How good does that look, lying there? I never cease to amaze myself.*

Satisfied his fake props were in position, he checked the depth gauge on his diving watch. Everything appeared to be in order. *Okay, time to get back.*

Resurfacing, Asho could see the group standing on the dive platform and that Fish had kitted them out in wet suits; relieved they fitted.

"How did it go, everything looking good, I hope?" Fish asked.

Asho made sure the group could hear before responding. "No problems," he said out loud. "It's absolutely amazing down there. We've picked a perfect day for a dive," he said holding up both thumbs. Then gathered everyone in a semi-circle to read them the riot act on the do's and don't's under water. Ending with his own made up story about not removing anything they see. His way of protecting his treasures from being swiped for souvenirs.

Fish grouped the students together for a final brief. "You all have your buddies. Once in the water, grab onto the Mermaid line running from the back of the boat and stay there until everyone is in the water and wait for further instructions. We will swim up current to begin with, making it easier on our return when we're all tired

Asho held back until Fish and their group were in the water, then he jumped in after them. Once they were fully masked, he led them to the ocean floor, leading them towards the shell, starfish and the pretend coin, then on towards the Phoenician ship. From their body language, they appeared to be lapping up the splendour of the underwater display and trickery. Realising the time, Asho bobbed his thumb up and down, indicating to the group it was time to head to the surface.

Using the anchor line, attached to the buoy floating on the surface of the water, the group was guided upwards to the boat and were soon clambering onto the dive platform, exhausted.

The four boys and four girls removed their air cylinders, peeled off their wetsuits and spread out under the canopy at the rear of the boat that gave a welcome relief from the unforgiving heat of the midday sun. The group chatted eagerly in their own language. Fish sidled next to Asho. "I haven't a clue what they're saying, but it sounds like everyone's happy," he beamed.

"I'm sure they are. I managed to steer the girls so they spotted the shell and starfish," said Asho

Fish got to his feet and rolled the top of his wet suit to his waist. "I'll make the lunches, you dive back down for our stuff. I'm sure everyone's ready for an Ozzie pie."

Asho listened to the group for a while before answering. "They'll probably hate the pies and would rather have Bratwurst and Sauerkraut!" He grinned. "Although I wouldn't mind a bit of German sausage either."

◆◆◆

Fastening his air cylinder to his back, Asho slipped back into the water and was soon back on the seabed, looking straight ahead.

I'm beginning to know this place like the back of my hand. He swam in the direction he'd gone earlier when he dropped them off; towards the volcanic lava rock. The shell and starfish were easy. Once he'd collected them, he searched at the foot of the rock with his eyes, for the bogus coin. It shouldn't have been that hard, he'd left the coin laying on top of the silt. Unable to see it by sight only, he sifted gently with his fingers. "*Got it,*" he thought, feeling something hard and holding it to his goggles for inspection. It wasn't his pretend, gold, doubloon, it was more of a blackened disc with slightly raised markings. He was intrigued.

Placing the object in his bag, he continued to search for his coin, finding it a few feet away. With his props and the disc, safely tucked away in his utility bag, he headed back to the boat.

Jenni was there to greet the newly initiated novice divers as they climbed from the boat, looking and sounding elated with their banter and bravado. Jenni handed out souvenir T-shirts to the group who thanked her with bear hugs. Asho couldn't keep his eyes off her as she bobbed from one to the other, listening to their stories and encouraging them to return or tell friends about their wonderful experiences. "She's a natural, they all love her. She's gonna be great for business."

"So, you think she's a keeper then?" Fish said with a sly grin, remembering what he had witnessed earlier.

Chapter 8

Asho lay on his bed, hands behind his head, staring at the ceiling thinking about his little find near the lava rock; his imagination running over time as to what it could be. The clock on the bedside clock said 3am. Flinging back the duvet, he leapt out of bed and dressed; deciding he would drive to the dive shop. Then he could check out the disc before Fish and Jen turned up. He'd said nothing to them about finding the disc, not wanting to look an idiot should it turn out to be nothing and had hidden it in the workshop.

The door to the shop creaked open, making him shudder as he stepped into the dark, empty room. The place was creepy and he hated being alone. Locking the door behind him, he hurried into the back workshop and clicked on all the light switches, and the little radio sitting on the work bench, to drown out the strange noises, the nights always bring.

Taking the disc from its hiding place, he held it to the light, turning it several times. At first glance, the disc looked uninteresting with only marking on one side, the other side flat; suggesting it could be identification disc, discarded from a passing boat.

Not to be discouraged, he placed the disc in the vice attached to the workbench and clamped it tight. Not even sure what metal it was, he grabbed the pot scrubber from the kitchen sink and rubbed gently. Showing no results, he used more pressure. The disc remained a murky green.

With the sinking feeling he was wasting his time, Asho scanned the workshop for ideas. A row of bottles, all shapes and sizes lined the shelf above the sink. Asho reached up and read each one out loud. "Dishwashing liquid, Jif, Drano. Hmm! Drano, that might do," he said, as he knocked over a small, brown bottle. Picking it up and reading the label, his eyes lit up. "Hydrochloric acid! Not sure why Jenni would have this. But if this doesn't work, nothing will."

Unscrewing the bottle, he poured a small drop into a jar of water and dropped the disc into the liquid. The liquid fizzed, turning the transparent acid into a cloudy froth. As the acid cleared, Asho's jaw dropped to see most of the green had disappeared. After a rinse under the tap and a quick buff with an old rag, he held it to the light.

"I don't believe it… how good is this!" He shouted out.

"How good is what?" A voice called out behind him, making him jump and dropping the coin.

He turned to see Fish, standing in the doorway of the shop. "Where the fuck did you come from. You scared the shit out of me, you *fuckwit*." Asho yelled. "What brings you here this early?"

"I could ask you the same. Call it telepathy, but I always know when you're up to something. I couldn't sleep so I called round to your house. When I saw your car was gone, I took a wild guess."

"Brilliant, Inspector Clouseau! You have good timing."

"Why… what you got there then?"

Asho held out his palm with the disc. "I found this disc yesterday when I swam down for our props. I thought I'd give it a clean. Find out what it is."

Fish picked it out of Asho's hand and squinted his eyes. "It certainly looks like a coin."

"At first I thought it was just an old discarded identity tag or something. After the acid wash, it looks more like an ancient coin."

"D'you think it might be worth something?"

"Could be, let's check it out."

The computer on Jenni's desk burst into life. Fish grabbed the mouse. "Right, where do we start?"

"How about trying the bleeding obvious, *antique coins?*"

Ignoring his sarcasm. Fish typed in the word coins, filling the screen with web pages and pictures of coins. He trailed his finger down the list, reading each one out loud.

"For fuck sake, this could take forever," Asho fumed. "Just click on any web page and see what comes up."

"Oh! Shut up and wait. You have to find one that's appropriate… I'll try museums," he offered, tapping the keyboard harder than necessary. A picture of an old bank building appeared, Fish's mouth moved as he read the text silently. "This could be it. There's a museum in the city that deals with coins. The Australian Museum of Numismatics."

"Sounds like a bunch of old people with stiff joints," said Asho and laughed.

Well, it's not, it's the study of old coins?"

After searching through the numerous coins that flashed across the screen, they could see there were similar coins to theirs. "Who knew there were so many coins in the world?" Fish said.

Being totally engrossed in what they were doing, neither of them noticed that Jenni had walked in and was standing right behind them.

"What are you both up to, may I ask?" Jenni interrupted, making them both turn sharply.

"Geez, what is it with you two, wanting to give me a coronary," Asho said, patting his chest.

"Ha ha, very funny. So what *are* you doing? This is *my* desk, *my* little domain," she said with a half grin. You should be out there getting everything ready for today's dives."

Asho looked at his watch. "Shit, is that the time," he said, pushing the coin into Jenni's hand. "I found this yesterday, next to where I left the pretend coin. Put it in the safe for me?"

Jenny scrutinized it. "Goodness, is it gold?"

"Your guess is as good as ours. Maybe when we're finished today, you and Fish could pay a visit to the Museum in the city. See if you can find out more information, maybe find out its history. We have to keep schtum and not tell anyone we have it or let it out of our sight, otherwise we will have every treasure hunter in Sydney spoiling our dive site."

"Why don't you go with Fish, I know nothing about old coins."

"I don't either," Fish butted in. "Why don't you two go?"

"Nah, sorry guy's, you two will have to go, I have to go the police station in the city. I've been summoned. It appears my biological mother died suddenly from a heart attack. I'm not sure why they need to talk to me, I hope it's not to identify the body or something," He said sounding a little perturbed.

"Are you okay Ash? You're not upset are you?"

"Yeah, yeah, I'm fine. It was a shock though."

Would you rather I come with you? The coin can wait another day," Jenni asked, sounding anxious.

"No, I'm okay, honestly. Besides, I'd like to know as soon as possible if we've had a lucky find. You never know, there might be more coins out there."

This time Jenni looked at her watch.

"Oh em gee," she said out loud. "You two better get going, our divers will be here in about an hour. I'll take great care of this don't you worry," she said as she scrunched it up in her hand and held it in the air.

Chapter 9

"Where are all your reports? What's taking you so long?" Inspector Dunn boomed. He'd been staring at the white board for a while, studying the photo of Laura Verwood with her personal details and time of death scribbled in black marker. Peter Ashcott's photo was pinned to the board next to her with the names of his adopted parents. Dunn was feeling agitated, the case was dragging on and they seemed to be getting nowhere. "Has anyone got anything for me?"

Detective Hunter, held up a hand. "Sir... Lloyd and I visited most of the tenants in the apartment block where Laura Verwood lived. All those who knew her said she was very pleasant and friendly. Sounds like she was a little eccentric. Just recently, she complained that someone was stealing from her. If you don't mind me saying, Sir, I'm not surprised, we found her car in the underground car park, unlocked. Which seemed a bit careless, seeing as it had quite a lot of stuff inside. And, although I'm no expert, some of it looked valuable."

"Did you find out why she was leaving for New York?" Dunn asked Lloyd.

"Apparently she travelled overseas often, according to her neighbours, but none of them knew where or why. Or were that interested, if you ask me."

Ellis headed towards the white board and picked up the black marker.

"As we already know, Laura Verwood was due to fly to New York on the ten thirty flight, with United Airlines." Ellis turned to the board and began writing notes with the black marker. "I checked her mobile phone for text messages. One was to a Julian Kent, saying she would ring him as soon as she arrived in New York. Then I checked her phone contacts for Julian Kent's number and gave him a call. It turns out he's the producer of the antique program Miss Verwood was a regular guest on. He explained what it was she did." After a short pause as he read his notes, he carried on. "It turns out she was scheduled to appear on the show being filmed the day after she arrived. Although that show won't actually be aired for two weeks, during prime time. Miss Verwood was an expert on antique jewellery and would give talks on the show about her heirlooms. This, in turn, helped sell them. Quite clever, don't you think?" He said, flashing a smile around the room. "The poor man was devastated by the news of her death, she was quite a star on the show."

The room went unusually quiet for a few moments until Inspector Dunn broke the silence.

"Well, that explains why she travelled often. What about her, associates or friends here in Australia?" Dunn asked.

"Hang on, there's a second message, to remind her to have a necklace cleaned which she was taking with her to New York. I then checked other contacts on her phone, I could see she had regular calls to a Dennis Sutton. I gave him a call and I explained who I was and asked what his relationship was with Laura Verwood. He was very cooperative, saying he was a close friend and associate in the antique business. When I informed him the reason I had phoned him, he sounded genuinely shocked, however, poor guy is convinced it couldn't possibly be Miss Verwood as she would be well on her way to New York." Ellis stopped and looked at Dunn.

"He has agreed to come into the station today, I knew you'd want to talk to him further."

"That's good, let's hope *he* can shed some light as to why this woman fell from her balcony." Inspector Dunn concluded.

◆◆◆

Dressed in faded commando shorts, a T-shirt that had seen better days and a pair of navy All Star ankle boots, Peter Ashcott walked into the police station with an air of youthful confidence. He approached the reception desk and flashed Inspector Dunn's business card.

"I've come to see Mr. Dunn," he announced'

"I think you mean *Detective Inspector* Dunn," The duty officer replied, looking at the card.

"Okay, I've come to see *Detective Inspector* Dunn." He replied, cheekily mimicking the officer.

"Can I ask the reason you need to see him, he's a very busy man."

"Actually, it's *him* that wants to see me. He left this card with my mother and asked me to come in here. I've no idea why he wants to see me, my name is Peter Ashcott."

The officer asked Peter to take a seat while he made a call to the main office. The phone rang on Sergeant Ellis' desk. Leaving the white board, Ellis reached across his desk to answer it. After hearing what the caller had to say, he placed one hand over the mouthpiece and looked directly at Inspector Dunn.

"Peter Ashcott is downstairs waiting to talk to you, Sir."

"Ah, that's good, tell the duty officer to take him to interview room one, I'm on my way."

Ellis moved his hand from the mouthpiece to relay the message, then hung up.

Before Inspector Dunn left the office, he called across the room. "Okay, Lindsay I need you to check out this Dennis Sutton. I want to know as much as I can about him before he turns up today and if it helps, we now know he's into antiques."

Lindsay mumbled under his breath. "A fancy word for junk, I reckon."

"Let's go Ellis, we've got a lot to get through today."

Draining the last dregs of coffee from a takeaway cup, Ellis threw the cardboard cup into the waste paper bin near his desk, but missed. Tutting loudly, he picked it up and placed it in carefully as he hurried to catch up to Dunn.

As the two detectives entered the interview room, Peter Ashcott was sitting at the desk playing with his mobile phone. Dunn nodded to the officer standing directly behind Peter, indicating he was not required. The officer left the room without saying a word.

"Good morning Peter, I'm Detective Inspector Stephen Dunn and this is Detective Sergeant Ray Ellis."

Peter immediately stood up and respectfully held his hand out and shook both their hands.

"Thank you for coming in to see me, please sit," Dunn said as he and Ellis sat on the chairs opposite him.

"We are investigating the death of your mother, Laura Verwood. First can I offer my sincere condolences for your loss," Dunn began before Peter butted in and leaned forward, placing both hands on the desk.

"With due respect to my parents, Inspector Dunn, I would prefer Laura Verwood not being referred to as '*my mother*'. She was just the woman who gave birth to me, my mum is Frances Ashcott and my dad is Graeme. They are the best parents anyone could ever have. They explained everything to me when I was very young, about my adoption. I know about the problems Laura Verwood was having after I was born. Then she went on to fame and fortune."

The fact is she had me adopted out when I was just a baby. She didn't want me, obviously a baby didn't suit her lifestyle. I met her when I was about fourteen, just before I started at Queens College. She seemed nice, but she's *not* my mother, as I said… my mum is Frances, always will be." He concluded sounding agitated.

"I apologize for my mistake, I didn't realise you felt that strongly about Miss Verwood. If it's any consolation, I know that Mr and Mrs Ashcott are very proud parents and love you very much, which was blatantly obvious when I talked to them the other day. You're quite a lucky lad," Dunn gushed.

"I have no doubts about that and I am very proud of them too, so why are you investigating Laura Verwood's death? Mum said she'd had a heart attack, what's the mystery?"

"Well, it's not that simple, unfortunately. That's just what we told your mum, I felt a little white lie was required. Can you tell us when you last visited Laura Verwood?" Ellis asked.

"It was about six weeks ago. What d'you mean it's not that simple? What has happened?"

"Be patient, we will come to that in a moment. Are you able to tell us why you visited her?" Ellis asked.

"Yes, yes I can. Although I'm a bit embarrassed to be honest. If you must know, I asked her if she would help, financially, with a business venture I was looking into at the time. I ran my plans past her about opening a scuba diving school." Peter sat up straight as he enthusiastically began to tell his story. "My friend, Fish, and I are both champion swimmers and love anything to do with water. It seemed like a great idea to open a business doing what we know best."

"What was her response, did she show any interest?" Dunn chipped in.

Peter's expression changed to sullen. "Actually, it didn't go too well if you must know. It was all quite bazaar, I didn't expect her to react the way she did. I started telling her my plan, and she was really enthusiastic, and quite excited about it all. She asked me about my friend. When I told her about my best friend, his name and family background so she knew he could be trusted, without warning, her attitude changed and she became very angry.

She started rambling on and had a go at me for leaving College and wasting all the money she'd forked out and that I had to learn to stand on my own two feet, going on and on about how no one had ever helped her and how she'd had to work hard to get where she is today, yada, yada," he said, mimicking a mouth opening and closing with his fingers. Inspector Dunn felt he was being rather disrespective towards the woman, not to mention sounding rather acrimonious.

"Have you any idea why she suddenly changed her attitude?" Ellis asked.

"No, I just got the impression she'd suddenly got the shits, realising I was leaving college. I got the message, she wasn't going to help me. Then she told me to leave. By the way, our dive school is now up and running and doing okay, no thanks to her,"

"That's good to hear. It must have made you very angry, her nagging you about leaving college *and* not wanting to help you with your business venture?" Ellis said, thinking they might be getting somewhere at last. "It must have made you mad? Did things become heated between you? Did you argue?"

"Argue? No, why would I have argued. I don't know what you're talking about. I tried to make her understand why I wanted to leave college and then I explained all the details about my idea about opening a scuba diving school. I gave her our business plan and projected figures, but when she gave me the reason she couldn't, or wouldn't help, I accepted that. Although, yes, I suppose I was annoyed… upset… angry, all the above."

"So obviously you knew she was a woman of substance. Is that why you went to her, for financial help? Did you feel she owed you something for abandoning you as a baby?" Dunn probed, observing Peter's body language. One thing for sure, this lad was certainly cool, calm and collected, or was he putting on a good act.

Peter leaned forward again and lay both arms on the desk in front of him. "Firstly, yes, I knew she wasn't short of a bob or two, but I did not and never have felt she owed me anything. As I said, I have great parents and I had a very good childhood, I wanted for nothing. Being abandoned by her, my biological mother, never entered my head."

"Why not ask your parents for help, they look quite comfortable, could they not have helped you?"

"Mum and dad *are* okay financially. I just had the idea that Laura Verwood, being a businesswoman herself, and with no disrespect to mum and dad, would understand the business side of things better.»

"Did you ever meet any of her friends?"

"Did I meet any of her friends? No, never, why would I? I was never in a situation where I would meet any of her friends. Just to let you know, I only ever met up with Miss Verwood when she came to my swimming tournaments or a school function. I can count on one hand the number of times I visited her apartment. On those few occasions, we got on well, she was a nice lady," Peter said as he leaned back in his seat with his arms folded. Raising his eyes to the ceiling in thought for a few moments. Leaning forward again, he rested one hand on the desk while twisting his lower lip between his thumb and index finger.

"Actually, come to think about it, she often mentioned a guy called Dennis, an antique dealer. I got the impression he was just someone in the same business as her that's how it sounded when she spoke about him, anyway."

"Did she ever mention to you why she travelled to New York often?" Dunn asked.

"*Yeah,* she told me she appeared on an antique TV show, sounded a bit ho-hum to me. Why are you asking me all these questions, have I done something wrong?" Peter asked sounding agitated.

"Please bear with us for a little longer Peter, I have a few more questions and then you can be on your way." Ellis advised, trying to sound as understanding as possible.

"When you met up with Laura, did she mention your brother?"

Peter looked at Ellis with a shocked expression.

"*Huh, i*s that some sort of joke? I don't have a brother and I think I *would* know if I had one. I'm an only child," he snapped, unable to comprehend the question.

Ellis gave Inspector Dunn a discrete frown.

"Peter, this might come as a shock to you, but we have positive proof that you *do* have a brother. Laura Verwood gave birth to a second baby about two years after you were born." Ellis said as gently as he could, then paused, allowing Peter time to digest the information.

"That's impossible, why would you say that? Surely someone would have told me before now. Where is he? Is he local? Can I meet him?"

Dunn was unable to detect whether Peter was happy or annoyed at this bitter sweet revelation. He was also surprised, if not shocked, that Peter had no idea about his brother.

"We're sorry you had to find out this way, we thought you must know already. We have no idea where your brother is, however, we're trying to locate his whereabouts to eliminate him from our enquiries. We were hoping you would know."

"How would I know where he is? I didn't even know he existed till just now. And what enquires, what's this all about? Is there something you're not telling me? How did Laura Verwood die? Are you saying her death was suspicious or something?"

Inspector Dunn cleared his throat as he leaned forward.

"I'm afraid it appears your mother, sorry, Laura could have taken her own life by jumping from the balcony of her apartment."

Peter instantly looked shocked as his eyes widened and his jaw dropped. His body slumped forward where he stayed motionless, without saying a word for some time. Sergeant Ellis and Inspector Dunn glanced at each other in sympathy, allowing him time to mull over what they had just revealed. Eventually he looked up, his eyes quite moist.

"I'm shocked, I don't know what to say, I just don't know what to say." He repeated as he pressed his thumb and index finger into his eyes to quell the tears.

"Fuck, why on earth would she do such a thing?"

"Can you tell us what her mood was like, last time you saw her? Did she seem depressed or worried?" Ellis asked.

"She seemed fine to me," Peter replied, shrugging his shoulders. "You said she'd had a heart attack, why would you say that," he said, putting more strength in his words.

"I'm sorry we had to be the bearers of bad news and you had to find out this way, but you understand, we needed to eliminate you from our enquiries."

"What enquiries? If she jumped why would you be investigating her death?"

"We have to check out all possibilities that she might not have jumped of her own accord. Until we can definitely be sure that her death was a suicide, it will remain an open case." Dunn explained.

"I can't believe she would take her own life. Not only was the business going well, she'd written a book on antiques and was planning a book launch. Doesn't this prove she had everything to live for? Another fact is, she hated that balcony and hated the thought of going out on it. When I arrived at her apartment a few days ago, the balcony doors flew open and she freaked. It took a while for her to calm down and wouldn't let me leave until I'd made sure they were well and truly secured. I'm not sure you have the right woman?" Peter said, the revelation suddenly lifting his spirits.

Dunn leaned back in his chair and thought for a moment. For the first time he felt the evidence they had was proving it wasn't suicide.

Having an idea, Ellis gave Peter a thoughtful look. "Well, there's one way we can make sure we have the right woman, would you be willing to identify the body? You don't really need to as we're positive the body is that of Laura Verwood."

"When would you like me to do that?"

"We can arrange it right now if you like." Ellis suggested.

"The quicker the better I think, then I can prove you have the wrong woman."

The two detectives stood up. Ellis held out his hand to motion Peter to stay sitting.

"Could you please wait here for a few minutes while I arrange someone to take you to the morgue, it's not too far away."

"I'll have to be quick, I have a boat to prepare for a dive tomorrow."

Inspector Dunn was amazed at how calm Peter had become being of the mindset there was a possibility the deceased was not his biological mother. Both detectives left the interview room and made their way to the incident room where Dunn ordered Detective Susan Hunter to take Peter Ashcott to Doctor Webb's lab and have him identify the body of Laura Verwood.

"Keep an eye on him, he's of the opinion we have the wrong person and the body in the morgue is not who we think it is. He might freak out when he sees it is Laura Verwood."

"Okay Sir, leave him to me," Hunter responded with a sympathetic smile as she left the incident room.

Ellis sat at his desk and thumbed through a pile of messages as Dunn headed towards his office

"Excuse me, Sir," Lindsay called out, halting Inspector Dunn in his tracks. "There's a Dennis Sutton, waiting to see you in interview room two. He's the antique dealer you wanted to see."

"Good. Hopefully this man will shed a light on a few details."

"He introduced himself as being Laura Verwood's business partner, he seems to think he was the last person to see her the evening she fell." Lindsay added.

"Ah, ha, now it sounds like it could be a classic case of a disagreement between business partners. They've argued, got into a bit of rough and tumble then whoops-a-daisy… over she goes," Ellis declared, demonstrating with an up and over hand movement.

"*Ellis,* don't be so bloody flippant," Dunn responded.

"Okay then, remembering what Doctor Webb said, he must be the lover."

“I need a break, Ellis. We need to go get some lunch. I’m sure Mr Sutton won’t mind waiting a bit longer.”

While Dunn grabbed the last empty table in the busy café, Ellis placed their lunch order at the counter. Taking the table number holder from the young girl he pulled her close. Her eyes widened wondering what he was about to say.

“Tell Tony not to fill my sandwich full of lettuce like last time,” he quipped.

The girl’s shoulders slumped forward with disappointment. “I’ll tell him,” she pouted.

As Sergeant Ellis dragged the chair out next to Dunn, their attention was drawn to a police patrol car passing driven by Detective Hunter. Sitting next to her was Peter Ashcott, looking decidedly unhappy.

“So, Ellis, what do you make of Peter Ashcott?”

“I thought he seemed genuinely distraught hearing the news about Laura Verwood. That was no act. Although I get the impression, he’s not too enamoured by his ‘birth mother’,” Ellis said, stressing the words with air quotes.

Dunn nodded in agreement. “I suppose he has good reason not to like the woman, after all she did give him away when he was a baby. But, by the same token, she did pay for him to attend Queens College.”

“D’you think he had something to do with her death?” Ellis asked.

“Honestly? No, I don’t, but in our game, who knows. Wait until we’ve talked to Sutton, then we’ll have more facts on the matter.”

They both fell silent as they began eating the sandwiches that the young waitress had placed on the table. Dunn engrossed himself in the newspaper he'd grabbed from another table. Ellis, who was idly gazing around the café, suddenly sat up straight, holding his sandwich halfway to his mouth.

"*Oh shit*, I'm in trouble… I won't be a sec," he announced, putting his sandwich back on the plate before bounding across the café to where an attractive blond was placing an order at the counter. Wrapping his arms around her in a familiar way, he began chatting incessantly as he waved his hands around, clearly explaining something. Then, after placing an affectionate kiss on her lips, he headed back to the table and continued eating his half-eaten sandwich.

"Phew, that was a close shave. That's Collette from the gym. I was supposed to take her out last night, but completely forgot. I don't think she was very happy with me standing her up. But with my irresistible charm, she's forgiven me." He laughed out loud. As the girl left the café with her coffee order, she turned and smiled sweetly at Ellis, as he mimicked holding a phone to his ear with his thumb and little finger to his ear.

Having watched the whole episode, Dunn folded the newspaper and slapped it down on the empty seat next to him.

"You never cease to amaze me, you have them eating out of your hand, don't you?" he said, with a hint of laughter in his voice. "Tell me Ellis, to change the subject, have you ever tried Scuba diving?"

"Yes, I have actually, a couple of times. Once on the Great Barrier Reef and another time when I was in Vanuatu. Why do you ask?"

"What did you think? Did you enjoy it?"

"It was amazing, quite exhilarating actually. Although it was just a touristy thing that I did, I always promised myself that I'd dive seriously one day. Again, why d'you ask?" Ellis paused. "Hang on… surely you're not thinking of joining Peter Ashcott's little group of novice divers are you?"

"No… no… not me, I was thinking more *you*," Dunn said smiling back. You're the rugged, athletic type, I was wondering if *this* could be the right time for you to learn how to dive properly. What do you think?"

"I see what you're getting at. Then I could keep an eye on Peter Ashcott. I can't go under cover though, he's already met me."

"So don't go undercover, be legit, tell him all about yourself, how you've always dreamed of scuba diving."

"Are you saying it will be all expenses paid?" he grinned.

"Whoa! Steady on Raymond, don't push your luck. Nevertheless, I'll have a word with the Green. I'm sure he'd sanction a couple of days, if it's going to help with our enquiries," said Dunn, sensing the excitement in Ellis' voice.

"I'll get on it right away, now let's go and talk to this Mr Sutton," he said as he stood up and walked out the café. Shaking his head, Ellis pulled out his wallet and headed to the counter to pay for the lunches.

"You never learn Ray, he gets you every time," The cashier chirped. As she placed a handful of change into his hand, he held onto her hand just a little longer than necessary.

"Have to keep the boss sweet now don't I," he said with a playful wink.

Chapter 10

A frosty atmosphere greeted Inspector Dunn and Sergeant Ellis as they entered the interview room where Dennis Sutton waited patiently. The well-dressed slightly balding man in his early fifties, drummed his fingers noisily on the desk in front of him. Jumping to his feet sharply, almost knocking his chair over, he gave them both a deathly stare, his bottom lip quivered with anger as he opened his mouth to speak.

Pre-empting what he was about to say, Inspector Dunn jumped in quickly. "Mr Sutton, I'm Detective Inspector Dunn, I must apologise for having kept you waiting, but you know how it is? Something urgent came up." Dunn said, covering up their inconsiderate behaviour. "This is Detective Sergeant Ellis, who you spoke to on the telephone the other day."

"I hope this is not going to take too long, I too am a very busy man," Sutton said, tapping his watch impatiently.

"That depends on how compliant you are Mr Sutton. Anyway, thank you for coming in so quickly and interrupting your busy schedule, I hear you're in the antique business?" Dunn asked.

"You heard correct, I am the owner of the 'Antique's Emporium' in the high street at Mosman. I've been there for almost thirty years, so I'm quite well known and respected in the antique world," Sutton replied.

"I take it you live above the shop?"

"That's right, I do, I have a very comfortable apartment and very convenient."

"That's good to hear Mr Sutton. Now my colleague here, Detective Ellis, informs me you called on Laura Verwood the night of her death, would you like to tell us the details of that visit?"

"Yes of course and that's correct, as your Sergeant here told you, I visited Laura around six o'clock. We always get together before she leaves for her trip to New York that's normal. We like to discuss what she will be taking and how she will present the items to their best advantage. We also meet up when either of us come across something interesting in an auction or a deceased estate sale. We like to discuss the items and research their true value." Sutton began to go off at a tangent. "It's quite a lucrative business if you find that little gem which turns out to be very valuable. When I say gem, of course I mean that metaphorically." He said, condescendingly.

"Laura's area is antique jewellery, mine is more furniture and objet d'art. We think highly of each other's opinions. If items turn out to be rubbish, then we discard them. Usually at Laura's apartment, hence the reason it's so full of stuff," He paused to laugh. "We sell our valuable items on, but not in Australia may I add. We sell to the American market.

That's why Laura made regular trips to New York. That and the TV show she appears on. Laura is quite the celebrity and is very popular in the American antique world. We have a good system, Laura presents three or four of our best pieces on the show then talked about them. Within hours people would be ringing wanting to buy, at ridiculously inflated prices. As I said, good business, don't you think?"

"Is that legal?" Ellis asked.

"We never break any laws, it's just being savvy and knowing how to play the market. Or a good advertising ploy if you think about it."

Ellis rolled his eyes while shaking his head.

Inspector Dunn held up his hand, halting their conversation, feeling they were digressing.

"Can we please keep to the point?" Dunn snapped. "Are you able to tell us what you talked about and how was the state of Miss Verwood's mind?"

"*Laura*, please, her name is Laura," Sutton said indignantly.

"Pardon me?" Ellis said, looking confused at being corrected unnecessarily.

"Her name is Laura," Sutton repeated, stressing her name as though it was important.

Ellis wondered why Sutton was making such a big deal with her name, putting it down to him being upset about her death.

"Okay then, *Laura,*" Ellis retaliated. "So, Mr Sutton, tell us about your visit."

"Laura phoned me early in the evening, insisting I go to her place which wasn't unusual as I said, we always caught up before her trips to New York. But this time she sounded agitated and not happy at all. When I got there, she was in a bit of a state because she couldn't find the expensive necklace she was taking to America. She knew exactly where she'd left it, but it was gone. So naturally she was sure someone had stolen it. In fact, she insisted there were other expensive pieces of jewellery were missing too, so of course she was very angry. I tried to calm her down, but she was in no mood to be calmed down."

"Are you able to describe the necklace," asked Dunn. "After all, you must have known the piece she was referring to, as you said yourself, you discussed what she was taking to America."

"Of course I can. In fact, I actually have a picture of it back at my place, as it appears in our catalogue. The necklace is made up of nine platinum filigree flowers set with diamonds and seed pearls. It has a large matching pendant hanging in the centre worth in excess of five thousand Australian dollars. I'd like to add it is also a genuine antique, meaning it is over a hundred years old."

"Make a note to call Sergeant Miller, Ellis, and let her know we now have confirmation there was a robbery and if she needs to speak to Mr Sutton, he's here in interview room two. I'm sure Mr Sutton won't mind staying for a little while longer," Dunn said. "So, let's get back to your story, Mr Sutton. You were saying Laura Verwood was angry?"

"Well, not very angry, more in a flap. I have to say, Laura can be a bit of a drama Queen. She would go on and on about not being able to trust *anyone.* Which I thought was a bit harsh and I'll admit, I took it a little personally.»

Sergeant Ellis tapped his pencil annoyingly on his notepad as he spoke. "There would have to be a lot of trust between you both. Buying and selling expensive antiques, there's always the chance that one could be ripping the other one off. Sounds like she could've been accusing you of robbing her, the evening she died. Did you argue?"

"Excuse me, Sergeant, we *never* argued, we were good friends and as far as ripping each other off, that's absurd. I take offence to that accusation."

Ellis shrugged his shoulders before speaking again. "To be quite frank, Mr Sutton, I'm not sure how she could notice anything missing, her place isn't exactly in order."

Sutton heaved a sigh. "To a layman like yourselves, you might be led to believe that, but I can assure you, we both know exactly what we have. When you are heavily involved in the purchasing of something, you don't forget it easily. You will find an inventory record in her desk at the apartment which gives a full account of purchases and sales. It will explain what her items were bought for and what she sold them for.

"Clearly she was accusing someone of robbing her." Dunn butted in. "Or was this a cry for help, making the whole thing up for attention?"

"I know where you're going with this. I've always known about Laura's depression and her dependence on sleeping pills." Sutton slumped back in his chair and lowered his eyes. He remained silent for a few seconds.

"Look, I have a confession to make. From the very first day Laura walked into my antique shop, I fell in love with her. Back then she knew nothing about the antique business, she'd worked in finance for years at a large bank in the city. Nonetheless, she was friendly, funny and eager to learn. Actually, I remember she was very impatient and wanted to know everything all at once, we often had little tiffs about that, she would say I was too slow and stuffy," A broad smile spread over his face at this recollection.

"My wife had just died from breast cancer, so I was pretty depressed and lonely at that time. Laura was like a breath of fresh air, she brought me back to life. And for your information, before you ask, we were never lovers, our relationship was purely platonic. We were really good friends, more like brother and sister I suppose."

"There goes our theory Sutton was her lover, which means he probably wasn't the last person to see her alive, or she definitely had another visitor that evening," Dunn thought to himself.

I taught her all the tricks of the trade and with Laura's infectious personality, we made a perfect business team," Sutton continued.

"So, on your last meeting with Miss Verwood… Laura, you mentioned that she was agitated," Ellis asked

"Yes, she was. I could usually pacify her when she got into one of her moods, but she seemed to have a bee in her bonnet that night, so I left."

Sutton looked up at the ceiling and sighed as he drifted into his own thoughts.

Bringing him back to earth, Ellis continued with his questions.

"We know she suspected someone of stealing, did you feel she was right? Did you know the pieces that were missing?"

"No, I can't say I agreed with her, if someone had robbed her apartment, I don't think they would have stopped at a few pieces. The place is like an Aladdin's Den for God's sake and I would definitely recognise any piece of jewellery someone tried to sell. I know every dealer in Sydney, it would only take a few phone calls to find *any* information regarding someone trying to sell stuff."

"One thing that puzzles me, Mr Sutton, you haven't asked us how she died. I would have thought that would have been your first question," Dunn said.

"I heard on the radio, a female had fallen from an apartment in Balmain East and then you phoned me asking if I knew Laura Verwood, I put two and two together." Sutton's voice began to tremble as he removed a handkerchief from his jacket pocket and blew his nose discreetly.

"I'm sorry, please excuse me, gentlemen, Laura was a popular and generous, kind person. I don't know how I'm going to cope with not having her around any longer." Sutton said then blew his nose again.

The room fell silent for what seemed like an eternity as both detectives gave him time to compose himself.

"Do you know anything about Laura's two baby boys that she had adopted?" Dunn asked

"Two boys? I think you will find it's only one. She spoke very little about the boy to me. I do know he's called Peter. It was a very private subject. All I know is when he was old enough to go to high school, she tracked him down. She contacted his adopted parents and persuaded them to let her pay for his education at a top school. They finally agreed and after that she stayed in contact with the boy. She never mentioned anything about another boy, not to me anyway."

"When you paid her a visit on that last evening, did you talk about anything else other than the stolen pieces?"

"No, Inspector, I wasn't there long enough."

"You both didn't by any chance, step out onto the balcony? Perhaps to talk."

"You must be joking, she hated that balcony. Why on earth she lived in an apartment that high when she had a massive fear of heights? No, that balcony scared her to death." A look of horror spread across his face, realizing what he had just said.

I'm sorry, bad choice of words. That's why there wasn't a stick of furniture out there. As far as I knew, the doors were kept locked and bolted.

As he allowed Ellis to continue to question Mr Sutton. Dunn sat quietly thinking to himself that the balcony story matched Peter Ashcott's except for the doors being locked. Peter had said they flew open when he was there and they were open wide when they visited her apartment the evening she died?

"Why didn't you call the police when she said things had gone missing?" Ellis asked.

"People don't see Laura as I do. Everyone thinks she's eccentric. When people know you suffer from depression, they think anything you do out of the ordinary is a cry for help. As you yourself, asked earlier."

Dunn sat up straight, thinking it was time to change the subject.

"Do you know why Peter Ashcott visited Miss Verwood, I mean Laura?"

"Yes, he was hoping she would help him out with a business venture. He wanted money. She said no… and before you ask, I don't know why she refused him. The woman is rich enough to buy him anything he wants or needs."

"Could he have been the one to have stolen her jewellery then? If he needed help financially. "

"Who knows, although I shouldn't think so, Peter hardly ever went to the apartment. It was mainly Laura that called on the Ashcott's."

Ellis' leaned forward and rested both elbows on the desk before speaking. "Just one more question, Mr Sutton,"

"When we visited Laura Verwood's apartment, the balcony doors were open wide, and the curtains were blowing wildly in the wind. Are you sure she would not have opened them?"

"Definitely *not*. I've already told you, she *hated* that balcony."

"Not even if she'd had a few drinks, or had taken a relaxant?"

"Not even if there was a million dollars sitting in a box out there."

Dunn felt he had enough to be going on with, and his hunch was beginning to hold some weight at last. He thanked Mr Sutton for his time and was just about to allow him to leave when Mr Sutton decided he still had more to say.

"Inspector Dunn, can I just ask? Where is Laura's body and who will be making the arrangements for her funeral?"

"Forensics have Laura Verwood's body, I would imagine it is still too early for them to release her. Mrs Ashcott has offered to take care of things, is that a problem?"

"What!" he exclaimed loudly. "It has to be me. My dear friend's funeral will be more than a backyard affair. I can assure you Inspector Dunn, Laura is... was a very influential woman.

Everyone in the antique world, not to mention her people in America, will want to attend her funeral and pay their respects to the wonderful woman." He paused for a moment. "It can't be arranged by the *Ashcott's*." he said, his voice trembling.

"I'm afraid you need to discuss this with Peter Ashcott. As far as we know, *he* is the only living relative, in which case, her affairs are to be taken care of by her next of kin."

"I'm sure you can communicate with the Ashcott's and resolve this. They are extremely approachable people." Dunn said, offering a solution. "Now, Mr Sutton, once again, I thank you for your time, Sergeant Ellis and I have other matters to attend to. I will phone you if I have any further questions.

Chapter 11

Not willing to drive into the busy city, Fish suggested to Jenni that they take the train to save time and then they could walk the short distance to the museum Asho was sending them to visit. To their disappointment, there was a light rain falling as they left the station. They weaved their way through the early morning commuters, ducking under shop awnings, to shelter from the rain which was turning torrential.

Thankfully, Asho's directions were easy to understand. Jenni and Fish reached the original old Victorian bank building which now housed the museum. The large carved timber doors were wide open, allowing them to enter hastily out of the rain. Being soaked to the skin, they began wiping themselves and shaking off the excess water from their clothes. A diminutive lady, appearing to be well into her seventies, waited patiently behind the reception counter for them to approach her. The large sign on the wall behind her, with the words 'The Australian Institute of Research in Numismatic Studies', confirmed they were in the right place.

After paying their entry fee, the lady handed them their tickets and a small folded pamphlet, pointing out it was a map of the four floors. Sounding very knowledgeable, the lady launched into a barrage of information, hoping they might find helpful. Fish and Jenni were finding it difficult to hide their impatience as they began walking backwards to distance themselves from her. Even though she was being kind, they felt she was wasting precious time.

"Okay, where do you want us to begin?"

"Well, according to this map, it makes sense to start at the bottom and work our way to the top. The ancient coins are on the first floor."

The lady at the desk overheard them and called out asking if they were sure she couldn't be of any help.

Letting out an impatient sigh, Jenni turned to answer her. "Basically, we're only interested in ancient coins,"

"Then you should go to the top floor 'Collections through the ages', start there and work your way to the ground floor. We have over forty thousand coins, medals, and decorations. You will see many of the world's most valuable coins and I'm sure you won't be disappointed." She added with a beaming smile.

Taking the elevator, they stepped out into a large gallery. The plain walls, painted stark white, set off the large oak frames hanging on each wall, displaying coins. The elaborate Victorian ceiling looked stunning with a flower feature picked out in gold. Dark timber and glass cabinets, filled with coins, ran along the centre of the room, leaving enough space to walk either side.

Being early in the day and the rain meant there were no other visitors, they had the room to themselves. Fish took out the coin to use for reference. The pair split up, taking a side of the room each.

As they strolled casually along the cabinet stopping several times to study the collection of ancient artefacts. Reaching the end of the gallery they turned and taking their time, began walking back to where they'd started.

"This is all very interesting, but there must be over two thousand coins here, and not one of them resembles ours," Fish said.

"Shall we go to the next floor?" Jenni suggested.

"I think we have to, let's hope we have more luck."

Deciding to take the stairs, instead of the lift, they discovered the third floor was the same as the one they'd just come from. They walked from one side of the huge room to the other with glass display cabinets along both sides, Fish held the coin above the glass and moved it around, hoping to find a match. As they returned to the beginning, Fish pushed the coin back into his pocket and looked at Jenni. "Okay, that's two down, two more to go." He smiled.

Using the stairs again, they reached the next floor to find that this gallery was totally different. Although there were the same ornate ceilings, the layout had changed. The display cabinets resembled tables that flanked both sides of the room with a walkway down the centre. A large sign on the left side, above the cabinets, read 'THE AVENUE FOR HOBBY COLLECTORS'. On the right-hand side of the room, tall timber and glass display cases contained military medals, each had a placard with information about the receiver of the award.

Both Fish and Jenni decided that this gallery was the least interesting. Finally, they reached the ground floor. Fish stood in front of a sign on the wall with bold lettering, 'WORLD'S RAREST AND MOST VALUABLE COINS'.

"Take a look at that Jenni, that old crow at the ticket office gave us a bum steer, we should've come here first like we said, the silly old bat."

Unable to share Fish's enthusiasm, Jenni wasn't so sure this was any more interesting than the other floors. Feeling sceptical, not to mention bored, about the whole coin thing, she decided it was more of a *boy* thing. She wandered around the display cases half-heartedly. Then her eyes followed along a corridor where she spotted the fire exit door, she had a giggle to herself thinking if only she could slip away.

Scouring the display units, Fish noticed a box with an assortment of small lumps of metal. The tag next to it stated, 'Coins minted circa AD10'.

"I think we're in the wrong place and what Asho found is not a coin at all, maybe he was right, it's just an old identification disc," Jenni said, stifling a yawn.

"Just be patient for a little while longer Jen, then I'll treat you to a cappuccino and cake. We may as well keep going now that we're here."

Fish sprinted ahead, taking long strides, skipping most of the display cabinets. When he reached the end of the room, he stopped dead in his tracks and stared into a cabinet. Seeing his expression change, she hurried over to join him to see his eyes fixed firmly on the glass window in front of them. Following his stare, she could see what had caught his attention.

There on the glass shelf was a row of six coins, matching theirs.

"I don't believe it, Jen, I think we've hit the jackpot." He called out trying to keep his voice low.

"Oh my God, Fish… they're the same," she whispered back.

"Whoa! Read the name underneath, it says 'Nubian gold'. Let's find the curator of this place and see what he has to say. Better not show him our coin, for the time being, let's keep it our little secret, eh Jen?"

"I agree, better not mention anything, we don't want them taking it off us, Asho would never forgive us," she added, pulling a face.

"Didn't he say whatever you find on the dive, you have to leave well alone?"

"Hmm, I'm not sure if that's true, or something he made up as a scare tactic to keep the divers in order," Fish replied, as they burst into a fit of giggles.

When they reached the reception, they approached a man, smartly dressed in uniform with an official name badge pinned to his lapel. Fish asked the man politely where they could find the curator and was it possible speak to him. The man gave a quizzical look for a few moments before replying.

"The Curator is *Miss* Caroline Hughes," he said, stressing the word Miss. "I can assure you, she is most definitely a woman. May I ask why you need to speak to Miss Hughes?"

Fish leaned close to Jenni's ear. "Funny how I assumed that a curator was a dude," he whispered. "Bit like a Doctor or a scientist." He continued.

Jenni slapped him on the arm, putting her index finger to her lips to hush him.

The man overheard Fish's comment but chose to ignore it.

"Just to let you know, young man, I think you will find, I'm capable of answering any questions you have, without bothering Ms. Hughes, who is a very busy lady,"

Thinking on the spur of the moment how he could reply, an idea came to him in an instant. He put on his best authoritative voice

"I'm sure you can, and under normal circumstances, I'd agree, but, our questions are for the purpose of scientific research. No disrespect, it's important we speak to someone who may have more knowledge on ancient metals."

Looking miffed, the gentlemen turned on his heels. "In that case, you better wait there and I will see if Ms. Hughes is free to speak with you,"

The man took off along the hallway, stopping at a door displaying the name 'Caroline Hughes, Curator' in gold lettering on a wooden plaque. He gave two raps on the door and waited before entering.

"That was quick thinking Peter, but how are you going to carry it through and talk about your research?"

"I'll just bluff my way through and with my wit and charm, I should be okay," he said with a smug expression.

"We'll see," Jenni smiled.

Fish and Jenni turned around sharply at the sound of the door bursting open at the end of the corridor. The man was walking towards them, followed closely by a tall, slender woman in her early forties with flame red hair tied up in a tight, unflattering bun. As they reached Jenni and Fish, the woman barged past the man, nearly bowling him over in an endeavour to reach them first. Jenni's first thoughts were that the lady had no thought for fashion. Her trousers looked two sizes too big, topped with an oversized, long green jumper that looked hand knitted by someone's dear old grandmother, hiding any curves she might have.

Reaching out, she took it in turns to shake their hands with gusto as she introduced herself in a husky voice. "Good morning, I'm Caroline Hughes, I'm told you would like to speak to me. I am the Curator of this fine establishment, and organizer of our collection here in the museum," she said, announcing her titles, with an air of authority.

"What can I do to help you today?"

"Thank you for taking the time to speak to us Ms. Hughes. I'm Peter Buckton and my associate here is Jenni Sherwood. We appreciate you finding time to talk to us, we'll try not to keep you too long." Fish announced as Jenni just gave a simple nod of her head.

"Because we're researching ancient metals, we thought we'd start with coins."

"Well then you've come to the right place," she smiled smugly. "We pride ourselves as having many of the most interesting and oldest metal coins in the world. In fact, we have artefacts that are over two and a half thousand years old," she exclaimed.

Leading them to a timber, glass-fronted cabinet, Ms. Hughes was unaware this was the cabinet Fish had discovered earlier which displayed exactly the same coin as theirs. There were at least a hundred coins displayed, all shapes sizes and colours.

"Most of today's coins are made of what we call Cupronickel. That is, before you ask, seventy-five percent copper and twenty-five percent nickel. You will find aluminium and bronze are also common elements in coin making these days," she said, sounding passionate about the subject.

"Any coins that are dated BC, were made from a metal called Billon. The Majority was a base metal, copper, and bronze," she said.

Ms. Hughes waited as Fish and Jenni examined the contents in the glass case as though they'd never seen them.

"We have many very interesting examples, take these over here, for instance," she said as she marched over to a timber picture frame with all the grace of a workman. The display was an assortment of crude handmade ancient coins.

"Often, the coins would be made from small quantities of silver, mixed with mercury. These alloys were regarded as a precious metal around the birth of Christ."

Waiting for a gap in Ms. Hughes lecture, Jenni bravely interrupted her.

"I thought gold was most precious at that time. Didn't one of the three kings carry gold as a gift to baby Jesus?"

"That's true, of course, but gold was only just coming into vogue at that time because of its softness. But, many still favoured silver because of its brightness. In fact, right up to the end of the Viking age, gold was rejected in favour of silver. It was all to do with the armour which protected the armies."

Fish was enthralled by Ms. Hughes information, finding it all very fascinating. Unfortunately, Jenni was bored again. It was all very interesting, but they weren't finding out much about their coin. The idea of coffee and cake was overpowering her thought. When Ms. Hughes wasn't looking and stopped talking for a second, Jenni began pulling faces at Fish to let him know how she was feeling. He knew what she was hinting at but he needed to steer the conversation back to their own coin.

"Were there *any* civilization that used gold for their coins?" he asked, when he got the chance to speak.

Without missing a beat, Ms. Hughes dived straight back into her wealth of knowledge.

"Funny you should ask that Mr Buckton, there was one exception and that was The Nubian Kingdom which was a region along the river Nile where gold was their prime source of precious metal. This was around 300BC. They turned their gold into coins, in fact, there's a few on display over here... come, follow me," she commanded, as she marched back to the original display cabinet. Unbeknown to her, it was exactly where they wanted to be. Fish was so pleased that he was asking the right questions without any suspicion.

"They say the Nubian people used their coins to trade with other nations. However, these are only rumours."

"Isn't that what coins are used for, anyway?" Jenni said stifling a yawn. Miss Hughes ignored her comment, taking more notice of Peter, who was pointing to a row of six similar coins to the one he had hidden in his pocket.

"What do you think the pattern on those coins represents?"

After studying the coins for a few moments, she began to explain.

"Looking at the shape of the coins and the arrangement of lines, we think it could represent the Coast of the Mediterranean, as it was known three hundred years BC."

"What about the pattern on the other side?" He asked.

Jenni gave Fish a look of disdain, giving him a sign his curiosity was making him sail a little too close to the wind.

"That's easy, there's no pattern on the other side. This is because; early coin makers would carve out a pattern in a block of wood, mostly cedar, then the molten gold would be poured into the mould. Then, with something hard, they would scrape off any excess. When the coins cooled, they would be removed, resulting in one side had a pattern, one side was flat," she said, pointing once again at the display cabinet, "If you examine the coins, you will see they have variations in their diameter's and their thickness. No two would be alike."

"What happens if someone found coins like these here?" Fish asked as he pointed to the coin, like the one in his pocket.

Now Jenni was very concerned. What Fish was asking this woman was getting too close for comfort and she wasn't stupid, she would know what he was up to.

"Well, first let me tell you, it would be highly unlikely that *anyone* would find coins like these," she replied. "However, if they *did*, they would have to hand them to the proper authorities so that proof of authenticity can be decided. If the coins are proven to be authentic, a certificate of authorisation would be issued. Only then they could be taken by the finder to do what they want with them."

"So what would a coin like that fetch?" Fish pushed on boldly as he pointed to the six coins displayed.

Jenni was now in panic mode, her hands were sweating observing the expression on the woman's face and the tone of her voice was changing. It was becoming blatantly clear, Ms. Hughes was becoming suspicious.

"Coins like these are not rare, maybe around thirty to forty dollars each. Maybe a little more if they are proved to be real gold." She replied, pausing for a moment.

"Where did you say you were from again?"

"We run a scuba diving school, we're asked constantly about finding treasure. Of course, we know only too well, there's no such thing around these waters. We like to have the right answers to tell people," Fish explained, hoping she was buying it.

"Are you sure you yourselves are not treasure hunters?" Ms. Hughes snapped. Neither Fish nor Jenni spoke for a second, giving Miss Hughes her answer.

"You are, aren't you, this has nothing to do with research has it? I think it's time you left, how dare you waste my valuable time," she said, sounding angered at his dishonesty, lying about his identity.

Turning to the man in uniform, Ms. Hughes whispered something in his ear. He made a halting gesture with his hands as she stormed down the corridor.

"Okay, you two, on your way before I call the police," He bellowed.

Getting the message, Fish and Jenni hurried towards the front reception and out of the building.

"I think we overstayed our welcome there," Fish said.

"You *think?*" Jenni fumed. "Fish, I could've clobbered you in there. Talk about walking on a knife edge."

"Don't be daft Jen, I think I did well, Asho will be pleased I reckon."

"I hope you're right and we haven't raised suspicion, I would imagine there's a lot of competition with treasure hunting, a very secretive sport. Woe betide anyone stepping on another's territory."

"How? They don't know who we are or where we live," he said, but had to admit, Jenni was probably right. Hoping to pacify her, he found a cute cafe and ordered her a coffee and two large chocolate eclairs.

Wiping a blob of cream off Fish's cheek, Jenni continued the discussion. "So anyway, that aside, did you get the information we need?"

"Yeah, two things, I found out the information about our coin and that we need a sack full just to buy lunch."

They both laughed hysterically at the ridiculousness of what they'd just encountered.

◆◆◆

After the unfortunate incident with the two young frauds, Caroline Hughes returned to her office and locked the door. She was furious at being taken in by a couple of kids and made to look foolish. Dashing to her desk, she picked up the phone and dialed a number, then waited for a response. Hearing the voice of the receptionist, Miss Hughes gave her name and asked if she could speak to Mr Pullman. After a few moments, the phone clicked and a man's voice boomed through the receiver.

"Pullman here,"

"David it's me... Caroline, Caroline Hughes from the museum," She paused as he greeted her with friendly banter. "Anyway, David, I thought you would like to know, I've just had a strange encounter with two young people here in the museum a moment ago. They spun me a line that they were making scientific studies about precious metals. They were asking questions about metals used in the making of ancient coins. Like an idiot, I was taken in at first."

"Get to the point woman," the man boomed, impatiently.

"Okay, okay… don't be so impatient. The young man prattled on about metals then pointed to one of the Phoenician gold pieces and asked pointed questions. He asked what was the procedure, should someone find one."

"You didn't tell them too much I hope?"

"Of course not! I was careful what I said. I told them all about the authenticity certificate. When he asked the value of one of our coins."

"Hmm, sounds a bit suspicious, what did you say to that?"

"I told them the coins were not as valuable as people think, in fact worthless. I'm sure they believed me. I think we need to look into this, I got the distinct feeling they might have discovered something."

"What makes you think that?"

"They said they ran a scuba diving school so I'm using my powers of deduction. Think about it David, Scuba diving... asking about gold coins, I think it's a forgone conclusion."

"Did they say where this scuba diving school is?"

"Well, no, that subject didn't arise. I don't know its location, however, I have a name. The young man's name was Peter Buckton and I think the young lady may have just been his girlfriend. I don't think it will be too difficult to track them down."

"You haven't mentioned this to anyone have you?"

"No, why would I? Will I be seeing you for our usual get-together soon?"

"Yes, and I look forward to it."

Ms. Hughes placed the phone down and donned half-rimmed tortoise-shell glasses on the end of her nose. She opened the drawer of her desk. Taking out a large zipped purse, she opened it and removed a small, neatly folded parcel made from tissue paper. Laying it on the desk in front of her, she unfolded the tissue revealing a gold coin. Unbeknown to her, Peter Buckton had the same one in his jeans pocket, standing right next to her. Picking up the coin, she rubbed her index finger gently over the coin and studied it for a few moments, a smile stretched across her face.

Opening the drawer, she swapped the coin for a book. Making her way to an armchair in the corner of the room, she made herself comfortable ready for some serious reading. Before opening the brand new publication, she trailed her fingers lightly over the title, 'Life without men', written by Barbara Scott.

Chapter 12

Opposite the Blue Horizons Scuba Diving School, two men sat in a Toyota dual cab utility truck, parked discretely under the thick foliage of a large gum tree. Dressed from head to foot in black, the two men had waited patiently for the sun to set. And with the lack of street lights in the area, the street was now plunged into darkness. From their position, they had a clear view of both the shop front and the marina.

Although the owners had locked up and left for the day, the men decided it best to play it safe and wait at least another hour. There was always the chance they might decide to return for some reason or the other.

The man sitting in the passenger seat removed a packet of cigarettes from his pocket and placed one between his lips. He pointed the pack at the man sitting in the driver's seat.

"No thanks, mate, and I wish you wouldn't smoke in my Ute," he whined.

Ignoring him, the man with the cigarette flicked his lighter, causing a bright blue flame to illuminate the cab. He touched the tip of the cigarette with the flame, making it glow red as he defiantly sucked in a mouthful of smoke and blew it out noisily through pursed lips.

"I wish you weren't ugly either, but there's bugger all I can do about that," the man said as he wound the window down and blew another puff of smoke out into the night air, ignoring the drivers scowl.

"How much longer are we going to have to sit here?" he asked, drawing on his cigarette and blowing out through the side of his mouth.

"Not long now, we have to be sure they're not coming back," the driver replied, waving his hand to dispel the smoke wafting his way. Taking out his mobile phone to check the time, he sat up straight. "Right… time to go," he said, pushing it back in his jacket pocket.

The tall man wound down the passenger window and flicked his cigarette into the darkness, sending a spray of glowing ash to the ground. He grabbed two woollen hoods from the glove box and tossed one to the driver. They pulled them over their heads and climbed out of the vehicle.

The two ex-navy men looked similar. Both with fit muscular bodies, squeezed into black cargo trousers, black T-shirts and black combat jackets; and their hair trimmed to a number one. The only dissimilarity between them was their heights. While one stood well over six feet, the other was much shorter at around five feet six. The short one retrieved a crowbar from the back seat of the dual cab and tried to tuck it under his jacket to hide it, wasting valuable time.

"What the fuck are you doing?" the tall man said sounding agitated. "Why bother trying to hide it, I think seeing a bloke dressed in black with a balaclava is more noticeable than a fuckin crowbar!" he fumed.

They glanced up and down the street, making sure it was clear before dashing across the street to the dive shop. Passing the front door, they headed down the side of the building. Taking the crowbar, the shorter man wedged it between the door and frame. Using brute strength, he forced the door open with a loud cracking sound. The taller man quickly entered the workshop and flashed his torch just inside the door for an alarm switch. Finding the simple security system, he snipped the wires and sneered. "Some people have bugger all idea how to protect their belongings, don't they realise there're criminals around?" he scorned, throwing his head back and laughing.

The man who forced the door attempted to push it back in the frame.

"Leave that, we haven't time, let's head straight for the room at the front."

Within no time, the room was destroyed as they both proceeded to pull out drawers, dumping the contents all over the floor. The files from the filing cabinet were scattered everywhere. The tall man opened a small cupboard in the corner of the room behind the desk.

"*Well bugger me! Come and see* what I've found," he called out.

His mate hurried over to see and slapped him on his back.

"Well done, leave it to me, stand back." He unhooked a large pouch from his utility belt and took out a small piece of a putty type substance and pushed it into the keyhole and around the handle of the safe. Taking out a small vial containing a liquid he pushed it into the putty then broke the glass allowing the clear liquid to drain out.

"Quick, get behind the desk," he called out.

Within seconds of them both ducking down, a deafening thud resonated through the small building. Once the smoke and debris had settled, the safe door now hung from its hinges. Both men stared into the safe, all that was in there was a small metal cash box. The short man grabbed the box and to his surprise the lid wasn't locked.

He raked through the contents with his fingers, disappointed to see all that was in there, was loose cash and a large wad of paper money and not what he was looking for.

Without his friend seeing he shoved the bundle of notes into his pocket and tossed the cash box across the room, sending the cash around the room with a clatter.

"Geez, how fuckin dumb are these people, haven't they heard of banks," he mumbled under his breath.

"So no luck there then?" the tall man asked.

"Nope, nothing here,"

"Okay, let's go mess up the workshop," the tall one said laughing. He picked up a chair and smashed it on the floor, causing it to shatter.

They both headed to the back room where the half-open door was swinging precariously from its hinges. Shafts of light from the semi-full moon streamed into the workshop.

"At least it's easier to see in here," The tall one said, as he walked the length of the workbench, searching through tool boxes and containers filled with an assortment of necessary equipment. Sending them crashing to the ground when he didn't find anything.

Yanking open the cupboard door, the short man rifled through the contents. After deciding it was a waste of time, he callously swiped his hand across the shelves, knocking the contents to the floor.

"It has to be in the boat," the tall one decided. "Let's get out of here."

Leaving by the door they had entered, they skulked back to the front of the shop where they stopped long enough to glance up and down the street to make sure there was no one around. As soon as they agreed that everything was clear, they headed towards the marina,

As they approached the locked aluminium gate, they both took turns at jumping up and grabbing the top of the gate. Then pulling their bodies up and swinging over, they dropped down on the other side, landing on the jetty without any effort.

"Do we know which boat?" the shorter one asked.

"Err, I wonder… how about the one over there with the words BLUE HORIZONS SCUBA DIVING SCHOOL written in big letters on the side. Is that a big enough hint?" the tall one said sounding exasperated.

Passing a line of expensive boats tied to the aluminium floating dock, they hurried towards the dive boat. Keeping their heads low, they clambered on board and tiptoed across the open deck to the locked cabin door. Using his crowbar again, the shorter man rammed it between the door frames and then jammed it with all his might, as he had done earlier with the shop. The door flew off its hinges and shattered, sending shards of wood into the air like missiles. A piece just missing the tall man by inches.

"For fuck's sake, it's only a fuckin plywood door, you could've pushed it open with your shoulder. Geez, you almost had my eye out," he ranted. "I need a smoke."

"No you don't, and shut the fuck up! You're like a bloody nagging old woman," the shorter one retaliated.

Storming the cabin, they ransacked the place, following the same MO as the shop. Standing in the middle of the steering station with his hands on his hips the tall man fumed. "*Bastards,* they must have taken it with them cos it's certainly not here, we've checked everywhere,"

"Shit, what we gonna tell the boss?" the short one asked, sounding concerned.

"How about, 'we didn't find anything boss' you dick head?"

"That means he'll send us to their houses to search."

"So… if we have to, we will now let's get out of here."

As they were just about to climb over the side rails of the boat, a small four wheel drive swung into the street, its bright headlights illuminating the whole area. Both men hit the deck. "Shit, don't tell me they've decided to come back, just stay down, I'll take a look." the tall one said as he raised his head just enough to see the vehicle slowing down near the marina. "Shit, it's stopping," he said in a throaty whisper.

The driver parked close to the marina's security gate and switched off the engine, plunging them back into darkness followed by silence. The men held their breath waiting for the occupants of the car to emerge. After several minutes, without hearing any movement, the tall man peered over the side of the boat once more to check what was happening. Seeing the two passengers locked in a passionate embrace, he gave a sly grin.

"What the fuck are they doing?" the shorter man whispered loudly.

Giving him a sharp nudge with his elbow, the tall one laughed. "Funny you should say that, I'd say that's exactly what they're doing. I suggest we settle down, this could be a long night."

The short man realised straight away what he meant. "You're joking! Haven't they got a home where they can do that sort of thing? Let me see?" he said, trying to get to his feet.

"No, you pervert, we're professionals, not fuckin peeping Toms," the tall one replied with a grin as he sat beside his mate. "Shit, I need a cigarette."

"God, I hope it's a quickie, I don't want to be here all night and what if someone else comes, no pun intended."

The tall one stifled a laugh. "If anyone turns up now, take it from me, that car will be the first to move," he said.

Peering over the rails again, he noticed the windows had steamed up, making it difficult to make out what they were doing. He slumped back down and checked his watch.

"Well, we now know that it's not just a quickie. Shit, I hope they're not gonna to be much longer."

"Yeah... and I'm feeling cold. It wouldn't be so bad if I could watch. It's okay for you, you're the one seeing all the action. I'm fuckin bored, sitting here like a spare prick at a wedding," the short one whined.

"Believe me, you're not missing a thing." Both men made themselves comfortable and took out their mobiles to while away the time.

The sound of another vehicle approaching broke the silence, the marina was illuminated once again.

"Stay down don't look until the lights go off," one of the men murmured.

A small hatchback stopped close by. The sudden continuous blast of the horn, pierced the silence. Not being able to contain themselves any longer both men peered over the side of the boat to watch the drama unfold before them. They watched as a shapely brunette appeared from the second car. Leaving the door wide open, she marched towards the first and banged loudly on the roof.

"Get out the fuckin car, you bastard, I know you're in there with that fuckin slag."

The back passenger door flew open, and a man struggled to clamber out, pulling his trousers up and fumbling with the zip.

"What do you want me to say? You've caught me red-handed," he yelled, throwing his arms in the air.

The brunette ignored him and headed back to her car as if to leave. She opened the boot and took out a large baseball bat and marched back to the man.

"Oh fuck, this is going to be good." The tall man on the boat said as he stifled a laugh.

The brunette returned to the man who was now looking very worried. Bringing the baseball right back behind her the woman took a huge swing at the roof of the car leaving a long thin dent.

"Get out of the car you fucking bitch, show yourself. Come on… show your ugly face?"

The man moved towards the brunette holding out both hands, in a pleading gesture, but the brunette ignored what he was saying and took a swing with the bat, narrowly missing him.

"You're a lying, cheating bastard, how could you? And with *her* of all people, the town slut. How could you insult me going off with that ugly cow?" she yelled, taking another swing, this time hitting him squarely on his forearm as he held it up to defend himself. He screamed out in pain.

"You stupid, fuckin bitch. Shit, I think you've broken my arm. And you wonder why I go off with other women, you fucking mad bitch," he yelled, as he rubbed his arm.

The brunette slammed the baseball bat repeatedly on the bonnet and side windows of the vehicle to the sound of breaking glass as it sprayed onto the road.

"*I said… get out of the car…* you bitch. I'm gonna rearrange your face, maybe I can improve it."

The car door opened and a mousy blonde woman stepped out gingerly.

"Why don't you leave us alone and accept the fact he doesn't want to be with you anymore? He wants to be with me. Why don't you just fuck off and leave us alone?"

The brunette threw the baseball bat down and lurched at the blonde, grabbing her hair, the momentum sending them both to the ground in a heap.

Forgetting the need to stay out of sight, the two men blatantly stood watching the performance from the boat.

“This is so much better than the telly,” the shorter man said with a smile.

As the two women grappled on the ground, the man tried desperately to pull them apart. Staggering to her feet with, the blonde took a swipe across the brunette’s face, knocking her sideways. This gave her enough time to hurry back to the car and jump in the front passenger seat.

The brunette picked herself up off the ground and retrieved the baseball bat from where she’d dropped it and stormed towards the man with a menacing look. He raced to the driver’s door and he too jumped back in the car and pressed the central locking. While frantically trying to turn the key in the ignition, the irate brunette took another swipe at the car, shattering the glass in the back window.

“You’re gonna be sorry, I’m gonna take you for everything, you piece of *shit*,” she yelled at the man. Finally, the engine burst into life, the car shot away from the curb with the wheels squealing as the driver threw the car into sharp a U-turn and sped away, fishtailing down the street before disappearing into the distance.

The brunette marched back to her vehicle and threw the baseball bat into the boot then slammed the lid closed. As she poised, ready to step into the car, her attention was drawn to the boat where the two men were standing. Their hoods now removed, not caring anymore if anyone could see them. She could tell by their body language they were laughing.

“So you think it’s funny, do you? Well, fuck you too,” she yelled, holding up her middle finger. She jumped into the car and slammed the gears loudly while making a three point turn before speeding away. The street fell silent and dark.

"Well, that was entertaining, to say the least. I wouldn't mind seeing the next episode." The tall man joked.

"D'you think she'll divorce him?"

"Nah, course not, they'll all move in together and live happily ever after." The tall one said sarcastically

"D'you think?"

The tall man did an exaggerated eye rolling while tutting loudly. "You're shitting me, right? Let's get out of here, this street has too much action for my liking."

The two men returned to the duel cab and drove away.

Chapter 13

For days, Sydney had suffered the worst weather. As the rain, lashed noisily against the windows of Dunn's office, he sat quietly at his desk; swinging from side to side on his swivel chair gazing into space. He mulled over what information they had so far; determined to unearth something that would lead to the truth about the death of Laura Verwood. With all his experience, he knew when something didn't gel. Dunn felt disappointed his team wasn't with him on this one. Their lack of enthusiasm was getting to him. Even Sergeant Ellis was losing interest. He himself was beginning to feel deflated at the slow pace they were making.

Fortis has made it abundantly clear he was just itching to pull the plug on the case if they didn't come up with something soon. Dunn was even more annoyed that, as far as the team were concerned, it was a clear cut suicide. Determined to follow his gut feeling, Dunn was eager to find *something* that would prove he was correct and that it was *not* suicide. Once again he stood in front of the white board, which was now covered in photos with explanations written in black marker.

"Okay, your attention please," he called out as one by one the team stopped what he or she was doing and listened. "I've asked Julie Miller to join us today," He began, nodding in Julie's direction. "Lovely to see you again Detective Sergeant Miller." Giving her full title.

She acknowledged everyone with a bright smile and a cute finger wave, without saying a word.

"There's a couple of reasons why Julie is here. First, when Ellis and I visited Laura Verwood's apartment, we found the place in such a state. There were boxes of antiques and artefacts everywhere, we both agreed the place could have had either a bungled robbery or it was full of stolen goods. I thought it best robbery check it out. The other reason for that will be apparent in a little while."

"Now on with the serious stuff, I need to remind you all, today is our last day to prove Laura Verwood was murdered. I know everyone suspects it was just suicide, especially the Superintendent. We need to pull out all the stops and find the evidence that will strengthen our case. Even the minutest scrap of evidence. First things first, I'm going through everything we have so far," he said as he turned to the board and picked up the black marker pen and removed the cap.

"These are the names of our main suspects, people who may have had good reasons to bump off Laura Verwood. We have Dennis Sutton, her business associate," he said, tapping loudly on the name Sutton. "I thought he seemed genuine enough, they had known each other for many years. He'd taught her everything he knew, and she sought out his opinions on business deals. By his own admission, he could have been the last person to see her alive. So what was his motive? We need to find *something* to connect him." Dunn moved the marker down to the next name.

"Then we have the building manager, Frank Farrow. So far, we have nothing on him at this stage except that he has keys to all the apartments, so has easy access to them. Lastly, we have Laura Verwood's son, Peter Ashcott. He was put up for adoption when he was only six weeks old due to Miss Verwood's medical problem. We know he paid a visit to her only weeks ago to ask her to help finance a business venture he was planning. We now know she refused, was this his motive to kill her?" Turning to face the group, Dunn continued as he pressed the lid firmly back on the marker and began rolling it over and over as he continued.

"The reason for Sutton's visit to Miss Verwood's apartment the night before she died, is that she was upset about the valuable pieces of jewellery that had gone missing. However, this was *not* reported to the police, which puzzles me and makes me even more suspicious. Could this be our connection to the murderer?»

I've deduced from the information we have so far, whoever it was, must have had easy access to her apartment or she knew the person and let them in. There was no sign of a forced entry and there was no signs of a struggle *anywhere* in the apartment. We now know she'd had a romantic encounter with someone hours before her death."

Ellis smiled inwardly at his description, he was such a gentleman.

Dunn paused, seeing the smirk on Ellis' face. "Have you something to add, Ellis?"

Wiping the smile off his face, he began to speak.

"Well, that covers all your suspects, Sir. As you said, the building manager has keys to all the apartments. He had no problem opening Miss Verwood's apartment and the first one he took us to, trying to put us off the scent."

Dunn scoured the room with his eyes looking for Detective Sally Hunter.

"Hunter, did you check out the manager by any chance?"

Flicking through the pages of her notepad, she stopped at the information she'd found about the man and began speaking out loud.

"Sir, Mr Farrow lives in an apartment on the ground floor, which comes with the job. He's ex-military, never married so there's no family, he lives alone. The tenants I spoke to all speak highly of him. The impression I get is he's a proud man and takes his job seriously. He has always made a point of knowing all the occupants of the apartments and likes to do small DIY jobs or run errands for them. An all-round nice guy don't you think, Sir?" she said as she looked around the room and smiled at everyone.

"I bet he has a nice little sideline in tips too, the bugger," Detective Skinner called out.

"Now, now, let's not begrudge the old man setting himself up for his retirement," Jones chirped.

"Oh, and another thing, on his days off, he has a car wash service," Hunter added.

"Very enterprising, I think," Dunn remarked.

"I also found out that he's a stickler for rules and likes the tenants to abide by them. Honestly, Sir, I heard nothing bad. I got the impression they were comfortable with him and his services," Hunter concluded

"Were you able to check out Miss Verwood's car?" Ellis asked.

"Yes Sir, we did," Lloyd called out and proceeded to read from his notebook.

"And you wouldn't believe it believe it, she only owned my dream car, a black Mercedes C class four-door sedan. I can tell you all, there's nothing I wouldn't do for wheels like that, even sell my body," he laughed.

The office erupted into an outburst of demeaning wisecracks.

"Too much information, Lloydy," Skinner called out.

"Not sure you'd make that much, sadly," another voice piped up.

"Does your wife know this?" Jones added.

As the room simmered down, Detective Lloyd continued.

"Cheeky sods, all I know it's a bloody sacrilege to see a car end up in that state. For a car only two years old, it was pitiful, it was filthy dirty, dented and scratched. It also looked like it hadn't been driven for quite some time looking at the dirt around the wheels and underneath. There was ornaments and painting all over the back seat and in the boot. A load of junk. "

"When you say junk, Lloyd, you wouldn't by any chance mean antiques," Ellis asked.

"No… what I saw was junk,"

"I take it you're not a fan of antiques, then?" Ellis continued.

"Nope! You can't fool me, antiques is just a fancy word for junk," Lloyd grinned.

Sally shouted to her partner. "I think you'll find it's now called by another fancy French word… ob- jay-dar," she said, speaking phonetically. "You've no class Lloydy."

Lloyd shrugged his shoulders. "Anyway… moving on... the car was unlocked, which I found strange because there was jewellery laying all over the front seat, which actually did look like good stuff."

"Is that it, Lloyd, are you done?" Dunn asked.

Lloyd nodded. "That's it for me."

"Sergeant Miller, what have you got?"

"Sutton gave me a picture of a very expensive necklace which I took around all my dealers and as many pawn shops we physically could, including those little pop-up gold buyers you see in the big shopping centres. I got nothing." Miller paused and looked directly at Dunn.

"However, Sir, we are trying a few different avenues, so I'll keep you updated," she concluded.

"We need you to continue looking, Miller. If you can find who stole the jewellery, it's possible we could find the person who may have caused her death. They may be one and the same."

Dunn continued to speak, directing his next question at Detective Lindsay.

"What information have you found on Mr Sutton, the business partner?"

Everyone's attention averted to Lindsay, who was staring at his computer, his dull mousy coloured hair falling into his eyes as he repeatedly brushed it to one side in annoyance. He looked away from the screen with a smug look on his face. This was always a good sign that he'd found vital information. "I think you're going to like this, Sir, especially as we believe he was the last person to see her alive. The first thing I discovered is that he lives above the antique emporium he owns in Mosman. I contacted his financial institution and had a long chat with the manager. He informed me that at this time, Sutton has a massive overdraft."

"Sounds like the man is having money trouble, but what connection does this have with Verwood going over the balcony?" Skinner called out.

"Hang on a minute," Ellis butted in. "According to Mr Sutton, when we interviewed him, they were making squillions between the two of them. Something's not right, Sir," Ellis pointed out.

"In that case, I think we need to pay Mr Sutton a visit at his premises in Mosman later, Ellis. Well done Lindsay."

Inspector Dunn paused for a moment, then turned to the whiteboard.

"That brings us to the other infant that was given up for adoption, the younger brother of this young man here," he said, tapping the photograph of Peter Ashcott with the black marker. "Has anyone managed to find out any information on her second baby and who adopted him?"

A loud sound made everyone turn to See Jones sucking the last dregs of a MacDonald's milk shake through a straw. He tossed the empty carton in the waist paper bin before reading out from his notes.

"I managed to track down the adoption agency, Laura Verwood went through to have her baby adopted. It wasn't easy, I can tell you. When I found the name of the agency, I got on the blower and told them I needed them to check their records for a Miss Laura Verwood. I gave them the information about her giving her baby up for adoption about eighteen years ago. I told them she'd used their agency. The lady I spoke to was very unco-operative. I told her that Laura Verwood had died tragically and that it was imperative we contact the adoptive parents. The lady informed me their records from back then were lost when they moved buildings a few years ago."

"And did you use that big word, Jonesey?" Lloyd called out.

"What word?"

"Imperative?"

Jones ignored him and carried on. "At first I thought, that was it, there's no more we could do. Then I had an idea, I asked about staff members that were around at that time and worked on her case. I thought it was worth a try."

Without any hesitation, she gave me the name George Lamar and then added he'd retired six years ago. I got the distinct feeling she sounded relieved at that fact hoping my enquiries would stop there." Jones looked up from his notes and glanced around the room. "As if that was going to stop me," he laughed.

"I scanned through the white pages on the computer and luckily there was only two entries with that name. Turns out they're both related anyway. When I phoned the first number and asked for George Lamar, old mate that answered, told me that was his brother and happily gave me his phone number and address, which I have for you here, Sir," Jones said holding a page from his notepad in the air.

"Pass it over to Ellis, he can call him later. D'you have anything else Jones?"

"No, Sir, but, I'm working a couple of other things I'm checking into."

"Okay, sounds good, don't stop, time is vital now."

Addressing the whole team, Dunn concluded.

"Everyone, we need to move fast, try to have your reports on my desk for when I get back. Ellis and I will head straight over to Mr Sutton's antique emporium to see what we can find out. Keep up the good work guys."

◆◆◆

The car's windscreen wipers were working overtime as the heavy rain lashed against the window, making visibility difficult and the car rocked with the strong winds. Ellis hated when Inspector Dunn drove. If there was ever a time he would've preferred to drive, this was it. For some reason, for the first time in months, his boss had insisted on driving this time.

Trying to spot Sutton's antique emporium, as the rain lashed against the windscreen, wasn't easy and neither of them were looking forward to getting out of the car when they did find it.

"That's it, Sir," Ellis called out, "Too late, we've past it. It was back there on the right. It might help if you drive a bit slower while we're trying to find the place." Ellis said, forgetting who he was talking to. Truth was, Dunn was annoying him, not to mention scaring the shit out of him with his driving. "Keep going, there's a mini roundabout further along this road, you'll be able to turn easily, then you can park in front of his building. I'm familiar with this area," he smiled.

"I won't ask how," Dunn replied, shaking his head.

Parking in front of Sutton's shop, the two detectives sat for a while, psyching themselves up to make a dash through the rain that had now eased slightly.

"You know you've parked in a loading bay for the businesses here, Sir? Shouldn't we move further along?"

"We're the police remember and we're working on a case, that should count for something,"

Sergeant Ellis was feeling even more irritated by his boss, but didn't dare argue. They both made a dash for the antique shop's large awning. Dunn tried the handle and found it was locked. He gave three loud knocks as Ellis peered through the large glass window.

"Phew! He certainly has plenty stock, the place is packed solid with furniture and stuff."

"Doesn't look like anyone's home," Dunn decided."

"Maybe we should try round the back, Sir, he could be in an office or storeroom and can't hear us," suggested Ellis.

They hurried down a path that led to the rear of the shop to find an area covered in tarmac. "Would you look at that. "Ellis exclaimed. "There's a whacking big car park back here. Do you want me to move the car, Sir?" he asked.

"Leave it Ellis. How many more times do I have to tell you, we don't have time?" Dunn snapped.

Two small windows on either side of the back door, were blacked out and iron bars stretched from top to bottom. In the centre of the building, fire escape steps led to a door with a plaque that said private residence. Dunn knocked loudly on the back door while Ellis took the fire escape steps, three at a time and banged hard on the door to the residence. There was no response from either. The two detectives were now soaked.

Damn, Ellis, I was hoping to speak to the man, what a bloody waste of time and now we're both sopping wet. Who would've thought he'd not be working at his shop today," Dunn said sounding peeved. "Seeing as we're out of the office, we might as well go over to the dive school and sign you up for some scuba lesson," Dunn grinned.

They hurried back towards the main street. As they turned the corner of the building, they stopped dead in their tracks as they watched a traffic patrol officer standing next to their car pushing a parking ticket under the windscreen wiper. Ellis lurched towards the car and pulled out his ID badge and flashed it at the officer.

"You can't do that," He called out as he continued to wave his ID frantically.

The Officer glanced at Ellis' ID without any expression.

"Well, all I can say is, you of all people should've known better than to park in a clearway, between six o'clock in the morning till ten."

"We happen to be working, you idiot," Ellis barked.

"There's always an excuse," the officer replied, still expressionless. He nonchalantly stuffed the ticket under the windscreen wiper, pulled on a pair of leather gloves and mounted his motorbike. Slamming his foot down hard on the accelerator pedal, the engine roared loudly as he sped off.

Grabbing the rain soaked plastic bag from behind the wiper, Ellis angrily crumpled it up in his hand. Without saying a word or asking Dunn, he climbed into the driver's seat, reached over and threw it into the glove box. In silence, Inspector Dunn climbed in the passenger side.

"I take it you're driving?"

"Yep," Ellis replied as he held his hand out for the keys, followed by a long silence.

Dunn slapped the keys into Ellis' outstretched hand. "Go on then, say it, '*I told you so*'," Dunn said, making a face as he spoke.

Ellis waited a while before replying. "Well, you have to admit, Sir, I *did!*." Ellis said gruffly as he started the engine and moved into the throng of busy traffic.

Chapter 14

For two days the rain refused to let up, Asho and Fish made an executive decision, not to open the dive school. The three decided not to rush into work and being efficient, Jenni had contacted the students that were booked to go out and postponed their dives till further notice.

Having stayed overnight at Jenni's, now their relationship had moved up several notches, Asho was enjoying a leisurely breakfast with her; and Jenni was concerned, they hadn't mentioned anything to Fish about it yet.

"We're gonna have to mention something soon, I'm scared he might catch us being a bit more affectionate than we should with each other and he's going to feel hurt that we kept things from him," Jenni pointed out as she cleared away the breakfast dishes.

"You big softy, Jen, but you're right, what we should do is all go out to dinner on the pretence of celebrating our new business, then just announce it after a few beers."

"Asho, that's a great idea," she said, throwing the dish cloth down and sitting on his knee. As she wrapped her arms around his neck, Asho slipped his hands into her pyjama top and stroked her soft warm flesh. Without warning, he jumped to his feet almost sending Jenni to the floor.

"Come on, it's still early, let's go back to bed for ten minutes," he said, grabbing her hand and leading her from the kitchen.

"Ten, minutes! You hoping to do it twice?" she giggled as they both hurried up the stairs to Jenni's bedroom and closed the door.

◆◆◆

At the Buckton's residence, Fish and his mother were having breakfast in the dining room, chatting and laughing, something he enjoyed doing. He loved his mother dearly, they had a special bond. Although he had no idea how she would react when he told her the news that he had quit college. He was dreading having to tell her, maybe he would take her out to lunch at her favourite restaurant. Neutral grounds, he thought. He could just slot it into the conversation, make it sound humorous and make her laugh about it. Another idea would be to invite Jenni and Asho to help soften the blow. He knew she was very fond of those two and Jenni could do no wrong in her eyes.

After giving his mother, her usual hug, Fish left the house and jumped into his car. Accelerating a bit too hard, the back wheels spun, causing a cloud of dust to billow into the air.

Watching from the front porch, Mrs Buckton shook her head as she let out a loud exasperated tutting sound. *I hate him driving, I don't know what I'd do if anything happened to my gorgeous boy! He seems a little distracted, I hope he's not having problems with his lessons. He's going to be under so much pressure having to follow his father's footsteps into law,* she thought.

Asho and Jenni arrived at the dive shop at the same time as Fish. Both cars pulled into parking bays near the Marina, directly opposite the dive shop. After making a dash for cover under the shop awning, Asho fumbled in his pockets for the door key. Fish glanced up at the sky.

"This bad weather will give us a chance to have a sort out in the workshop and clean the boat, then I think we should take it out, what'd you say Asho?"

"I'm game if you are," he replied with a mischievous grin, holding up the key's he'd discovered were in the leg pocket of his cargo pants.

"No, you're bloody not," Jenni said loudly, "If you think for one minute you're going out on that boat in this weather, you're both very much mistaken. It's far too dangerous."

"Excuse me, who made you the boss," Fish said as he pushed her playfully. I'll have you know, our boat is more than capable, regardless of the storm." He pointed out. "Come on, Asho, open the bloody door, we're getting soaked here."

"Well, be it on your heads, don't come crying to me when you drown,"

Asho and Fish looked at her and then at each other and began to laugh.

As the door swung open wide, all three entered the shop, chatting good-humoredly. They stopped dead in their tracks, horrified at the sight in front of them. Jenni's hands shot over her mouth, dumbfounded as she mumbled something incoherent about the place being ransacked, then burst into a fit of sobbing. Asho wrapped his arms around her shoulders as his eyes scanned the room.

"Who could've done this and why?" Fish fumed, as he picked his way through the files and paperwork strewn all over the room. As his foot slipped on a pile of paperwork, almost sending him crashing to the ground, he became enraged. "Why, why us, what have we done to deserve this?"

Leaving Jenni's side, Asho walked over to Fish and placed his hand on Fish's shoulder.

"I'll go and check the workshop,"

Asho made his way through all the debris and went through to the back room.

"It's the same through here," he yelled "What a fuckin mess."

Jenni had a sudden horrible thought. She hurried to the cupboard behind her desk where the safe was kept. It was wide open. Suddenly her legs turned to jelly as she took the few steps towards the safe. She could see the door had been blown clean off and it was now empty. The bundle of notes that she'd put there the day before, was gone.

With both hands on top of her head, Jenni stood traumatised. "The takings are gone," she cried out.

Asho appeared from the back room. "What did you say? They've taken all the money?"

"Well the bundle of notes, that is, they obviously had no need for the cash, that's been hurled around the room." Jenni whimpered as she sat down heavily on her office chair and put her head in her hands. Asho hurried to her side and hugged her head in an attempt to comfort her; which was hard as he was fuming from what he'd discovered in the back room. "The bastards have come through the back door, it's hanging off its hinges and our poxy alarm system has been cut, very efficient, I don't think," Asho said sounding furious.

"We better call the police," Fish suggested pulling his mobile out from his pocket.

He dialed triple zero and was soon relaying the details to the person on the other end of the phone. Ending the call he turned to Asho and Jenni.

"Okay, you two, they said they'll be here as soon as possible and have given strict instructions we are not to touch *anything*," Fish advised. "How about we go and sit in the boat. It's too depressing here, I'm sure it'll be nicer than sitting in this mess."

"The boat, shit, I'd forgotten the boat," Asho called out. "Let's hope the bastards didn't trash the boat as well." He stumbled through the piles of broken furniture and paperwork and raced out the door. Fumbling with his keys, he finally opened the aluminium gate and made his way to the boat with Jenni and Fish following closely. The three jumped on board, then stood in silence as their eyes focused on the mess before them.

"Fuck, they've wrecked this as well," Asho said out loud.

"Surely they can't think we keep money on the boat, if that's what they're searching for," Fish said.

"Maybe its drug addicts and they were hoping to find something they could sell," Jenni offered.

"How the hell did they get over that bloody gate?" Fish suddenly thought. Geez, we have great security in this place!"

"This is not a robbery, or someone looking for money," Asho said.

"How can you say that?" Jenni asked, thinking he must be mad, coming to that conclusion.

"Think about it, the workshop is full of expensive stuff, electric tools, diving tanks and equipment, the boat has the most sophisticated electronic equipment known to man, worth a small fortune. Yet none of these things were taken. No, this wasn't a robbery, this is either sabotage or someone looking for something."

"But Ash, what on earth can we have that someone would want that badly they destroy our shop and boat to find?" Jenni sighed.

"I wish I knew, and I'd like to find out," Asho said as he rubbed his forehead.

Then a thought struck Fish.

"No, it can't be."

Both Jenni and Asho spoke at the same time.

"What?"

"At the museum yesterday, Jen, did we mention where we lived, or where our dive school is?"

"No, definitely not, the subject never came up. Do you think this might have something to do with us going to the museum yesterday?"

"I'm not sure. I did tell them our names, and that we *had* a dive school. I suppose it wouldn't take them long to find us if they joined the dots."

"And you did make that woman very angry," Jenni added.

"What is it you're trying to say, Fish?" Asho asked.

Before he had a chance to reply, they were interrupted by a car pulling up, right outside the shop. Assuming it was the police arriving as promised, they climbed off the boat and made their way back to the shop just as Detective Sergeant Ellis and Inspector Dunn were walking away from their vehicle. The three distressed friends, hurried towards them.

"Phew, I wasn't expecting you this soon," Asho said as he reached forward and shook both detective's hands. "Actually, we've met already when I came into the police station to talk about Laura Verwood, I'm Peter Ashcott, remember?"

"Yes, of course we remember you," Ellis replied.

Fish also shook hands with both detectives as he introduced himself.

"I'm known as Fish, Peter's friend and business partner. I'm so pleased you got here so soon, we haven't touched anything in the shop or the boat." Fish said sounding desperate.

Replicating the two boy's, Jenni shook their hands and introduced herself.

"I'm Jenni Sherwood, also a business partner, as you can imagine we're very distressed about this. We're completely baffled as to who could've done this awful thing, or why."

The two detectives looked at the three young friends and then to each other with curious expressions.

"We're totally confused, you all appear to be upset about something, what's going on?" Dunn asked.

"The *break in*, I called you about fifteen minutes ago, we've been robbed," Fish explained.

"Everything has been smashed to pieces, like a bomb has gone off," Jenni added.

"It's a coincidence, we actually here on another matter. But seeing as we *are* here, you might as well show us the crime scene," said Ellis.

Entering the dive shop, both detectives were noticeably shocked at the mess and commiserated with the three friends. Assuring them that the officers in charge of robbery, would arrive soon and take all their details.

"Someone's certainly done a number on you. You haven't touched anything I hope," Ellis asked.

"No, we only just arrived ourselves a short while ago," Fish replied.

"Good, unfortunately you will all have to stay away from the site for the rest of the day while the robbery squad and forensics go over the place. You'll be questioned and then fingerprinted. Don't be alarmed, this is just to eliminate you from the crime. They're also going to need to know what is missing. You're going to have to make an inventory."

Glancing around the shop at all the destruction, Ellis turned to Asho.

"Do you think this might be sabotage? Could this be the work of another dive school by any chance?"

"When we set up here, we made sure we were not stepping on anyone's toes and encroaching on other diver's territory. Although we can't stop other dive schools from visiting our dive site."

Ellis shook his head and tutted loudly.

"Well by the look of all this, Mr Ashcott, someone's not happy with you."

"By the way, why have you come? Do you need to talk to me again about Laura Verwood because I honestly don't have anything else I can tell you?" Asho pointed out.

"No, that's not why we're here, but it's not important now. If you must know, I was just wanting to sign up to go out on one of your dives." Ellis replied, sounding deflated.

"Have you had much experience, Sergeant?" Asho asked.

"Well, actually I have, I did a bit of diving on holiday in Vanuatu a few years ago and again in North Queensland last year," he said proudly.

"Well, in that case, you're advanced enough to dive by yourself?"

"I am, although I might be a little rusty. Although I suppose it's like riding a bike, once in the water, it all comes back," Ellis said smiling.

Asho had taken an instant liking to Sergeant Ellis and had a good feeling about him. "Then why don't you come out with us when this weather improves. You'll be helping us out. With three instructors out there, we might be able to catch up on our lost days, due to this rotten weather."

"*Whoa,* steady on, I didn't say I was an instructor," Ellis exclaimed.

"Don't worry, our novice diver's will be none the wiser, you just need to follow my instruction."

Ellis smiled as he thought to himself, how he'd advance to an instructor already, how easy was that?

"Well, count me in, I'll just clear it with my boss. What time?"

"We have an early start, you will need to be here no later than seven, and then you can help us set up. It'll give you a chance to familiarize yourself with the equipment,"

While Ellis talked to Asho, Inspector Dunn made a quick phone call to Sergeant Miller to find out how long she was going to be. He explained to Julie, they were not there for the robbery that it was a coincidence, but they'd hang around till she arrived. Dunn called for everyone's attention.

"Just letting everyone know, robbery will be here in about fifteen minutes. I suggest you three head off, Sergeant Ellis and I will stay here and speak to our officers on your behalf." Dunn suggested, as he raised his arm to check the time on his watch. "I need to speak to the Sergeant who is on her way. Remember, you will need to be fingerprinted at some point as we mentioned earlier."

"We were thinking about heading out on the boat? We've checked it out and fortunately it wasn't touched. The bastards who did the shop, couldn't have got through the aluminium security door to reach the boat thankfully," Fish lied.

"I don't see why not, it might even help you get over the shock of this ordeal," Dunn said with compassion, waving his hand around the room.

Without any hesitation, all three grabbed what they needed, pulled on their heavy duty rain coats and made a dash to the marina. Dunn and Ellis stood under the awning of the dive shop and watched them clamber onto the back of their boat which rocked unsteadily in rough water. Fish drove with precision past the row of crafts swaying madly in the wind. Once out into the open water, he picked up speed and headed out to their site. The two detectives stepped back inside the dive shop where Sergeant Ellis, began telling Inspector Dunn everything Peter Ashcott had said about going out with them as an instructor.

"Well then, if you feel you can handle it, I won't stop you. As if I could," Dunn said.

◆◆◆

All three congregated in the steering station, chatting endlessly about the morning's drama as Fish steered through the rough waters.

"By the way, Fish, I was meaning to ask you, what happened to the coin after you took it to the museum?"

"Don't worry, It's well hidden in a very safe place where no one will find it," he smiled proudly.

"Good, let's keep it hidden for the time being."

Chapter 15

Hearing the sound of vehicles pulling up outside the dive shop, Ellis and Dunn stopped speaking and headed out the door. They stood under the awning, protecting them from the pouring rain and watched as Sergeant Julie Miller and an officer climbed from their vehicle and made a dash towards them. A forensic officer from the vehicle behind followed. Miller looked pleasantly surprised when she spotted Dunn and Ellis standing in front of the shop doorway.

"Nice weather, Sir," Julie called out as she scuttled out of the rain.

Detective Sergeant Julie Miller had worked with Dunn's team for over two years before being promoted to Sergeant and head of robbery squad. Everyone on Dunn's team loved her. Julie's sunny personality was engaging. Although only in her mid-thirties, Julie had a tendency to mother the younger team members. She was admired for keeping Ellis in line with her quick comebacks when he teased her. Julie reckoned she must be the only woman in Sydney that wasn't taken in by his charm; always ripping him for his hair length. Secretly, her attentions were firmly set on Detective Inspector Stephen Dunn, whom she admired immensely and liked everything about him. From his fastidious habits to his quiet, peaceful nature. Not to mention his distinguished good looks.

Miller knew she was no beauty, she had more of a 'girl next door' look. She lived in hope that one day she'd win him over and perhaps put a smile on his face.

"What kept you?" Ellis started on her immediately. "Did you go via Newcastle?" He grinned.

Julie walked straight up to him, ignoring Inspector Dunn.

"Hi Sergeant Ellis, this rain must be cramping your style, well your hairstyle at least," she said as she reached up and patted his head before turning to Inspector Dunn who was stifling a laugh.

"Come on you two, call it a truce, please," Dunn begged.

"We're only joking, Sir, Julie knows I worship the ground she walks on, err yak, what's that you're standing on," he said, laughing out loud.

"Sergeant Miller, good to see you again," Dunn said, ignoring Ellis' wisecracks as he stepped out of the doorway to allow her and the officers to enter the ransacked premises.

"Just to remind you, we're not meant to be here, in case you're wondering, Ellis and I came on a private matter. I've sent the three young owners of this establishment away for a few hours, they were extremely upset. They would most likely have just gotten in the way if they stayed."

"That was good thinking, Sir, and thoughtful of you," she said, flashing him a smile. "What's the MO then, Sir?" Miller asked Dunn as she walked ahead and entered the shop; treading carefully through the mess scattered all over the floor. As she kicked a file out of the way with her foot, she turned to listen to Dunn as he gave her the information.

"It looks just like a break in and robbery. Although they've made a hell of a mess just to steal the day's takings, which, according to the young girl, Jenni, wasn't that much I might add. So we were wondering if there's more to this than meets the eye," Dunn continued to speak as he followed Miller across the room. "Ellis asked them if they knew of *anyone* who could've done this, but they had no idea. All three are a bit wet behind the ears. From what I can see, they've opened this scuba diving school having no business acumen. Despite all their enthusiasm, they still need to know how to run a business for heaven's sake," he smiled, throwing his hands in the air.

"Well, they've been baptized with fire, that's for sure, poor buggers," Miller said.

Inspector Dunn headed into the workshop leaving Miller to talk to Ellis.

As Miller made her way to the back of the shop where she spotted the safe with the door blown open. Hunkering down, she examined it closer.

"I admit, when I first walked in, I was thinking perhaps a gang of kids, maybe drug addicts wanting to find something to sell. However, *this* changes everything, this is the work of a professional; and you say there was only a small amount of money in this safe?"

"Maybe that explains the damage, they got angry with the slim pickings, so they trashed the place." Ellis offered.

"No, I don't think so. I've never come across a safe cracker that trashed the place after robbing it. I'd say, whoever did this, was after something other than the money taken from the safe. They've been searching for something, hence the damage. Then they've found the safe, blown the door off and maybe found whatever it was they were looking for. The money was a bonus. But it's not kids or opportunist that's for sure." She concluded.

"I wonder what the hell it was they were looking for," Ellis said, running his fingers through his hair.

"Are the young owners positive that there's nothing else missing? Also, are they likely to be keeping something from us?"

"Come and take a look at the mess in the workshop, it might confirm your deductions," Ellis said as he squeezed past the two forensic officers and headed to the back room. Inspector Dunn was now standing in front of the broken door, twisting his bottom lip between his thumb and forefinger as he studied it. Hearing a voice behind him, he turned to face Detective Miller.

"What's your thoughts so far, Julie?"

"As I discussed with Ellis, I'm convinced, whoever came in here was looking for something other than money. I think you need to put pressure on the three owners and get them to fess up to whatever it is they're not telling us. My guess is that they know something. If they're scared, then we need to make sure they are made to feel safe," Miller suggested as she moved around the workshop, taking in the extent of the damage. She pointed at the mess on the floor. "Looking at the damage, I'd say whatever it was these people were looking for, it wasn't something large. The jars filled with small goods like nuts and bolts, etc., have been taken off the shelves and then dropped on the floor and smashed. Every drawer in the desk was yanked out and the contents flung far and wide. This tells me they weren't annoyed at not finding what they were looking for, they were just on a mission to find it.

Then there's the safe, it's not exactly big, is it? So whatever it was they were looking for must have fitted in the safe; for them to go to the trouble of blasting it open. Maybe they were looking for documents or valuable jewellery. We don't even know if they found what they were looking for. If the owners say there's nothing missing, then maybe they're keeping something from us."

"Did you ask them if they've trodden on anyone's toes, opening this place?"

"Geez… now why didn't I think to ask them *that*?" Ellis answered, as he looked up to the ceiling and tapped his chin with his forefinger. "Let's see… ah yes, because I *did*." He said, leaning his face towards Miller.

"And?" she replied, ignoring his sarcasm. "What did they say?"

"They all have no idea of course, what d'you think they'd say?"

"*Ellis*." Dunn snapped in annoyance. "Perhaps you should see if you can contact them on your mobile and repeat the questions, only put on a bit more pressure."

"I'll see what I can do, but I'm sure there's no coverage out where they are," he mumbled under his breath as he walked back into the shop.

Watching him leave the room, Dunn shook his head, then turned and pointed to the simple alarm system hanging off the wall with its wires severed.

"Take a look at this, Julie, its rubbish, bought at the local DIY no doubt."

Miller studied it for a few moments. "It's such a pity stores are allowed to sell these things. People buy the systems and probably feel smug they've covered themselves for break in's. There's no backup system, no CCTV so no footage we can check through. These things can be snipped so easily. In other words, no protection at all from invasions," she said with sympathy.

Ellis returned and Ignoring Inspector Dunn and Sergeant Miller, he strolled towards one of the forensic officers and began talking technical regarding boat and land communications.

Dunn glanced at his watch, deciding it was time they moved on. "I think we will leave you to it, Julie, we need to be somewhere else and we're already late," he said as he caught Ellis' attention and bobbed his thumb towards the door, letting him know his intentions. "Just one more thing, Julie, did you have any luck with any of the pawn shops you were visiting regarding the stolen jewellery, allegedly taken from the Verwood apartment?"

"Actually, yes, Sir. I've left my report on your desk for you to look through. You might need to keep an eye on Frank Farrow. Turns he's been selling bits and pieces around town."

"Hmm, I had my suspicions about him. How did you find that out?"

"Simple really, I flashed a photo of him to a few local dealers and one of them recognised him straight away. Apparently, he's a regular and often visits this particular pawn shop to sell small items. However, he added, the items are never worth that much."

"That's very interesting… you haven't interviewed him yet, have you?"

"No, not yet, Sir, I only found this out yesterday afternoon."

"Good, I'd like you to leave him to us, I'd like to talk to him if you don't mind."

"Whatever you say, Sir. The robbery is all very sketchy, apart from the expensive necklace, we haven't a clue what else was taken, which makes it difficult."

Dunn placed his hand on Julie's forearm.

"You're doing a great job, Miller."

She acknowledged his compliment with a smile. It felt good to be appreciated, especially by someone, she admired so much. If only he could see her as a desirable woman and not just 'Detective Sergeant Julie Miller, she sighed inwardly.

From the other side of the workshop, Ellis had witnessed the look on Julie's face and smiled inwardly. He knew enough about women to know that look. Then the thought crossed his mind, he was going to have to do something about those two. Surely Dunn couldn't be that blind.

As Miller turned to talk to her team, she could see out the corner of her eye, Ellis, waving his arms, looking like an idiot. Changing his arm waving to mimicking holding a drink, he pointed to her then to himself, followed by pretending to hold a phone to his ear with a grin. Julie understood, he wanted to meet for a drink and would phone her later. Nodding, she held up both thumbs with a beaming smile.

Chapter 16

"Do you have Lamar's address?" Dunn asked as Ellis pulled away from the curb.

"I do, Sir, he lives right next to Coogee beach. Hope you've brought your swimmers," He joked.

After a few seconds. Dunn replied "No, I didn't bring them, there's a hole in the knee."

Ellis frowned at Dunn for a split second before realising the joke, then gave the loudest laugh Dunn had ever heard.

Dunn was forced into making a faint smile as Ellis carried on laughing, not so much at the joke, but the fact his boss had made one.

After they both settled down, Ellis started the engine and drove towards Coogee following the winding road to the beach. Driving past the horseshoe-shaped beach, they both remarked on how quiet it was because of the bad weather. The rain had not stopped all day, although the wind had now died down.

"This is it, this is the address of George Lamar," Ellis announced as he parked directly in front of the house.

The two story federation style house looked old and weathered from the outside, but both men agreed that houses around this suburb did not come cheap. Bracing themselves, they made a dash through the pouring rain to the house. The overgrown garden almost covered the path, forcing them to walk in single file to the front door. Ellis pressed the doorbell, and rolled his eyes at the sound of a whimsical chime being played.

The door opened almost at once by a bare-chested man in his late sixties, dressed in faded orange board shorts and orange leather mule slippers. His grey, receding hair cut so short, he appeared bald, and what he lacked on his head was more than made up with body hair. A large silver pendant, hanging on a chain round his neck was almost hidden by the thick mat of grey chest hair. He wore several silver chains on each wrist and every finger had a silver ring, including his thumbs. His leathery, over-tanned skin, proved he spent many hours in the sun.

"Oh! You're not who I was expecting," said the man, waving his arms in a dramatic fashion. "I thought you might be those church people. They're always coming around, trying to convert me," he began, with a cheeky grin. "But I can see you are police officers, am I correct?" the man asked, sounding effeminate.

Dunn held up his ID card. "Very perceptive of you, what gave us away?

"Let's just say instinct darling," he said with a sycophantic grin.

Would you be George Lamar?" Dunn asked.

"Yes, that's me, have you come to arrest me?"

"Why? Have you broken the law?" Ellis replied sharply.

"Oh… Touché, young man," Lamar replied. "Now how on earth can I help you two handsome police officers today?"

"I'm Detective Inspector Dunn and this is Sergeant Ellis. We believe you worked for an adoption agency before you retired, is that correct?" Dunn asked.

The man's cheery expression suddenly changed to serious. "I did.... A lifetime ago. Why?"

"We would like to ask you a few questions."

"Then you better come inside, darling," he said as he turned and minced along the hallway, assuming the two detectives would follow. Entering into the lounge, both men were surprised at the decor. The exterior of the house certainly belied the interior with a colour scheme of predominantly blacks and whites with splashes of reds and oranges. The leather furniture looked expensive, although a little avant-garde. Lamar had style, albeit risqué with a shameless display of oil paintings on every wall of the same naked young man in various stages of repose. Lamar noticed both Detectives eyeing the portraits.

"Ha! As you can see, I was much younger then," he said with a frown. "Aging is such a bitch!"

Sergeant Ellis pointed to the paintings with raised eyebrows. "That's you?" He gasped, with more shock in his voice than intended.

"Hard to believe I know. But, sadly, as you can see, good looks don't last. Make the most of them young man! And don't think the aging process won't happen to you... I'm testament to that," he lamented, pointing to a black and white leather, retro, sofa and gestured the two detectives to sit. Sergeant Ellis looked at the sofa, then at Dunn, deciding it was far too small for two and politely moved to a matching chair.

"Now, gentlemen, may I offer you a nice cup of tea? Or perhaps something a little stronger?" He asked with a smile.

"No that won't be necessary, this shouldn't take long."

Lamar draped himself over a large seat covered in a black and white cow hide and began toying with the large medallion laying on his chest. "Okay, what do you need to know? May I remind you it was some years ago when I worked there."

"I understand, but anything you can remember would be appreciated. Hopefully we won't take up too much of your time," said Dunn,

"No need to worry about taking up too much of *my* time, Inspector. I have *all* the time in the world, now I'm retired," He said, waving his hand with a flourish down his torso. "As you can see by my lovely sun tan… my *all* over sun tan," he emphasised, looking directly at Ellis, and giving him a sly wink, making Ellis shift in his seat.

Dunn was beginning to lose his patience. "Unfortunately, we can't say the same, Mr Lamar, we don't have a lot of time. Can we be serious, I need to ask you a few questions about the agency. Are you able to cast your mind back twenty years, there was a couple called Frances and Graeme Ashcott who adopted a baby named Peter. Do you recall the case?"

"Well, that's asking a lot darling, I saw hundreds of babies go through the agency while I worked there and you are talking *twenty* years ago. I think you need to talk to the agency. You are aware they keep records?" he said with a hint of sarcasm.

"Of course… we're well aware, please give us credit," Ellis snapped.

"We've spoken to the agency," Dunn cut in, seeing Ellis was not looking too enthused by this man. "We were after information about the mother who gave her baby up for adoption. Does the name Laura Verwood ring any bells?"

The colour appeared to drain from Lamar's face at the sound of the name, followed by silence. He rose to his feet and moved slowly across the room to a cabinet with an assortment of spirits and a cut glass decanter of port. Removing the large glass stopper he poured himself a drink, then held the decanter in the air.

"I know it's rather early, dears, but would either of you like a port?"

There was a resounding '*no thanks*,' from both detectives as they replied in unison. Mr Lamar pushed the ornate glass stopper back into the decanter and wiped around the silver tray, clearly stalling for time.

"Well… what can you tell us?" Dunn asked.

"I've told you, you need to talk to the agency, it's all far too long ago for me to remember anything," Lamar replied, sounding impatient.

Noticing the sudden animosity, Ellis left his seat and began strolling casually around the room, stopping in front of a painting and studying it without saying a word. He absent mindedly picked up a white, marble figurine of a naked boy.

"Are you married, Mr Lamar," Ellis asked, knowing damn well what the answer would be.

"What has *that* got to do with anything?"

"Just that, your place is immaculate. I live on my own and my place looks like a bomb's hit it. Women are much more fastidious than us men, don't you think? I was wondering if you have a wife and what she thinks of your paintings and ornaments," Ellis asked, sounding facetious.

Without saying a word, Mr Lamar placed his drink on the occasional table, trounced towards Ellis and removed the figurine from his hands and placed it back on the shelf. He returned to his seat, picked up his drink and with one leg draped over the arm of his chair, he swirled the port around the glass for a while before speaking.

"If you must know… I *was* married once, many years ago."

Not expecting that answer, Ellis sat down. "You were?" His startled expression noticed by Lamar.

"Not what you're thinking. Anyway, I divorced the bitch. I ended the union when I found out he was messing about with other men. Good riddance to bad gay men, I say." Lamar said, as he turned his head to one side and placing the back of his hand over his mouth in a mock display of emotion, making him look even more effeminate.

The room fell silent for a few seconds. "Hang on, it's not legal… Gay's being allowed to marry I mean," he said, blatantly.

Turning to face Ellis, Lamar responded. "Well, when I say *married*, what I mean is, my partner and I had a small private ceremony to bless our union and promised to forsake all others. Ha! That turned out to be a joke." He pouted.

Seeing the man was becoming emotional, Ellis had an idea. "How about I make us all a cup of tea? Which way to the kitchen?" he asked as he jumped to his feet.

"Through that door, you'll find everything you need in the cupboard above the red kettle. So, when you find the kettle, you will find everything else. I'm a methodical bitch about certain things," Lamar blurted out, suddenly sounding more cheery. "By the way, I like mine hot, black and strong."

"I bet you do!" Ellis said under his breath as he headed towards the kitchen.

Dunn heard and struggled to keep a straight face as he continued with his questions.

"Mr Lamar, when I mentioned the name Verwood, it appeared to strike a chord, why was that? Did the name bring back memories by any chance?"

"Yes, It's that name, I knew one day it would all come back to haunt me, I should never have agreed to it. You know don't you Inspector?"

"Know what? I know nothing, that's why we're here. What can you tell us?"

Ellis returned carrying a tray with three teas in an assortment of cups and a sugar bowl and set it down on the low retro table. No one spoke until Ellis had placed a cup in front of each one of them, and sat down. "Sorry it's black for everyone, there's no milk in the fridge."

"You were saying Mr Lamar," Dunn continued, feeling he was getting somewhere at last.

"Okay, okay, I'll tell you everything I know. The first baby Miss Verwood had adopted was easy, the baby went to a lovely couple. I forget their names, but they were perfect and everything went smoothly. Two years later, Miss Verwood returned to us, after giving birth to another boy. Both boys were named Peter, for reasons only known to Laura Verwood.

About that time, I found myself in a spot of bother after being involved in a dreadful altercation with a bitch of a woman while driving to work one morning. We ended up on the pavement, shouting and hollering. She was saying dreadful things, even though the bingle was entirely her fault. When she called me an ugly faced poof, I snapped and hit her."

Ellis tried hard to stifle a laugh that Lamar observed. He gave him a filthy look and continued. "I'm not a violent man Inspector Dunn and I was as shocked as she was after I did it. The police were called and I was carted off to the station." Lamar paused to take a sip of tea, noticeably saddened at the memory.

Dunn placed his cup back on the table and butted in. "Just a minute, can I stop you there, what has this got to do with Laura Verwood?"

"If you wait a minute, I'm coming to it," Lamar snapped. "I had to appear before the Magistrate. Naturally, I was sick with worry how this would affect my job. Do you know the stigma of being homosexual in the workforce Inspector Dunn? Especially back then, and I had a mortgage to pay? However, when I arrived at court, the prosecutor took me aside and told me if I cooperated, the matter would disappear.

As you can imagine, I was confused but delighted at the same time."

"Hang on a minute, so you're saying the prosecutor offered to remove the charges… make them simply go away," Dunn exclaimed as he flicked his hand sideways.

Both detectives were now on the edge of their seats listening.

"He talked about how his wife was desperate to adopt a baby after years of heartbreak, unable to conceive. Then went on and on about not being able to face going through the right channels and the trauma it would cause his wife; the baby would be well looked after and would want for nothing. The man was almost begging me.

The strange thing is, he knew about Miss Verwood's baby and was determined this was the baby he had to have."

Ellis looked at Dunn in disbelief. "Did you have any idea that what he was asking you to do was an indictable offence and that you risked a possible prison sentence? Not a place to be with your persuasion," Ellis said.

"He offered to have my charges disappear, and I'm sorry, but the Verwood baby was just another baby as far as I was concerned," Lamar said, sounding heartless.

"What was the name of this prosecutor?" Ellis asked.

"That's easy, he's often in the papers. His name is Buckton.

Inspector Dunn had just taken a mouthful of tea, which sprayed over his knees hearing the name, Buckton. Retrieving his handkerchief, he quickly wiped his mouth and chin.

"Buckton? Not The Honourable Chief Justice Clifford Buckton, the high court judge?" he asked.

"Yes, that's right, only he was just the prosecutor back then. You have to understand, I meant no harm, I only wanted to help them out."

"And yourself of course, if, as you say, your case was inexplicably dismissed," Dunn said.

Lamar didn't say a word, just nodded.

Inspector Dunn stood up. "Well, well, it looks like we need to talk to the Honourable Chief Justice Buckton as soon as possible."

"Please don't tell him I gave you this information," Lamar whimpered. "I might end up with concrete boots at the bottom of Sydney Harbour."

"You understand, I can't promise anything and I'm not sure what to do about you, you will need to let me sleep on it," Dunn said as he headed for the door. "We might want to talk to you again and it goes without saying Mr Lamar, this conversation is to be kept between the three of us. Is that understood?"

Mr Lamar said nothing, just made out he was pulling a zip across his lips.

"No need to show us out and thank you for the tea."

After making a dash to the car to avoid the rain, Dunn gave Ellis instructions to drive straight to Buckton's house.

Ellis looked a little dubious. "I'm not sure the Super will be happy when he finds out you've paid a visit to the Chief Justice Clifford Buckton and his wife, Sir."

"That's why we're going straight there now before he knows about it. Now let's go, I'll direct you."

"You know the way to Judge Buckton's house?"

"We go back a long way, old Clifford Buckton and me. That's one of the reasons why I'm not too worried about getting permission."

"Nice, in that case, let's go."

The rain lashed against the windscreen as Ellis picked his way through the chaotic morning traffic. He merged into the lane that would take them over Sydney Harbour Bridge, then out towards the affluent suburb of Vaucluse, where Chief Justice Clifford Buckton lived. At the end of a narrow cul-de-sac, with barely enough room for two cars to pass, they stopped in front of large ornate wrought iron gates set between two high concave sandstone walls. In the distance, a magnificent white mansion stood majestically with a hundred and eighty degree views of the Tasman Sea behind.

"Good grief," Ellis gasped. "Look at the size of the house. Well, this is a first for me, going inside a mansion, this should be interesting.

"Just drive as close as you can to the intercom over there on the right… and let me do the talking, okay?"

Sergeant Ellis stretched is arm out and pressed the button in the centre of the intercom panel, which buzzed loudly. Within seconds a man's voice crackled through the speaker in a formal sounding voice.

"To whom am I speaking?"

Dunn leaned over in front of Ellis and spoke in a precise manner. "It's Detective Inspector Stephen Dunn, is that you Charles? I'm hoping I'll be able me to speak to The Judge?"

"Ah! Inspector Dunn, it's been a while. Is he expecting you?" The voice replied with the melodious tones of a Scottish accent.

"Sorry, Charles, no he isn't, this is spur-of-the-moment and I'm sure his nibs won't mind a little visit from an old friend," Dunn said, hoping he wasn't pushing his luck, turning up out of the blue; especially now his old friend Clifford was The Honourable Chief Justice Buckton and had become such an influential man.

The sound of laughter crackled through the intercom.

"Just hold on a moment, I'll find out if he is receiving guests." The intercom fell silent.

"That's Charles the butler, can you believe, he now has a butler?" Dunn smiled.

Dunn had known Clifford Buckton for many years, long before he became Chief Justice of the Supreme Court. All this formality was very different to how they visited each back in the day. However, as the man was now in a high position, Stephen felt he'd better be respectful and follow the protocol or at least some of it.

It must be at least five years since the last time he'd socialised with Clifford and Felicity Buckton. They were an eccentric couple and interesting. Felicity was notorious for throwing parties, boasting A-list guests. Lady Buckton was the archetypical Lady, with her clipped British accent. She was loud and quite jovial, her conversations often peppered with idioms, everything was *a piece of cake* to Felicity.

Lady Felicity had moved to Sydney from England as a teenager with her father, Lord Jeremy Fairfax-Crone, hence her title. It was because of Lady Buckton that Cliff had gained his wealth, even his station as she was a hard taskmaster. So when Lady Buckton told Clifford Buckton to jump, he asked, *how high my dear?*

The sound of Ellis' voice brought Dunn back down to earth.

"Do they have maids too, Sir? You know, the ones who wear little black dresses with white frilly aprons and black stockings?" Ellis asked, grinning slyly.

Dunn gave a loud tut. "Ellis I'm begging you, please behave yourself, when we're inside. I don't want you chatting up all the female staff. D'you hear?"

"As if?" Ellis said, grinning like a Cheshire cat

After what seemed an eternity, the gates began to rattle open. The gravel covered driveway, crunched under the wheels of the car as Ellis made his way to the entrance of the house. An abundance of different coloured roses decorated the garden beds on either side of the driveway giving it an English feel. Ellis parked in front of the imposing entrance porch. Charles, the smartly dressed butler, was waiting on the doorstep to greet them, an umbrella poised at the ready.

"Nice to see you again Inspector Dunn, it's been a while," The butler said as he held the umbrella high to protect them from the relentless rain.

"I see you have Sergeant Ellis with you this time, very nice." The butler added with a grin, as they scuttled under the porch.

Ellis gave Dunn a very quizzical look.

"Your reputation precedes you," Dunn whispered, out the side of his mouth.

Ellis wasn't sure how to take that comment as he stepped in line and followed Dunn into the large imposing reception.

"Justice Buckton is waiting for you in the library. This way, please, gentlemen."

As they approached the double doors leading into the library, the butler halted them before pushing the doors open and taking a step into the room.

"Detective Inspector Stephen Dunn and Detective Sergeant Raymond Ellis are here to see you, Sir," he formally announced, stepping aside to allow the two detectives to enter. Then backing out through the doorway, he closed the doors behind him as he left the room.

Sergeant Ellis's eyes scanned the huge room trying not to look overwhelmed at the sheer size and opulence. Three walls of the large library were covered from floor to ceiling with ornate wooden shelving, filled neatly with books. A large mahogany display cabinet with glass doors stood at the far end of the room, filled with an assortment of trophies; ranging from traditional, solid silver cups to the up-to-date style of figurines balanced on blocks of marble. The figurines were all of swimmers, in many stages of swimming strokes. An elegant solid timber coffee table, surrounded with two extra-large, deep burgundy chesterfields and a matching leather, high back chair, took up the centre of the room.

Justice Buckton was sitting behind a large mahogany desk. He removed his reading glasses and hurried towards the two detectives. Dressed expensively, he looked every bit the distinguished gentleman in his beige coloured Armani trousers with a Ralph Lauren navy blue and white striped shirt; the famous logo emblazoned on one side. He looked of a similar age to Stephen Dunn, although this man's thick mane was predominantly grey.

The Hon. Chief Justice Buckton spoke in a strong, precise manner.

"Stephen, my old friend, what a surprise, how are you? Still a handsome bugger," Buckton said, as he grabbed Dunn's hand and pulled him close, for a friendly man hug. "I see you're not as grey as me yet either," he added pointing to his own hair.

Turning away from Dunn, he held out his hand. "And who do we have here?"

"This is Detective Sergeant Raymond Ellis and I'm warning you, hide away any female staff," Dunn said, looking at Ellis with a proud smile.

"Yes, I can see why you would say that," Buckton said as he shook Ellis' hand. "He's a good-looking man."

"Excuse me, I *can* hear you know," Ellis said, as he pointed to his ear.

The three men laughed as Buckton ushered them to the large Chesterfield sofa's and beckoned them to sit as he reached over to his intercom system on his desk and ordered Charles to serve tea and chocolate cake. Dunn smiled, as he remembered how wonderful Lady Buckton's cakes were.

"Not the famous flourless chocolate, cake?"

"The very one, Felicity's signature dish," Buckton said, his face breaking into a proud smile, flashing perfect white teeth. As the two old friends indulged in some catching up, Ellis leaned across the coffee table and pulled a magazine towards him with the title, *House and country.* He idly flicked the pages, becoming bored quickly. He got to his feet and wandered over to the glass cabinet to study the trophies. A photo on the shelf next to the cabinet of a young man, taken by an official photographer, made him do a double take.

"Is this your son, Sir?" Ellis asked as he positioned the framed photo allowing Dunn to see.

"Yes, that's Peter, he's a handsome devil, takes after his father," He joked, then changed the subject.

"Anyway, Stephen, so what do we owe the..." Buckton was interrupted mid-sentence when the double doors burst open. An older woman of ample proportions flounced into the room.

"Ah! Felicity, Darling, look who is paying us a friendly visit."

Dunn rose to his feet and watched as she stood next to her husband.

Buckton slipped his hand into hers and held it in the air. "Here she is, the apple of my eye, the light of my life," he said with pride. He leaned towards Dunn and whispered, "At least I hope that's why you're here?"

The apron Lady Buckton wore, stained with an assortment of ingredients, and covered an expensive turquoise two piece, accessorised with a single string of pearls and matching earrings. Her salt and pepper hair, once neatly folded into a French pleat was now dishevelled and fell in loose ringlets around her face.

"Stephen... Darling, when did you arrive? Goodness gracious, Clifford why did you not call me?" Lady Buckton said, in a Lady-of-the-Manor accent as she pulled away from her husband and flounced towards Dunn, proffering both hands for him to take; then reached forward and air kissed him on both cheeks.

They all resumed their seating positions as they listened to Lady Buckton who remained standing as she removed her apron revealing a deep cleavage. Both Dunn and Ellis averted their eyes out of politeness.

"I was in the kitchen baking when Charles said he was to serve tea and my chocolate cake in the library as we had visitors. Well, darling, I just *had* to come and see who these visitors were.

This is such a wonderful surprise, Stephen. It's been so long since we last caught up." She gushed as she took the spare seat next to her husband then slapped his knee playfully.

"You are a scoundrel, Cliffee, I'm an absolute mess," she said as she smoothed her hair into place with the palms of her hands. "What must you think?"

I have to say, my dear, you look like you've been through the wringer," Buckton joked, then laughed loudly.

Throwing her husband a dirty look, Lady Buckton turned to Stephen.

"And who is this nice young man?"

Before Dunn had a chance to reply, Buckton answered for him. "This is Detective Sergeant Ray Ellis and I have it on good authority we must lock up all our female staff," He laughed again.

"Sorry to disappoint you, Sergeant Ellis, our only female is our German cleaning lady, Ingrid and she will scare the life out of you." Lady Buckton said making a snorting sound as she laughed.

"Don't tempt him Felicity, he would look at that as a challenge," Dunn responded.

Sergeant Ellis scowled at Dunn. He was finding it hard to comprehend everything, he'd never before encountered anyone who spoke with a plum in their mouth. Although a little intimidated, he was also amused. Lady Buckton seemed a mismatch for this distinguished and refined figure of a man. She was loud and on the large side, even scary. This relationship was definitely a case of the wife wearing the trousers.

Noticing the frown on Ellis' face Lady Buckton gave him an apologetic smile.

"Take no notice, my dear, we're just teasing you. Now Stephen, please tell me there's now a Mrs Dunn waiting at home and keeping you in order."

Realising it was that long since they last saw each other, the Buckton's would have no idea he'd married and was now divorced. He decided it was best to say nothing on that matter.

"Now you know very well, Felicity, the only woman I ever wanted to marry, ran off and married a judge," Dunn replied, making Lady Buckton smile.

"Did you hear that, Cliffee? You had better behave yourself, no running off and have an affair. Looks like I have an admirer," she said, giving Buckton a sideways glance.

"Joking aside, Stephen, we have been expecting you, in fact, you've just helped me win a bet, and I'm now ten dollars richer. You can pay me when you're ready, darling."

"Okay, how did I help you win a bet?"

"When we heard the name of the woman who tragically fell to her death in Balmain, we knew it wouldn't take you and your team long to work out she was the mother of our boy, who we adopted eighteen years ago. Fliss said you'd be here in a week,

I said it would only take you two or three days, and ta-dah, Here you are." He said as he outstretched both his hands towards Dunn.

They were all interrupted by a light tap on the door, followed by Charles pushing a trolley, laden with Royal Daulton crockery and matching teapot; a chocolate cake taking pride of place in the centre.

After painstakingly pouring the tea and serving everyone, Charles retreated through the doors, allowing Buckton to continue.

"Just in case you're wondering," Buckton began, directing his conversation at Ellis. Your grumpy old boss here and I go back a long way. We must have worked on thousands of cases together, isn't that right Stephen?"

"That many eh? Yes, that was back when you were a mere messenger boy for a big law firm," Dunn joked.

"You cheeky bugger, I beg your pardon, I was the duty solicitor," He said with pride.

"Hang on, if you knew about Miss Verwood, why didn't you contact me?" Dunn said, now sounding a little curt.

Sir Buckton let out a robust laugh. "Come, come, Stephen, what's the fun in that? I'll make another bet it was that spotty faced computer nerd, Lindsay, who found out all your information so you could make the connection between Laura Verwood and us."

"Well, not quite, I'll admit he did the ground work and it was he who found a man called George Lamar,"

Dunn watched as Judge Buckton sat bolt upright at the mention of the name.

"Goodness, that name's a blast from the past. So what did Lamar have to say? The adoption agency was given strict instructions not to reveal any information about the adoption and especially our names. Surely you understand why we insisted on that, Stephen."

"I think you know what Lamar revealed to us, don't you Clifford?"

The expression on the Judge's face was that of horror as he tried to give Dunn a signal to desist from saying any more in front of his wife. Bobbing his head sideways towards her as he mimicked with his hand, as though slitting his throat.

Dunn took absolutely no notice of his pleas. As he continued. "Sorry Clifford, I have to talk about this, according to Lamar, it seems you jumped the queue, pulled a few strings and cut through the red tape to secure the adoption of baby Peter. Even making Lamar's criminal offence disappear, isn't that right?"

The Judge cleared his throat with a nervous cough. "Come on Stephen, all I did was move things along, Felicity had been through hell losing three babies through miscarriages and being disappointed month after month. I couldn't stand to see her being so unhappy."

"Clifford," Lady Buckton exclaimed. "I knew nothing about all this, why on earth did you not tell me at the time?"

"There was nothing to tell you, my dear," He said to his wife as he leaned over towards her and patted her knee. "All I did was to help with our predicament and it all had to be kept a complete secret from everyone, especially the press."

"Well, it certainly *was* kept a secret, in all the years I've known you, even I had no idea your son was adopted," Dunn said.

The problem is, I'm now investigating the *murder* of Laura Verwood."

The sound of a cup and saucer rattling caused Dunn to stop talking as the three men looked at Lady Buckton.

"Oh, my apologies, Stephen, but that's dreadful, that poor woman," Lady Buckton said as she covered her mouth with one hand, looking shocked.

"Just a minute, we heard on the news she committed suicide by leaping from her balcony. There was no mention of her being murdered!"

"Unfortunately, that's not altogether true. Don't believe everything you hear in the media. There are a few things that make me suspicious, so I don't think this is just a cut and dry case of suicide."

A silence fell over the room for a few moments before Dunn carried on. "You realise I won't be able to keep your names a secret if it turns out she was murdered? We are still collecting evidence as there are certain anomalies with the fall that puzzles us."

Buckton jumped in. "You know she had attempted suicide before? Twice actually," he said, holding two fingers in the air, emphasizing the number.

"Yes, we are well aware of Laura Verwood's medical history and her suicide attempts. What we are trying to find out is, why?" Dunn said, sounding more assertive. He was feeling the pressure of knowing the people personally connected to his case.

"I see, very astute of you Stephen. I know only too well how you work, never leaving a stone unturned till you find the answers."

"Can you tell me what you know about Laura Verwood?"

Buckton had a strong desire to end the conversation, he thought perhaps he could pretend to have another appointment he had to attend. He knew, however, this would not go away and Stephen Dunn would never give in.

"Perhaps my wife can explain, she's better at this than me."

Lady Buckton placed her cup and saucer down, composed herself and cleared her throat. "We had no idea who the mother of our baby was at first. I was informed by the adoption agency that their policy was not to encourage meetings between the adoptive parents and the biological mother, for many reasons. I understand full well, the agony these mothers must go through having to give up their newborn babies.

"Being extremely pedantic," she faltered for a moment while she reached over and placed her hand on her husband's knee affectionately before continuing. "Clifford went to great lengths to investigate the mother of our son. Please understand, he did it in all good faith. We needed to know the girl's history, was she a drug addict, conceived through incest? The list goes on. Naturally, we needed to know these things, I think that is fair to say," she paused, rearranging herself on the sofa.

"Clifford hired a private detective so could check everything out thoroughly. I have to say, I was amazed at the information he obtained about the woman; it was as if he knew her personally," she said as she turned to her husband giving him a knowing look.

"After all, we couldn't possibly take a baby whose parents were from a low class or were criminals or infected with some disease." She added and for the first time, sounding snobbish.

Dunn drifted for a moment as he considered some of the things Felicity Buckton was saying. It sounded like Cliff had pulled the wool over her eyes, even if it was in her best interest. He also thought she sounded a bit unfeeling. Surely if a woman wanted a baby badly enough, she'd take any baby, *even* the ones that *are* disadvantaged. That way she could mould them into a fine upstanding citizen. It wasn't unheard of that offspring of the hierarchy turn out to be little shits.

Felicity Buckton could see Dunn wasn't listening so put an emphasis on his name with her next sentence. Hearing his name, brought him back to earth.

"*Stephen*, I need to stress, our son knows nothing about his adoption. We have gone to great lengths to keep everything from him. Naturally, that means he knows nothing about his biological mother and that's how we would like to keep it. You must understand, we have great plans for our son. The next few years will be difficult for him and crucial for his career in law.

After he has his undergraduate degree, he will then attend law school where he will obtain his Juris Doctor degree. After that, he must pass the Bar and other exams, become appointed or elected to the court then finally complete Judgeship training. Then our wonderful boy will become a judge, like his father and his grandfather before that. As they say, the apple doesn't fall far from the tree."

Lady Buckton finished her speech, then leaned forward and picked up the antique silver cake slice lying next to the chocolate cake.

"Now then, you must all have a slice of my lovely chocolate cake," she announced as she carefully placed a wedge of cake on the dainty bone china plates with a small gold fork and handed them out one by one, ending with Ellis.

"I've given you two slices, I think you need feeding up more than these two," she laughed.

"Thank you Lady Buckton, I refuse nothing when it comes to food, especially chocolate cake, my weakness. And if it's as good as these two say, I might even come back for a third slice," he responded with his famous Raymond Ellis charm.

As they all ate, there wasn't a sound except for the clinking of forks against bone china. Ellis had devoured both pieces before the others were half way through theirs.

"I think that piece there has my name on it, Lady Buckton," Ellis said as he pointed to the last slice.

"I'll have it put in a container for you to take home," she smiled.

"Sorry, Felicity, this one has a bottomless pit of a stomach, yet look at him, not an ounce of extra flesh," Dunn commented.

"What he doesn't tell you is I'm at the gym at six o'clock every morning, while he is turning over for a second sleep."

The room erupted into laughter and derisive comments aimed at Dunn.

"Did you know that Laura Verwood was a rich woman?" Dunn asked, silencing them instantly.

"No, we didn't, how would we know that? Sir Buckton replied, giving his wife a sheepish look.

Dunn noticed the look, but ignored it.

"Ironically, your son could be in for a large inheritance," Ellis added.

An exasperated sound emitted from Sir Buckton as his pulse spiked.

"Take a look around gentlemen," he said as he made a circular movement with his arm.

"Do you honestly believe Peter will need an inheritance? The boy wants for nothing, he also has his own money, which he inherited when his grandfather, Felicity's father, The Right Honourable Sir Jeremy Fairfax-Crone, died two years ago.

"Shouldn't we let Peter decide that?" Ellis asked.

Lady Buckton looked deeply concerned as she leaned forward and spoke quietly.

"We have already explained, Peter must be told nothing about Laura Verwood. He must stay anonymous to her solicitors and it must be kept out of the public eye. He must be allowed to pursue his career with no hindrance. Surely you understand, Stephen?"

Dunn glanced at Ellis and then back at the Buckton's. "Or are you more concerned this could cause a scandal?" he said curtly. "Okay, if I agree to mention nothing to Peter about Laura Verwood, his biological mother, will you agree to let us to a DNA test on Peter? That way we can eliminate your son from our enquiries.

"Stephen, is that necessary?" Buckton asked.

"Well, yes, I'm afraid to say," Dunn replied, trying his hardest to sound sympathetic.

Lady Buckton glared at her husband with a look concern as he continued.

"Okay, if that's what it takes to keep you quiet and I'm sure Peter has no need to worry."

Lady Buckton struggled to her feet, then made her way towards the large glass cabinet displaying trophies and proceeded to point to each, relaying who they belonged to.

"Peter is a champion swimmer, Stephen" she announced as though it had relevance. "Clifford taught him to swim at an early age, being concerned he might wander out to our pool and drown. Clifford was also a champion swimmer when he was a young man, hence all the trophies you see here. Honestly, those two are like two peas in a pod," she said proudly.

Unfortunately Peter is out with his friends, swimming as we speak, so you will need to return at a later time, to do the test," Buckton announced.

"In that case, he will need to come to the station," Ellis replied. "It's not our job to do a DNA test."

Lady Buckton began clearing the coffee table, she noisily piled the plates on the trolley. This seemed like a signal it was time for the two detectives to leave. The three men rose from their seats at the same time and proceeded toward the door. Buckton placed his hand on Dunn's shoulder.

"I will bring Peter to the station personally, as soon as I can, if that's okay. I'll make up some story as to why you need his DNA."

"Yes, yes, that will be good, then you can see where all the real work is done," Dunn laughed.

"It was good to see you, Stephen. Even if it was under strange circumstances. And nice to meet you too, Detective Sergeant Ellis," Buckton said as he gave them both a handshake. He stopped at his desk and pressed the intercom button on his desk, "I'll have Charles show you out, I have a stack of work I need to attend to. I'm going through a big case at the moment. It's very draining, so I trust you will let things stay as they are?"

Dunn smiled at Buckton then turned to Lady Buckton to give her a farewell kiss on the cheek. Not knowing the protocol, Ellis faltered as he stood in front of her, appearing gauche. Easing his embarrassment, Lady Buckton took his hand and leaned towards him, offering the side of her face for him to kiss, to which Ellis obliged.

"See, that wasn't so bad was it, kissing an old woman," she said, throwing her head back and laughing raucously.

"Not at all, you're a lovely woman, Lady Buckton," Ellis replied, as he continued to hold her hand, giving her one of his cheeky winks.

Dunn shook his head and rolled his eyes as he watched his little display.

"I need to get him out of here, Clifford, looks like Felicity is falling under his spell," Dunn said under his breath.

The double doors were opened by Charles, who beckoned them to follow him.

Lady Buckton linked arms with Sergeant Ellis and walked ahead through the doorway, chatting and giggling as though they were sharing a joke. Sir Buckton held Dunn back to walk with him. Then spoke in a low whisper.

"Let me know how you're going with all this, keep me in the loop with all your enquiries. No need to bother Felicity. Just do your tests, then leave my son well alone."

"For the time being, your secret is safe with me, but, you must understand, I will not compromise my investigations for anyone, even you, Clifford." Dunn expressed with indifference.

In the reception area, Buckton slipped his arm affectionately round his wife's waist.

"I'll see you very soon, Stephen."

The Buckton's returned to the library as Charles walked the two detectives to the front door.

"No need for an umbrella Charles," Dunn said, leaving him standing on the doorstep as they made a dash to their car to avoid the rain, Charles opened the gates with the remote allowing them to leave. Neither Dunn nor Ellis said a word until they were well on their way into the city.

"Drive me straight home Ellis, it's been a long day, I don't know about you, but my head is buzzing."

Ellis agreed but needed to ask a few questions to satisfy his curiosity.

"Sir, did you recognise the lad in the photo?"

"I sure did, it was the young man from the scuba diving school, the best friend of Peter Ashcott who he calls Fish. Come to think of it, we've never been given his full name. There was another photo of him on Buckton's desk."

Neither of them said a word for a few minutes before Ellis exclaimed. "Oh my God! D'you realise what that means, Sir? If the Buckton's adopted son is Laura Verwood's second baby and Peter Ashcott's biological mother is Laura Verwood that makes them brothers, well, half-brothers. Unless they have the same dad, whoever and wherever he may be." Ellis said as he pulled up outside Dunn's home and sat with the engine idling. "They're a strange pair, the Buckton's, I reckon.

"It might just be you're not used to mingling with the upper social classes," Dunn grinned.

"Well, I picked up on some strange body language back there, and I've decided, those two are definitely not well matched. Geez, I nearly fell off my seat laughing when Lady Muck gave that huge talk about their plans for their son Peter. I would love to be a fly on the wall when she finds out he's left college to be a plain and simple scuba diving instructor,"

"I take it you're not too enamoured by the Buckton's? I've known them for a long time and they are the most hardworking, down to earth honest individuals. Lady Buckton is a philanthropist and is the director of many charities. It's tragic to think he could be caught up in this adoption mess and I have no idea where it's all going to go. Let's just take one day at a time, eh, Ellis?"

"Is that why you promised not to say anything to their son Peter as to who his mother really is? Do we actually have the right to stay silent? After all, this is possibly a murder case."

To answer your questions, if you want to be technical, I promised not to say anything, I don't remember you promising," he smirked.

Ellis broke into a smile as he thought to himself, *the cunning bastard!*

"What have you in mind for tomorrow, Sir?"

"I need you to contact Sutton as early as you can and warn him we will visit him at his shop during the morning and make sure he will be there this time. So on that note, I'm off, there's a glass of the best malt whiskey waiting for me," he said, climbing out the car. Slamming the door shut, he banged twice on the roof with the palm of his hand and watched Ellis drive away.

Dunn closed the front door of his two story terrace and leant his back against the cool, stained glass and closed his eyes for a moment, reveling in the peace and quiet. Scooping up the pile of letters his cleaning lady had left on the hall table, he headed into the small but comfortable lounge. After pouring himself a large malt whisky, he sat in his favourite leather reclining chair and proceeded to sift through his mail. Seeing there was nothing of importance, he took a sip of his drink and gazed around the room.

A sudden wave of sadness crept over him and for the first time in years he felt lonely. He held his glass in the air. *It's time for Stephen Dunn to start getting out more, meet a nice lady and stop being such a serious loner*, he declared as he knocked back his drink in one go.

Chapter 17

Asho was relieved Inspector Dunn hadn't questioned his story the intruders hadn't touched their boat and was thankful he'd agreed to let them take it out for the rest of the day. He knew it was risky in the stormy weather, but it was a risk all three were willing to take. The thought of finding more coins had them intrigued and excited. As they'd cruised away from the marina, Fish was surprised how easily they cut through the three-metre swells. A short time later, as the marina became a small dot in the distance, the swells doubled in size; causing them to rock from side to side violently.

Being a competent sailor, Fish knew the logical thing was to aim the bow of the boat into the swell. As larger waves appeared, putting their small craft in danger, he was beginning to think perhaps they shouldn't have ventured so far from the mainland after all. For safety reasons, Asho had insisted that everything should be fastened down or stowed away, making sure their expensive gear wouldn't end up overboard and lost forever.

Feeling a little queasy, Jenni decided to stay close to the toilet cubicle.

"Do you want me to help with the steering?" Asho asked Fish, watching him struggle with the controls.

"Nah, I'm sure I can handle it, okay, but you do realise if it gets any worse, we will have to turn back?"

"Having come this far, let's hope that's not the case."

At that moment, a large wave crashed down on the port side, giving them a start. They both grimaced at the sound of Jenni, being sick in the small toilet cubicle.

"That doesn't sound good, does it? What's your thoughts on what we should do?" Asho asked.

"Sorry, no time to *think*, I need all my concentration to control this bastard."

The heavy rain clouds rolled over, blackening the sky as the steady rain had turned torrential. It was impossible to see through the windscreen and the wipers were useless. Asho had volunteered to brave the extreme conditions and headed out on deck to act as a lookout; returning ten minutes later, drenched to the skin. "We're here," he yelled to Fish. "Slow down and I'll guide you to the buoy and I'll tie her up."

Fish followed Asho's instructions. Once they were fastened securely, he shut down the engine.

"Sorry Ash, there's no way I'll be able to join you today. I feel like shit," Jenni moaned, just managing to finish her sentence before having to dart to the toilet to throw up again. Asho followed her and placed his hand affectionately on her back and rubbed it gently.

"Is there anything you want me to do? Do you want a sip of water," he asked sympathetically.

"Just leave me alone, I want to die, just let me die in peace," she groaned as she sat on the floor next to the toilet, her head slumped forward. Asho knelt beside her, looking concerned as she wiped her mouth with the back of her hand.

"I'll go and find you a towel or something, hang on in there Jen." He leapt to his feet and began scratching around in the cupboards in the hope he'd find something he could use. He hurried back to find Jenni was back over the bowl, now dry reaching. Trying to stand up, Asho grabbed her arm to steady her. Handing her the towel, he could see she was as white as a sheet. It was killing him, not being able to hold her in his arms and make her pain go away. But he knew Fish was close by. He felt helpless.

"I'm so sorry Ash, I never get seasick, maybe it's all that business back at the shop," she wailed. I have to say, it did make me feel nauseous seeing that mess."

"Let's get you over to one of the bench seats, they're under cover, but unfortunately, everything is soaking wet. You'll feel a bit cooler. He guided her to the bench seat and sat her down gently as he whispered in her ear.

"We're going to have to tell Fish soon, this is agony not being able to hold you."

"I know, I just want a hug, except I now stink of vomit," they both laughed.

Fish appeared from nowhere. "Looks like it's just me and you then."

"Not necessarily," he replied as he pulled out the wetsuits from the storage trunk and took one to Jenni.

"Sorry Jen, I have to be cruel to be kind. Put this on, I want you to come with me."

"Not now Ash, I have a headache," she whispered and giggled like a school girl.

Asho laughed, then placed his finger on his lips and made a shushing sound as he nodded his head towards Fish. He then continued with his advice. "Believe me, the way this boat is rocking, you're going to be hugging the toilet for the rest of the day it's much calmer on the seabed. Trust me. You'll be much better under water."

Jenni let out a groan. "Sorry Ash, Just leave me here to die. Going for a dive is the last thing I want to do at this minute," she wailed.

"He's right, you know Jen," Fish called out. "Just give it a go and if you still feel rotten, we'll pack up and head for land."

With all the strength she could muster, Jenni reluctantly, pulled on her wet suit. She wasn't completely convinced they were telling the truth, but knew nothing could be worse than the way she was feeling and she didn't really want to miss the dive.

"Do we have a plan of action?" Fish asked.

"I think the best thing would be to start where I found the coin and work backwards. The way I see it, if there's one, there must be others. It's just a case of sifting through the sandy silt slowly and being extremely careful."

Without warning, the boat took another hit from a large wave, causing Jenni to fall off balance and stagger against Asho, who automatically wrapped his arms around her waist and held her tight.

"Shit, that could've been nasty, you must hang on to something, anything," he chastised, slightly embarrassed they'd ended up in a compromising position. Fish could see his discomfort and smiled to himself, wondering whether he should tell them both he knew about their relationship. Then decided he'd let them squirm for a bit longer.

"Now, listen, you two," Fish announced, taking control. "It might be dark and cloudy down there if the storm has churned up the seabed. Hopefully the LED headbands should help our visibility."

As soon as they were kitted out, the three made their way to the diving platform at the rear end of the vessel. Choosing to go first, Fish jumped in the choppy waters. Before he had a chance to bob back to the surface, Asho slipped his arm around Jenni and gave her a quick hug. Wearing mouthpieces prevented them from speaking, Jenni blew Asho a kiss before he disappeared into the churning sea. As she was about to follow the boys, something caught her attention in the distance. Straining her eyes, she could see it was another boat about two hundred metres on the starboard side.

Although it was a fair distance away, she could just make out the silhouettes of two figures standing on the rear deck. Unable to find out as to whether they were male or female, all she could tell was that one was tall the other short. A light reflected off the forehead of the shorter one making her think they were using binoculars. Thinking no one would be daft enough to enter into these stormy waters, Jenni decided it must be the coast guards. She edged to the end of the platform and leapt into the briny deep to join Asho and Fish.

Once on the seabed, they faced each other and gave the okay sign with a thumb and forefinger forming a circle. Before heading off on the quest to hopefully find treasure, each one reached up and flicked on their headband torches. Without waiting for the other two, Fish took off on a mission. Asho grabbed Jenni's arm and made circular movements on his stomach, meaning was she feeling better. Jenni gave him an exaggerated nod while making the okay signal back at him.

Arriving at the place they were now becoming familiar with, Asho took out his small scraper and began pushing the sand back at the base of a large black stone. The other two joined in, combing their fingers through the spaghetti-like seaweed as they searched. A large shoal of brightly coloured fish, glided past, then dispersed into smaller groups taking off in all directions. It was quite tranquil on the seabed as all three were soon engrossed in their search to find another coin.

◆◆◆

With great difficulty, the two men balanced on the rear deck of their boat as it rocked perilously on the rough sea. The men watched and waited until the three friends had left their boat unmanned. Letting his binoculars fall onto his chest, the shorter man called out to his mate who was fully kitted out in a wetsuit and an air tank strapped to his back, ready to make a dive. "They've gone down, you're all clear to go," He yelled.

The man in the wetsuit turned with his back to the water and gave a wave before rolling backwards into the ocean, disappearing out of sight. The man left on deck, looked at his watch to check the time. After fifteen minutes had passed, he raised his binoculars to take another look at the boat in the distance, now deserted and vulnerable. The name 'Blue Horizon Diving School' boldly sign written on the side. He could see his mate, dragging himself onto the aluminium deck at the rear of the boat and removed his flippers, mask, and tank. He waved with both hands held high in the air, then staggered towards the steering station.

Once inside, the tall man took out his two-way radio from his diver's utility belt, switched it on and began calling his mate, back on their boat. "Are you there?"

"Are you there?" There was no answer. "Hello, is anyone there?" Still no answer.

"Are you there? You little dick head," he bellowed.

The two-way burst into life. "Sorry mate, I was having trouble with these binoculars" the man replied. "Why are you bothering to talk to me on this thing anyway? I can see you, you big oaf, just search the fuckin place and be quick about it, before they decide to return."

Switching off the radio, the tall man staggered back to the covered deck. Spotting a pile of clothes, he rifled through the pockets, then searched the deck area before returning to the two-way radio.

"Are you there? Nah mate, can't find a thing here so I'm going down, see what they're up to. I just have to hope they don't see me."

"Yeah, they might mistake you for a big whale."

"Hah! Bloody hah! Very funny."

Slipping his diving gear back on, he quickly dropped into the sea and made his way to the seabed in record time. In the distance he could see three figures a few feet apart, crouching down. They appeared to be sifting through the sand looking for something. Making sure to keep out of sight, he circled them and headed towards the sunken relic. Taking up his position behind a large jagged rock, he was able to observe them while staying out of their line of vision. After watching for a few moments, deciding it wasn't such a good vantage point, he edged along the sandy surface, making his way to the bow, only metres away from Jenni. Kneeling down and narrowly missing a spiky sea urchin he leapt backwards, causing a cloud of silt to billow around him.

Something out the corner of Jenni's eye made her turn. A school of coloured fish swam past in perfect formation, satisfying her fear. Moving her hand over the soft sand, her heart skipped a beat as she noticed a round, flat object the size of a twenty cent piece. Clutching it in her fingers, she held it high to take a better look by the light from the torch.

The man watched, dumbstruck seeing Jenni holding something that looked like a coin. "Well, I'll be buggered," he thought to himself. "That's typical, we've been looking for months and haven't found a bloody thing. These kids come along and bingo! Find something straight away."

Seeing the other two divers were so deeply involved in their own search, and hadn't noticed their friend holding something up high, he made his move. Gliding swiftly over the top of the unsuspecting Jenni. Taking her completely by surprise, he reached down and plucked the object from her hand, knocking her off balance, sending her reeling to one side. The man took off, clutching the item; casting a shadow over Asho and Fish as he swam over them. They both froze, thinking it was a shark.

They looked up to see the shape of a diver swimming past. Both turned their gaze towards Jenni, who appeared to be swaying precariously. Asho desperately wanted to head over to her, but thinking quickly, he knew he was a stronger swimmer than Fish and he needed to go after whoever it was and find out what they wanted. Grabbing Fish's arm to get his attention. He motioned to him that he should go to Jenni while he himself would take off after the stranger. He had no idea if the person was male or female. One thing for sure, he intended to find out.

Asho cut through the water like a dart making it clear the rogue diver was no match; even after a head start, the gap between them soon narrowed to within arm's length. The diver suddenly turned and with great force, kicked Asho, sending him careering off sideways. This gave the diver, enough time to reach down and pull out a long, double bladed knife from its sheath strapped to his lower leg. Asho was horrified when he saw the glint of a large bladed knife.

Having no protection himself, he needed to think quickly. It was futile to try and overpower the person. He floundered backwards through the water as the diver came at him, waving the knife threateningly. Fearing the worst, Asho was now scared out of his wits. His life suddenly flashed before him, fearing he was about to die at any moment. He closed his eyes and waited for the searing pain of a sharp knife, to go straight through his wetsuit and puncture his heart. After a few seconds, when nothing happened, he opened his eyes to discover he was alone.

Disappearing into the far distance he could just make out a dark figure.

The diver made a dash back to the boat where his accomplice was waiting patiently on the dive platform. Clambering on board, the man lay on the deck, gasping for breath; still holding the knife in one hand, the disc he'd grabbed from Jenni in the other.

"Don't tell me you've used a knife on those kids, you dumb Arse. What the hell happened down there?"

"I had to, one of the little shits chased me and bugger me he swam like a bloody Dolphin. He was just about to grab me. So I pulled out old faithful here," he said as he held the intimidating knife in the air.

"Please don't tell me you used it on one of them?"

"Nah, just scared the shit out of him when he saw the knife, so I was able to get away," he sniggered.

"Let's hope he didn't die of shock."

"Stop your whining, wait till I show you why they were chasing me, look what I grabbed from one of them," he announced proudly as he held up the perfect round flat disc shaped item.

"What the fuck... a *shell!* You grabbed a piece of shell?" Geez man, you really are an imbecile.

The tall man looked closer at the disc in his hand, unable to believe his eyes.

"You have to admit, it does look like a coin," he said as he threw it to his mate who examined it closer before throwing it into the sea. They both looked at each other and began laughing hysterically.

◆◆◆

Asho pulled himself together. "*What the fuck was all that about?*" he thought to himself.

Slowly making his way back to where he'd left Fish and Jenni he pointed to his wristwatch and held his thumb in the air, bobbing it up and down, indicating it was time to head to the surface.

A short while later, all three climbed onto the aluminium platform, sitting for a few moments to catch their breath, before removing their scuba gear.

"Are you okay Jen?" Asho asked, sounding concerned. He crawled across the deck and sat down next to her. "Tell us what happened, did he hurt you?"

Jenni scraped her wet hair back off her face with both hands.

"I'd just picked up what I thought was a coin and was holding it up to see it better in the light of my torch; when suddenly this black figure came out of nowhere and grabbed the thing out of my hand, which knocked me off balance. But I wasn't hurt, don't worry. I just got the shock of my life."

"Fuck… *you* got a shock? He groaned, I thought I was going to be stabbed to death down there." With a horrified look on the faces of Fish and Jenni, Asho launched into the details of his narrow escape.

Jenni ached to hug him, hearing his story, but instead placed her hand on his arm.

"Well, it's now clear that whoever they are, they're looking for coins, obviously, that's what that diver, thought I had.

"Hang on a minute, what's that doing there?" I don't remember bringing the two-way radio out here," Fish called out.

"We didn't, it's not ours. Shit! Someone's been here, probably the person I've just chased," Asho fumed as he jumped to his feet and legged it into the cabin with Fish close behind him. Feeling left out, Jenni leapt to her feet and followed. As she crossed the deck, she spotted a vessel she'd noticed earlier, was still there.

"Look, you two, over there, It's the same one that was there earlier," Jenni called out, as she pointed into the distance.

Asho and Fish hurried out from the cabin. They followed her finger to where she was pointing to with their eyes. They could see a boat, pitching and rolling in the distance.

"It was there when we went on our dives. I could just make out two figures standing on the back deck looking through binoculars. I thought it must be the coast guard," she said now beginning to feel foolish not taking it more seriously.

"Obviously, they were waiting for us to leave the boat unattended, then they've made their way here and searched the place. At least there's no damage this time."

"D'you think it's the same people that wrecked it before, and the shop?" Jenni asked.

"Who knows, but it's a horrible feeling knowing someone's been rummaging through our belongings. Suddenly the colour drained from Fish's face.

"Fuck, the coin," he shouted with fear in his voice.

Both Jenni and Asho stared at him, confused.

"Don't tell me you brought the coin with you? You bloody idiot," Asho said furiously.

For fuck's sake Asho, get off my case, it's well hidden, no one could possibly find it," he said, covering the way he felt as he suddenly doubted his clever hiding place.

"I thought it would be handy to compare it with any coins we might find today.

"You're a bloody idiot, we've just had the boat ransacked, it had better be hidden *really* well, cos if not, it's now gone, mate."

Fish couldn't help thinking, Asho was overreacting a bit, or maybe he was just showing off in front of Jenni. Either way, he was now feeling extremely embarrassed as he led them back into the steering station, his hands were sweating with fear that the coin would not be where he'd left it. Asho and Jenni followed him with bated breath as they watched him hunker down and lift the corner of the carpet, then slowly rolled it back. To Fish's relief, it was still there, looking small and insignificant, lying on the bare ply board floor.

The look of sheer relief spread over Asho and Jenni's faces

"You see, I'm not an idiot, I'm quite ingenious," Fish said, with a weak laugh trying to sound more confident than he was feeling.

Asho stretched his arms out and enveloped Fish in a big man hug.

"Okay mate, I apologise, I was a bit out of order just then, I think this coin malarkey is making me obsessive,"

"You think?" Jenni exclaimed as she watched her two favourite people. "It's affecting all of us. I would love to know who it was that destroyed our shop and now seems like they're following our every move."

"By the way, Jen, what was it you had in your hand that the diver grabbed?"

"I just managed to work out what it was before he took it. It was a well-worn piece of shell, so whoever it was is not going to be too pleased when they find out they went to all that trouble for a shell," she giggled.

"I take it he's from the boat over there, so let's go over and ask them what they're playing at, stealing shells," Fish said, lightening the mood.

"Yeah, let's go and ask, please mister, can we have our shell back," Jenni said, pretending to be a child.

Once they were untied from the buoy, Fish took his position in the driver's seat and fired up the engine. He yanked the steering wheel sharply to the right, then pushed the throttle down hard. All eyes were on the boat in the distance, which hadn't moved.

Watching through his binoculars from the back of their vessel, the shorter of the two men realised the dive boat was heading straight for them.

"Oh no you don't, you mongrels," he called out. The binoculars fell to the deck as he dashed into the cabin and within minutes was revving the engine ready for his get-away from the pursuing boat. Fish managed to close the gap in no time. Then, as if by magic, the boat ahead appeared to levitate above the water. Two hydrofoils, flanked on either side of the boat appeared out of nowhere. As the boat thrust forward, the hull raised high in the air and skimmed over the surface of the water, leaving Asho and Fish's boat to roll precariously in the wake.

"Look at that," Fish yelled.

Asho's jaw dropped as he stared in disbelief at the disappearing craft.

"What just happened, guys? I've never seen anything like that, *ever*."

"Me neither, the bastards have just left us for dead," Fish replied. "There's only one boat, capable of doing that. Although I thought those things were still experimental."

"You look worried Fish, what is it? Is there something you want to tell us?" Jenni said.

"Well, it's either someone extremely wealthy, or we're facing the Australian Navy."

"What? Are you serious? How do you know this?" Asho asked.

"And what's so special about that coin," Jenni added.

"I suggest we check out that sunken ship a bit more. We may have accidentally gotten ourselves involved in something we know nothing about," Fish summed up, as he headed for Congwong Bay. Asho and Jenni set about tidying up as they chatted quietly to each other knowing they were out of Fish's earshot, who looked like he was a million miles away.

As he manoeuvred carefully into their berth, they could see a police officer standing close to the marina. His blank expression turned to delight at the sight of them. Once on land, the officer met them at the gate.

"I was ordered to stay until you returned to keep an eye on things and to let you know that forensics have finished, you're free to tidy the mess up now," he said, sympathetically. "I don't envy you one bit. I'll be off and leave you to it."

The officer began to walk away, then having an afterthought, he turned back. "Oh, one more thing, you'll need to call an emergency locksmith to fix the back door. It's quite mangled and you need to make the premises secure before dark."

The memories of the morning flooded back as they walked through the front door and saw the mess. Taking command, Jenni suggested they get stuck in and clear the place up. The boys looked at each other and shrugged their shoulders.

"Okay, you two, I'll take the office, while you two can tackle out the back, we need to be up and running as soon as possible." Seeing the look of despair on their faces, Jenni offered to drive to the café a few blocks away and buy them food. This did the trick, they both looked much happier as they headed for the door to the workshop.

As Asho glanced around the room and saw the mess, his heart sank, they didn't deserve this," he thought to himself.

"Let's hope Sergeant Ellis turns up, at least we will have help with the scuba lessons," Asho said, wondering where to start.

By late afternoon, the place was just about back to the way it was before the break in. The sound of someone whistling, made Jenni look up from behind her computer to see a dark skinned man with an afro hairstyle standing in the shop doorway. The man, dressed in overalls over a multi-coloured t-shirt and carrying a tool box, stopped whistling and gave the broadest grin.

"How, you doin young lady? Hope I didn't give you a fright, I have a habit of doing that, but honestly, I'm quite friendly. I'm Jock Smith the locksmith," he said, then gave out a loud belly laugh, flashing perfect white teeth. "That's not really my name, I just love seeing the look on people's faces when I say it," he laughed once again. "So, tell me young lady, where's the damage?"

Taken aback by this odd person, not really knowing how to take him, Jenni stood up. "You better come with me," she said, as she headed into the workshop where the boys were still sorting the mess.

"The locksmith's here," she called out to Asho and Fish. The man followed right behind her holding out his hand in readiness to shake theirs.

"I'm Ruben, I hear you've had a spot of bother," he said in a strong Cockney accent.

Completely spellbound by the way he spoke and hearing his stories, Fish and Asho hadn't noticed the time, forgetting why he was there. Not hearing any work being done, Jenni decided to investigate by peering through the doorway. Seeing no one doing anything constructive, Jenni stormed in the room. "What's this? Having a little men's pow-wow are we?" she said, stomping towards the kitchenette and filling the kettle noisily, making her point.

Taking the hint, Asho explained to Ruben what they needed him to do. "We better leave you to get on, I think we're in trouble" he said, slowly moving towards the front office.

"No probs mate, nothin Ruben ere can't fix, just leave it to me," he said watching them walk away. "By the way, miss, I take two sugars in my coffee," he called out with a cheeky grin, holding up two fingers.

Jenni placed four cups of coffee and an open packet of biscuits on a tray and headed towards the front office, stopping at Ruben on the way. "Yours is the large mug and grab a few biscuits before the boys get their hands on them," she offered.

As Jenni placed the tray on her desk, Fish took the packet of biscuits and tore the packaging completely and grabbed four.

Asho did the same before flopping down on one of the seats in the waiting area. “Wow, Jen, this looks better than it did before, you’ve done a great job in here,” Asho said, glancing around the room.

“Not only have I straightened this place, you should see what I’ve found on the computer. There’s a whole bunch of information on the relic we’ve discovered.” She said excitedly.

Asho and Fish grabbed a chair each and sat either side of Jenni with their cups of and listened intently as she read out the information that flashed across the screen. Skipping past a few paragraphs, she found the history of the Phoenicia, an ancient civilization, composed of independent city-states which lay along the coast of the Mediterranean seas. All three were intrigued as the information described how, at the request of the Pharaoh, Nacho, instructed the Phoenician sailors to circumnavigate the African coast. Scrolling down once more, they read, that Nacho, commissioned a ship with a crew that comprised of a High Priest, who was to master the vessel and one hundred oarsmen to move the vessel from the calmer Mediterranean waters to find new territories through unchartered waters. There were pictures of the merchant ships, called Bireme’s and described how they were built for carrying cargo for trading and that the Phoenicians were expert sailors.

“Listen to this, legend has it that the High Priest was given one hundred solid gold pieces, to trade with other countries in textiles, spices, and other merchandise.”

Asho sat back in his chair. “I reckon we’ve accidently stumbled right into someone’s treasure hunt territory, and that’s what all this crap we’ve been through, is all about,” he said, sounding concerned.

Turning from her computer, Jenni sat bolt upright, glancing from one to the other.

"If none of us told anyone about our find, how did those people out there today find out?"

"It had to be that wranger woman at the museum, Hughes. I thought I'd hoodwinked her into thinking we were studying metals. Bugger, she must've guessed what we were really up to," Fish replied.

"So, you two, what d'you think, should we have given her the coin?" Jenni asked, raising her eyebrows.

"I'll be honest, there's a time I would've said yes, but not now, no way, never. Not after all they put us through today." Asho said angrily.

"Your quiet Fish, what's going through that head of yours," Asho asked, reaching up and tousling his hair annoyingly.

"I've been thinking,"

Asho and Jenni looked at each other and grinned.

"No, listen, hear me out. I've been thinking, if we are looking for these gold doubloons, what we need is an underwater metal detector,"

"Oh my God, he's right, that's it. Good thinking little man, there's more than sawdust in that noggin of yours" Asho said as he tousled his head again.

This time, Fish jumped up to retaliate and grabbed Asho's head, putting him in a headlock. Following through, Asho wrapped a leg around Fish's ankle, knocking him off balance, making them both crash to the ground in a heap.

Having witnessed this behaviour so many times, Jenni picked up the three empty cups and casually walked out to the workshop and placed them in the sink, leaving them to it. On her return to the shop, the boys were both sitting rubbing where it hurt and laughing uncontrollably.

"Are you both done? Can we get on, you two?"

The two boys stopped laughing and gave each other one last punch for good measure.

"As you were saying Fish," Jenni said, sounding agitated.

"As I was saying," he replied, rubbing his elbow. "We should hire a metal detector, it will save us so much time and will make a much thorough job than scratching around with our hands on all fours."

As Fish was talking, Jenni started searching on her computer. "There's a number of companies, there's even one in Botany Bay, not far from here. Making a note of the number, she reached over and picked up the phone then dialed the number. Within seconds she began talking to someone on the other end of the phone.

"That's fantastic, we will be there in about thirty minutes," she said before clicking off the phone and turning to the boys. "How easy was that? They've got one and we can pick it up now."

"*Woohoo,* you're the best," Fish called out as he grabbed Jenni's head and kissed the top of it in a rough but friendly movement. "We can go in my car, it's the biggest." Fish added, excitedly.

The banging from the other room stopped and within a few minutes, Ruben the locksmith appeared at the door of the office, wiping his hands on a dirty rag. "Just letting you know, I've done my best, I've put a new lock on the door, fixed the hinges and replaced the door jamb on one side; where it had been smashed to pieces. But I recommend you buy a new back door. Let it be a lesson, there's no such thing as too much security, especially around these remote parts," the locksmith advised. "I'll send you an invoice. You should be able to claim through your insurance," he paused. "That's if you *are* insured," he added, whistling merrily as he turned to leave.

◆◆◆

A short while later the trio pulled into the car park of a hire company specialising in metal detectors. A grey-haired man in grimy overalls limped towards them, introducing himself as Mr Denton the proprietor and beckoned them to follow him to a large warehouse. They were confronted by rows of tools, air compressors, jackhammers, earth moving equipment. Possibly everything and anything anyone would ever need.

"This is it," Mr Denton said, as he stopped at a large, torpedo-shaped machine, about the size of their boat. Fish leaned towards Asho and whispered into his ear, hoping the old man couldn't hear.

"It's fucking *massive,* I imagined it would be much smaller than that."

The old man stood proudly next to the very large metal detector.

This is an eight-ton, remotely operated vehicle known as an ROV. It's launched from your vessel wherever it is you want to do your search. "What is it you want this for by the way? You didn't say on the phone?"

Asho hesitated as he tried to think of an answer, without sounding foolish.

We run a scuba diving school and we've discovered a wreck. We thought there might be some artefacts, maybe old weapons around the area where the wreck is situated. It might be interesting for our pupils to try a bit of metal detecting while they're on their dives."

Fish looked at Asho and winked, as he thought to himself what a clever bit of subterfuge, putting the man off the scent.

"You're kidding me? I'm a metal detectorist myself. Nothing underwater mind you, I prefer land. I go to beaches all around Sydney. You wouldn't believe the stuff I have found."

Asho looked at the man in disbelief as he thought to himself. *"Bugger, I wasn't expecting that response. Who would've thought he'd be so friendly."*

"Actually, Mr Denton, we did give that a try once," Jenni jumped in. "But seeing as we're scuba diving now, we thought we would try something a bit more adventurous."

"Oh, I wish I was twenty years younger, I'd love to have a go, but I think I'm far too old to go scuba diving at my age, I'll be seventy-five next birthday," he said proudly

"Not at all, we take people your age down all the time, after a little training, you'll get the hang of it, Asho said encouragingly, not wanted to pass any business down.

Jenni and Fish glared at Asho, thinking he was treading on very thin ice. The man might suddenly decide to take him up on it. Then came his response.

"I might take you up on that young man, give me your card so I can give you a call. Now do any of you know how to use one of these babies?"

The trio looked blankly at each other without saying a word.

"I thought not. You do know this one is not something you push along the seabed?"

They looked at each other and shrugged their shoulders.

"No, this little beauty hangs from the back of your boat and it floats above the ocean floor. You do have a boat, I hope?"

"Of course, we do, we have a thirty-five footer," Fish said with pride.

"That's a good size boat, however, you will need something a bit bigger for this size detector. These are what we supply the oil companies with. Looks like I'm not going to be able to help you out after all. You do know that the size depends on the depth you intend to go. The water pressure can tear a small detector apart. What depth had you in mind?"

"No more than about twenty metres," Asho replied.

"Sounds like you only need the smaller model."

The man stopped speaking for a few seconds.

"Actually, you know who might be able to help out, but it's a long shot, the police. You don't happen to know a nice friendly policeman, do you? They have special ones for shallow waters." He advised.

"You've been very helpful Mr Denton," Fish said as he shook his hand again.

"Well, I've got your card, I might just take you up on those scuba diving lessons," the gentleman said as he gave a friendly smile.

The ride back to the dive shop was made in virtual silence. The rain had eased and the weather forecaster had assured them it was going to clear up by morning. The three were feeling disappointed that the metal detector hadn't worked out. Hoping to start up a conversation and feeling a little embarrassed she'd sent them on a wild-goose chase, Jenni began chattering about their preparations for the next day's dive.

Chapter 18

Ray was thankful the foul weather of the past two days had subsided and the early morning sky glowed red as the sun peeked over the horizon. Although it was only seven o'clock in the morning, it was already warm as he headed out to the dive school. The conditions were looking favourable for the scuba dive Asho and Fish had arranged for him.

At the same time, Inspector Dunn made his way to Dennis Sutton's antique emporium for his prearranged meeting. Avoiding a repeat performance with parking after his last visit, Dunn had the forethought to drive to the rear of the building; remembering there was an actual car park. He parked next to a white van, assuming it was Sutton's.

After giving two sharp raps on the door, there was a sound of movement within the building. The door was opened slightly by a worried looking Dennis Sutton; still wearing his dressing gown and slippers. Seeing Inspector Dunn, he gave a sigh of relief, opening the door wide.

"Ah, Inspector, I *was* expecting you, just not this early. I do apologise for my attire, I don't open till ten, so I have a leisurely breakfast and read the paper. "Sutton invited Inspector Dunn in and without waiting, he turned and took off along a dimly lit hallway, leaving Dunn to close the door. The place smelled musty as he squeezed down the wide hallway, stacked on either side with boxes, stuffed with ornaments and bric-à-brac. He followed Sutton up a narrow wooden staircase to the apartment on the first floor,

The landing at the top of the stairs led into a large spacious kitchen, where the theme was continued with more boxes. Sutton had resumed his seat at an old style dining table covered with a white damask tablecloth. A single setting of fine bone china was laid neatly in front of him with a matching teapot, cream jug and sugar bowl. He pushed a plate with a half-eaten slice of toast to one side and methodically folded his newspaper and placed it on the far edge of the table.

"So, Inspector Dunn, please take a seat and tell me, what's this all about?" Sutton asked.

"Mr Sutton, I hope my Sergeant explained why I was visiting you today, I'd like to question you on the statement you gave us at our last meeting," Dunn began, as he pulled out a chair and sat down.

"Yes, yes, Sergeant Ellis was quite clear. I have to wonder what questions you haven't already asked," he said with an air of confidence. "Before we begin, can I interest you in a cup of tea? I have only just brewed a pot of my favourite tea, Lapsang Souchong. I don't know if you're familiar with this tea, I can highly recommend it."

"As coincidence would have it, I do have a penchant for that particular tea."

Sutton ceremoniously placed the tea strainer over the fine bone china cup, picked up the matching tea pot and poured the almost clear liquid. As he handed the cup to Dunn, he suggested he'd go and make himself more presentable. Inspector Dunn had no problem being left alone for a while, having found it difficult to be serious, talking to a man in silk pyjamas.

Within fifteen minutes, Sutton returned, suitably dressed and with an overpowering aroma of cologne. He beckoned Dunn to follow him downstairs where they weaved in and out between old glass display cabinets and chairs stacked high. They finally reached a room which doubled as a storeroom and office. Sutton placed the tray on the solid antique oak desk with a deep burgundy leather inlay which sat majestically in the centre of the room; leaving very little room to move. Sutton squeezed behind the desk and sat in a dark leather office chair looking like it had seen better days.

With no direction from Sutton, Inspector Dunn sat on the only other seat in the room, a classic red leather Queen Anne winged back chair. A three drawer, metal filing cabinet, against the far wall, looking out of place, standing next to a highly polished, ornate, rosewood chiffonier. Sutton poured two cups of tea and sat back in his chair.

He noticed a slight pause in Dunn's actions, as he inspected the chair before sitting. Being a salesperson, Sutton had no desire to miss an opportunity for a sale.

"I can see you admire the Queen Anne, wingback? Have you any idea how much it's worth?"

"I've really no idea, sorry."

"Go on, take a guess, just humour me," he chuckled.

"You're probably going to tell me something ridiculous like a thousand dollars?"

"Well, you'd think wrong," Sutton replied, feeling miffed at his lack of knowledge. However, he was willing to forgive him, especially him being a Lapsang Souchong tea drinker, he thought to himself as he leant over and refilled Dunn's cup.

"What would you say if I told you the price tag on that chair is three thousand dollars? And sadly for me, in two weeks, that chair will sit in the beautiful home of a well-known American wrestler in uptown Missouri, in the US of A. Strange as it sounds, he has a thing for antiques. Actually, it's his wife, seems he has to keep her happy. These people have more money than sense," he smiled. "But it keeps me in business. Now do you want to know how much I paid for it?"

Dunn was beginning to feel agitated with the guessing games.

"I have no idea Mr Sutton, but I'm sure you will tell me."

"The guy I bought it from wanted a thousand, but I knocked him down to four hundred dollars," he said with pride. Good business sense, eh?"

"If you say so… look, Mr Sutton, I'll come straight to the point… when we last spoke, you told me Laura Verwood and yourself were making a stack of money."

"That's correct, what's your point?" Sutton said, looking sad at the mention of Laura's name.

"I'd like you to explain something if you don't mind. I had one of my officers make enquiries with your financial institution.

He discovered that you are in quite a lot of debt and your bank account is overdrawn by a substantial amount of money."

"You have been busy," Sutton said indignantly. "Are you allowed to check into my business affairs and speak to my bank without my permission?"

"That's exactly what we can do *if* we are investigating a serious crime or a murder. Now, are you able to explain the discrepancy in your statement?"

There was a moment of silence.

"I wonder, Inspector Dunn, did your officer talk to my bank manager or a teller?"

Suddenly Dunn realised he couldn't answer that question as he didn't know. He cursed inwardly. So as not to lose his credibility with Sutton, he continued.

"My officer spoke to a man called Julienne Carmichael."

Sutton threw both his arms in the air and brought them down hard on the desk in front of him.

"I rest my case. That is *not* my manager. The man you spoke to, clearly does not understand how the antique business works. Please, follow me and let me show you something."

Sutton stormed towards the office door and beckoned Dunn to follow him into the shop.

"First, as you can see, what we have here is two shop fronts knocked into one. Upstairs, there are two large apartments. I bought this property over thirty years ago and now this property is worth an enormous amount of money, and I mean *enormous*. Second, you probably think that this place is full of junk and that there's far too much of it. Let me tell you, about a month ago, I was at an auction where I won the bid for a deceased estate of a titled man who lives not far from here. It cost me a fortune, half of the stuff is here, half is at my warehouse, which I *also* own."

Walking towards a large timber table, he gently trailed his fingers across its surface.

"Take this Tudor oak dining table for instance. To the right person, I will sell this for five thousand dollars, I only paid *two*. Let me tell you, Inspector, Tudor is the latest buzzword in the antique circles."

Sutton moved over to the far side of the showroom. "This here is my personal favourite. It's a Jacobean oak farmhouse corner cabinet in perfect condition. This should fetch around six thousand dollars."

"Okay, okay, I get the picture, I do have a little knowledge of antiques, Mr Sutton. I understand, you have your money invested in your stock."

"May I show you my pièce de résistance? It will only take a second,"

Sutton made his way to the far side of the shop and pointed to the display window.

"What do you think of this?"

Dunn stood dumfounded, unable to hide his utter dislike to the vulgar piece of furniture Sutton was pointing at.

"Lost for words, inspector? Don't worry, ninety percent of the world's population would have the same reaction? In case you're interested, this is a Gothic, library table. It's ugly, not something I would usually buy and is valued at ten thousand dollars."

Inspector Dunn looked shocked. “Nothing personal you understand, but I wouldn’t give it house room. Having said that, I do appreciate the workmanship that’s gone into the making of it.”

“I know what you mean, but you will be shocked to know that it is sold,” Sutton said, pausing, to watch Dunn’s reaction. This is where Laura was invaluable as you know she had her own slot on an American antiques program which showcased our more expensive stock. Within days of her appearing on TV, we’d have our stock sold at a nice profit.”

“Okay, okay Mr Sutton, you’ve cleared up a few questions and you’ve made your point.”

Sutton ignored Dun’s hint to stop talking shop and continued. “Ours is a difficult business, however, like many businesses we have to spend money to make money. Let’s go back to my office, I think it’s time for another Lapsang,” Sutton decided. They made their way back to the office. Sutton collected the tray of crockery and headed to the kitchen to make more tea; leaving Dunn alone.

While waiting for Sutton to return, Inspector Dunn picked up a magazine lying on the desk. Flicking through the pages, something caught his eye, making him stop on a page and stare in disbelief. There in front of him was a full-page article with a coloured picture of Laura Verwood. He raised the magazine towards the light for a better look.

“Well, well, so that’s Laura Verwood,” Dunn thought to himself, scrutinising the colour photo at the top of the page. He hastily scanned through the article before Sutton returned. His first thoughts were that she looked a classy lady; in her haute couture navy suit with silk, cream coloured shirt. He couldn’t say

she was beautiful, she had more of a classic look with the palest skin and crystal blue eyes; her auburn hair was cut into a sleek jaw length page boy.

The article was well written, mostly about her TV programs in America. It also touched on a couple of personal topics, giving Dunn an insight into this tragic woman.

So engrossed in the article, Dunn didn't hear Sutton return with the tray of teas.

"You've found the article? Laura was quite a celebrity in the antique world. Let me tell you, Detective, she's left a massive hole in the lives of everyone who knew her."

"Do you have any idea how much Laura's collection would be worth?" Dunn asked.

"How long is a ball of string? Unfortunately, she was stubborn and dare I say it, a scatter brain. I told her time and time again to catalogue everything as soon as she bought it. But it was like talking to a brick wall. I can assure you, the stock she owns will be worth a lot of money."

"Did you know, even her car was filled to the brim with antiques, yet it was unlocked."

"Don't talk about that car to me... biggest waste of money if you ask me. Laura hates driving. Almost as much as she hates the balcony. She was given it by the chap she sees, has been seeing for many years now. However, don't ask me who this elusive man is. After all the years I've known Laura, I have no idea who he is. She's kept that information to herself. And to be honest, I've never questioned her."

Dunn made a mental note regarding her secret friend being the purchaser of her car.

"Laura was spending a lot of her time writing as she was given a deadline to finish the book, so naturally, it took precedence in her life."

"I think we'll leave it there, Mr Sutton. You've given me food for thought as far as the comings and goings of the antique business is concerned. I've checked out the price tags on some of your furniture and now know the markup."

"I don't know what you're inferring, Inspector, I'm a businessman, I'm not a shark. Unlike Laura, my stock is written up in an inventory, I can account for every piece I possess. Everything is completely above board."

"Glad to hear it. I'll be in touch if I need to speak to you again, thank you for the tea, very nice," he smiled.

Before driving away, Dunn took out his mobile and checked for messages, surprised to see none. Sutton's words ran through his mind. *Everything is completely above board.*

"If he's not a crook, I'm a monkey's uncle," he said out loud with a twisted grin.

Chapter 19

Sergeant Ellis wondered what he'd let himself in for. There had to be a big difference between scuba diving for fun while on holiday, to being responsible for peoples' lives. His concerns subsided when he reminded himself, being a policeman for fifteen years, he knew very well how to make sure people were safe. And anyway, the thought of spending a day scuba diving, rather than being stuck in an office outweighed the negatives. He had to admit to himself, he was elated.

His heart sank seeing the place deserted. Swinging the car into a space close to the marina, across the street from the shop, he switched off the engine to wait. A quick check of the time confirmed he wasn't too late. Maybe he got the day wrong. His mind drifted to the previous day at the Buckton's. Although good friends of Inspector Dunn, he wasn't too enthralled with the Judge. He'd been blown away with the revelation Asho and Fish were true half-brothers, both being the offspring's of Laura Verwood. He would have preferred not finding out the truth about Peter Buckton, worried how it would impact on how he reacted to him now. It's one thing to try and keep an adoption a secret, but these things have an awful habit of rearing up out of nowhere, wreaking havoc to all concerned.

A car pulled up right next to him alleviating his concerns about the day's dive. He could see Asho and Jenni. Before they noticed him sitting there, they both leaned towards each other and gazed into each other's eyes affectionately as they talked, then they kissed.

"*Whoa, I had no idea, they were an item!*" he thought to himself, as he opened the door, alerting them to his presence before they got more frisky.

When Asho caught sight of Ellis, his expression changed to one of horror. He leapt from the driver's seat and bounded towards him, reaching out for a handshake.

"So glad you made it Sergeant Ellis," Asho, sounding uncomfortable.

"Good to be here and, please, call me Ray, I'm not on duty now. "So… you and Jenni… you're… you' know… together… a couple?" Ellis stammered, wagging his finger from one to the other.

Asho looked concerned when Fish's car pulled in next to him. "It's not official, can I ask you not to say anything to him," he said nodding towards Fish.

"No worries, my lips are sealed," Ellis said as he shrugged his shoulders. "Your call."

With a cheery smile, Fish headed straight for Sergeant Ellis to greet him. "Blimey you're keen, you're here right on time, good to see you, Sergeant Ellis," Fish said, holding out his hand.

Ellis gripped it giving him a firm handshake. "As I said to Asho and Jenni, I'm Ray."

"Phew, am I glad we've sorted that out, I was a bit worried about calling you Sergeant in front of our novice divers today, not sure it'll go down well," Fish said as they all laughed.

Taking out a bunch of keys from her large tote bag, Jenni unlocked the door to the dive shop. After flicking on the lights from a central panel she hurried to her desk.

"I have all the forms ready for you to fill in and sign, Ray. This is a pre-requisite before you're allowed to dive today. Please, sit here at my desk and don't miss any questions, if there's something you don't understand, just ask."

"Hmm, a bit of a bossy boots," Ellis thought to himself. *"Nice pair of pins, though, I have to admit."*

Taking a pen from his jacket he sat down and began reading through the form.

"Declaration waiver and indemnity," he read out loud. "I declare that I am physically fit and have trained sufficiently to dive, that's a tick.

"I agree to adhere to all rules and conditions set out by Horizons Professional Diving School, another tick. So far so good," he smiled at Jenni, giving her a wink.

He carried on reading down the lengthy form ticking every box. After what seemed like an eternity, he finally came to the end of the questions and signed in the final box at the bottom of the last page.

"Goodness, I feel like I've just read and signed the Magna Carta," he joked. "It asked for everything except the colour of my underwear and what I had for breakfast." Jenni slapped him on the arm as she took the form, studied it then slipped it into the top drawer of her desk.

"Okay, now let's get started, I'll show you where we keep the air tanks and regulators. It's imperative we check them thoroughly, we don't want anyone to drown out there," "Especially *me*," he remarked. "Inspector Dunn would never forgive you if you lost his main man," he laughed.

"Now then Ray, I'll be your dive buddy today, which means we watch out for each other," Asho said

"No problems, I hope I don't let you down, remember, I've never instructed."

"Look, if you're as good as you say you are, you'll be fine. Just bluff your way through, like I do," he chuckled.

As Jenni set about preparing lunches and packing the cooler box, Fish, Asho, and Ellis loaded the equipment onto a large buggy ready to take to the marina.

A minibus pulled up right outside the dive shop and eleven Japanese students scrambled out, chatting and giggling incessantly. Jenni hurried to greet them, seeking out the spokesperson then repeated the instructions she'd given to Ellis.

"I have paperwork for all of you to sign before any of you can dive today," she called out, not being too sure they understood as they disappeared into the shop.

Asho and Fish briefed Ray, giving him a thorough demonstration, showing him the ropes. The three were now togged out in their dive gear. Ellis's cheeky wit and humorous banter had the boys entertained. It was clear they'd both taken to him.

The sound of chattering was getting louder as the Japanese students approached the boat. They were helped on board and ushered to the bench seats on the rear deck. Asho and Ray instructed them how to put on their wetsuits and attach their breathing apparatus; while Fish and Jenni disappeared into the cabin.

The boat glided away from the marina and before long they were out in the open sea. Ellis looked across at Asho and gave him a wink, his sign to mean everything was going well. The Japanese students were clicking away merrily with their cameras, insisting on taking photos of Ray and Asho with their arms around the girls as they giggled.

"I will take four and Fish can take four, that leaves three for you Ray, you should be able to handle three,"

"If I get into difficulties, I'll yell out,"

"Ha, ha, funny, I see we're all going to get on well."

As they arrived at the dive site, Asho tied the boat securely to the floating buoy and then ordered the novice divers to line up for their pre-dive inspection. Once he had their attention he spoke loudly.

"Now you're not to worry about the current carrying you away, if I can't find you, the search and rescue boat will be along in two days."

Ellis let out a loud laugh while the group remained silent with blank expressions. Asho looked directly at Ellis and shrugged his shoulders as Ellis responded by waving the flat of his hand across the top of his head, meaning the joke had gone over their heads. One by one they entered the water to squeals and nervous laughter, before disappearing below the surface.

Reaching the seabed with his three young divers, Ellis guided them towards the wreck. Having not seen it himself, he was fascinated by what was around him. He wished, at this point, he was on his own with no responsibilities. Taking his group towards a large cluster of coral bommies resembling columns rising from the sea floor, schools of brightly coloured fish appeared out of nowhere and darted around them.

The rays of sunlight bounced off the coloured fish and transformed the calm blue water into a light show; his three divers appeared worried. Ellis moved his body in front of them and made the dive signal with his index finger and thumb, meaning everything was okay. They all nodded as they returned the signal.

His last port of call was to see the Kelp forest, where two metre high fluorescent green and brown fronds waved elegantly with the movement of the water. Looking at his dive watch, he was surprised to see how much time had passed. He made his way with his group towards Asho who bobbed his thumb up and down, showing the sign to say it was time to return to the surface.

Half an hour later, everyone had removed their dive suits and were back in their own clothes enjoying the lunch, Jenni had prepared. The only place Ellis could find to sit was to perch on the rail of the deck. As he sat precariously, eating a meat pie, he held it in the air and called out.

"Nice pie, Jen, you've no idea how much this has hit the spot," he said, with a wink.

Asho agreed, flashing her a cheeky smile. The sound of everyone talking at once about their dive was deafening. They were soon back at the dive shop where the Japanese students scrambled back onto, their minibus, still chatting amongst themselves and were soon gone. Waiting patiently on the Marina, the second group of novice divers were ready to board the boat.

The whole procedure from the earlier group was repeated. As the boat returned to Congwong Bay for the second time that day, Ellis reflected on his day scuba diving. He was exhausted but exhilarated. When all the pupils had left, the boat had been hosed down and the equipment thoroughly washed and stowed away, they all made their way to the shop.

While Asho grabbed four ice cold beers from the fridge, the other three found somewhere to sit. As the only three seats were taken, Asho positioned himself on the floor, next to Ray, interested to hear what he had to say. "Well, Ray, what'd you think? You ready to give up your regular job to become a scuba diving instructor?" Asho asked.

"If the pay was right, I'd do it in a shot. It's obvious to me why you want to do this for a living. It has a more glamorous ring to it than being a detective." He grinned.

"I'm not so sure about that, I did like the way the female students were hanging on your every word, and you're a bit of a charmer, Ray" Fish announced.

Jenni added her observations. "Actually, that goes for all of you, I can see I'm going to have a lot of competition," Jenni added, as she took four more beers from the fridge.

"It's all a hobby at the moment, we're not making that much money," Fish said as he held his bottle in the air. "I'd like to say, thank you for your help today Ray, you were a great help. If you ever want to join us again, just say the word."

As Fish headed to the workshop, Jenni busied herself collecting bottles and tidying up, Ellis got to his feet and put on his jacket. Taking Asho aside, he asked him a delicate question.

"Will you be arranging the funeral for Laura Verwood?"

Asho looked shocked and lost for something to say for a few moments.

"Hang on, I hardly knew her," he exclaimed.

"Well, it turns out, you are her next of kin, her only known blood relative, so the responsibility falls on you," Ellis said, choosing his words wisely.

"In all honesty, I hadn't even given it a thought, I suppose I *would* be expected to attend. But not organise it!"

Jenni called out from the other side of the room.

"It's okay Ash, I know you had little to do with her, but she was your birth mother. Fish and I will help you."

Making his way back from the other room, Fish overheard the discussion. "She's right and you should say a few words too,"

"Steady on Fish, why did you suggest that. How to ruin a great day."

"I'm probably speaking prematurely as the body's not released yet. But it's something you need to think about."

Jenni went straight to Asho and placed her arm around his shoulders.

"And I will help you write something, don't worry."

Ellis turned to Fish.

"This is probably not the time and place, but I need to ask, where were you on the night Laura Verwood fell to her death?"

"Me? That's easy, I was at home. Mum was in a shitty mood for some reason and we rowed over me playing a game on my laptop, instead of studying, so I stormed off to my room. She can be a nag when she has a bee in her bonnet about something. Mum will vouch for me, no worries."

"Okay, sounds feasible, but, we will need to check it out. Now, sorry to be a party-pooper, but I will have to go. Thanks for a great day guys."

After shaking the hands of Asho and Fish, he placed both hands on Jenni's shoulders and gave her a kiss on the cheek.

"That, Miss Jenni, is to thank you for the best meat pie I've ever eaten," he smiled as he walked over and placed his empty bottle on Jenni's desk, he noticed the bronze coloured coin lying next to the keyboard.

"Whoa, what have you got here?" he said, picking it up and holding it to the light. "I collected coins as a kid, as you do, but I've seen nothing like this before."

Asho rushed over to Ellis and roughly, snatched the coin from his hand then turned to Fish.

"What the fuck is this doing just lying on the desk?" he fumed. "It should be locked away in the safe."

"Keep your wig on, if you remember, we don't have a safe any longer," Fish retaliated.

"Well put in a *safe* place, you fuck-wit,"

"So it's all down to me… you're not capable of hiding it? Why you blaming me?"

"Oops, I think I've stirred something up here, sorry guys, this has nothing to do with me," Ellis said, as he held both hands in the air as though having a gun aimed at him.

"It's not your fault Ray," Jenni butted in, as she attempted to pacify the boys. "Asho meant nothing. But being threatened by a knife wielding diver, followed by two undesirable looking men and then the break in and having our place trashed..."

Ellis stopped her mid-sentence, holding up the flat of his hand towards her. Hang on a minute, go back! What d'you mean, threatened with a knife? And what men were following you?"

The room fell silent as Asho, Jenni and Fish hung their heads, not knowing what to say. Fish raised his head and looked directly at Asho.

"You may as well tell Ray, I think it's time he knew what's been going on. I'm sure we can trust him, or even ask his advice"

Asho lifted his head slowly, wondering where to start.

"You're right. Okay… so where do I begin?"

"At the beginning, I hope," Ellis replied sounding curt. He walked around the desk and made himself comfortable in the office chair as Asho sat on the corner of the desk and launched into their story. He started with them finding the coin and Jenni and Fish's trip to the museum. Jenni butted in to talk about how they'd upset the curator lady when she sussed out they were interested in ancient coins.

Asho finishing with the dive incident. As all three talked incessantly, making sure they left nothing out, they all waited for Ellis' response as he listened intently, looking from one speaker to the other as he adeptly twirled a pen between the fingers of one hand.

"At the museum, did they tell you the value of the coin?"

"Well, yes and no." Fish explained. "We didn't show them the coin, we only touched on the subject of coins and their value. We pointed to one like ours pretending to be just interested and not that we had one."

"The woman told us they weren't worth much, so naturally, we were disappointed," Jenni added.

"You didn't by any chance tell this woman your names or where you lived?"

Fish looked coyly at Jenni before he answered.

"We gave our names when we introduced ourselves, but neither of us mentioned where we lived. Unfortunately, I said we had a dive school. But I never mentioned where it is."

Ellis looked in deep thought for a while as he toyed with the pen.

Asho suddenly had a bright idea. "That's it, we all need another beer," he announced as he jumped up from the desk and made his way to the fridge.

Removing the cap from his bottle of beer, Ellis gulped back a mouthful before speaking. "It's all becoming clearer to me now. If I'm correct, my guess is that the coin you have found is worth more than you've been led to believe. I'm guessing if someone wants it that badly, they won't give up till they've got it. They may even think you have more than one. Which means you are all in danger."

"I can vouch for that… being threatened with a twelve-inch knife was no laughing matter."

"Who knows what their next move might be. It might not be just a threat to scare us, it could be a lot worse…" Fish trailed off.

"I don't think you need to worry too much there, it sounds like these people just want to scare you, so don't let your imagination run over time. However, their scare tactics are very distressing, so it's still not good. If it's the same people who wrecked your shop and are now threatening you, which I'm convinced it is; I think you might want to consider shutting up shop. At least till it's all sorted," Ellis concluded, feeling concerned for the three of them.

"I'd like to say I agree with you," Asho responded. "But, sorry, no way am I running away. We've worked hard to set this place up and we now have a small database of students and tourists. You yourself said it's great. Sorry Ray, but I'm not letting these shits intimidate me," Asho said bravely.

"I'm with you there Ash, I've spent a small fortune on this place so I'm not prepared to give it up now," Fish added.

"Okay, then I suggest that you hide that coin in a safe place, preferably not here. Make sure you have the best security system for both the shop *and* the boat. I will talk to my boss, Inspector Dunn. Perhaps we might arrange to have police protection set up for a few weeks."

"Thanks, Ray, I'm not sure it will look good for business to have a policeman standing guard at our front door," Fish joked.

"We're a bit more discreet than that, you dope," Ellis said as he leaned over and gave him a playful punch on his arm.

"Ouch, that hurt," Fish called out as he rubbed his arm. "All I know is that we have a group booked in tomorrow and we can't afford to lose them. We could put the word about that we have a police sergeant as an instructor. That might ward off the baddies," Asho suggested.

"Hold on a minute, that's not exactly ethical. Leave it to me for the time being."

Taking the last mouthful of beer, Ellis stood up to leave.

"Just one more thing before you go, Ray," Fish piped up. "We've always thought there must be more coins where we found this one. Now, after what you have just told us, I'm now convinced there is," he said as he looked sheepishly at Asho and Jenni, taking a deep breath before continuing.

"We need a metal detector and we have it on good authority that the police have them. Do you know anything about this? If so, what's the chances of us being able to borrow one?"

"Hmm, it's not something I'm aware of, but leave it with me, I'll make enquiries. Again, I will need to run all this past my boss. Now, I really must be off, I don't know about you lot, but I'm buggered."

Ray sat in his car for a minute before starting the engine. If what they were telling him was true, this needed to be checked out. One thing for sure, he had plenty to tell Inspector Dunn.

Chapter 20

Closing the file on her desk, Caroline Hughes looked at the clock hanging on the opposite wall. Seeing it was now fifteen minutes past six, she breathed a sigh of relief; the museum was now closed. She got up from her desk, smoothed down her clothes with the palms of her hands and walked slowly towards the filing cabinet. Sliding the top drawer open, she slipped the manila folder back where it belonged.

The loud ring of the doorbell made her look up sharply at the clock for the second time. "*Good, right on time*," she thought to herself. Leaving her office, she made her way to the double timber entrance doors of the Australian Institute of Research in Numismatic Studies. She unlocked the door and opened it hesitantly. A look of surprise swept over her face, not expecting to see three men standing on the doorstep.

"David, you're right on time, as usual, you better come in, quickly," she said, giving the two strangers a quizzical look.

"Caroline," The man said in a booming voice, as he placed his hands on her shoulders and gave her air kisses on both cheeks. The two men followed and stood to one side.

"No need to look so worried, I've brought along my two trusty men, and I knew you wouldn't mind,"

"No, I suppose not, as long as they behave themselves," she snapped, looking decidedly put out.

Ms. Hughes stepped outside and looked up and down the street, making sure there was no one about, before retreating back inside and slamming the door shut and locking it.

"Let's go to my office," she said, as she walked briskly ahead of the three men.

David Pullman followed close behind Ms. Hughes. The bespectacled gentleman in his late fifties spoke with a loud authoritative voice. With his brash, overpowering manner, it was clear no one would dare argue with the man. The bright fluorescent lights, bounced off his receding head, making it appear larger than normal. Although a big man, David Pullman was smartly dressed in a bespoke suit with a silk tie and matching silk handkerchief poking out from his breast pocket. The two men lingered in the hallway not knowing what they were supposed to do. Ms. Hughes sat at her desk as Mr Pullman pulled out the chair opposite her and made himself comfortable.

Leaning right back and craning his neck to see where the two men were, he called out loudly. "Excuse me you two, were you intending to join us at any time?"

Entering the room as though they were marching, the men stood behind Mr Pullman, side by side, feet slightly apart, their hands clasped in front of them as though protecting their private parts. Caroline felt intimidated by the men, dressed in black t-shirts and cargo pants tucked into black laced boots, resembling the military. Apart from their heights, they looked identical.

Pullman turned around in his chair and pointing to the tall man on the right. "This one is called Todd McPherson, the other one is Ewan Wallace. Two strong Scottish names that suit my two strong boys," he gushed. "But to make it easy for me to remember I call them Lurch and Shorty. I'll let you guess which name goes with which," he laughed

"Boys, this is my good friend and ally, Caroline Hughes."

The tall man tapped his forehead with his index finger as though saluting. "Nice to meet you, Miss Hughes."

The shorter one bobbed his head towards her. "Miss Hughes,"

Pullman sneered. "Man of few words, our Mr Wallace, I'm afraid, "Pullman pointed out.

"Gentlemen, nice to meet you," she said, with a nod.

"So Caroline, do you have the coin I gave you to check out?" Pullman asked.

Ms. Hughes opened the bottom drawer of her desk and took out the makeup bag containing the ancient coin. Unzipping the bag, she removed a small paper tissue parcel and unfolded it slowly and methodically, as the three men watched with trepidation. As the coin was finally uncovered, she pressed it in Mr Pullman's hand.

Holding it up to admire, he thanked her for the information she'd given him earlier. He was extremely impressed with its history and the fact that it was pure gold.

"You did well, Caroline, it's a real treasure and is something that should be kept under lock and key," he said, sounding concerned. "Come take a look, boys." Holding the coin in his outstretched hand. "That is what a gold coin looks like, I took from a gullible diver last month, who I convinced was worthless. I threw him twenty dollars and he was happy," Pullman bellowed.

Both men moved towards Mr Pullman, McPherson took the coin from his hand and began to inspect it before handing it to Wallace.

"We would have had another one if you two had done your jobs right. Unfortunately, you weren't able to do a simple task I asked you to do," he boomed. How hard could it possibly be to take a coin from those naïve kids? They probably have no idea what they're holding in their possession? It should've been as easy as taking candy from a baby."

McPherson spoke for the first time.

"As I told you, we searched the place from top to bottom, including their boat and couldn't find it anywhere. We even broke into their safe, the obvious place to put something of value. But it wasn't there either. In our defence, something as small as a coin could be hidden *anywhere*, probably in one of their wallets,"

"Or for that matter, in that young girl's bra," Wallace joked, which went down like a lead balloon. "We did trash the place as you instructed," Wallace then added proudly, hoping to exonerate himself.

Hearing the last comment, Ms. Hughes was horrified. Pullman saw the expression on her face.

"It's okay Caroline, the boys just had to make it look like kids had broken in. Nothing was taken, they only wanted the coin."

Wallace took a big gulp of air, remembering the bundle of money he'd slipped into his pocket.

"Our problem is, what do we do now? We know there's more coins where this one came from, according to your information. That is if what you say is correct."

"*Excuse me,* I take umbrage at that remark Mr Pullman," Ms. Hughes said indignantly. "I can assure you, having studied everything pertaining to that coin till I was blue in the face, the information I gave you is exceedingly accurate. When the ancient ship sank to the bottom of the sea almost three thousand years ago, over one hundred solid gold coins went with it,"

"I'm sorry Caroline… that was callous of me, to say such a thing. I do appreciate everything you've done. The question I asked was what do we do now? Do we let these young ones do their dives, and hopefully find more coins? Then somehow steal them. Or do we scare them away, drive them out of town so we can search ourselves and hopefully find the coins without any hindrance."

"Any of those decisions will be difficult. If these people are as keen as you are to get their hands on cold coins, they're not going to leave without a fight; or allow you to take their treasure easily. Ms. Hughes advised. "Also, I will not condone any acts of aggression. The two choices you're making, reek of violence."

"No, no Caroline, no one is going to hurt anyone, or even threaten them. Isn't that right boys," Pullman said, looking menacingly at the two men standing behind him.

"That's correct, Mr Pullman, Wallace or I would never threaten anyone, it's just not in our nature, is it Ewan?" McPherson announced as he elbowed his mate in the ribs.

"Correct," Wallace snapped as he threw McPherson an evil stare as he rubbed his side.

"You know, there's more than one way to skin a cat. I have an idea, why don't we talk to them, join forces," Ms. Hughes suggested.

"*What*? And have to share the treasure fifty, fifty? No way on earth," Mr Pullman barked, sounding disgusted at the suggestions. "When we find these coins, we will melt them down and sell the gold before the authorities find out," he sneered.

"It seems such a pity to melt them down, in fact, its sacrilege if not illegal. It will be destroying history, they're something we should preserve forever."

"Don't worry Caroline, I will donate a couple to your museum for your collection," he smiled sarcastically.

McPherson cleared his throat, making everyone turn their attention towards him.

"I think Ms. Hughes is right, we could sign up for lessons at the dive school and lull them into a false security. Find out what their plans are, what they are up to."

"Better still," Wallace began. "McPherson and I have our scuba diving credentials, we could even see if we could join them as instructors. What d'you think of that plan?"

"I think that's a brilliant plan and by all intents and purposes, you shouldn't bungle it up. That's settled then, you will call them tomorrow and do what you have to do, get into their confidence and *hey presto*. Now you two men can run along, Caroline and I have a lot to discuss."

She stood up and motioned the two men to follow her to the large wooden entrance doors. As they disappeared out of sight, she closed the doors and made sure they were locked securely.

Returning to her office, Caroline opened the door slowly to see the lights had been turned down low. She pulled her baggy knitted sweater over her head and stepped out of her slacks, revealing a black lace bra with matching suspender belt and black stockings. Her outer garments clearly hid the temptress that lay beneath. She made her way to her desk where Mr Pullman was waiting, stark naked holding a horse crop. Ms. Hughes took the crop with her right hands and began slapping into the palm of her left hand.

"I hear you've been a very bad boy Mr Pullman and you need to be punished, now *lie down*," she ordered, holding the crop in the air as he sprawled face down on the desk. Pullman's face contorted with a mixture of pain and pleasure as she brought the crop down across his bare buttocks.

Chapter 21

At the sound of a car pulling into the driveway, Inspector Dunn glanced at his wristwatch and smiled. “Good, right on time,” he muttered to himself. He scooped up the notes he'd been studying and placed them neatly into his briefcase then snapped the lid shut. Making his way to the front door, he stopped briefly before opening the door to check himself in the hall mirror and smoothed down a tuft of flyaway hair on the side of his head. Sergeant Ellis was standing on the doorstep with a beaming smile.

“Morning Sir,” Ellis chirped.

“Good morning, Sergeant, you look happy, does it mean everything went well yesterday?”

“You bet. Everything went like a dream, it was one of the best day's I've had in a while. They're a lovely bunch of kids, In fact, they've all but convinced me to join them. So I'm contemplating leaving the force for the glamorous life of being a scuba diving instructor,” he mocked. “Only trouble is, I'd have to do it for love, cos there's no money to be made yet,” he said, smiling. He opened the car door and slid behind the wheel; and prattled none stop on the drive to the command centre.

"Sounds like you got along really well with the three young ones,"

"You can say that again... we're like that." said Ellis, indicating their closeness by holding up a hand and crossing his fingers.

"You gave them the Ellis charm then? Did you find out anything useful to help with our murder case?"

"Well, I'm now convinced, Peter Ashcott, whose nickname is Asho, had nothing to do with his mother's death. He had little to do with the woman. And he showed no interest or made any reference to an inheritance. I realise it's not something he'd bring up in front of me. After talking to him and watching his body language, I think we can omit him from being a suspect."

Ellis stopped talking for a moment as he turned off the main road and into the Command Centre. He drove up to the electronic roller gates and reached his arm out of the car window and swiped his pass across the intercom system. As the doors rumbled open he finished his conversation.

"When I pointed out to him that it was his responsibility to arrange the funeral, being her only real family member, he wasn't happy. His concern was that he really wasn't that close to her and it didn't seem right. He did look genuinely shocked, I have to say."

"I hope you didn't divulge anything about them being brothers?"

A frown spread over Ellis' face. "No, why would I?"

"Good, let's keep it to ourselves for the time being."

Squeezing his car between two patrol vehicles, Sergeant Ellis and Inspector Dunn, left the car and headed to the eleventh floor where they parted ways. As Dunn walked into his office, he was taken by surprise to see Fortis Green, Standing with his back to him, gazing out the window at the harbour. Fortis turned as Dunn passed behind him as he made his way to his desk and dropped his briefcase down with a clatter.

"So… Fortis, to what do I owe the pleasure?"

"Morning Stephen, I've just come to see if you're still in the land of the living. Are you trying to avoid me," he started.

"I don't think so, how can you say that? I've been flat out with the Verwood death investigations and you did give me a deadline, remember."

"Okay, but please tell me you're making headway and you've found some proof it was murder and not just suicide. I hope you're not just barking up the wrong tree."

Both men took a seat at the desk before continuing with their conversation.

"Rest assured, I'm not barking up the wrong tree, as you put it. From all the evidence I have so far, I'm now convinced it *was* murder, in fact, I have two possible suspects. People who visited her on the night of her death."

"And a motive?"

Dunn paused for a moment, wishing he didn't have to explain everything. He just wanted to be left alone to do his job, not to mention having to prove to Fortis he was right. As always, he was looking forward to that sweet moment when he announced his successful result.

"Well, that's a bit of a sticking point at the minute. We're positive it has something to do with her stolen jewellery, so we're piecing things together now. I have a few irons in the fire, however, I'll admit it has been slow going."

Dunn clicked the clasps on his briefcase, which sprang open. Removing a manila folder, then placed it to the side of his desk out of the way.

"I just need a few more days and you'll have a result, then we'll be making an arrest."

Fortis brought the flat of his hands down on his knees with a loud slap before rising to his feet.

"Okay, Stephen, you're twisting my arm, but I know you too well, you won't give up, will you? Okay then, I'm giving you two more days, then I want it wrapped up," he stressed, as he backed towards the door, almost careering into Ellis who was standing in the doorway holding a takeaway coffee in each hand.

"Good morning, Superintendent Green, if I'd known you were here I would've bought you a coffee."

Fortis turned sharply, hearing his voice. "No worries Ellis, I'm just leaving. I hope he's not working you too hard." Green asked, bobbing his head towards Dunn.

"As if, Sir. Although he does crack the whip, keeping everyone on their toes." Ellis joked.

Green gave a half grin and stepped aside, allowing Ellis to enter then had a second thought; turning back to Dunn. "Oh, Stephen, I almost forgot, Sarah has invited you for dinner tomorrow evening, what do I tell her? Remember, she won't take no for an answer."

"In that case, how can I refuse?"

"So that's confirmed, we will see you about seven. Feel free to bring a date," he added with a grin.

Ignoring the sound of sarcasm in his voice, because knowing Green, that was exactly how he meant it to sound, Dunn replied. "Seven it is then," feigning a smile as he watched his friend leave his office.

Sergeant Ellis set the two coffees down, "Don't tell me he was here to close the Verwood case was he, Sir?" Ellis asked, taking a seat opposite Dunn.

"No, well, yes and no… he's pushing to have it all wound up as soon as possible, in two days if you must know. Then he's closing the case, which means we have to move on what we have so far."

As both men sipped their coffee in silence, Ellis plucked up the courage to run an idea past his boss. "Sir, can I make a suggestion?"

"Go on… I'm all ears."

"I might have a way we could find out who our jewellery thief is? And, with a bit of luck, it could be the same person causing Laura Verwood to fall to her death."

Ellis launched into his story, explaining how Asho and Fish had found a coin at the dive site. He felt sure there was a connection between their find, and the break-ins at the pro dive shop. He went on to fill Dunn in about the underwater incident the three instructors had endured."

Inspector Dunn raised his eyebrows as he heard the last piece of information regarding the incident.

"I advised that we could give them some sort of protection, or suggested they at least close the shop for a few days till things are sorted. However, they refused point blank."

"If they didn't take your advice, there's not much we can do. Anyway, what has this got to do with our Verwood investigations, I think you've digressed. So, what's this idea of yours?"

"Well, I was thinking that we could borrow the coin from the boys and drop hints to Sutton and Farrow that a very valuable coin is at Laura Verwood's place. Then we go there and put it in a place where it won't be too difficult to find. We hide in one of the rooms, and wait to see if either one takes the bait and goes to the apartment to search for it."

"Hmm, not bad, I think I like that idea. I just wonder why are you're bringing Farrow into the mix? I can understand Sutton, he was the last one to see Laura Verwood, as far as we know, that is."

"Only that Julie Miller told us he was selling small items of jewellery around the local dealers. That and the fact he has a key, therefore, has access to the apartment."

Inspector Dunn sat with his elbows on the desk cradling his face in both hands as he thought for a moment.

"Okay, let's do it, can you arrange it for tonight, though, I have a dinner invitation for tomorrow night," he warned, screwing his face like he'd sucked a lemon. "But, any excuse to get out of it," he said, breaking into a half smile. "You better let Sergeant Miller know our plans. Or, see if she can join us, after all, she's robbery."

"I'm on it, Sir, leave it to me." Ellis felt elated that his boss had agreed to his suggestion. It could take up a whole evening, he quite liked the idea of catching the culprit red-handed, if it all goes to plan.

◆◆◆

Sergeant Ellis hurried to his desk and phoned Asho before they left for their dive to ask if they'd hold off for half an hour as he needed to talk them urgently.

Asho agreed but insisted it would *have* to be only half an hour as they had a tight schedule. Ellis bolted from the office to head to the school on a mission to persuade the boys to help him with his little plan. Turning out of the Command centre, into the busy traffic, he had the bright idea to switch on the car siren and high beams, allowing him to cut through the city much quicker.

After speeding through three sets of traffic lights with ease, the thought crossed his mind, there were advantages in being a cop after all. He could see a police patrol vehicle in his rear-view mirror and was aware their siren had burst into life as his radio crackled and a voice called out.

"This is patrol car Yankee, Delta, Uniform, seven, nine, four. We are directly behind you, do you require assistance? Where are you heading?"

Reaching over for his receiver, Ellis called back.

"Detective Sergeant Ellis, not this time lads, just trying to get home before my dinner gets cold," he joked.

"Okay, hope you do and you enjoy it," The voice called back as the siren silenced and the car moved to the outside lane to overtake Sergeant Ellis's' car. The officer bounced his index finger off his forehead as he passed by.

Without any further interruptions, Sergeant Ellis was soon screeching to a halt outside the dive shop. He spotted Fish and

Asho on the marina and bounded over towards them. With the sun shining brilliantly behind the boys, Sergeant Ellis could see for the first time the strong resemblance between them. Both had dark hair with a slight red cast and not only did they have exactly the same build, they shared the same stance.

They greeted him enthusiastically.

"I really appreciate that you agreed to stay back so I could talk to you," Ellis said, breathlessly.

"So what's the urgency, nothing wrong, I hope," Fish asked.

"No, no, nothing's wrong, I just wondered if I could borrow the coin you found, just for one night."

The boys looked puzzled. Not wanting to give too much information away, Ellis gave an abridged version of the reason why he needed the coin. How he was setting a trap to catch a thief that stole from Laura Verwood's apartment."

"It's only okay with me, if I can come with you, I'm not letting that coin out of my sight," Asho said, sounding irked.

"I suppose I could say yes, as it's your coin, but unfortunately, it's out of the question. We're talking about a crime investigation. You can refuse, but it's in your best interest that you comply and anyway, you'll be helping me out, big time."

"Well, I don't mind and I think you're being stupid Ash, we couldn't ask for a safer place to keep the coin, with the cops and anything that helps our boys in blue is okay by me," he scoffed. "I suppose you have to try everything if you want to catch your man, isn't that right Ray?"

Asho shrugged his shoulders, the look on his face said it all, he was not happy.

"I'll go and get it then," Asho mumbled as he climbed onto the back of the boat and headed towards the cabin. A few minutes later he was back, holding the coin in front of him.

"You keep the coin on the boat?" Ellis asked.

"Why not? You know what they say, if you have to hide something from someone, put it right under their noses, they'll never find it,"

Ellis' brow furrowed. "Well, if you say so."

To Sergeant Ellis' relief, Asho handed him the coin.

"Phew, you've no idea how grateful I am that you both agreed to this. I promise I will look after it with my life," Ellis vowed. "I'll call you with further instructions when you get back from your dive, okay?"

"Sure… and by the way, what happened about the metal detector?" Asho asked.

"I'll talk to Inspector Dunn when I get back, I've been a bit preoccupied with murders and robberies. I haven't forgotten, though, don't worry. The fact that you're both helping out this way should help persuade him. I'll let you know." Ellis took out his wallet and placed the coin safely in the section with a zip, then pushed his wallet back into his pocket.

"Anyway, I must dash, there're people to see, places to be and all that. Have a great dive today, wish I was coming with you," he called back as he hurried to his car and sped off into the distance, surrounded by a cloud of dust.

Back at his desk, Sergeant Ellis picked up the phone and made another call.

"Hi Julie, it's Ray, do you still have the key to the Verwood apartment? The reason I ask is Inspector Dunn and I are heading over there tonight. We're planning a stakeout and hopefully catch the thief who stole her jewellery, red-handed. We're hoping this person will shed a light on Laura Verwood's death."

"Why, Ray? Robbery is my jurisdiction. If you're planning to apprehend someone, surely I should be there too?"

"That's right and if you wait, I'm coming to that. Because you have the key to the apartment, I need you to go there and let us in. Don't bring anyone with you, we don't want the building Manager, Farrow, to know we're there. Going on what you said about him selling to the local antique shops, he's one of our suspect."

"What makes you think he'll go into her apartment tonight?"

"We're setting a little trap. Look, I'll explain when we meet, can you be there for six. Park on Bent Road, at the back of the apartments. Be prepared for a long night. Better bring your lippy and whatever else you women need to keep yourselves beautiful," he joked.

"Well, don't forget your hair dryer and rollers... see you at six."

Ellis clicked off the phone and dragged both hands through his hair. It struck him what he'd just done. Everyone was right, he did do a thing with his hair. He shrugged his shoulders and picked up a sheet of paper with scribbled notes on what to say. Taking a deep breath, he dialed Dennis Sutton's number and was answered immediately.

"Mr Sutton, it's Detective Sergeant Ellis, I hope I'm not interrupting anything."

"Not at all Sergeant, I'm having a quiet day, I was expecting a call from a customer and hence why I answered so quickly, I thought you were he."

"I wondered if you can shed a light on a historic gold coin we discovered in Laura Verwood's apartment."

"A gold coin, you say? No, sorry, I know nothing about a coin and Laura never mentioned anything about a coin, which is unusual, she always told me everything," Sutton replied, sounding annoyingly calm at Ellis' question.

"Well, I'm no expert, but I think this could be a very valuable coin, it looks solid gold. Anyway, we will just leave it where we found it in the glass cabinet in the lounge."

"It certainly sounds valuable, I would very much like to see it. Perhaps I could assess the value for you."

"Unfortunately, that's not possible, everything in the apartment has to be left intact at this moment in time. Look, sorry to have bothered you, I'll leave you to whatever it was you were doing."

Ellis ended the call before Sutton had a chance to say another word; hoping he'd given the man just enough information to whet his appetite and take the risk to go to Laura Verwood's home.

"If that doesn't have him racing round there, I don't know what will," Ellis called over to Lindsay, who just gave him a blank look, not having a clue what he was talking about.

"Now Peter Ashcott, it's your turn." He looked at his watch to check the time, it was one thirty. There was a good chance they were now back from their morning dive. Picking up the phone once more, he dialed Asho's number.

"Hi, Asho its Ray again, here's what I need you to do. I want you to go to Laura Verwood's address this afternoon? You've met the building manager, Mr Farrow when you visited her, so he knows who you are. This will make it easy for you to approach him and ask for the keys without any suspicion. I want you to tell him you have to drop off a gold coin, say it's for an antique dealer who will be picking it up in a few days."

"But I don't have the coin, you have it."

"I know, just listen. He will probably refuse to let you in and will make some excuse as to why you can't have the keys. You must be insistent, if he suggests he accompanies you, don't let him; you must go by yourself. Then I want you to take the lift to the eleventh floor, wait five or ten minutes, there's no need to even go into the apartment. But I need him to see you *have* taken the lift to the eleventh floor. Then go back to the reception and give the keys back to the manager and leave.»

"It's vital you phone me the minute you leave the building… is that clear?"

"Is this all necessary? It's a bit cloak and dagger isn't it?" Asho responded with a mocking tone.

"Yes, absolutely," Sergeant Ellis replied indignantly. "It's all part of my master plan. I'll be eternally grateful and I will make *sure* Inspector Dunn agrees to borrow the metal detector."

"Okay, leave it to me, if that's what it takes to get our metal detector, I'll do it."

Once again Ellis hung up his phone and then headed into Inspector Dunn's office.

"The traps are set, Sir. We're meeting Sergeant Miller at six at the rear of the building."

"So… Sergeant Miller has agreed to join us?" Inspector Dunn replied as the hint of a smile spread over his face that did not go unnoticed by Ellis.

"Let's hope this all goes to plan Ellis and we're not left with egg on our faces. Talking about eggs, it must be lunchtime, I'm starving."

"It's half one, Sir, you want to go to our usual?"

Dunn nodded as he pushed his chair back, allowing him room to stand.

Eating lunch at their favourite cafe, Inspector Dunn picked up a newspaper from an empty table and engrossed himself in the crossword, while Ellis chatted incessantly about football with a fellow officer sitting at the next table. Sergeant Ellis' mobile phone lying next to his plate began to buzz, interrupting their conversation.

"Hi Asho, what's up?"

"Just letting you know, I managed to get the key from Mr Farrow. You were right, he insisted he had to come with me to the apartment. But I was able to fob him off by saying I needed some privacy to remember Laura Verwood. He was actually quite sympathetic and seems a nice guy. He went on quite a bit about how he thought the world of her."

"Well done. I'll see you tomorrow to return your coin safe and sound." After the call, Ellis looked at Inspector Dunn, who was waiting to hear what the call was about.

"All sorted, we're set to go, that was the last bit of skullduggery and the final part of the plan put into place."

Inspector Dunn rolled the newspaper and shook his head.

"Devious little bastard, aren't you Sergeant?"

"All in a day's work," Ellis replied, as he opened his wallet and pulled out two twenty dollar notes. "It's okay, I'll get this, Sir,"

Ellis offered, making sure Dunn would be in a good mood when he asked him about the metal detector. “Sir, there’s something I need to ask you”.

“Uh huh! This sounds ominous and you look worried.”

“Well, you might not like what I’m about to ask. The boys at the dive school wanted to know if I’d like to make another dive, they’re convinced there’s more coins where they found this one,” he said patting his breast pocket. “Trouble is they need a metal detector. So,” he gulped. “I was wondering, would it be possible to borrow one from the marine area command?”

“You’re joking? You do realise what you’re asking?”

Ellis gave a sheepish grin. “Yeah! Of course, but I thought with your clout in the force, it wouldn’t be a problem, Sir!”

“You want me to ask if we can borrow an expensive piece of equipment for some overzealous treasure hunt you’ve got yourself involved in… Jesus Christ, Raymond, do you realise the ramifications in that request?” Think the responsibility of borrowing something so valuable.” Dunn got to his feet, slipped the café newspaper under his arm and turned to walk away.

Ellis stood, leant forward and removed the newspaper from under Dunn’s arm, making him turn. “Not sure they’d appreciate you taking their property, Sir. So, can I can take that as a *maybe*,” Ellis grinned “Can I just point out, the lads are helping with our enquiries. And because of them, we could catch our man tonight, solving the mystery of Laura Verwood’s death, or the stolen jewellery.”

With a questioning look, Dunn looked straight at Ellis without speaking, then turned and picked his way through the tables towards the door, leaving the cafe. Ellis made his way to the till and handed his money to the diminutive elderly Scottish lady cashier, holding on to her hand as she handed him his change. "When you gonna ditch that old man of yours and marry me, Alice?"

"Och, Raymond, you're a cheeky bugger, if only I was five years younger," she replied, making Ellis laugh as she giggled like a school girl and pulled her hand free.

Ellis gave her a wink and hurried to catch Dunn, who was waiting patiently, poker-faced.

"Personally, Ellis, I think you've had a brain snap. However, I know how much this means to you and you *do* have a very persuasive manner. As it happens, I do know someone in the water police. Although be warned, I can't promise anything."

"Thanks, Sir, you can't say fairer than that," Ellis said, wanting to jump for joy, but instead, kept cool, calm and collected. "Back to the grind, then, eh?"

Chapter 22

Sergeant Ellis glanced at the time in the right-hand corner of his computer, making him sit up straight. "Shit, is that the time?" he said out loud. Leaping to his feet, he made a dash into Dunn's office. "We should get going, Sir, it's almost five o'clock."

"What's the rush? I thought we weren't meeting till six and it's only around the corner."

"We still have to drive there and the traffic at this time of the day will be hell."

"Okay, just give me five to finish what I'm doing," he called back.

Reaching under his desk and pulling out a sports bag, he patted it twice. "Right, I'm all prepared to stay all night if I have to," he said to no one in particular. "I have everything I need and some."

Detective Sally Hunter leaned over from her desk towards Ellis and bobbed her head towards Inspector Dunn's office. "Hope you have fun with Mr Happy tonight… you deserve a medal," she whispered just as Inspector Dunn appeared at his office door, giving Hunter a cold stare.

"Don't you have work to do, Hunter?"

"No, Sir, I don't, I'm off home," she replied, sounding too cocky for Dunn's liking. Tossing her bag over her shoulder, she headed for the door. "Hope you all have an exciting evening, no getting up to anything you might regret," she laughed out loud as the door slammed behind her.

"Let's go, Ellis, what we waiting for?"

Reaching the car park, Dunn threw the keys at Ellis. "You can drive."

"That makes a change," he muttered under his breath, as he caught them with an overhand action.

"I heard what you said there. You better be careful, otherwise, I'll drive and I know how you hate my driving," he frowned.

Ellis decided he better keep quiet as that was a helluva threat."

The street behind the apartment block was unusually quiet, making parking easy. Ellis switched off the engine and reclined his seat as far as it would go. He shuffled around making himself comfortable, stretching his long legs out with his arms folded across his chest, he closed his eyes. Inspector Dunn remained sitting upright, his head tilted to one side as he stared into the darkness, allowing his mind to drift.

With no warning, the rear door, behind Ellis, yanked open, startling them both. Sergeant Julie Miller flounced into the car. "What's up, boys? Sorry, did I wake you, Ray?" she said, boisterously, knowing it would annoy the shit out of him.

"Jesus Christ, Julie, I nearly had a heart attack there!" Ellis called out as he sat bolt upright.

"Where on earth did you come from?" Dunn asked.

"Sorry Sir, I thought you'd seen me pull up behind you," she replied with a nervous laugh.

"Did you bring the key?"

"Sure did Sir, I have it right here," Julie said as she opened her bag and took out a key ring with only one key and held it in the air.

"How do you want to do this then?" Julie asked.

"I have an idea," Ellis began. "If Julie approaches Farrow and tells him she needs to get into the apartment for further investigations, Farrow wouldn't be suspicious, and he knows she's the investigating officer. When Julie gets into the elevator, we can sneak in behind her. Once we are inside the apartment, she can go back down to Farrow and tells him she's finished and pretends to leave.

But then, she makes her way back to us by the stairs. As far as he's concerned, the apartment is empty. With Asho's little white lie, saying he'd dropped off a valuable coin, if he's the culprit, he will sneak up to the apartment right into our trap," he said, reveling in his cleverly orchestrated plan. Inspector Dunn brought him back down to earth with a thump. "Are you mad Ellis? The apartment is on the eleventh floor."

"But Sir, there's nothing else we can do, once Julie leaves, that's it, she's supposed to be gone. If she sneaks back up in the elevator and goes back up to the eleventh floor, he'll suspect something. It has to be the stairs or nothing," he wailed. "Anyway, I'm sure Julie wouldn't have a problem, she's fit, or so she keeps telling me."

Julie reached over the back of the driver's seat to swipe him with the flat of her hand across his head. Pre-empting her action,

Ellis ducked forward covering his head with his arms in an over exaggerated movement. "Not the face, not the face," he cowered.

"That's enough, you two," Inspector Dunn called out. "Sorry Julie but Ellis is right, the stairs are the only way. Just one more thing, though, Ellis, give Julie some money so she can buy us all a coffee and maybe a round of sandwiches. It could be a long night."

Frowning, Ellis reached into his pocket for his wallet and pulled out a fifty dollar note. With no hesitation, Julie snatched it out of his hand.

"That will do nicely, Mr Money Bags, can I keep the change?"

"No, you fucking can't, that's all I have left to last me till next payday."

Julie slipped from the car, then walking around to the front passenger window to where Inspector Dunn was sitting.

"Wish me luck," she said with a playful grin.

They both called back in exact unison. "Good luck."

Both Detectives watched her in silence as she hurried away. Julie looked good. Her slim but curvy figure was emphasized in black leggings tucked into black commando-style boots and a short black puffer jacket. The only colour she wore was a pink cashmere scarf, casually thrown around her neck. Her blonde short curls fell loosely around her face, giving her a mischievous look.

"She's a little pocket rocket," said Ellis, turning to Inspector Dunn. "Admit it, Sir, she's a lovely lady, don't you think?" Ellis asked, probing to see how he felt. He now had it on good authority, Julie had a thing for Dunn. Although he had to admit, he wondered why?

Inspector Dunn waited for a few seconds before answering. He shrugged his shoulders and mumbled "I suppose," giving nothing away. "Now, Ellis, back to business."

Disappointed at his response, Ellis decided it must be a self-preservation mechanism. No one could be that blind to the charms of a woman. He knew of two bitter experiences Dunn had had that were responsible for him being wary. One was when his wife left him and married his best friend and then there was the intense affair a few months back that didn't end well. Ellis understood where he was coming from and decided it was time to change his boss' attitude towards women; and help him to find romance. It might even put a smile on his face. Ellis smirked to himself at the thought.

They waited a few minutes before following her, keeping a safe distance, making sure they wouldn't be noticed. When Julie entered the lobby, Farrow was taking a phone call with his back to her. As she approached his desk, her interruption seemed an inconvenience. He turned, acknowledged her presence with a flick of his hand, then to her amazement, turned his back and continued his conversation.

With no hesitation, Julie made her way to the lifts and pressed the button. As the doors of the lift opened, she stepped inside and turned to see Ellis and Dunn appear from nowhere, slipping in beside her as the doors slid closed behind them.

"Phew… that was easy," Ellis announced.

"I think we could have all just walked in brazenly, the man was too preoccupied to be bothered by you two, Sir," Detective Miller commented.

As they reached Laura Verwood's apartment, Miller unlocked the door and the three of them climbed through the blue police tape. Once inside, Detective Miller took out her notepad and leaned on the kitchen bench to write the sandwich order. After fifteen minutes had passed, they agreed it was time she headed down to the foyer so as not to raise too much suspicion.

The apartment hadn't changed since Ellis and Dunn had first walked in the day Laura Verwood fell to her death; the only deviation was that the two balcony doors were closed and locked with the key still in the lock. Left alone, the two detectives strolled around for a while before saying anything.

"Someone should come and clean this place," Ellis said as he trailed his hand over a pile of boxes.

"Not yet, it's a bit too early. Now then, where do you suggest is the best place to set ourselves up?"

Ellis tried the door leading off the dining area to find it was the master bedroom. Walking in without turning the light on, he closed the door behind him leaving it open about an inch and peered through the crack. Flinging it open he stepped back into the room where Inspector Dunn was waiting for an explanation as to what he was doing.

"Right… this will work. If we keep the door open about an inch and with the light off, we have full view of the main entrance door all the way across to the kitchen."

Dunn made his way to the door Ellis was referring to. "I take it we're setting up camp, in the master bedroom, then?" Inspector Dunn supposed. He entered the room and sat in the only chair. Ellis meandered around the apartment going from room to room, picking up and examining ornaments and trinkets appearing bored. Once he'd explored all avenues of interest, he joined Inspector Dunn in the bedroom. Standing at the foot of the bed, he dived headlong onto the bed, landing face down.

Rolling onto his side, he propped himself up on one arm. "Well, this was a boring idea and what's more, I'm not so sure anyone *will* come here after all," he sulked.

"That's a defeatist attitude, Ellis, don't be so miserable."

Ellis looked at his watch. "I wonder what's happened to Julie, she's been gone a while… I'm starving."

No sooner had he said it, there was a strange sound at the apartment door. Ellis pulled himself to the edge of the bed and both men stared at each other, then both headed towards the entrance door. Hearing the sound of heavy breathing and the husky sound of a female voice.

"It's Miller you bastards… open the door!"

"Shit!" Ellis exclaimed, as he opened the door wide to see a red faced Detective Miller, holding a large plastic carrier bag in one hand while balancing a cardboard takeaway cup holder with three coffees in the other. Bent over and gasping for breath, Julie leaned on the door frame for support. Inspector Dunn gallantly hurried to her aid and lifted the blue tape and helped her through the doorway. As she stumbled into the apartment, Ellis took the bag and coffees from her, while Dunn steadied her by holding her elbow. He led her into the lounge where she slumped onto a sofa. Neither of them had seen her so angry.

Then her voice began to tremble as though she was about to burst into tears. "Never ask me... to do anything... like that again... Sir and you too Ray!" she stammered. "I thought... I was going to die on the fifth floor... and I still had six to go! You bastards," Julie cursed, feeling no respect for her superiors at that moment.

"We owe you big time Julie," Inspector Dunn mumbled, forgiving her for the sudden lapse of respect and at the same time feeling retched for making her climb eleven floors. He placed his hand gingerly on her shoulder in a feeble attempt to make her feel better. Julie ignored him and lay her head on a scatter cushion, and curled up in a ball as she waited for her breathing to return to normal.

As Ellis watched her lying there, he thought how small and vulnerable she looked. Even he felt like he wanted to hold her in his arms. Surely Dunn could see it. He needed to make her feel better, he couldn't stand seeing her so unhappy, it wasn't like Julie. "Oh come on Julie, it's not that bad, just think of the calories you've burned. You'll thank us one day," Ellis said, in an attempt to cheer her up, the only way he knew how, by being sarky. He sat on the sofa and patted her back, prompting her to sit up. He put an arm around her shoulders, pulling her close to him.

Julie pushed his arm away roughly," fuck off Ray, I'm not in a good mood.

Refusing to give up on winning her over, Ellis wrapped both arms around her shoulders and gripped her firmly side on, as her head flopped forward.

"Don't be mad, you know we love you, we'll make it up to you, Inspector Dunn has promised he will take you out for dinner to thank you. Isn't that right, Sir?" He said daringly, as he flashed a look over Miller's head towards Inspector Dunn and winked. Dunn raised his eyebrows looking surprised.

"*I did*?" he asked, then seeing the scowl on Ellis face, changed his tone. "That's right, *I did*."

Hearing Inspector Dunn, Julie looked up and pouted. "I'm holding you to that, Sir and it will be somewhere fancy," she replied, throwing her head back and smiling at last.

"Now we must eat, drink and be merry," Ellis announced as he stood up and pulled Julie to her feet. They moved to a small round dining table where Ellis spread the food out and passed round the coffees. Before long everything was back to normal with Julie and Ray sparring with their silly quips.

After clearing away the mess from their hastily eaten meal, Ellis placed the coin in a glass cabinet, Ellis explained to Julie, their plan for the evening. He turned off all the lights, plunging them in darkness. All three stumbled to the master bedroom to wait. Hopefully someone would take the bait. They discussed the case for a while and then one by one, drifted into their own silent thoughts as they waited. It crossed Julie's mind that it was a pity Ray was there, this would've been a good opportunity to be with Inspector Dunn on his own.

After an hour had passed, Ellis yawned and stretched. "Looks like Farrow or Sutton are not the ones we should be concerned about."

"Well, if nothing happens tonight, we will know for sure we're going down the wrong path, Inspector Dunn replied. "Let's give it a couple more hours, then we'll pack up and go home." He suggested.

"I know, let's play I spy," Miller piped up attempting to lighten the mood.

"I think we will just sit in silence if you don't mind," Dunn replied, being in no mood to play silly games.

Ellis yawned again, then stopped mid yawn as the sound of the apartment door creaked open, startled them. The three detectives looked at each other holding their breath, not wanting to make a sound. The door clicked closed, followed by the sound of rummaging. Putting his finger to his mouth, Dunn indicated to the others to be quiet, he then tiptoed to the door and peered through the crack. To the surprise of Ellis and Miller, he flung the door wide open.

"Why Mr Sutton, and what do we owe the pleasure of this visit?" Dunn asked sharply as he stepped out from the bedroom.

Dennis Sutton froze on the spot, with a look of horror.

"I... I... I expected no one to be here," he stammered.

"Obviously," Dunn replied.

"I was just looking for something"

Ellis and Miller appeared from the bedroom.

"You wouldn't by any chance, be after Laura Verwood's jewellery would you, Mr Sutton?" Miller asked

"No, no, you've got it all wrong, it's not me taking Laura's jewellery. I wouldn't do that, we were friends," he pleaded, sounding pathetic. He slumped down into one of the dining chairs and hung his head.

"Okay, I'll come clean, I wanted to see the gold coin you mentioned on the phone today. My curiosity got the better of me,

I found it hard to believe Laura would have such an item and not tell me about it, Laura told me *everything*."

"You realise this is a restricted area, a crime scene, didn't you notice the blue police tape across the door?"

"Yes, I did, but I thought no one would be here, I didn't think it would be a problem. Believe me, I had no intentions of taking the coin, I only wanted to take a look at it. That's the truth."

Ellis placed both hands on the table in front of Sutton and leaned closer towards him.

"What happened Sutton? Did Laura catch you stealing some of her antique jewellery, you argued and things got out of hand. Did you push her or did she jump to get out of your way because she was scared?" Ellis' demanded in a raised voice.

"No, no, for God's sake, I would never harm Laura, as I said before, I loved that woman. I couldn't resist checking out the gold coin you mentioned. Naturally, being an antique dealer, I was intrigued, I couldn't pass up an opportunity like this. And that's what makes me a *good* antiques dealer." He said, failing to sound confident as the fear of being caught made his voice falter.

The apartment entrance door opened, making everyone stop talking and turn round. A woman's face peeped through the door. Seeing the group of people, the woman backed out and closed the door with a bang. Without any hesitation, Ellis bolted towards the door, flinging it open. After detangling himself from the blue tape, he chased the woman to the end the corridor. Not able to go any further, being a dead end, the woman stopped and turned, with a look of despair to face Ellis.

"Mrs Ashcott," Ellis blurted out, sounding shocked. "It's you, what on earth are you doing here? You'll need to come back with me so you can explain what you're doing here.

Lowering her head, she gave no resistance as Ellis held her elbow and guided her back to the apartment. As they entered the lounge, Dunn's jaw dropped when he looked up to see Mrs Ashcott being led into the room by Ellis.

"What's going on? How long have you had a key to this apartment Mrs Ashcott?" Dunn asked

"Laura gave me a key when I first cleaned for her, I always give the place a thorough going over when she's on one of her trips to America," she replied, her voice trembling.

"You better sit down," Miller suggested, seeing the woman shaking like a leaf. "Do you need a drink of water?"

"Yes, please."

"Now Mrs Ashcott, what are you doing here?" Dunn asked.

Taking the water from Julie she took a sip before launching into her story. "Laura has such gorgeous things. Sometimes, when I'm here alone, cleaning, I try some of the beautiful pieces on. A few months ago, when I was cleaning her bedroom, I came across a silver locket and yes, it *was* in a jewellery box and yes, I shouldn't have been looking in the box, I know that," she said regretfully. "I couldn't believe it, the locket was exactly the same as the one my grandmother always wore."

"I don't know what made me do it, maybe I was swept up in a moment of nostalgia, thinking about my dear grandmother." Mrs Ashcott said, with her eyes fixed on her hands. "I put the locket around my neck and admired it for a while then carried on cleaning. I left the apartment and went home. When I had a shower that evening, to my horror, I was still wearing the locket," she raised her head and looked at Inspector Dunn pleadingly.

"I wanted to take it back, but I knew Laura was due home the next day and I had no idea what time. I didn't want to get caught. How could I explain the locket was in my possession? My plan was that I would slip it back in the jewellery box, the next time I cleaned the apartment. I hardly slept for weeks, waiting for that dreaded phone call from Laura. But after about four weeks, it crossed my mind how strange it was that I'd heard nothing. No one made a fuss about the locket disappearing.

When I turned up at the apartment, Laura was there and was her usual lovely, friendly self. I thought that if nothing was said then it mustn't really matter. Perhaps the locket wasn't important or she had so much stuff she hadn't noticed it was missing. So I put it out of my mind, the weeks turned into months until here we are six months later. You must believe me, I never stole it,"

"Well, technically Mrs Ashcott, you did," Sergeant Miller replied, sympathetically.

"So why have you come here this evening?" Sergeant Ellis asked. "Don't tell me you're here to bring the locket back?"

"That's exactly what I was doing. Peter came home today and told me you were going to hide here in the apartment, hoping to catch the person who has been stealing Laura's jewellery. I almost had a heart attack, thinking you meant me."

Mrs Ashcott opened her handbag and took out a velvet draw string pouch. Slackening the cord she tipped the contents into her palm, revealing an ornate silver locket.

"I thought you would be gone by now, so I dashed here to put it back where I found it. I'm so sorry, Inspector Dunn sorry, it was just a huge misunderstanding, I meant no harm," she said as she burst into tears. Dennis Sutton pulled out a neatly folded handkerchief and handed it Mrs Ashcott and cleared his throat ready to speak.

"I need to explain something to you all, including you Mrs Ashcott which will shed a light on this matter. Laura Verwood knew the locket was missing and guessed you had taken it," he said, looking at Mrs Ashcott, whose hands shot up over her mouth, shocked at the revelation.

"You mean to say, all this time I've been sick with worry, she knew and didn't *mind*?" Mrs Ashcott said, her voice going up an octave at the end of her sentence.

"Not exactly, I wouldn't say she didn't mind. She was a little hurt at first thinking how you could deceive her, when she thought you were friends. She couldn't say anything to you for fear of embarrassing you and you couldn't say anything to her. Bit of a Catch 22 situation."

"Anyway, she chose to forgive you because she was grateful to you for raising her son Peter to be a fine upstanding young man. As she said, she felt forever in your debt. A small locket was little price to pay for what you have done for her son."

"Looks like we've lucked out here then," Sergeant Miller interrupted. "If nothing was taken other than the locket, perhaps she was attention seeking or having a neurotic tantrum, carrying on about her jewellery being stolen. May I remind you, I have no idea what is missing, no one has yet given me a list of any missing items. Apart from the necklace," Miller concluded.

"That's a bit harsh. I can assure you, Sergeant Miller, if Laura Verwood said things had gone missing, then they had. She mentioned something about them being heirlooms she was particularly fond of. Unfortunately, I don't know which pieces she meant as she didn't tell me either."

Sutton turned to Inspector Dunn. "If you're finished with Mrs Ashcott, why doesn't she wait downstairs in the lobby and I will give her a lift home. There's just something I'd like to talk to you about, in private. It will only take a minute."

"Okay, Mrs Ashcott, but before you go, are you able to account for where you were the night Laura Verwood fell to her death?"

"Where I am every evening, at home with my husband."

"In that case, we *will* need to confirm that with him at some time. If you would like a lift home, you're free to go, Mr Sutton will be down very shortly. Dunn said with an understanding smile.

"Thank you, Mr Sutton and thank you Inspector Dunn," she said, handing him the key and leaving the apartment.

"Just changing the subject for a moment, I was wondering if I could be allowed to see the coin. Be assured, I just want to see it, not take it away, don't panic" Sutton begged

Inspector Dunn considered his question for a moment, then looked at Sergeant Ellis before replying.

"I suppose it wouldn't do any harm, maybe he could do a quick valuation, I'm sure you're dying to know, admit it, Sergeant."

"You're not wrong, and if it's just a bit of rubbish, it will save me having to beg for the metal detector. Hang on, I'll go and get it."

Sergeant Ellis walked over to the glass cabinet where he'd put the coin earlier and rummaged about for a second; everyone watched in silence.

"That's funny," he said, pretending it wasn't there. "Ah, it's here," he announced as he held the coin in the air. With great reluctance, he placed it into Sutton's outstretched hand. He began examining it very closely, turning it over a few times.

"Hmm, it's small and a strange bronze colour, amateurish in its making, a pattern on one side plain on the other and misshapen. If it's genuine, it means it's very old, very old indeed," he deliberated.

Sutton clenched the edge of the coin between his teeth to try and bend it. After a few moments, he looked across at Dunn, who was waiting in anticipation.

"Well… what's your thoughts, Mr Sutton?"

"I'll give you one hundred dollars for it," he said humorously.

Ellis answered at once, making sure Sutton understood the situation. "Not ours to sell and I'm damn sure Asho and Fish have no intention of selling it,"

"I was just kidding, I wouldn't sell it either. I estimate if it's genuine, it's worth around ten thousand dollars, at least."

The room suddenly quietened as the three detectives were stunned at the estimation. No one uttered a word until Inspector Dunn broke the silence.

"You are kidding me, right?"

"Well, to be honest, I am, that's because I don't really know the true value.

Although I don't think I'm far out, in my opinion, it is solid gold," he advised, holding the coin towards the group as they looked on in amazement.

"Well, I'll be damned. Asho and Fish are going to be very pleased," Ellis remarked.

"I know I said I didn't want to take the coin, but I do happen to know someone who could give us a professional valuation. Then we will know the exact worth" Sutton offered. "These people are experts in their field, they…

"Take it easy Sutton," Inspector Dunn replied. "The coin belongs to the two young friends, Buckton and Ashcott, it's not our decision to let you take it. If you're as honest as you say, you need to talk to them. My thoughts would be, the less people that know about the coin, the better at this stage.

"Okay then, with your permission, I would like to speak to the two boys," he said as he took out his wallet and removed a business card, handing it to Inspector Dunn together with the coin.

"I'd appreciate if you could give them my card."

"I'm sure Ellis will be happy to do that," Dunn replied, passing the coin and card to Ellis and glancing at his watch. "It appears there's no more to do here. I think it's time we called it a day,"

"And I need to take Mrs Ashcott home," said Sutton, remembering she would be still waiting for him. "If you need me, Inspector Dunn, you know where I am."

"Before you go, I'll need your key."

The three detectives waited until the door clicked shut behind him. "What's your thoughts, Sir?" Miller asked. "Do you think Mrs Ashcott was telling the truth about the locket and she's the jewel thief?"

"Funnily enough, I do believe her story. We still don't know who *has* been stealing from this apartment. Without evidence or a lead, I doubt we ever will. And as you said Julie, was jewellery actually taken?"

Ellis was unusually quiet as he left them on their own and strolled towards the doors leading to the balcony and gazed out over the city lights.

"Thanks for tonight, Julie, I appreciate you joining us," said Dunn.

Assuming Ellis was out of earshot, he took the opportunity to speak to her in private. "Julie, about that dinner date, would you like to join me tomorrow evening?" When her face light up, he quickly added. "Don't get too excited, it's at Superintendent Green's home, I've been invited for dinner and they said I could bring someone along. I would really like it if you could join me."

He placed his hand on the small of her back as he walked her towards the door.

Julie's heart almost skipped a beat. It wasn't the dinner date she would have preferred, but it was a dinner date. "I'd like that, Sir," she said, trying hard not to sound as ecstatic as she felt.

"That's a relief, I thought you'd say no."

"It's been an interesting evening you have to admit, Sir," she said with a smile. Ellis seemed a million miles away with his back to her. Julie shrugged her shoulders. "Say cheerio for me," she said then skipped out of the apartment.

Finally, the two Detectives were on their own. Ellis turned and called from across the room. "I'm sorry Sir, that wasn't the best plan was it?"

"Don't be so down on yourself, Raymond, we had to try something and it wasn't a complete waste of time when you think about it." Dunn replied as he strolled towards Ellis, at the balcony doors and turned the key in the lock. An unexpected strong gust of wind caused the doors to swing open, almost knocking him off balance and sending the flimsy gauze curtains billowing into the air. After composing himself, Dunn looked directly at Sergeant Ellis with a look of indignation. They both stepped out onto the small balcony and battled the strong gusty winds. Gripping the glass and chrome hand rail, Inspector Dunn leaned over to view the soundless empty street below. The blue temporary tent that had hidden the body on the pavement was gone and there was no sign a tragedy had ever occurred.

Shaking his head and without saying a word, Dunn returned to the apartment. Ellis followed through the doors, closing them behind him. As he made his way across the room to join Inspector Dunn, a sudden gust of wind triggered the double doors to burst open once again. Ellis lurched forward and using brute force, pushed them closed, locking them with the key. His attention was drawn to the area surrounding the handle. Deciding to try something, Ellis turned the key to unlock the doors and stepped back. After a few moments, they blew open.

"What is it Ellis?"

"Farrow's right, I can see here the lock has been replaced recently, the paint is badly chipped, exposing bare wood. Bit of a shit job as far as I'm concerned." Pushing the doors shut and locking them, Ellis tugged on the handles, using pressure. This time the doors remained closed. "It appears that the doors *have* to be locked to stop them from blowing open, which is not good."

Leaning in for a closer inspection, Dunn agreed. "Let's just try something, Ellis, unlock the doors but keep them closed. If my theory is correct, watch this."

Inspector Dunn bounded to the entrance door and waited as Ellis unlocked the balcony doors and stepped to one side. When Dunn released the latch and opened the door slightly, the balcony doors burst open. Dunn slammed the entrance door closed and made his way back to Ellis, who was struggling with the balcony doors.

"As you have just witnessed, if the doors are not securely locked, the draught from the front door opening, causes the balcony doors to fly open." Inspector Dunn pointed out.

"This could explain why the doors were wide open when we entered the apartment that first day," Ellis said. "I had to wedge the door closed with a chair before we left, because if you remember, they wouldn't stay shut."

"It puzzled me why Farrow didn't make sure the doors were locked before he let us in the day Laura Verwood died. After all, he said he'd checked the apartment to see if everything was okay. Now we know it was because the lock was broken."

"We have two possibilities, if she jumped of her own accord, chances are the doors would've been left open. If someone was with her and she was pushed, they probably would've closed the doors but didn't lock them. As they left the apartment, the doors would have burst open as we have just demonstrated. Lock up Raymond, I need to talk to Farrow again,"

Ellis rattled the handles making sure the lock was firmly closed. "He's probably tucked up in bed, Sir" Sergeant Ellis said as he checked his watch.

"Well, he'll have to get back up, then, won't he?" Inspector Dunn said, deadpan.

There was no sign of life in the lobby, the reception desk where Farrow sat, was deserted.

"Do we know where Farrow lives?"

"I'd say it's the one with the plaque that says Building Manager," Dunn frowned. "I know, I know, Raymond, it's been a long day," he grinned.

Pressing the bell on the side of the door, Ellis stepped back to wait. Within seconds the door flung open. A red-faced, sweaty Mr Farrow, standing in tracksuit bottoms and an old baggy singlet, greeted them breathlessly.

"Oh! It's you two… what time is it? He asked. "How can I help you at this time of night?"

"Sorry to call so late, Mr Farrow, there's a couple of questions I need to ask you," Dunn demanded.

"I apologise for the state of me, I have a little workout regime I do every evening, the place might be a bit hot and sweaty," he smiled sheepishly.

"No worries, Mr Farrow, there's nothing we haven't suffered in our line of duty," Sergeant Ellis pointed out.

Farrow took a step back to allow the two men in his apartment and pointed along a small hallway.

"Just follow your nose into the lounge,"

"Phew, literally," Sergeant Ellis remarked, wrinkling his nose. "I can see why he's not married," he mumbled under his breath.

"Now Detectives, what's this all about eh? Has there been a new development?"

"We've just come from Laura Verwood's apartment." Inspector Dunn began, ignoring the confused look on Farrow's face.

"We noticed that new locks have been fitted to the balcony doors in Laura's apartment. Were they replaced before or after Laura Verwood fell from her balcony?"

Farrow hesitated before answering. "It was a day before, Laura had complained to me that the doors would blow open, even when she'd securely locked them. Why d'you ask?"

"Was it your handy work?" Dunn asked, ignoring his question.

"Certainly not… I always use a reputable company to fix or replace the locks in the building. I have no choice, the new regulations insist a qualified locksmith must do the work in this apartment block. There's been many tragic accidents over the past few years of people falling from balconies. But you must know that, being in your job."

"When we first came into the building, you wasted our time by showing us the wrong apartment, sending us on a wild goose chase." Inspector Dunn began. "At your admission, this was to give you time to go to Miss Verwood's apartment and check if it *was* her that had fallen. That's correct, isn't it?" Without waiting for an answer, he continued. "However, when we entered Miss Verwood's apartment that day, the balcony doors were wide open. If that was the case, why didn't you close the balcony doors and make sure they were locked and secure before we entered?" This time he paused for an answer.

Farrow lowered his head with embarrassment. "Because I, I didn't go in… I… I wanted to, but… but I just couldn't," he stammered, before looking up to face the two detectives, who were staring at him; waiting for him to finish. "I stood outside Miss Verwood's apartment for a few seconds, then changed my mind. I headed straight back to where I'd left you just as you were both coming out of the wrong apartment. As I've already told you, Miss Verwood was a lovely lady and was always good to me. I guess I was in shock," he said, sounding troubled. "You must understand, I don't think I knew whether I was coming or going that day."

Inspector Dunn was beginning to feel weary, it had been a long day and he felt they'd achieved very little. He was beginning to wonder why he was even talking to this man.

"Mr Farrow, you say you had the locks fixed days before Laura died. Well, I can assure you, the doors have not been fixed. They still blow open when unlocked as we have just discovered; either due to the strong winds that occur on those higher floors, or if the entrance door into the apartment is opened, causing a suction.

Farrow hung his head. "I was worried they hadn't been fixed properly. I've had a few complaints about the workmanship of the locksmith I use. So when I heard Laura had fallen. I was terrified they'd blown open and she'd tried to close them and fallen to her death.

"Are you able to give me the name and address of the Locksmith Company? I think we need to pay them a visit. However, you need to have a more reputable company check these locks Mr Farrow."

"Yes, I use *Concord Locksmiths,*" Farrow replied as he walked towards a cork board near the kitchen and unpinned an advertising flyer and handed it to Inspector Dunn.

"This is the company I use. As you can see, he only uses a post box so I have no idea where they're located. I guess the clue is in their name," he said with a watery smile.

"I believe he's only a one man operated business. Come to think of it, you both passed the guy on the way to Miss Verwood's apartment the day she died."

The two detectives looked at each other questioningly. After a moment or two, Sergeant Ellis remembered passing a man carrying a small ladder and a tool box. But hadn't taken much notice, having other things on his mind. Inspector Dunn studied the flyer then he too recalled seeing a tradesman in the hallway.

"Do you have a name for this man?" Dunn asked

"His name is Brad, that's short for Bradley."

"I know what Brad is short for," he snapped, sounding exasperated. "Do you have his surname?"

"Sorry, I never asked that, I just accepted his quote and let him get on with the job,"

There's a slight problem though, I've been calling all day trying to speak to the man with no luck. I'm not happy with his locks, they're rubbish and I've had so many complaints from the tenants that they are not working properly."

Farrow continued to ramble on how his phone has never stopped ringing with complaints which reflected badly on him and his ability to do his job properly. He was concerned, he could even lose his job.

Now looking noticeably disturbed, he continued to explain that the locksmith had seemed like an honest man. Farrow stressed he'd had no reason to think the man was not a good tradesman when he'd quoted the job.

Inspector Dunn noticed the change in Farrows demeanour. He had reason to suspect that Concord Locksmiths had been cheap which suited Farrow and his little money making schemes on the side. However, it appeared he was now in an awkward position with his tenants.

"Luckily, Locksmith's have to go through rigorous police checks before they can obtain their licences. It shouldn't be too difficult to find out this man's full name and hopefully his address."

"On another matter, Mr Farrow, we now have it on good authority, that you are known in the local antique shops for selling small items of jewellery. Can you explain this?"

A shocked look spread across Farrow's face.

"*Oh no…* I bet I know what you're thinking, but you're wrong. There's no way I stole from Laura. I take exception to you even thinking that. The fact is, I did small jobs for her. I carried boxes, ran errands, fixed things around her apartment and she paid me with things that she thought I would like, but truth be known, I didn't. I had no use for some of the things she gave me, so I sold them. I think she knew, so it was her way of passing stuff on without the bother of selling it herself."

"Sounds like you had a nice little arrangement going, a nice little money making scheme" Ellis scoffed.

"You need to understand, I am nearing retirement and when I do, I'll be out on my ear from this place. So, I have to prepare myself for that day. I've set myself up in a permanent caravan on a park up north. After this business, I'll be relieved to move away."

"Sounds like you've got it all well planned, good luck with that," Sergeant Ellis said.

Inspector Dunn held the flyer a few inches from Farrow's face before folding it neatly into a small square and pushing it in his jacket pocket.

"Just one last thing before we leave, so you can get back to whatever it was you were doing. I suggest you find yourself a *good* locksmith as soon as possible and have all the locks on this building replaced before another tragic accident occurs. This might have been a high price to pay for the sake of saving a few dollars. I'll say no more on the matter."

"That could cost me thousands, where am I supposed to find that sort of money?"

"Not our problem." Ellis added, condescendingly, as he turned and headed towards the entrance door then out into the foyer. Once out of earshot, Dunn pinched his nose between his thumb and index finger, can't say I'm sorry to get out of there, it's good to be back in the fresh air."

It was now late as Sergeant Ellis picked his way through the evening traffic.

"By the way Raymond, with everything that's gone on tonight, I completely forgot to tell you. You'll be pleased to hear I've spoken to my old mate in the Marine Area Command. The good news is, he doesn't have a problem loaning us the underwater metal detector. I've said we needed it for one of our cases. He took some convincing we didn't require his assistance," Dunn grinned. "Be warned, do not take your eyes off it for one second. Which means, where the machine goes, you go, understood?"

"Geez, Sir, that's the best news I've heard today, thank you so much. Did he say when we can pick it up?"

"He suggested as soon as possible, they never know when they might need it."

"Those three at the dive school are going to be thrilled shitless."

The car ground to a halt outside Inspector Dunn's house.

Here you are, Sir, right to your door."

"And I can hear my bed calling me," Dunn said, as he pulled himself from the car. "I'll see you in the morning, we need to go through everything with a fine-tooth comb from tonight's little exercise." He grimaced before slamming the door shut

Chapter 23

Jenni tutted loudly when the telephone on her desk rang, interrupting her concentration. Stretching over a pile of reference books, she picked up the receiver. Using her best telephone manner, she rattled off her well-rehearsed greeting. Hearing Sergeant Ellis' voice, her face lit up.

"Hi Jen, it's Ray... you busy?"

"Well, yes and no, I'm just mucking about on the computer, I've bought a bookkeeping software thingummy-bob, so I'm trying to get my head round it, and it's difficult, I can tell you."

"I'm sure you'll work it out, you're a clever girl. Is Asho or Fish there? They will go nuts when I tell them my news."

"Ooh… tell me… what is it? Sorry, I'm being nosy, I'll call them. They're just out the back." Jenni placed her hand over the mouthpiece and called out that Ray was on the phone.

Asho bound into the office and grabbed the phone.

"What is it, Ray? You haven't lost the coin, have you? Please tell me you haven't lost it," he said, breathlessly.

"Excuse me! What do you take me for? No, I haven't lost your bloody coin. And if you calm down, I'll tell you what I've found out. Which is… its solid gold and worth around ten G's."

A silence followed. “Did you hear me? Are you still there?” Ray asked.

“You’re kidding me, right?”

“Why would I?” That’s what the expert advised me, I’m assuming he knows his stuff.”

Fish stood next to him with a worried expression. “What’s he saying, Ash, tell me, what’s he saying,” Fish cried out in panic, shaking the sleeve of Asho’s shirt.

“Hang on Fish there’s more, just a sec,” Asho said, pulling his arm away from Fish’s grip.

“So, what’s the other thing you had to tell us?”

“The other thing is… Inspector Dunn has arranged for us to borrow the underwater metal detector.”

Without replying to Sergeant Ellis, Asho dropped the phone with a clatter and jumped up and down punching the air as he shouted hysterically.

“He’s done it, he’s got us the metal detector, I don’t believe it… he’s done it.”

Asho reached out to Jenni and threw his arms around her waist. Holding her tight, he lifted her off her feet and swung her round, full circle as he jabbered on with all the news Ray had given him. Fish picked up the phone and spoke into the mouthpiece.

“What’s going on Ray, Asho is acting like a maniac.”

“So he should be, it’s all good and when he calms down, he will tell you all the news.”

Asho reached over and grabbed the phone from Fish’s hand.

“When can we pick it up, Ray? D’you think we can go get it this afternoon?”

"I don't see why not, do you have a large vehicle? Preferably a utility as it will be big.

"Bugger, we don't, I can't even think who might have one," He replied.

"You're in luck then, one of our men here is in a band and has a van to carry all their equipment. I'm sure he won't mind me having a loan… leave it with me."

"If we push this morning's group through in record time, we can be finished by lunch time, would that suit you, Ray?"

"No problem, I'll organise the van and will see you at the dive shop about one o'clock," he said before the phone went dead. Placing the phone back where it belonged, Asho turned around and looked from Fish to Jenni.

"Fuck… that man is incredible, he's the brother I never had," he said in a state of euphoria. "And true to his word… he said he would see about borrowing a metal detector and he's managed to borrow one. We're picking it up after lunch, after our dive this morning. Shit, I can't even think straight," Asho garbled.

"So what was the first thing Ray told you that made you swear your head off," Jenni chided.

"Oh, yes, you're not going to believe what else he said, he said the coin is definitely solid gold and could be worth up to ten thousand dollars."

It was now Fish's turn to be excited. He held both fists in front of him and pulled them sharply into his waist. "Yes," he called out before grabbing Jenni, giving her a hug in a more gentle fashion. A frown spread over Asho's face for a split second feeling a hint of jealousy, but shrugged it off, knowing fine, well how he and Jenni felt about each other; realising Fish must be thrilled too. Fish pulled away from Jenni thinking he may have crossed the line.

"He certainly has helped us out these past few days. I was worried he was all talk. I don't know how we're going to thank him. But for now, let's get everything ready for the morning group so we can be back as soon as possible," Fish trailed off, as he disappeared into the workshop to prepare for the dive.

Both boys worked diligently, checking all the equipment carefully. After completing the usual procedures with a new contingent of divers, they were soon on their way.

Sergeant Ellis collard Detective Skinner as he was leaving the office. He raked his fingers through his hair before speaking. "Skinner, can I ask a favour?"

"What you up to Sarge? I know there's something, you do that thing with your hair when you're being shifty," Skinner scoffed.

Sergeant Ellis laughed as he began telling Detective Skinner a little white lie about wanting to borrow his van to move a table to his apartment. "I didn't realise I did anything with my hair," Ellis said, sounding curious. Detective Skinner threw his keys at Ellis, warning him to look after his pride and joy with his life or there'll be hell to pay. Ellis suddenly realised how much responsibility was hanging over him as he swapped his car keys with Skinner.

He wondered how on earth he'd gotten himself into all this, after all, he'd only just met the young, unworldly, energetic trio. Although he had to admit, he too was feeling enthusiastic about the whole treasure hunt thing. Truth be known, he was doing all this for his own pleasure.

Driving up to the marina, Sergeant Ellis spotted Asho and Fish looking busy in front of their boat. Parking in front of the gate, he gave two small peeps on his horn to catch their attention. They both waved eagerly. Asho held up five fingers, indicating they'd be five minutes. Sergeant Ellis decided to head straight to the shop and wait. Jenni's brow furrowed as she stared in deep concentration, at the computer. A beaming smile spread over her face as she looked up to see Sergeant Ellis standing at her desk.

"Oh high Ray, I didn't know you were there. You'll be pleased to hear I'm mastering this thing, it's awesome once you know what you're doing," Jenni giggled.

"I take it you're talking about your accounts thingum-my-bob?" Ellis joked.

Jenni began thanking Ray endlessly for helping the boys out. She described how Ash has been unable to contain himself for days with the thought of borrowing a metal detector. When he heard you'd done it, he was ecstatic.

"He's kept me awake for the past few nights, he is so excited, I hope he doesn't fall asleep today from sheer exhaustion," she divulged, before realising what she'd said about them sleeping together. Jenni's cheeks suddenly reddened.

Noticing Jenni's embarrassment, Ray discreetly turned to a brochure rack and picked up a scuba diving magazine. Flicking through, a full-page advertisement for 'The Horizon Professional diving School' jumped out at him. After scanning down the page and reading the text, Ellis was impressed. The advert looked good, offering everything from PADI courses to training for novice divers and more. They certainly knew their stuff, he thought to himself.

Jenni was thankful that Ray had walked away, giving her a chance to get over her embarrassment. Seeing him holding the magazine she changed the subject. "You've spotted the advert I see? I have a great idea I want to run past the boys. I reckon we should arrange diving vacations. We could go to exotic places such as the Caribbean, Fiji or Tahiti. The places are endless," Jenni rambled with excitement. "I have a friend who is a travel agent, we could work together on this and it would be amazing to travel the world."

"Hmm, sounds a great idea to me. A lot of planning and organising, but hey, don't let me dampen your spirit," Ellis said, hoping to sound encouraging.

Asho and Fish clattered into the shop carrying some of their diving gear.

Holding the magazine in the air, Ellis called out. "Nice ad, very professional, I'm impressed. Let's hope it does the trick and customers come flooding in, eh?"

The boys dropped the equipment on the floor next to Jenni's desk.

"It had better… it cost us a small fortune, that ad. Should we go get this metal detector?" Asho said excitedly, not wanting to wait another minute.

"That's why I'm here. We have to head across the city to the Police marina on Sydney Harbour at Balmain. It's going to take at least an hour depending on traffic, so let's go."

Squeezed into the front seat of the van next to Ray, the two boys almost drove him to distraction as they yakked throughout the whole journey, without taking a breath. After reaching their destination, Ray ordered them to stay in the van while he headed into the police building. Twenty minutes later he emerged through the gates of the loading dock, keeping pace with a small forklift truck; driven by a middle-aged man dressed in navy blue overalls. The two boys leapt from the van and waited in anticipation.

Securely strapped onto the forklift was a large black and silver flight case. The driver approached the van and manoeuvred his machine as close as possible to the back door. He began raising the load carefully, to align with the floor of the van. Asho and Fish, looked on, dumbstruck with anticipation.

Ray removed the straps and helped guide the case carefully into place. The man sped away on his forklift and disappeared through the gate as Asho and Fish helped Ray to secure their load.

"It looks heavy," Fish commented.

"It's not too bad, about seventy kilos, easy enough for two people to lift," Ellis pointed out.

The forklift driver returned with a smaller load and repeated the performance, placing it in the back of the van.

Ellis bade his farewells to the forklift driver, shaking his hand vigorously.

"That's it then, Rob, we've got everything, so we're all set to go. Rest assured, I will guard this thing with my life, as will my trusty friends here. Isn't that right boys?" he said as he brought his hand down heavily on Fish's shoulder, who was standing nearest to him.

As all three climbed back into the vehicle, a wave of apprehension poured over Ellis at the sudden thought of being responsible for not only the metal detector but also the van. He hoped and prayed, nothing would go wrong or he was in deep shit. Taking his time, making sure the equipment in the back wasn't shaken around, the drive back through the city to Congwong Bay, seemed to take forever.

At the marina, all three leapt out the vehicle and opened the side and back doors. They unloaded one of the cases, carefully placing it on the ground. Ray knelt down and lifted the lid, revealing a shiny yellow projectile; about four feet long and six inches in diameter resembling a small rocket. They gawped at it in silence for a few moments.

"Geez, I hope it came with instructions," Asho said being the first to speak.

Sergeant Ellis got to his feet and swiped his hand across the top of his head. "There's nothing in this case, let's hope, they're in that other one," he said, pointing at the large case still in the van.

Suddenly a voice called out from behind them. "Nice piece of machinery you've got there."

They all turned to be confronted by a short, stocky man with close-cropped ginger hair. He seemed to have appeared out of thin air. Ray wasn't happy about the interruption, especially as time was flying by.

Ignoring them, the man knelt down and patted the metal detector with the flat of his hand.

They threw curious looks at each other over the man's head as he carried on talking.

"Ah ha! A series 10 model, very nice, a great little machine, used by the police I believe," he said as he stood up.

"How do you know that?" Fish asked,

"I'd say the police blue and white chequered labels on the case is a dead giveaway," Sergeant Ellis said sarcastically. Feeling uncomfortable and feeling a little suspicious about someone who turns up out of the blue and just happens to know about an uncommon piece of machinery. "If you must know, that's who we've borrowed it from."

"I meant how do you know about the tow fish, you sound familiar with *this* model?" Fish continued, taking no notice of Sergeant Ellis' comment.

"I sure am… what you have here is the one I operated while in the Navy."

The man held out his hand, volunteering a handshake.

"I'm Ewan Wallace, Ex-Navy, I'm new in town and I've just discovered this place, lovely spot," he added, waving his arm around the marina. Are you three the owners of the diving school?" he asked as he took it in turns to shake their hands with a firm grip.

"No, only me and my friend here are the owners," Asho said as he pointed to himself then to Fish. "I'm Peter Ashcott, better known as Asho and my friend here is Peter Buckton, known as Fish."

"I can see why you'd be called Asho, but how come Fish? Don't tell me… you're a good swimmer," the man laughed, then turned his attention towards Sergeant Ellis. "And you would be?"

Seeing Asho was about to speak, Ray held his hand up to stop him from speaking, not wanting it mentioned he was a police officer.

"My name is Ray Ellis, what is it you want? We're busy here," he barked.

Asho felt Ray was being unreasonable, the guy was just being friendly. Clearly, he was hiding his Police officer status, the way he cut in just then. Hoping to encourage the man to move on, he made a suggestion. "If you're wanting to book in for a dive you will need to go over to the office and speak to our receptionist, Jenni," Asho said, sounding impatient, eager to get this thing out of the truck and be on their way.

"No, sorry, I don't want to book a dive, I'm hoping you might need an instructor… I'm looking for work. I'm a qualified diving instructor and have my C card," he explained as he held up the black plastic ring binder he was holding in his hand. "You will find all my qualifications in this folder."

Sergeant Ellis turned his head away and rolled his eyes to no one as he went back to unloading the second case; leaving the three of them to talk as he untied the ropes.

"Correct me if I'm wrong, but something tells me, you're not just scuba diving instructors are you? Judging by this machine here?" he added, pointing to the detector with his foot.

"Well, yes, no, hmm, we *are* just instructors," Fish stammered.

Asho jumped in. "What he means is… If we're going under water to scuba dive, why not have some fun searching the sea floor? You never know we might find some pirate treasure," he joked, hoping the guy bought it.

"Why not? I say. I would do exactly the same in your shoes, or flippers," the man said then laughed at his own joke.

"Are any of you familiar with this equipment?"

Not wanting to appear completely clueless, Ellis spoke. "I'm familiar with metal detectors, but not this one. As far as this model is concerned, I was advised that the instructions are all here in this box," he said, pulling the flight case towards the back of the van. "We're not fools and it's not rocket science."

"Maybe not, but you still have to know what you're doing, there's more to it than just lowering it down under the water and towing it behind the boat. I take it they supplied the computer system?"

"Of course… it's all in this box here," Sergeant Ellis snapped, pointing to the second box. Not happy with the interruption from this arrogant man, he was beginning to lose his patience. He just wanted to put the boxes on the boat and get going.

"Good… you must make sure you map out the area you're going to search first, this will help provide you with a record for future searches."

It was Asho's turn to sound impatient. "Thanks, mate, we'll do that," admitting to himself, he certainly knew his shit.

As the three turned away from Wallace and returned to checking out the equipment, he continued talking to the back of their heads.

"One more thing,"

The three turned to hear what he had to say. Ray gave a loud tut and rolled his eyes. "What's that?"

"Which one of you's is gonna use the computer on board the boat?"

"We will take it in turns," Asho shouted back. "Sorry, Mr Wallace but we need to get going. Give your resume to our receptionist and leave your contact details. We'll be in touch if we need someone." He smiled.

"Okay, I won't hold you up." Mr Wallace called out, shrugging his shoulders as he turned and headed towards the dive shop.

Ellis bent down to close the lid on the box, then straightened up before he offered his opinion.

"You do realise I have never worked one of these in my life. I'm wondering if, all said and done, Ewan Wallace might be the right person to show us the ropes."

"Funny you should say that I was thinking the same thing," Fish answered back. "Much as I hate to say it, Asho, I think Ray's right. We could waste hours trying to fathom this thing out, not to mention damaging the bloody thing in the process."

"What you suggesting, you dope? That we tell a total stranger we're looking for ancient gold coins, nice one Fish," Asho said, aiming his insult at Fish.

"No, stupid… we don't have to tell him anything. We just stick to the story that we're just having a bit of fun. If we're careful what we say to each other in front of him, we could use his know how and then piss him off at the end of the day. And don't call me a dope,"

"So don't call me stupid," Fish replied, landing a heavy blow across Asho's back. Retaliating, Asho grabbed him by the wrists. Turning his hands round, made Fish slap his own face.

"*Whoa,* what's going on?" Ellis yelled out. "I've been thinking, it's not a bad idea and as Fish said we just have to be extremely vigilant as to what we say in front of him. We stick to the story you are scuba diving instructors, but think it will be good for business to trick the divers into thinking they are hunting for treasure."

Sulking, Asho responded. "I suppose, if you put it like that, it does sound workable, I'll go and see if he's willing to come out with us now, I suppose it wouldn't hurt and he may be helpful."

Asho bounded into the shop to find Ewan Wallace casually chatting to Jenni; in her hand was the plastic ring binder Wallace had given her. Trying to appear casual, he took it from her and calmly began flicking the pages, checking out the numerous certificates displayed in plastic pages; putting his mind at rest that the man was, without any doubt, extremely qualified.

"We were just having a quick discussion and wondered… if… by any chance… if you have no plans for the rest of the afternoon, we were wondering if you'd like to join us. We could call on your expertise and at the same time, check out if you're as good as you say you are. What d'you say?"

Ewan Wallace was no fool, he knew damn well they didn't have a clue on how to use that metal detector. His little plan was working better than he thought. However, he knew he was going to have to watch everything he said to these three.

"You're in luck, as I'm in between jobs, I was heading off to visit a few more dive schools to see if they had any vacancies," He lied, giving more strength to his pretence. "I'm sure that can wait until tomorrow, so I'm completely free. It will be my pleasure to join you this afternoon," he said as he stretched his arm out towards the door, gesturing to Asho to show him the way. "Lead on, Macduff," he chuckled.

Once back at the marina where Ellis and Fish were lifting the second box onto the ground, Mr Wallace took complete charge.

"We need a couple of small digging utensils for starters and do you have the torch headbands?"

"We have those things on the boat already," Fish announced.

"Okay, let's get this lot on board so we can be on our way," Wallace commanded as he set off along the aluminium boardwalk ahead of everyone, with an air of confidence.

After the boxes were safely on board, Ellis watched as Ewan Wallace, Asho and Fish were deep in conversation about the boat and its equipment. He couldn't help thinking to himself there were a few questions he needed to ask this stranger. For a start, he couldn't help noticing how familiar he seemed to be around their boat.

Hoping for the opportunity to have a word with Ewan on his own, the chance came sooner than he thought, when the two boys headed into the steering station.

"Bit of a coincidence you turning up like that," Ellis began. "Not sure what your game is, the boys might be taken in by you, but you're not fooling me."

"Now why should you say that?"

"Just a gut feeling, so be warned, Mr Wallace, I'll be keeping an eye on you,"

"You sound a bit cynical, you're not a policeman by any chance are you?"

"What makes you think that?"

"Just a guess, I find it easy to recognise the signs. I have navy buddies who are now in the police force, working for the Marine Command in Balmain,"

"Well, you've guessed right. I'm Detective Sergeant and have been with the Police for fifteen years.

That wasn't what Wallace wanted to hear, deciding he better change the subject, not wanting Sergeant Ellis to press him for any further information on that falsification.

"Have *you* ever served in a conflict zone?" he asked.

Ellis assumed he was asking the question, hoping to get one over on him, make him look a wimp. "Depends on what you mean by *a conflict zone.* When I was a police officer in one of the less desirable parts of Sydney, I witnessed things I would like to forget, including seeing my partner and best friend, shot at point blank range. He died in my arms and left a wife and unborn son. That's something I wouldn't want anyone to go through. He was just doing his job. So where is this leading to Mr Wallace? What's your point?"

"Heavy stuff, and I'm truly sorry for your loss Sarge, but I was talking conflict in a *war zone.* My point is, I have and have no desire to be sent back there and that's why I'm looking for a job. No need to be suspicious about me, I was just in the right place at the right time, pure coincidence. You obviously need help with the metal detector and I know how to use one. You could say the stars were aligned," he said with a chuckle. "How about I show you the ropes today, if there's no work with the boys, I'll be on my way and you'll never see me again. Simple as that."

The man was beginning to sound genuine, he was certainly convincing Sergeant Ellis he was above board. Police training and being in the force had made him to be always on his guard, not to trust anyone or take things at face value. Maybe he should give a bit of slack to the guy.

"No need for that, let's just see how the day goes, you never know the boys might be pleased to have someone to help them out. How about you wait and see." Ellis said as he offered his hand to the man.

"Truce?"

"Truce." Mr Wallace replied. "I think we're going to get on just fine," he beamed.

Fish and Asho approached the two men.

"Well, I can see you two are getting on well," Fish said with a smile. "Just letting you know, everything is in place and we're ready to leave."

"So, Fish… you're a good swimmer I hear? I'm not bad myself, I was school champion. Perhaps we should have a race sometime?"

"Hold your horses, Ewan, these two are Olympic standard swimmers," Ray warned.

"Yeah, and not being cheeky Mr Wallace, but it looks like it's been a while since you were in school," Asho joked.

"Geez, how to put a man down. In that case, I've changed my mind," Ewan said, letting out an infectious laugh as the others joined in.

While Fish fired up the engine and moved away from the marina, heading towards the dive site, everyone made themselves busy, including Wallace, who glanced around the boat and mentally congratulated himself on how convenient it was for him he'd won them over so easily. A dark cloud swept over him as he had to admit they were a likeable bunch, even the Sarge. Maybe this would not be as easy as he thought. *Bugger I'm getting soft in my old age.*

As the boat cut through the water, Ray and Ewan Wallace began unpacking the equipment from the flight boxes.

"It's a powerful detector you have here, it'll detect metals in about a three-metre radius and at least two metres deep. It's clever how these things ignore mineral substances and hones in on metal targets only."

Ellis was feeling relieved that Ewan Wallace knew his stuff, and he was finding it all extremely interesting.

Pointing to the large slim projectile object laying in the box, Ewan continued with his lecture.

"This here is the side-scan sonar, or tow fish, as it's more often known. We have the search coil and fifty metres of tow cable, which should be more than enough for what we need."

Carefully lifting the surface control unit, the GPS and the laptop computer out from the second flight box, Ewan laid it on the deck.

"Okay Fish, as the driver, you have the honour of operating these little devices here on the boat, while we mess around below the water. I'll give you a quick demonstration."

"Why me? I've never clapped eyes on any of this, let alone operated them."

"Relax, it's very easy, a five-year-old can work one of these," He taunted.

"Just remember, you are in control of the boat and our lives are in your hands. If we get into trouble by any chance, it will be up to you to haul us back up to safety."

"No pressure then," Fish said, trying not to sound as nervous as he felt. "You do know we've dived many times in this area, it's as safe as houses."

"Ah ha, that's where you're wrong, this time, it will be different. You obviously haven't swum with something that looks like a giant fish. *We* know it can't be eaten, but you try stopping those man-eating creatures from trying. You do realise you're going under water at the worst time of the day? Our enemy the shark will be coming out to eat about now," Ewan sniggered, when he saw the look on Fish's face.

"In that case, I'll stay with the technical equipment here on the boat," he said with a forced smile.

Listening to the conversation, Ellis was hoping that Ewan was joking.

After Ewan had completed his demonstration of the software to Fish, he turned to Asho and Ray.

"Okay, now for you two," He said, sounding serious for the first time since they'd met him.

Wallace suggested they first map out the search area, to which they agreed. Following his instructions they attached the tail-fins securely with wing-nuts and fastened the safety cable and the tow cable to the tow fish. After testing the equipment to make sure everything worked, they dropped the yellow torpedo shaped scanner into the water, lowering it down to about three metres above the seafloor.

He explained how the tow fish will drag behind the boat. The same principal as a flag on the back of an airplane. Ewan decided that as Asho was such a great swimmer, he would be the one to swim close to the scanner. He was to watch for the blue light at the top of the scanner to flicker, which meant a target had been detected. He was to give a signal to Ray and himself, letting them know the location. They would head to that area of the seafloor and investigate further, using the small digging tools they'd tied to their belts.

He explained to Fish how the software on the boat will show the path of the boat as it moves over the search area. The readouts and coordinates change colour so Fish will see where and when a target is detected. It was then up to him to circle around the area.

"Have you all got it?" Wallace asked

There was a resounding sound of affirmatives as the three looked at each other feeling elated.

When they arrived at the dive site, Asho tied the boat to the floating buoy as he'd done many times. They all pulled on their wetsuits in preparation for the dive including Fish. Asho advised it would be a good idea in case he needed to make a dive for some reason.

Ellis and Wallace carefully lowered the tow fish deep into the water as Asho jumped in after it. Making the okay signal he disappeared below the surface of the water. When he reached about three metres from the sea floor, he gave the cable two tugs letting them know his position and to stop lowering the side scanner any further.

"See you in a while Fish," Ellis called out before slipping into the water with Wallace and they too disappeared out of sight. Fish watched from the dive platform with a feeling of foreboding. Although he was excited, he wasn't too happy with what Ewan Wallace had said earlier about sharks. He untied the boat and headed to the steering station. He manoeuvred the boat with great care, back and forth, following the path displayed on the laptop diagram. The sea was behaving itself and had remained calm throughout the dive, but he was disappointed an hour passed without a single hit, registering on the computer.

Wallace looked at his dive watch and felt disheartened seeing how much time had passed. He gave the thumbs up signal to Ellis and Asho for them to begin their ascent.

As they all clambered onto the dive platform, Fish was waiting to greet them.

"Not sure the computer was working properly, Ewan. I was able to follow your every move, but I got no signal to say we'd had a hit."

Wallace sat on one of the long bench seats and began removing his air tanks.

"It's not the computer, we never *had* any hits. I don't know if you were hoping to find anything, but there's one thing for sure, there's nothing around that shipwreck down there."

"That's because we need to be searching around the lava rock," Asho blurted out.

"What makes you so sure what you're looking for is there?" Wallace asked inquisitively.

Asho could've bitten his tongue off for saying that as the other two gave him daggers.

"Let's just say it's a hunch of mine?"

"A hunch about what?" Wallace said with a look of

surprise.

Ellis suddenly thought they'd better calm down talking about treasure. Wallace might start to be suspicious if they sounded hell bent on finding something. And the boys were sounding too enthusiastic for his liking.

"We're not looking for anything in particular, just idle curiosity that there might be something near an old shipwreck that's all. Don't old shipwrecks and treasure go hand in hand?" Ellis asked, trying to sound as flippant as he could.

"Let me tell you, Sarge, if you think there's any treasure from that old ship you're wrong. I can tell you, this whole area has been thoroughly checked out, hundreds of times. I would say it's been searched to death."

Ellis frowned, wondering how he would know that, didn't he said he was new in town?

"Yeah, I think you're right, but what harm can it do to take another look," Asho said, still sounding enthusiastic about the whole treasure hunting thing. Especially now they had the sophisticated equipment.

"If your game I'm game, it's your boat, your equipment. I'm just here for the ride." Wallace said, raising his eyebrows. "Only one thing, it's getting late, it'll be dark soon. I suggest you leave it now till tomorrow."

Asho jumped to his feet. "What? No way, no time like the present, I say. We can just go down for another hour. What do you think Ray?"

Wallace butted in before Ray had the chance to answer.

"Be it on your head, I have to warn you that sharks feed at

dusk

"That's two hours away and I must admit," Ellis pointed out. "I'm keen to get back down there, it's fascinating."

Throwing caution to the wind, Ellis and Asho slipped back into the water and were soon out of sight. Ewan shook his head and rolled his eyes at Fish.

"You know what to do, keep a vigilant eye out for anything that might look strange," he warned before slipping into the water himself.

Being familiar with the lay of the land, Asho pointed the tow fish towards the kelp forest and the two-metre high lava rock. Ray settled on a clear patch of white silty sand next to the tall waving fronds of the kelp forest. Ewan took up his position just past Ellis near the large lava rock, straddling the winding crack along the seafloor.

Ellis was a little concerned to see Asho swimming erratically, moving from the continental shelf that dropped off into a dark green abyss; and then crisscrossing from left to right with no particular direction. As he appeared to have his own agenda, Ellis decided all he could do was to wait patiently and keep an eye on his movements.

A large dark shadow swept over Ellis. Curious, he looked up and was horrified to see the bulky bodies and pointed heads of four dark coloured sharks emerging from the kelp forest. Seeing their spiky teeth clearly, he momentarily froze to the spot. Then without any hesitation, he positioned himself to make a dash for it. Ewan anticipated Ray's move and made a dive towards him, pinning him down on the sandy surface as best he could.

Not understanding what Ewan was playing at, he tried to

wriggle free until he saw Ewan was shaking his head and had placed his finger over his mouthpiece, warning him to shush. Then, with the flat of his hand, he raised it up and down, signalling to lay low. Ellis understood at once. An inquisitive shark left the group and swam within a foot of the two men's faces.

Ewan reached down and whipped out a long-bladed knife he had strapped to his lower leg. Ellis thought he was about to lash out, but instead, he held it close to his chest.

Staying stock still, Ellis didn't want to breathe as two more sharks broke away from the school and headed their way. Approaching so close, Ellis could see the reddish brown spots on their backs as they taunted the two men, bumping their noses against Ewan's air tank and baring rows of white spiky teeth.

Asho had watched the whole drama unfold from behind the lava rock, completely mesmerized as he watched the sharks heading towards Ellis and how Ewan had dived on top of him, forcing him to lie still. Assuming the sharks had now all gone, Asho waved his arms above his head to show he was okay.

A slow moving shark, he hadn't noticed glided majestically through the water, heading straight for him.

He pulled his arms down and slumped down behind the rock as the shark closed in, nuzzling the rock right next to Asho's head. The shark swam round and round for a few minutes, grabbing unsuspecting small fishes, swallowing them whole.

Glancing down at his dive watch, Ellis realised an hour had passed since the sharks had appeared and wondered how long it would be before they could escape their advances; wondering if they should start thinking about making a dash for it. Ewan must have read his thoughts as he tightened his grip on Ellis, keeping him firmly in one place.

A school of small, brightly coloured fish swarmed in the open waters, causing a frenzy of the four sharks; the larger one of the pack taking all the spoils. An even larger school of fish headed towards Asho as though they were under the impression he could protect them. One of the sharks observed the move and headed straight for Asho, its jaws wide open, revealing a double row of lethal looking teeth.

Asho watched as the school of fish, in perfect formation, gracefully split into two groups and swam in different directions, leaving him in full view of the shark. As he stood, not daring to move he closed his eyes, fearing the worst and waited for the inevitable.

After a few moments, he opened his eyes. To his amazement the shark was following a school of fish, its mouth wide open, scooping them up; swallowing them whole.

Asho slid down behind the rock, keeping out of sight for a few moments longer. He could see from his vantage point, the larger shark disappeared back into the kelp forest as the other sharks followed. He waited a few minutes before daring to move.

Making his way tentatively towards Ewan and Ray, he gave the thumbs up to signal that it was definitely time to surface. The other two didn't have to be told twice. To their surprise as they reached the boat it was dusk. The red glow of the sun had dropped below the horizon. Fish stood over them with both hands on his hips as they all lay on the aluminium platform exhausted and breathing heavily.

"What the fuck kept you, I thought you were only going

down for an hour, you've been gone almost two hours. You can't imagine how worried I was," he spat out.

Asho removed his diving mask, throwing it to one side. Bringing his knees up and placing his elbows on his knees, he cupped his face in his hands without uttering a word. Ellis too pulled his mask and flippers off and dragged himself to his feet. Putting his arm around Fish's shoulders, he led him onto the back deck of the boat and motioned him to sit on the bench seat with him.

"We've all had a big shock, just give us a few moments and a couple of beers," he said as he shook the water out of his hair then smoothed it back with both hands.

"I want to know what happened,"

"Fuckin sharks, that's what happened," Wallace shouted, as he climbed onto the back deck to join Ellis. "I tried to warn you, their favourite feeding time is dusk."

Fish bolted into the cabin and brought back four beers, then handed them around, ending with Asho who had now sat next to Ellis and was pulling his wetsuit down to his waist.

"Well, I'll be the first to admit I was shit scared down there," Ellis said.

Wallace threw his mask down on the deck, then pulled off his air tank.

They could all see that Ewan was not happy. The drama that had unfolded on the seafloor had obviously infuriated him.

"In all my years in the navy, I've never experienced anything like what just happened down there. What were you thinking Sarge? What the fuck was going through your mind? Did you honestly think you could outrun a school of sharks? Man, they'd have eaten you in one gulp."

Fish handed round more beers. Wallace swapped his empty bottle for a new one. He twisted the top off and took a long swig, taking a few moments before continuing.

"Your friend here," pointing to Asho. "Nearly got us eaten alive or drowned. We were all put in great danger."

Seeing everyone was in a state of shock, Fish tried to alleviate the situation, not to mention get Wallace off their backs.

"Don't blame Asho, he was just caught up in the thrill and excitement of trying to find something around the old shipwreck, which clouded his brain. I can't see it ever happening again."

"I realise how fucking eager you all are, but when it comes to working under the ocean, there're rules. There's certain things take priority over everything else. It's an unknown quantity down there, there's never two dives the same and you have to be prepared for everything and anything that can and will happen. Just promise me the next time you decide to dive for treasure, you'll call me and let me give you some instructions on what to do if and when danger strikes," he demanded, securing a further dive with these people.

There was an uncomfortable silence while they all peeled off their wetsuits and dressed.

Ellis was feeling wretched and knew only too well that if Wallace hadn't been there today, he could've easily died. Asho too was feeling very embarrassed by the whole episode and didn't want to speak. He felt stupid, he'd only just met Ray and really like him. Thinking he could've died because of his own stupidity gave him the shivers.

While they all wallowed in self-pity, Fish pulled up the cable and raised the scanner, laying it carefully on the deck; he made his way to the steering station and headed back to the marina.

As they bounced across the waves, Ray turned to Wallace.

"I have to thank you, you saved my life today. I hate to have to say this, but I panicked, something as a police officer, I should never do."

"Don't think about it, Sarge, it's over and hopefully you have all learned a lesson today. It goes without saying, had the shoe been on the other foot and all that, eh?" he offered, sounding genuinely sympathetic.

"Or flipper," Fish called out, hoping to lighten the mood.

They all grinned as Ellis pointed his bottle towards Ewan, who clinked it with his bottle.

"I'd just like to thank you again, from all of us."

They arrived at the marina in complete darkness, with only the weak lights of the boat and one street light at the marina gate. They were exhausted but Asho insisted that everything should be washed down and packed away before anyone headed off home. Jenni had hurried down to meet them and was helping with the work.

"I take it you didn't find anything,"

"Only about a dozen sharks," Asho exaggerated.

"*What,* please tell me you're joking."

Ewan looked at Jenni and with a concerned voice began to explain.

"We were lucky today, your friends here insisted on diving,

even though I'd warned them it was a bad time. Dusk is when the sharks rear their ugly head and guess what? I was right, that's exactly what they did,"

"Oh, what kind of sharks were they," Jenni exclaimed, showing no concern about how Asho was feeling.

"Jen," Asho said out loud. "Is that all you got out of that conversation?"

Ewan butted in, showing off his knowledge of the ocean.

"If you must know, they were Sand Tigers, they're easy to recognise with the brown spots on their backs. Despite them looking fearsome, they don't attack if you lay still. So it's not a good idea to try to outrun them," he said, aiming his glance at Ellis. "Or wave your arms around like a madman, offering yourself on a plate." Looking at Asho. "They have a nasty bite so could take a limb with no trouble."

As they all reached the marina gates at the end of the boardwalk, Ewan gave them all a friendly handshake offering his services if they ever needed him, and walked away. He felt confident he'd made a good impression and was convinced he'd be hearing from them again. He just hoped he hadn't come down too hard on them.

"Fuck it, they needed to be told, no one should be wrapped in cotton wool if they want to survive in this world," He thought to himself as he climbed into his silver duel cab utility truck.

Before they all took off in different directions, Jenni placed her hand affectionately on Asho's arm.

"By the way Ash, there's a message from Inspector Dunn when he called earlier. He wanted to let you know that they are releasing Laura Verwood's body tomorrow and as you are her only relative, it's up to you to arrange her funeral."

"Well, if I wasn't depressed by today's dive, I certainly am now," Asho grumbled as he pulled his arm away from Jenni's hold.

Jenni gave Ray, a look of humility at both Asho's harsh action and his lack of empathy.

"Ash, don't be like that, I'm sorry to be the one to tell you, but someone had to," she begged.

Ellis gave her a sympathetic wink and placing a hand on each shoulder, moved her out of the way.

"Asho the first thing you must do is talk to Dennis Sutton. He was her best friend and business associate. I know for a fact he was keen to be the one to arrange Laura's funeral. I don't think you have any need to be worried." Ellis said as he opened his wallet and took out the business card Sutton had given him.

"Give him a ring tomorrow, he knows all about you and he's expecting a call anyway. Now, folks, I have to love you and leave you, I have an early start tomorrow, I'll have a mountain of catching up to do, having had a day out of the office."

He shook Asho and Fish's hands and gave Jenni a light peck on the cheek then headed towards Skinner's van. Having an afterthought, he stopped dead in his tracks turned back.

"Make sure you guard that scanner with your lives or else," he called out as he swiped his index finger across his throat pretending to slit it.

Chapter 24

An early morning bingle in the city centre, between a government bus and a car, had caused horrendous traffic conditions, meaning Inspector Dunn and Ellis arrived late at police headquarters. The Duty Officer on reception made hand gestures to attract Inspector Dunn's attention. Without saying a word, he nodded towards the waiting room, not wanting to be overheard by the two visitors, who'd patiently waited to see him.

With confused expressions, they looked in the direction the Officer was pointing. Even with the daily newspaper propped in front of him, it was clear the person reading it was Clifford Buckton. The young man sitting next to him, leaning back in his chair, his legs outstretched, completely oblivious to everything around him as he immersed himself on his smartphone. Dressed smartly in beige trousers, a navy linen jacket over a pale blue shirt, with dark glasses perched on his head, he resembled a young movie star or at least, a male model.

Inspector Dunn made a beeline towards Buckton without paying any attention to the young man. "Clifford!" Inspector Dunn called out, his arm outstretched for a welcoming handshake. "I'm not usually this late arriving in the morning, we've been caught up in traffic for the past hour."

Buckton hastily folded his newspaper and placed it carefully on the seat next to him. With a serious expression, he leapt to his feet and took hold of Dunn's hand. Ushering him to one side, out of earshot from Peter, he pulled Dunn close and leaned into his ear. "Don't' forget what we said, you're not to mention anything to Peter about what we discussed at our meeting," he whispered. Saying it more as a threat than a plea. Dunn responded with a nod and narrowing his eyes. If there was one thing Inspector Dunn did not respond well to, was being spoken to in that way. Sergeant Ellis overheard the conversation and watched his reaction. Buckton was making a big mistake, speaking that way to Detective Inspector Stephen Dunn. Glancing over Buckton's shoulder, Dunn could see the young man clearly, now he was on his feet. He recognised him straight away and was just about to say something when he noticed the lad was glaring at him and shaking his head piteously. Realising there was a problem and thinking on his feet, Ellis gave Buckton's hand a welcoming shake and diverted his attention with jovial banter. Grabbing the opportunity, Fish began speaking secretively to Inspective Dunn, he begged for him to say nothing about the dive shop or even having met him, in front of his father. Seeing the look in the boy's eyes and after the way Buckton had spoken to him, Dunn nodded and winked as he shook the boy's hand. The fact was, not only was he keeping things from Peter on Clifford's behalf, now he was having to keep things from Clifford on Peter's behalf.

"So you are Peter Buckton?" Dunn said, as he began the performance of a lifetime.

Hearing Inspector Dunn's voice, Buckton turned sharply. "Yes, Stephen, let me introduce you. This is my son Peter, chip off the old block, don't you think, eh?" he said. Peter, this is Detective Inspector Dunn, a very old friend of mine. The two acknowledged each other with a nod.

"Nice to meet you, young man, you're much bigger than when I last met you," he said, then added. "Which was at your christening when you were a baby, would you believe?" Dunn said, making Peter Buckton smile.

"Goodness, I hope I'm bigger, I'd look odd if I'd stayed the size of a baby."

"*Peter,* don't be cheeky," Judge Buckton chided.

"That's okay Cliff, it was a daft thing to say. "I hear your called Fish these days?"

"That's right," he said, flashing Sergeant Ellis an awkward half smile.

"Hello there Fish, I'd forgotten you were coming in today," Ellis butted in. "How's Asho today?"

The Judge gave a quizzical expression as he looked from Ellis to Peter.

"You two know each other?" he questioned, wagging his finger from one to the other.

Fish stared at Ellis pleadingly.

Realising what he'd said, Sergeant Ellis made up something. "Yes, we met at Peter Ashcott's home when we interviewed him a few days ago."

Fish let out a silent gasp as though he'd been holding his breath for half an hour, then gave Ellis a smile of sheer relief. He was thankful that Sergeant Ellis had not mentioned anything about the dive the day before. What's more Inspector Dunn was doing a good job of pretending not to know him.

"Asho is fine now, we think it was just one of those twenty-four-hour bug things, he'll survive. He's a tough bugger."

"*Peter*," his father reprimanded him again.

Ellis winked at Fish and smiled as Dunn changed the subject.

"Have you spoken to the duty sergeant yet?" Dunn asked.

"No, I was waiting for you, I thought it would be better to talk to you first. I didn't think there was any need to bring attention to myself and explain who I am, you do understand don't you?"

Inspector Dunn leaned in close to his ear and speaking in a low voice, assured him that everyone was well aware that he was The Honourable Chief Justice Clifford Buckton, giving him his full title.

"Ellis, will you go and ask the duty sergeant if he knows where the doctor is while I take Judge Buckton and his son to interview room one for some privacy."

As Inspector Dunn led the Judge and his son to the interview room, he searched his brain for something to say to alleviate the silence between them. "How's Felicity?"

"She's well and after your last visit, I think you might be invited to dinner soon. Although one of the stipulations will be that you bring along your Sergeant. I think she was taken in somewhat by his charm." He mocked.

"Ah, speak of the devil," Dunn said as Sergeant Ellis popped his head round the door.

"Apparently, he's on his way, Sir," Ellis announced to Inspector Dunn then turned to Judge Buckton. The duty Sergeant will let you know when he arrives."

Inspector Dunn turned to leave the interview room. "I'll catch you later Clifford, I'm supposed to be at a meeting with my team and I'm over an hour late! I need to go crack the whip. You know the way it goes, with these subordinates," He said nodding his head sideways at Sergeant Ellis. "Tell Felicity to ring me," he called back over his shoulder before disappearing through the door.

The incident room was unusually quiet as Inspector Dunn and Sergeant Ellis entered. The team all appeared busy. Without hesitation, Inspector Dunn marched towards the white board. In order to attract the team's attention, he began tapping loudly with his pen on the photograph of Laura Verwood, hoping it would have the desired effect. Turning his back to the board and facing the team, he could see the tapping hadn't worked.

"Okay everyone I want your undivided attention, I need you to listen carefully to what I am about to say. Stop whatever you're doing and listen," he said loudly before turning back to face the photo of Laura Verwood, this time pointing with his finger.

"Unfortunately, we're getting nowhere with this case. We're still no further forward in establishing who was stealing her Jewellery or if she met with foul play, causing her death."

He pointed from one photo to another as he called out their names.

"Our main suspects, the business associate Dennis Sutton, the building manager, Frank Farrow and her son Peter Ashcott have all been eliminated from our investigations, so where does that leave us?"

The room fell silent, you could hear a pin drop until Lindsay called out.

"I checked out the Department of births, deaths, and marriages, but unfortunately, the only name written on the birth certificates of the two boys is the mother, no mention of the father's, which of course is legal… annoying… but perfectly okay."

"Hunter, how did you go with your door knock?"

"I spoke to all but two neighbours and everyone said the same thing. Laura Verwood was a very private lady, an unknown quantity. In fact, all the tenants in that block appear to keep themselves to themselves," Detective hunter advised. "As far as anyone was aware, there were no gentleman caller," she added with a smile.

Inspector Dunn admitted he'd had the same response from her business partner of some twenty years. "When I questioned Dennis Sutton, he could not shed a light on who the person was that she'd been seeing. Although he confirmed there definitely *was* someone and had been around for many years."

"I'm absolutely dumbfounded that anyone could hide a relationship, or keep it a secret, for that long," Skinner piped up. "Especially a woman,"

Suddenly, a pen flew past Skinner, from the direction of Detective Hunter, narrowly missing him.

"Fuck off Hunter, you nearly had my eye out. You must admit, though, I'm right. Come to think of it, what women would put up with 'an affair' for years?" He said, making inverted commas with his fingers. "Surely if old mate is married, she'd be nagging the shit out of him to leave his wife?"

"Maybe she was nagging him and that's why he's half heaved

her off the balcony, a man can only take so much nagging," Jones added, as a build-up of laughter spread around the room.

"Well, if he's been putting up with it for years? I think he's a bloody martyr," Skinner added.

"Hang on you lot, I think you might all have a point," Dunn called out over the noise. "Why would a woman hang around for years, hoping a man would leave his wife? We know why a married man would have an affair for years, he's getting the best of both worlds." He paused allowing everyone to snigger. "However, a woman would never put up with it. There's got to be something in that, thanks, Skinner, you're not as daft as you look," Dunn added.

"D'you wanna bet," a voice called out.

Ellis reached over to Skinner and ruffled his hair as the room filled with jeering. Sitting back in his seat, Ellis noticed a large white envelope lying on his desk. Picking it up, he could see it had been opened then resealed. Pulling out the contents, he scanned the page to see it was the DNA results from Peter Ashcott.

"According to the report I've found on my desk, after running the DNA through our database, apart from Laura Verwood, there were no other matches. In other words, there's still no record of his biological father."

"That came yesterday while you were out enjoying yourself. That's why I decided to give my permission to the mortuary to release the body. Now we know Peter Ashcott is the next of kin I left a message for him advising he can start arranging the funeral," said Dunn.

Ellis hadn't dared tell his boss about the shark debacle. Apart from being unbelievably embarrassed by it, he wanted to try and forget the whole episode, least said about it the better. It was ironic that Inspector Dunn was thinking he was out enjoying himself.

"Yes, I know, Sir, I was there when Jenni gave him the message which he didn't take too well. I gave him Dennis Sutton's business card and told him to contact him. Hopefully, Dennis will arrange the funeral, he seemed to be of the understanding it was his duty to arrange the funeral when we spoke to him just after Laura's death."

"Lindsay I need you to check the bank where Laura Verwood worked. See if there's anyone still employed there that may have any recollection of her. Were they aware of a boyfriend or partner, she may have had at the time? Skinner, you can find out more about the Mercedes, who bought it, who registered it."

The Inspector left the incident room and made his way to his office where he stood gazing out of the window, deep in thought. The telephone on his desk buzzed, bringing him back to earth with a thump.

"Inspector Dunn."

"Good morning Inspector, Dennis Sutton here. I just wanted to tell you, I have had a call from young Peter Ashcott and he agrees I should make all the arrangements for Laura's funeral. I've managed to book it in for Monday at two-thirty at the Rookwood cemetery. The wake will be held in the hall next to the chapel."

"Thanks for letting me know, I would like to attend to pay my respects. I'll see you there."

No sooner had Inspector Dunn replaced the receiver, it burst into life again. This time, it was Superintendent Fortis Green sounding irate.

"Stephen, drop everything and come to my office, there's something we need to discuss."

"Give me ten minutes." He answered. *Now what's got his goat? For crying out loud,* he thought.

On his way to meet with Fortis, Dunn approached Ellis' desk and perched himself on the corner.

"I've been summoned," he said, trying to smile. "When I get back, we are going to head over to Laura Verwood's apartment and search it with a fine tooth comb. There's got to be *something* that will prove there was a man in her life, a photo, a scribbled note, something that might hopefully reveal his name."

"Yeah, I have to admit, Sir, I'm not convinced anyone can have an affair all that time without there being some evidence. If there's anything there, we'll find it."

"I'm off to see what the hell I've done wrong this time,"

"Any idea, Sir?"

"No, and there's only one way to find out, see you in half an hour," he said, walking away, knowing exactly what it's about.

After giving two light knocks on the door, Dunn entered the office to find Fortis was at the far side of the room standing in front of an open cabinet. Without saying a word, he ceremoniously opened a bottle of Gentlemen Jack whiskey and poured two glasses filled with ice cubes. Picking them up, he turned and handed one to Stephen.

"Hoping to soften the blow, eh?" Dunn asked as he accepted the drink.

"Something like that. Geez, Stephen, you bloody know how to push my buttons," Fortis said brusquely, as he held his glass towards Dunn's, inferring they chink them together. Fortis sat at his desk as Dunn sat on the chair opposite.

"Stephen, as you can imagine, I'm trying hard to keep my cool. So… can you *please* explain to me, why in God's name did you interview The Hon. Justice Clifford Buckton without my permission? Do you realise he is one of the most respected men in Sydney? You know the rules when it comes to the legal hierarchy."

"*Of course, I do*, and I've known Chief Justice Clifford Buckton since he was a mere post boy, running errands," Dunn exaggerated.

"You know him personally?"

"I certainly do… and I didn't think of it as an interview, more like visiting an old friend. I didn't think I needed to ask your permission to do that. It was a spur of the moment thing. I'd just interviewed someone who gave me vital information and I thought I'd follow it up."

"And this information involved The Honourable Chief Justice, Clifford Buckton?"

"Well, yes, strange as it sounds. I had just found out that the baby Lady Felicity and Clifford Buckton gave a huge, pomp and ceremony christening for, which I attended, was actually adopted as newborn baby boy. It turns out the baby's mother is none other than Laura Verwood, her second child who she gave up for adoption, eighteen years go. Which means Peter Buckton is the half-brother of Peter Ashcott, they have the same mother."

"You are joking? What about the father or fathers?"

"Ah, well, that's where we've drawn a blank, we are leaving no stone unturned trying to find at least one of the fathers."

"How did the boys take it when they found out they were blood-related?"

"Peter Ashcott was delighted he had a brother, however, when we gave him the news, we ourselves had no idea the identity of the sibling. We haven't disclosed that information to him yet. In regards to Peter Buckton, I have promised faithfully to the judge and Lady Felicity that I will say nothing to the boy. At least for the time being.

Turns out they have kept his adoption a complete secret from him all his life. He has no idea Felicity is *not* his real mother. Although things like this have a way of rearing their ugly heads sooner or later. Would you believe, I too had no idea their son was adopted and, as I said, *I* was at the christening,"

Fortis picked up the two empty glasses and returned to the drinks cabinet to refill them. Dunn had no intentions of refusing another drink. He was thankful Fortis had no grounds to haul him over the coals. They'd been friends far too long for anything to come between them and Stephen hated when Fortis had to pull rank.

"The Buckton's are also adamant that Peter has no claim to any inheritance."

"Do you still suspect foul play?"

"Well, I have to tell you, my team are not exactly behind me a hundred percent any longer. Every one of them has tried to convince me that we're possibly wasting our time. But you know me Fortis when I think I'm right, I usually am. Okay, I'll admit, it's all been a bit feeble, but I think we're on to something with our new line of enquiries," he said, with a little more enthusiasm.

"I'm certain if we find the man she's been seeing for many years, or at least one of the fathers of the two Peter's, or father if it's the same man, we will have some answers. I'm hoping they might turn up at the funeral to pay their last respects. If not, *then* I'll throw the towel in," he announced, knocking back the last dregs of his drink and banging the empty glass on the desk in front of him. The whiskey had given him the desired effect, he was now feeling relaxed.

"Right then, I'm off to Laura Verwood's apartment with Sergeant Ellis. We're going to scour the place for any telltale evidence she had a lover and hopefully put a name to him."

Dunn walked towards the door ahead of Fortis then stopped and turned suddenly. Fortis hadn't anticipated him stopping so abruptly and careered straight into him, their faces ending up inches apart.

"By the way, I'm looking forward to dinner tonight?" he announced, sounding more than a little inebriated.

"Steady on Stephen, I thought for a minute you were going to kiss me." He said as they both broke into laughter. "By the way, I will be bringing a lovely lady, you better be on your best behaviour."

"Goodness Stephen, there's hope for you yet! Let's hope she can put a smile on that craggy old face of yours. Anyone I know?"

"Wait and see," he winked.

Inspector Dunn returned to the main office to find it a hive of activity. Seeing Ellis, perched on the corner of Detective Skinner's desk, deep in conversation, he called out to him to catch his attention; then pointed towards his office indicating he needed to see him.

"Okay, Sir, what was it this time? What did he have to say?"

"Can't you guess? Turns out he bumped into The Honourable Chief Justice, Clifford Buckton in reception and after chatting with him found out I'd gone to his home a few days ago to interview him, without running it past him first."

"So, do we still have jobs?"

Inspector Dunn gave Ellis a quizzical look,

"Why d'you ask that Raymond? You know me better than that, I had him eating out of my hand within five minutes," he said, looking smug. "Now let's go, we're running out of time."

Sergeant Ellis could tell, his boss had indulged in a couple of malt whiskies so he'd be mellow for the rest of the day. Plus, he wouldn't be driving.

Before leaving the main office, Inspector Dunn stopped to make an announcement to the team.

"Sergeant Ellis and I are heading over to the Verwood apartment one more time and tear the place apart if we have to. There has to be *some* incriminating evidence that there was a boyfriend and I'm determined to find it."

"Maybe the boyfriend dumped her so she's got upset," Ellis said. "You know what they say about a woman scorned?"

"Oh yeah, you would know all about that, wouldn't you Ray?" Sally Hunter shouted out to the sound of muffled giggles. With his palms outstretched, Lindsay bobbed them up and down to quieten the team.

"No, hang on, that's right, she phones him up, they have a big row, she threatens to kill herself to make him feel bad, then whoops-a-daisy, over she goes," Lindsay called out, making an up and over gesture with a curved hand. There was a sound of low chattering amongst the group as they appeared to agree.

"Great assumption, Lindsay," Dunn said, shaking his head and scanning the faces of the team.

"So that's it then, you're of the same opinion that Laura Verwood jumped to her death of her own accord; and according to Lindsay here, it was to teach her boyfriend a lesson and punish him for ending their relationship."

"Well, no Sir, that's not what he meant. But you must admit, the case is getting weaker by the day," Ellis said feebly, not wanting to upset his boss.

A feeling of disappointment swept over Inspector Dunn at the lack of support he was getting from his team, especially from his sergeant. Yet he himself was now convinced it wasn't just a hunch. There was definitely a mystery surrounding the death of Laura Verwood and he wasn't going to rest till he solved it.

"Okay you lot, can I ask you to just humour me and carry on assuming she was murdered for the time being. At least till we find out who the fathers of her babies are and who the mystery boyfriend is. I need you all to go over again everything and anything you have on this case." He announced before storming out the main office door and headed along the hallway to the elevator, not bothering to check if Sergeant Ellis was following behind him.

Sergeant Ellis hated it when his boss gave the silent treatment. However, he'd been with him long enough to know that it was best to give him a wide berth while in this mindset. He decided to concentrate on driving while he waited patiently for Dunn to make the first move. After what felt like an eternity, Dunn finally spoke. "I know what the team is thinking, Ray but what are your thoughts? Am I chasing my tail? Barking up the wrong tree?"

"Hmm, lots of canine metaphors there, Sir," Ellis grinned, trying to lighten the mood and relieved his boss was back in the land of the living. "If you must know, my thoughts are, that if that bloody locksmith had done his job right, the door wouldn't have burst open and maybe Laura Verwood would not have gone out on the balcony. Maybe Lindsay is right about her being in a turmoil over her relationship. It could have been a threat or a cry for help. Unfortunately, we might never know."

"Maybe you're right, of course, but as you know, I hate being proved wrong."

Sergeant Ellis gave him a sideways grin as he swung the car into the apartment block car park. The Commissionaire, Frank Farrow, greeted them, holding a pen in one hand and a folded newspaper, showing the daily crossword in the other.

"Ah, I see you and Inspector Dunn have something in common, he likes crosswords." Ellis pointed out to Mr Farrow.

"I'm usually very good, but this last clue has me bamboozled," Farrow replied, scratching his head.

"Go ahead, ask the genius here, he'll solve it for you in a second,"

With his pen poised over the crossword, Farrow read out the clue.

"Ghost ran, spooked by rainforest fern?"

Thinking Farrow was speaking in Swahili, Ellis averted his eyes from the Commissionaire to Inspector Dunn waiting for an answer. Hoping like hell he wouldn't disappoint him by not knowing the answer after giving him a big rap.

"Ask me a hard one for God's sake… the answer is *stag-horn*."

"Uh, well, I'll be blown!" Farrow said, filling in the boxes, then throwing the paper down, triumphantly. "How's the investigations going? Wrapped up now I suppose? Does that mean I can remove the blue tape that's pinned across Laura Verwood's apartment door? It doesn't look too good and I think it's stressing the other tenants."

"I don't see why it can't be taken down, but first I need the key to the apartment.

We're going to take one last look before the case is finally wrapped up."

"I've just found out the funeral is to be held on Monday, Inspector. There're a few tenants in the building and of course I myself will be attending to pay our respects. I can't believe I'll not be seeing her cheery face passing through here again," he said sadly.

"Tell me, Mr Farrow, are you absolutely sure you never ever saw Laura Verwood with anyone or had anyone call on her, either male or female?" Ellis asked sounding desperate.

"Honestly, I never saw anyone visit her. Except, of course, Mr Sutton, who came here on a regular basis; and of course young Mr Ashcott a couple of times."

"So how come you don't have CCTV in the reception, surely there's always the chance of undesirables entering the place." Ellis asked.

"It's never been necessary as long as I've been here. I'm at my station here during the day and as you know I live just there," he said pointing to the first door on the left.

"I still don't think that's right in this day and age," Ellis continued, catching the keys effortlessly that Farrow threw at him.

"I'll have these back to you when we're done," he called back over his shoulder as he joined Inspector Dunn in the elevator taking them to the eleventh floor.

Reaching the apartment door, Ellis pulled the blue and white tape to one side. Raising his hand to push the key in the lock he could see the lock wasn't fully engaged. "Check this out Sir, this isn't locked," he said." He placed his fingers over his lips. "Shh! I think there's someone in here," he added, pushing the door open carefully.

To their amazement, the man they'd passed in the hallway, the day Laura Verwood died was standing at the dining table, frozen to the spot. A look of horror spread over the man's face as the two detectives appeared in front of him. They could see he was holding a handful of necklaces

"What the hell are you doing in here?" Dunn called out.

The man jumped. "Sorry, I was just being nosy, I'm here to check Laura's locks," the man spluttered.

"I'll be on my way then," he added, placing the jewellery he had in his hand on the table.

"Not so fast, you'll stay right where you are. I'm Detective Inspector Dunn and this here is Detective Sergeant Ellis," Dunn announced as they both held their ID's in front of him. "And you are?"

"Wilson, my name is Mark Wilson, I'm the locksmith for the building. Mr Farrow employed me to fix all the locks. As I said I'm just here to check the locks on Laura's apartment."

"I think you're a bit late to be checking Ms. Verwood's locks, don't you think?" Ellis remarked.

"Let's see if that's all you are doing Mr Wilson. Empty everything out your pockets," Dunn ordered.

The man obliged at once as he gingerly began taking one necklace after another from his pocket. Cunningly managing to keep one hidden in his hand, thinking the detectives wouldn't notice.

"*Everything*, Mr Wilson," Ellis demanded.

Wilson reluctantly finished emptying the haul from his pockets and stood silently.

"Can you explain all this," Dunn asked, referring to the jewellery he lay on the table.

"I don't think Laura will be missing any of this lot now she's dead," he said callously.

"Whether the lady is alive or dead, Mr Wilson, what you are doing is stealing.

"Okay, okay, I get it. It was a moment of weakness. But Laura's loaded, I don't think she'd miss anything, especially not now. I suppose it's a good job you came in when you did and stopped me, I would have regretted it the rest of my life no doubt. Believe me, I'm no thief, it's just what I think I'm owed" he garbled. "Can I go now?"

"By rights, Mr Wilson, I should be arresting you. However, I think today is your lucky day. As it turns out, I have much more important things to do, so I suggest you leave now before I change my mind and throw the book at you."

Sergeant Ellis looked on in shock, unable to say a word. Both detectives watched in silence as Wilson closed his toolbox and scuttled out through the apartment door closing it loudly behind him.

Ellis was about to speak when Inspector Dunn held his hand up to halt him. He hurried to the door, opening it a few inches, enabling him to watch as Wilson disappeared into the elevator.

"Quick, let's go,"

"Go where, Sir? What the hell is happening? What did I miss?"

"Just follow me."

They both bounded down the corridor, stopping at the fire exit. Dunn pushed it wide open and beckoned Ellis to follow him.

"You do realise we're eleven floors up?" Ellis called out as they both began descending the concrete steps two at a time.

When they reached the ground floor, puffing, and panting, Dunn opened the exit door just enough to see if Wilson was anywhere in sight. The foyer was deserted except for Farrow, his head just visible over the counter, slumped forward. Clearly, he was fast asleep.

He watched as Wilson crossed the car park and climb into his van. The name 'Concord Locksmith', handwritten on the side looked faded and amateurishly done. The van inched out of the car park and headed in a northerly direction.

"Quick Ray, the car, we need to follow him and see where he goes, hopefully, his home. Keep your distance, we don't want him to suss we're following him."

"Surely if he's called 'Concord locksmiths' his premises will be in Concord? It can't be that difficult to look up."

"Believe me, Raymond, this way is so much easier. Just follow him and let him take us directly to his place. Then we'll be able to pay him a visit and while we're there, we can check out his premises. He's just given us a good indication that *he's* the one who's been stealing from Laura. With a bit of luck, we might find some of her stolen items. I have a sneaky feeling he's just about to lead us to them.

"Without a warrant?"

"Goodness Raymond, there's more than one way to skin a cat."

"Okay, I'll say no more, Sir."

"Good."

Sir, didn't you think it was strange he kept referring to Laura Verwood by her name, seemed a bit familiar, him being just the locksmith."

"You didn't last long, I thought you were going to say no more," he smiled. "If you must know, I had noticed, maybe he's the secret lover." Dunn let out a cheeky laugh.

Inspector Dunn took out his phone and made a call to Detective Lindsay who answered instantly.

"Lindsay, I need you to find out anything you can about a company called 'Concord locksmiths' the proprietor is a Mark Wilson. Ring me back the minute you have anything, I'll be waiting for your call."

Without waiting for an answer, he ended the call and pushed his phone back into his pocket.

"We're now in Concord, Sir. He should be pulling up soon.

Wilson continued through the high street and out to the busy Parramatta road.

"Where the hell's he going now," Ellis called out.

Just then, Dunn's phone gave out a loud shrill sound. Pulling it out of his pocket and opening it up, he could see Lyndsay's name.

"What you got for me?"

"You'll be interested to know, Sir, the owner of the business, Mark Wilson, has form. He spent nine months at Silverwater gaol for embezzlement. He was caught passing bogus cheques or something.

Then not long after he got out, he applied for his locksmith licence. He obviously slipped under the radar as he met all the criteria required to obtain his licence. The justification for licensing certain locksmith activities is to protect the general public."

"What about Concord Locksmiths, is it a big company, or a one man band?"

"Mark Wilson registered the business, Concord locksmiths and works on his own, there are no other staff members. The only address I have is a post box in the suburb of Five Docks."

"Five Docks?" Dunn said out loud. "So that's where he's heading, that's the next suburb. Is there any mention of a wife in his file?"

"Not on the police data, it's not a requirement when applying for a license," he replied, border lining on sarcasm.

"Okay, how about DNA, any chance he did a DNA test when he was taken into custody."

"Actually, yes, for some reason. I'll put a copy of it on your desk. Any reason why you're investigating this man?"

"All in good time," Dunn replied before ending the call.

"I was right to follow the man, there's only a post box on file and who would've thought a business called 'Concord locksmiths' is *not* in Concord," Dunn exclaimed.

They were now in an older part of Five Docks. The van made it through the lights as they turned from amber to red. Ellis screeched to a halt, unable to make it and watched helplessly as the van followed the line of heavy traffic ahead.

"Shit, that's all we need," Ellis fumed. "Let's hope that traffic up ahead holds him up, otherwise, we'll lose the bastard."

After what felt like an eternity, the lights turned green, allowing them to continue their pursuit. The van was nowhere to be seen. Cursing inwardly, Ellis cruised past three, run-down old shops covered in graffiti. The two buildings on the outside looked empty and derelict, their windows now relegated to billboards, covered in posters, advertising local events and graffiti. The premises sandwiched between, looked slightly more presentable.

"That's it! Stop the car, Raymond, read the sign above the door, CONCORD LOCKSMITHS"

Ellis pulled up sharply in front of the door to the scruffy, run down shop. The shop front window was blanked out with a coating of white paint, etched with offensive illustrations.

"I'll drive around the back, Sir, I'm assuming that's where the entrance to the upstairs flat must be. That's most likely where he is."

Sergeant Ellis turned into the next street, guessing there must be a service lane behind the buildings.

A thicket of overgrown bushes practically obscured the entrance to the narrow lane-way. Swinging the car sharply into the lane, he ran headlong into the van. Both drivers slammed on their breaks simultaneously, avoiding each other by inches.

The look of annoyance on Wilson's face turned to sheer panic when he recognized the two detectives sitting in the car in front of him.

Both drivers stared at each other for a few moments deciding who was going to reverse. Sergeant Ellis brazenly inched forward, letting Wilson know who was master.

"Stop the car, Ellis," Inspector Dunn yelled, then climbed out of their vehicle and stormed towards the driver's side window of the van and banged hard on the glass.

Wilson rolled the window down and leaned his head out. "What is it you want now?" Wilson pleaded, "I thought we'd said everything, I have nothing else I can tell you."

"Mr. Wilson, I suggest you back your van up and park. Whether you like it or not, my Sergeant and I need to have a few more words with you."

Wilson slammed the gears angrily into reverse, causing the wheels to spin, spitting gravel and dust into the air as he hastily backed along the lane. He swung the van into a parking bay and turned off the engine. Sergeant Ellis inched forward and parked next to Wilson.

The three men stood in silence at the back door of the shop as Mark Wilson took out a bunch of keys and began unlocking a series of locks.

"I'll get you to wait here while I nip in and turn off the alarm system, I won't be a moment," Wilson advised as he disappeared through the door.

"*He has an alarm system*!" Ellis exclaimed, rolling his eyes. "Not to mention thirty thousand locks. What the fuck does he have in this place that needs so much security?" he added as they both muffled a laugh.

Wilson returned and asked them to follow him through a room which looked like it doubled as a kitchen and a store room then into the shop area. As Inspector Dunn entered the musty smelling shop he shuddered. It was his idea of purgatory being in a place like this.

The old wallpaper was peeling in places and cheap hand painted shelves around the room were stacked with grubby boxes containing lock components.

A rack with keys of all shapes and sizes hung on the wall near the counter on which an electric key grinder was conveniently set up. Years of grinding dust lay on every surface around the place. A large collection of framed photos and paintings of racehorses took pride of place behind the counter.

A wooden staircase to one side of the shop with a sign that read 'Private', hinted it lead to the living accommodation on the next floor.

"Please Inspector, take a seat."

Glancing at the oddments of dusty furniture placed around the room, Inspector Dunn couldn't think of anything he wanted to do less.

"I'll stand if that's okay Mr. Wilson and I'll get straight to the point. Do you remember passing Sergeant Ellis and myself in the hallway of the Balmain apartments? It was the morning Laura Verwood fell from the balcony of her apartment. You were fixing new locks in the building I believe," Dunn began tersely.

"As it happens, I do remember you and your sergeant. If you're questioning the locks, I can tell you now, I had no choice fitting the cheapest locks I could find. The Manager at the apartments, Mr. Farrow, said if I reduce my quote he'd make sure I got the job. I don't like cutting corners, but you have to understand, I need the work. Things haven't been going too well for me lately." He rambled.

"I'll tell you another thing… that man is ripping off the residents of that building. I know because I've spoken to most of them. I can assure you, there's a massive discrepancy between what they have paid for their locks to be fixed and what I'm being paid. So he's obviously pocketing a tidy sum," he said, sounding agitated.

"Calm down, that's not what we've come to talk to you about, you can take that matter up with Farrow if it bothers you so much. I don't even need to talk to you about you stealing Laura Verwood's jewellery earlier."

"So what else can I possibly tell you?"

It was a long shot and he was scraping the barrel, but he thought he'd ask anyway. "When you were fitting the locks on Laura Verwood's apartment, do you recall her having any visitors? Did you ever see a boyfriend or partner or overhear a telephone conversation, sounding as though she was talking to a close friend or a partner?"

"No never, I just got on with my job."

"Okay, I'll ask you another question. When we spoke to you in Laura Verwood's apartment, you referred to her by her first name. How come you're so familiar? Did you know her more than just a customer? You visited her on a number of occasions, is there something you're not telling us?"

There was a long pause as Wilson moved a pile of old magazines from a stool and sat down. "You're right, I did know Laura and I know what lies she's capable of telling. In answer to your question about a partner, the answer is no… no, I never saw anyone else at the apartment. However, I know only too well how secretive she can be, the deceiving bitch." He spat the words out, then wiped his forehead with the handkerchief he'd taken from his pocket.

"So you *did* know Laura Verwood?" Ellis asked, bewildered at the revelation but trying to sound casual. "What d'you mean, you know how secretive she could be?"

Mark Wilson suddenly sounded agitated, his voice rising a few octaves.

"I'll tell you how I know… because during the three years we were together she was carrying on with some bloke behind my back. *Three fucking years,* can you believe it?"

The room fell silent as the two detectives digested what had just spouted from Wilson's mouth.

Trying hard not to sound stunned at the information he'd just heard, Inspector Dunn asked the question. "So what happened?"

"I fucking left her, that's what happened. I know it was a long time ago, but you never forget when someone does what she did. She was my life, I thought we would be together forever, we'd be married and have kids." He continued, his voice now lowering and beginning to sadden. "Have kids, Ha! That's a laugh."

Inspector Dunn decided, against all his better judgement to sit on one of the grubby chairs thinking the conversation was becoming interesting and could take a while.

"Did you know she lived in those apartments?"

"No, I hadn't clapped eyes on the bitch for nineteen, twenty years. When I knocked on the door and she opened it, I got the shock of my life. The old feelings came flooding back, a mixture of hate, but at the same time, sad. I couldn't help thinking how good she looked, why did it have to all go wrong?" He said, bowing his head. "You have to understand, Inspector, I was crazy about the woman all those years ago, but what she did was unthinkable."

"So what happened when she opened the door? How did she react? You must have become angry, did you argue?"

"She was shocked, we both were, and no, we didn't argue, well not a real argument. She didn't realise I was there to fix her locks, she said if I was there to cause trouble I was wasting my time and that she'd call the manager. I explained to her I was only there to fix the locks and that I wasn't there to cause trouble."

"Do you expect us to believe that Mr. Wilson? The woman caused you so much pain, as you say, yet you act all humble and mealy-mouthed. What did you mean by, you didn't want to cause any trouble?" Ellis asked without showing any compassion.

Dunn spoke before Wilson had a chance to answer. "What trouble were you expecting?" After all, you'd separated over nineteen years ago. I've done my sums Mr. Wilson, is Laura's first child yours by any chance?"

"You would be forgiven for thinking that… as I did. The truth is, after three years of being together, my precious ex-partner, announces she's pregnant. Naturally, I was ecstatic, I wanted us to get married. Then she drops a bombshell and tells me it's not my baby, that she'd been having an affair for six months. I was devastated, so we argued, boy how we argued. The upshot was, I said if she were to have an abortion, I was willing to forgive her affair and even still get married. But one thing for sure, I didn't want a baby there as a constant reminder of some bloke she'd been shagging.

"Of course, she flatly refused to have an abortion for all sorts of reasons, mostly moral. The final solution was that she carry on with the pregnancy and that she'd have the baby adopted. You have to understand, it wasn't my kid, so how do you think I felt?" Wilson said as he jumped to his feet and began pacing up and down as he continued to talk. "I couldn't bring up another man's kid. But I loved Laura and was willing to forgive her. After the baby was adopted, we carried on as though nothing had ever happened. Or so I thought." He stopped pacing and leant against the counter not speaking for a few moments as the memories flooding back.

"This must be difficult Mr. Wilson but you can see how this information is impacting on our investigations." Inspector Dunn informed Wilson, who looked up and nodded.

"I suppose I should've seen the writing on the wall, I thought she'd gotten over giving up the kid, it was never mentioned. Then she tried to top herself ending up in some clinic for people who've gone loony," he said, demonstrating by twirling his index finger in a circular motion near his temple. "Our relationship had gone from bad to worse and although she was shutting me out, I clung on with both hands hoping we would get back to the way it was at the beginning."

Wilson sat on the arm of an old chair before continuing.

"Anyway, the crunch came when she got pregnant again, this time, I knew it wasn't mine."

"And how could you be so sure this time?" Ellis asked.

"Because I was working away for nearly a year, so it couldn't have been mine," he said, bowing his head down again.

Inspector Dunn and Sergeant Ellis looked at each other wide-eyed, knowing exactly what he meant by 'working away'. Detective Lindsay had filled them in on that piece of information.

"So tell me Mr. Wilson, why were you in prison?" Ellis asked, waiting to see his reaction.

His eyes darted from one detective to another, shocked at the question. Before replying, his shoulder's slumping forward

"Of course… you of all people would know," he said with a sigh. "I'm not proud of myself, I can assure you. Truth is, I like to have a flutter on the horses and as you can see, I'm not exactly good at it," he said as he waved his arm around the room pointing out the state of the place. "You win some, you lose some, same old, same old for people like me with this affliction. I got in with the wrong crowd, owed money to the wrong people who forced me into doing things I shouldn't have done. You know how it goes. But I've paid my dues to society, end of story."

"Okay, if you say so, now carry on with your story," Ellis said impatiently.

"I found out on the grapevine that the kid was adopted as soon as it was born and Laura tried to top herself for the second time. Again she was lucky that someone, conveniently called and found her in the nick of time and rang for an ambulance. She was carted off to spend time in the same posh clinic. When I got out she hated me and refused to have anything to do with me. I have to say, by then, the feeling was mutual."

"Why do you think she called both babies Peter? Is there a connection somewhere?"

"I have no idea and to be honest, I couldn't care less either. No doubt she was so upset at losing the first baby, she called the second one Peter as well. Or it could've been she just has no fucking imagination," he smirked.

"Now the million dollar question, Mr Wilson, do you have any idea who the fathers of her babies are?" Ellis asked.

"Fathers!" Wilson exclaimed, nearly choking on the word. "You mean *father*... singular. Both her babies are by the same bloke. I thought I mentioned that. Laura wasn't a tart, she was having an affair with the same *man*, the man she'd met when she was working at the bank. Apparently, he had a wife. From what I've also heard on the grapevine, the fucker was still stringing her along all these years later and he's never left his wife.

"Both babies have the same father?" Dunn said out loud. A shocked look spread over his face, realising the implications this meant. "When you say she met the man at the bank, was he a colleague? Meaning did he work for the bank, or was he a customer?"

"He was a customer, a very influential man. I only found this out when I was visited by a private investigator who was checking up on Laura in regards to the adoption of her second baby. Although I have to say he seemed more interested in me and what I was up to, which I thought was strange at the time."

"So you met him? Do you know his name?"

"Nah, what I meant was, the adoption agency asked all the questions on his behalf."

"Do you mind if Sergeant Ellis takes a look upstairs, I presume that is where you live?"

"Hold on a minute." Wilson's eyes almost popped out of his head. "Yes, that is my flat, don't you have to have a warrant to snoop around people's private stuff. Isn't that how it's done?" Wilson said as he jumped to his feet. "You can't just search someone's home."

"As it happens, yes, we can, if we suspect them of stealing, or worse, pushing someone off a balcony."

Wilson turned to Inspector Dunn with a look of indignation on his last comment.

"What the fuck? Surely you don't think I had anything to do with her death?"

"I don't know, you tell me. You certainly had a motive. As you have just admitted, Laura Verwood treated you like shit and then you meet up with her twenty years later and there she is, a lady of fame and fortune. It must have stuck in your craw seeing her after all these years and she's done well for herself, while you," Inspector Dunn paused as he rolled his eyes around the room in an over-exaggerated manner. "Clearly, you haven't done that well for yourself, have you, Mr. Wilson?"

Wilson slumped back in the chair.

"Go ahead then, looks like I can't stop you," he said, flicking his hand towards the stairs.

Sergeant Ellis sprinted up the stairs two at a time and disappeared through a door at the top as Dunn continued with his questions.

"You say the private investigator seemed more interested in

you, have you any idea why " Dunn asked as he strolled around the shop, idly picking up items, studying them and placing them back where he found them.

Ignoring his question, Wilson said, "I'm supposed to be at a job now, I only came back to pick up a ladder from the back lane. I'll no doubt lose that job, which I can't afford to happen at the moment, he rambled, trying to change the subject.

"I asked you a question," Dunn said, sounding impatient.

"Alright, alright, I'll tell you," he snapped, as he sat bolt upright. Inspector Dunn sat on the arm of a chair opposite Wilson.

"It all started when I was asked to do a job in an office in the city, a solicitor's office, a classy joint. For some reason, I was accused of stealing money. My tool box was searched and an envelope filled with a large wad of money was found. I swear Inspector, I honestly don't know how it got there. I was framed and had no idea why."

"A solicitor's office in the city you say?"

"Yes, then two evil looking hard nuts paid me a visit. They gave me an ultimatum, they told me that they wouldn't report me stealing the money providing I never ever contacted either of Laura's boys. They said they would leave me alone, but if I ever tried, they'd be back to sort me out. I was shit scared. I'd already been inside and I certainly did *not* want to go back."

As Wilson talked, Inspector Dunn had a flashback after hearing something Wilson had said. He remembered Felicity Buckton telling him that Cliff had had Laura Verwood investigated. If what this man said was correct, about feeling the investigators seemed more interested in him; that would make sense. What they were really doing, was checking him out.

Dunn snapped out of his thoughts to hear Wilson finish off his conversation.

"Why I would want to contact either of those two kids had me bamboozled, I can't think of anything I would want to do less," he concluded.

At that moment, Ellis' face appeared over the bannister at the top of the stairs.

"Sir, you better come and have a look at this."

Mark Wilson glared at Inspector Dunn with a look of panic. They both headed up the stairs to join Ellis. The flat was marginally better than the shop. The dimly lit sitting room was sparsely furnished with a sofa, coffee table and TV that filled the room.

The well-worn carpet was dotted all over with stains, especially at the far end of the room where there was a small kitchenette with a round table, completely covered by a daily newspaper, opened on the horse racing page.

Inspector Dunn and Mr. Wilson followed Ellis into the bedroom where he pointed to the bed covered in a tangled mess of bedding. Perched on the bed was a cardboard shoebox with the lid removed.

"Take a look in the box I found under the bed," Ellis said sounding triumphant.

Peering into the box, Dunn could see, perched on top of several pieces of jewellery, a diamond and pearl necklace; matching the description of the necklace that had allegedly gone missing from Laura Verwood's apartment. He turned to Wilson, who looked stunned.

"This little lot wouldn't belong to Laura Verwood by any chance?"

Realizing he'd been caught red-handed, Wilson had no choice but to confess.

"Okay, okay, what can I say? It was a moment of weakness. When I visited the apartment the first time and saw the way she was living and the way she looked. Yeah, I was pissed off, she looked like she was loaded, and that apartment is fuckin something else! The memories of the suffering she'd put me through all those years ago came flooding back and I hated her. Yes, it crossed my mind, she owed me, that's all I could think of. That woman owed me big time." He indicated with a circular motion of his arm. "Because *this here,* is what I've been reduced," he cursed.

"And here she is, living in the lap of luxury. I got my chance when she left me in the apartment to get on with the job. There was stuff everywhere, there's no way she would've missed a couple of trinkets. I could sell them and make myself some ready cash."

"Did it ever occur to you that the woman had worked hard for what she had?" Ellis fumed.

He just shrugged his shoulders as though that had never occurred to him or that he didn't care.

"I have no idea about all this antique mumbo jumbo, I just thought it must be worth a bit, she's done so well out of it. Unfortunately, when I tried to sell it, I hardly got anything. So I made an excuse that I needed to go back to the apartment and when she went out the room I grabbed another necklace. As I said, I didn't think she'd notice, the place was full of stuff spread all over the place and clearly she was now rich."

Inspector Dunn insisted they left the bedroom and make their way back downstairs as the smell of the flat was making him nauseous. He asked Ellis to call Detective Miller to give her the heads up about the thefts. As it was, her jurisdiction, he felt she should make the arrest.

"Mr. Wilson, did you go to Laura Verwood's apartment the night she died?"

"Definitely not and before you ask I have a cast iron alibi for where I was that evening. I was at the races and was on a winning streak. Hard to believe, but I won that night and paid for a round of drinks with a few of my mates. They will vouch for me."

"Well, we will certainly follow it up."

"I know it was a long time ago when I was with Laura but the way I remember it, when she tried to top herself the two times before, I think she had no intentions of doing it. I believe she was being a drama queen, doing it for effect. It was strange that both times she popped a load of pills it was at a time when she knew she could be found. I think you call it, a cry for help. Jumping off a balcony is not a cry for help, it's final, and I don't think that was Laura's style."

"Thank you, Mr. Wilson, your comment has been noted."

A loud rap on the shop door gave them a start. Wilson pulled out his bunch of keys and unlocked the door and pulled two bolts across. The door creaked noisily as Wilson opened it, allowing Detective Sergeant Miller and her accompanying officers to enter. Inspector Dunn handed Julie the shoe box and introduced her to Mark Wilson. "I'll leave him in your capable hands and I think you'll find what you've been looking for in this box.

Sergeant Miller instructed the officer to take Wilson to the paddy wagon. After they'd left, she gave Inspector Dunn a puzzled look. "Okay, Sir, what made you suspect it was the locksmith who did the robberies?"

"Elementary my dear," he laughed.

Ray and Julie looked at each other. Had Inspector Dunn just said something funny?

"Easy really, Ellis and I found Wilson in Laura's apartment a few hours ago. We caught him red-handed, pilfering a few trinkets. I recognised him straight away as the locksmith we passed in the hallway the day Laura Verwood died. I suddenly realised, being a locksmith, everyone would trust him. Quite often leaving him alone in their apartments to get on with his job. So I decided Ellis and I would follow him, and I was right."

Dunn thought for a moment. "You might want to check with the other residents in the building, see if anyone else was robbed too. Anyway, I'll leave it with you Julie," Dunn ended as he left with Ellis by the back door.

"So now we know there's only one father, he's very influential and has a wife, well that narrows it down Sir," Ellis said mockingly.

"What we need to do now is to watch out to see if an affluent looking man turns up at the funeral to pay his last respects."

Opening the car door, Inspector Dunn hesitated before stepping out the car.

"I will see you on Monday morning, pick me up about one which should give us plenty time to get to Rookwood cemetery for the funeral. Don't forget to wear a suit."

"I won't. Okay, I'm off to have dinner with a lovely lady so I'm on a promise tonight," he said with a sly grin.

"And who is it this time?"

"Erica, my old faithful, when there's no one else… we have a special arrangement," he said with a wink.

"Well, if you must know, I too have been invited to dinner tonight."

"Don't you find it odd having dinner with your ex-wife and her new husband?"

"Strangely enough, no. I admit I was a lousy husband. You might be interested to know, Julie has agreed to accompany me."

Ray did a double take. "That's great, Sir. Hang on... are you calling it a date, or a diversion for Sarah, someone for her to talk to while you two indulge in your 'memory lane' conversations?"

"I don't know what you mean, I didn't realise we did that. Although I have to admit, I never thought about it as a date."

"Hmm, I wonder how Julie sees it."

Changing the subject quickly. "Will you talk to the team and see how many can attend the funeral. We need them to mingle and listen in to conversations between the mourners, to see what we might pick up about this elusive man."

He reached down to the door handle. "Anyway, have a good night... one way or the other... I'm sure you will." Dunn said, shaking his head.

"You too, Sir, and try not to talk shop all evening, remember, Sarah is not in the Force."

Ray watched his boss walk to his front door. He couldn't be happier he'd asked Julie and was guessing there was more to it than he was letting on. There was definitely a spring in his step. He enjoyed working with Inspector Dunn, he admired him as a person and respected his work ethics. Although only fifteen years older, he looked on Dunn as the father he never had. After hearing so much about Detective Inspector Stephen Dunn five years ago, he'd jumped at the chance to join his team in homicide; and during that time they'd worked together as a great team.

The one thing that was missing in the man's life was a good woman at home. Someone who would take care of him and make it all worthwhile. Someone to put a smile on his face.

Chapter 25

"How are we doing for time Raymond?"

"Okay, we still have another fifteen minutes. We should be there soon if we don't get lost."

A light rain fell as Sergeant Ellis and Inspector Dunn made their way by car to Rookwood Cemetery on the outskirts of Sydney where Laura's funeral was to be held. Ellis had surprised his boss by wearing a black suit and tie for the occasion. With his hair slicked back and a fashionable five o'clock shadow, he oozed charisma. As he turned off the main road and entered through the gates, both detectives were dumbstruck at the sheer size of the place. Gravestones of all sizes and shapes disappeared into the distance where the city skyline peered over the horizon.

The network of narrow, one-way roads that lay ahead had Ellis bamboozled not knowing which direction to take.

"We're looking for, All Souls chapel so just follow the signs, Raymond."

"What signs? So far I've seen one, and that said, way in!" Ellis snapped. "Point out a sign and I'll follow it."

"Well, I don't think she was Asian and according to the names on those gravestones, we're in the Oriental section" Dunn retaliated.

Creeping past whole sections of the cemetery, dedicated to every religious belief, they both marveled at the magnitude of the place. Ornate buildings representing each denomination appeared every now and again in the midst of the graves and floral tributes.

Rounding the corner of an ivy-clad, red brick building with traditional stained glass windows, they spotted people gathered in front of the wooden doors leading into the chapel.

"This must be it, looks like she's drawn a sizeable crowd," Ellis said, sounding surprised. "I'm interested to find out who they are. From what I've picked up, I got a distinct impression she was a private person, a loner. Even though she was a celebrity in the USA."

"Sutton mentioned there'll be a contingent of Americans. He's expecting the producer of the TV show she appeared on, to be at the funeral."

"I'll park here and we can walk the last bit if that's okay, the rain seems to have eased.

Meandering towards the throng of mourners, Ellis spotted Detectives Skinner and Hunter looking inconspicuous, and gave them a knowing wink. They responded with furtive nods, acknowledging they knew of the situation.

It was imperative, friends and relations were not to know police officers were in their midst. Dunn was counting on his men to listen in on conversations that might reveal information; which would help with their investigations.

The crowd dwindled as everyone entered through the arched doorway leading into the chapel. Dennis Sutton was standing to one side, his solemn facial expression spoke volumes as he greeted Laura's friends as they passed by. Raising his head, he spotted Sergeant Ellis and Inspector Dunn over the heads of the mourners and beckoned them over.

"Thank you both for coming, no doubt you see many funerals in your line of work. After the service, I'll introduce you to Laura's people from New York. She was close to the Producer, Julian Kent, who has taken her death badly, for many reasons, not least the fact she's stuffed up his TV program," Sutton said, devoid of emotion. "You should question him, he may have further information for you, although I can't see what he can tell you I haven't already said.

Sounding bitter, he wagged his finger into the chapel. "I was closer to Laura than any of those so-called pseudo friends."

In the distance, a white hearse carrying a white coffin, adorned with one purple and green floral arrangement came into view.

Taking it as their cue, the two detectives made their way inside the chapel and stood at the back out of sight.

"Check out Lindsay and Jones, Sir," Ellis said, out the side of his mouth as he nodded along the line of people standing next to them.

Inspector Dunn leant forward for a better view. They were both engrossed on their mobile phones.

"No doubt they're playing games, I'll be having words with those two," Dunn remarked in a low voice. "Can you see Lloyd?"

"Not yet, he's probably snuck behind a gravestone having a sneaky smoke"

No sooner had he finished his sentence, Sergeant Ellis peered out through the arched doorway to see Lloyd, a few meters away, stubbing out a cigarette with his foot and blowing out a mouthful of smoke before entering the chapel. Glancing sideways at Inspector Dunn and Sergeant Ellis he gave them a slight hint of a smile, as he walked past, before turning to the opposite side of the chapel and stood almost to attention behind the rows of pews. The Ashcott's, Peter Buckton and Jenni were sitting together right at the front.

As the moving sound of Eric Clapton's 'Tears in Heaven' filled the chapel, the coffin appeared through the doors being carried by four well-dressed men with sombre expressions. Inspector Dunn did a double take, seeing Peter Ashton as one pallbearer, it crossed Dunn's mind how poignant it was that he should carry his birth mother's coffin at her funeral when she'd given him away as baby.

After a short speech given by the Minister, the plasma TV burst into life with the image of Laura Verwood splashed across the screen. Friends and family watched in silence as her slot on an episode of the American antique programme played in its entirety.

"What a waste," Ellis whispered," "She was gorgeous."

"Puts a different slant on it, seeing her animated," Dunn responded.

As the video continued to play, Ellis drifted off, remembering his date a few nights before with Erica, the stunner from Denmark. The trendy Mexican restaurant had been a good choice and had worked out well, with amazing food. He smiled at how she could drink him under the table with tequila sunrises and how the drinks had had the desired effect later in the evening.

The sound of Dennis Sutton's voice brought Ellis back to earth, as he delivered the eulogy which went on for some time. He took it as a cue to immerse himself once more in his own thoughts. After a memorable night of no holds barred sex, he'd woken up with the gorgeous, leggy blonde lying next to him, her long hair spread over the pillow like melted marshmallow. There was nothing the girl didn't do, no position she wouldn't try. She'd shown him a thing or two since they met. But Erica was a tough cookie, not the girl you took home to meet your parents.

He recalled how he'd trailed his fingers over the contours of her body. When he'd moved closer to her, pressing his naked body against her soft warm flesh, she'd recoiled. Instead of giving him a sign of encouragement, her face crinkled as she moaned about having to go to work.

He'd watched her tall, slender feminine shape as she slid out of bed and with no inhibitions, stomped across the bedroom floor, disappeared through the bathroom door and slammed it closed behind her. He'd listened to the water pouring from the shower faucet. Then, as he lay on his back, feeling rejected, the door had opened again and to his surprise, Erica appeared, beckoning him to join her.

Ellis' face broke into the biggest grin as he recalled what followed.

"Penny for your thoughts," Dunn said, nudging him in the ribs.

"It'll cost you more than that, Sir," he replied giving a sly wink.

"You might want to wipe the stupid grin off your face, this is a funeral," Dunn whispered, tilting his head towards Ellis and speaking behind his hand.

To Dunn's amazement, Peter Ashcott took the stand. With his well-rehearsed eulogy, he rose to the occasion. He maintained his emotions as he remembered his biological mother; while throwing affectionate glances towards his adopted mother, Mrs Ashcott, at regular intervals.

Once the service concluded, the four pallbearers each held a corner of the coffin and ceremoniously walked down the aisle to the waiting hearse outside. Peter Ashcott gave Detective Ellis a watery smile as he passed by while Dennis Sutton resumed his position at the entrance, accepting condolences and inviting everyone for refreshments in the assembly hall after the internment. An entourage of cars followed the white hearse, making its way at a slow pace, through the labyrinth of roadways as it headed towards the Church of England burial site. Pulling their car over onto the grass verge, Ellis was about to open the door when Dunn held him back. "Just sit for a moment and watch."

Only half the mourners attended the graveside. As expected at a funeral, the rain had started up again, soaking the ground, making it muddy to walk on. They could see Mr and Mrs Ashcott, talking to the two Peters and Jenni. Everyone else looked mystified what they should do until the Minister drew them in close.

"Sir, I think we should wander over and show our faces."

"To be honest, Raymond, I'm not sure it's our place to be there, it's quite a private thing, watching the coffin disappearing into the ground don't you think?"

"The American producer is there and I'd like an introduction. Let's just go get it over with."

After a short and emotional few words from the Minister, the four pallbearers each took an end of the straps and lowered the coffin into the grave. While crying in silence, Mrs Ashcott accepted a tissue from Jenni as she slipped an arm around her shoulders with a reassuring hug.

"I can't see anyone who fits the bill for an affluent lover, Sir, how about you?"

"No, no one. I'd say the group on the left are the American's. They have that flamboyant look."

Dennis Sutton appeared from nowhere and grabbed Dunn's elbow, ushering him towards the colourful man walking away from the graveside.

"Inspector Dunn, there's someone you need to meet," he said, guiding him towards a man texting on his smartphone. Dunn's first thoughts were, he was inappropriately dressed for a funeral. His pale aqua blue jacket with a lemon cashmere scarf draped around his neck stood out a mile. Although Dunn had to admit he could be forgiven for his outfit as he looked interesting, maybe even taking the edge off a sombre occasion. As they neared the man, Sutton began his introductions. "Mr Kent, this is Detective Inspector Dunn, if you have a moment, he'd like to talk to you about Laura."

Dunn was intrigued by the man's manner, unable to ascertain whether he was gay or just eccentric.

"Darling, you must call me Julian," he declared in a strong American accent. "This is a shocking business Inspector and has saddened us, Laura is leaving a huge void in our lives, let me tell you. I have no idea how we will manage without her. The TV viewers are devastated, the tributes have flooded in. If only she could see them. Everyone loved that lady." He said wistfully, not stopping for a breath.

"Mr Kent, I mean Julian, let me introduce you to Detective Sergeant Ellis," Dunn said as he turned to include Ellis in the conversation, only to find there was no one there. Directing his eyes a few meters away, he could see him talking to a stunning lady with an American accent.

"Hmm, cool guy looks like he's chatting up my assistant Toni. You may need to let him know *'she'* is not a woman if you get my drift," he added as he threw his head back and laughed.

A smirk stretched across Dunn's face. He wondered if he should warn Ray, then decided to let the charmer find out for himself.

"So, Laura made a big impression on your antique show?"

"Let me tell you, Laura *was* the show, not only did she know everything there was to know about antiques, she was charming and bright. Everyone loved her cute Australian accent and hung on her every word. I tried time and time again to persuade her to move to New York, If only she'd listened; she'd still be with us," he said with a sad look.

"That would have been impossible, moving away and leaving her loved ones behind," Dunn said, hoping to trick Mr Kent into revealing something new.

"I'd say that was the main reason for staying here," he replied, then a thought struck him. "Hey, where is the bastard, I'd like to meet the fucking dumb ass. Do you know which one he is?" he asked, craning his neck to scan the people at the graveside.

"No, we have no idea. I was hoping you could tell us."

"I have no idea either, you'd think he would be here at her grave paying his last respects. Maybe he's back at the chapel, I wouldn't mind giving the ass hole a piece of my mind."

"As I said, I know nothing about her partner, in fact, nobody does. We don't know his name or how he looks."

"Well, that darned fucker made her unhappy I know that much. D'you know how many times I overheard her talking on the telephone, sounding pissed like she was having a fight with the guy?"

"Were you aware he was a married man?"

"He had a *wife*? You're shitting me?"

"Do you recall any of the phone conversations she was having, did you overhear anything?"

"Yeah, I sure do as they were always about the same thing. There was this one time, while on her last visit, I overheard her speaking quite angrily on her cell phone as I walked past her dressing room. Now I'm not in the habit of listening in on other people's ding dongs, but I couldn't exactly avoid this one."

"Go on," Dunn said, being drawn in.

"Oh, let's see, she was hollering about what a dumbass he was, she said something about how she'd been patient for twenty years. It must've been her guy because she shouted about having his babies. I wasn't able to catch everything, you understand. She said something about how she knew her kid, her son, was with him. I know I shouldn't have been listening, but it was sounding interesting and I'd never heard her get sore like that."

"Did she say his name during the conversation?"

"I don't think so, if she did, I don't remember. There must've been legal stuff going on because she said something about not being difficult for him, he should be the judge, or words to that effect, and she intended to reveal everything. That's all I heard, she turned round and saw me and closed the door."

"Did you ask her about the call, who she was talking to?"

"No way, man, it was private," he grinned. "I wasn't supposed to be listening. Anyway, I was due on set."

"I'm sorry, Inspector, I have to go talk to my cameraman, who's filming the funeral for our audience back home," Kent said, shaking Dunn's hand before flouncing away.

Seeing Mr Kent leave, Sergeant Ellis made his way towards Inspector Dunn.

"Find out anything interesting?"

"It's amazing what people will reveal when they're emotional," Dunn smiled. "Let's find the team and grab something to eat."

"Sir, Sutton has talked to Asho and Fish about Miss Verwood's belongings, in particular, the expensive jewellery. He's put them in touch with some of the dealers and has given them the name of the solicitor, Randal Goldthorpe, who is also Miss Verwood's executor. I can assure you he will take care of them."

"Let's hope so."

They made their way to the All Souls chapel where the catering company that Dennis Sutton had arranged were bustling between guests, serving hors d'oeuvres and pouring drinks. Strategically positioned round the room, the team continued to chat to all and sundry as they tucked into the refreshments; hoping to appear inconspicuous. Dunn gave a surreptitiously sign to each officer, letting them know it was time to leave. One by one they made their excuses to leave and headed for their vehicles in the parking area.

"Okay, I don't want to be seen standing here talking so let's get back to the command centre, then we can have our discussion in private."

Once again, Inspector Dunn chose not to talk during the drive. Deciding the silence was deafening, Sergeant Ellis spoke.

"Everything all right, Sir?"

"Not altogether, we have a major problem."

"What is it, do you mean we're no further forward? We certainly didn't achieve any leads there today did we?"

"Just wait Ellis, I'll explain when we get back to the office. It's complicated."

Inspector Dunn appeared to be on a mission as he barged towards the white board in the main office. He picked up the black marker and removed the lid.

"So, how did you all get on? Hunter, did you hear anything while you mingled?"

"Sorry, Sir, I heard nothing negative. I suppose it's to be expected, it's a funeral after all. The people I chatted with were mostly antique dealers, they all said she was a lovely lady and knew her stuff. Nothing about a lover and no one knew *anything* about her having children."

Each member of the team reiterated everything Hunter had said with the exception of Detective Lloyd who wore a beaming smile. While talking to the cameraman from the American party, he'd gleaned some interesting information. He discovered that Laura and he had formed a strong bond as they were in a similar relationship. The cameraman had divulged to Lloyd how they commiserated with each other whenever she was in New York. However, although Laura confided in him, she never revealed a name or who the man was. He also said, Laura was at the end of her tether with the relationship and had given her lover an ultimatum. The cameraman insisted the last time he spoke to her, she sounded confident and that her life was going to change for the better. Apparently her lover was about to leave his wife at long last and set up home with her."

"After hearing what he said, my thoughts were, if the lover didn't agree to her demands, she might've got hysterical, leading her to jump."

"Very interesting, Lloyd, thanks for that thought."

Sounding excited, Lindsay called out while keeping his eyes fixed on his computer screen.

"I've found out something interesting, Sir. I never expected in a million years."

"What is it Lindsay, don't tell me you're on a dating site and someone's agreed to go out with you?" Hunter called back.

There was a wave of snickering throughout the group. Inspector Dunn made a loud rapping sound on the white board with the marker.

"Okay you lot, that's enough."

"Lindsay, please continue, let's hear what you have. I need *something* that will help solve this God forsaken case," Dunn demanded.

"It's the car… the Merc, Sir, you'll never guess who the original purchaser was?"

"Queen Elizabeth?" someone called out.

Ignoring the comment, Lindsay carried on.

"I've found out information you will find interesting," he said, as he tapped the computer screen with his pen. "The car belonging to Laura Verwood is unregistered and uninsured and has been for the past twelve months."

"So?" Ellis said, feeling impatient that Lindsay was dragging it out and taking forever to explain. Lindsay pushed his hair to one side, out of his eyes, before continuing. "It's a known fact that when you buy a car brand new, the registrations for the first year is included in the purchase price. That Merc is now two years old."

"You wouldn't believe *that* if you saw it."

Everyone averted their attention at Detective Lloyd as he called out from the back of the room, sounding appalled. Without responding to Lloyd's outburst, Lindsay continued once more.

"The vehicle was an ex-government car, used to chauffeur the judge. It was subsequently bought by C & F Holdings and registered in the same name. However, since lapsing it has remained unregistered and uninsured. Hence, according to our good friend Lloyd over there, left to rot,"

"There's another thing you might be interested in, Sir," Jones added.

"I was talking to my mate in traffic on an unrelated matter and I found out Judge Clifford Buckton's Merc was caught on a speed camera in Rozelle, a five-minute drive away from the apartments in Balmain where Laura Verwood lived. It was clocked at ten, twenty on the night she died."

After listening intently to what Jones was saying, Inspector Dunn looked up.

"Well, well, well, you have all confirmed my suspicions from information I picked up at the funeral today," he said, turning to face the whiteboard and in bold capitals, wrote the name 'The Honourable Chief Justice Clifford Buckton' highlighting it by drawing a circle around it. Underneath, in smaller lettering, he added, the biological father of Peter Ashcott and Peter Buckton.

The office erupted into a cacophony of voices from the team all venting their opinions. When Inspector Dunn called out for quiet, the room soon fell silent.

"I am now certain that the father of the two boys is the Honourable Chief Justice Clifford Buckton," he announced banging the marker on the name he had just written in bold letters. "I have deduced that *he* is the married man that Laura Verwood was having an affair with for the past twenty years. The annoying thing is, it was right under our noses all along."

"What made you think of it, Sir," Ellis asked.

"I've had my suspicions from the information that's been coming in. But it was when I was talking to the American producer, Julian Kent, at the funeral. He gave me the run down on a telephone conversation he'd overheard Laura Verwood having in her dressing room. What he described, was more of a row. The things he could hear her saying were that she'd been faithful for twenty years and even had his *children*, plural. She added in her fury he had the luxury of having the perfect, cosy family, the life she craved."

Inspector Dunn motioned Skinner to move out of his seat, allowing him to sit down. "I might not have connected this with Judge Buckton until I heard what Mr Kent had to say. Things he didn't understand himself. He'd overheard her saying to the person on the other end of the phone, it should be easy for him, something to the effect of, 'and he should be the Judge'. Apparently she yelled that she'd had enough of the lies and deceit. Kent said the last words he heard were, she was going to tell his... It was at that point she caught him eavesdropping and closed the door on him. That was all he could give me.

Had Laura not spotted Kent listening, I'm sure what she would have continued to say was, '*I'll tell your wife*.' That's enough incriminating evidence to be going on with. That, and now the fact, Laura's Mercedes was a government vehicle, used by the Judge's chauffeur."

"What if the Judge denies all this? After all, Laura Verwood is now dead and we've struggled to find any concrete evidence or witnesses," Detective Hunter added.

"That's why we have DNA, you know that," Dunn snapped. "Once we've proved he is undeniably the father, then we will go from there."

"You realise you will need to run this past the Superintendent. He won't like you interviewing the Chief Justice again," Ellis pointed out.

"I'm about to find out as I'm about to pay him a visit."

"Good luck Sir," Ellis called out.

After giving two raps with his knuckles on the door of Superintendent Fortis Green's office, Dunn barged in without waiting for a response. Taken aback by Stephen's entrance, Fortis sat bolt upright and pushed his chair away from his desk and got to his feet.

"Stephen, what a surprise? Do you want a drink?"

"If you're having one?"

"That's sorted then, take a seat and make yourself at home. You look like you have something on your mind."

After pouring two drinks, Fortis handed a glass to Dunn and walked back to his chair and sat down. Stephen took a large gulp of his whisky before launching into the revelations of the day.

"I'm almost a hundred percent sure I can name the father of Laura Verwood's babies."

"Did I hear you correct? Did you say father as in singular? So you're positive it was just one man?"

"No, I said *almost* a hundred percent, however, with your permission, I need him to have a DNA test."

"With my permission!" he exclaimed. "What's this all about? How come at last you're asking for my permission? "That's not like you Stephen."

"There's more, I have it on good authority that this is the man she was having the affair with for over twenty years, the usual scenario, he's a married man and doesn't seem to want to leave his wife, obviously likes having the best of both worlds.

Anyway, Laura Verwood was overheard having a massive row, threatening to tell his wife, giving him an ultimatum. This is where it gets messy. The man had the perfect reason to want to kill Laura Verwood. I'm almost certain the father of her children, the man she was having a relationship with for over twenty years is the man who murdered her."

"So who is this maniac, murderer," Fortis asked as he took a mouthful of his drink.

Stephen paused for a few seconds before announcing the name.

"It's the Honourable Chief Justice, Clifford Buckton."

Fortis' body lurched forward as his drink sprayed from his mouth, all over his desk. "For fuck's sake, Stephen… "*What are you saying?* Please tell me you're joking. The Honourable Chief Justice, Clifford Buckton? What on earth has brought you to this conclusion?"

"Well, do I need to point out I've been flat out on this case for the past week, sifting through everything I could get my hands on. Do you think I like all this? Geez Fortis, Cliff and I go back a long way. I've visited his home and had dinner with him and his wife Felicity for God's sake. I myself, had no idea whatsoever their son was adopted and I've known the baby since birth. So think about it, if he can keep that a secret and the fact he's been keeping another woman for twenty years behind his wife's back, he's capable of anything."

"So you think we can now just march up to him and ask him to do a DNA test?"

"Yes, why not? Whether you like it or not, this is what I'm doing, Fortis."

"You realise that you can't see him, it's not ethical."

"Yes, I know, we must get Raymond to see him, I'll brief him when I get back to the office.

Stephen stood up and placed his glass on the desk. Not uttering another word, he sauntered towards the door.

"Stephen."

Dunn turned, expressionless, to hear what Fortis had to say.

"You better be right… it's my head on the chopping block, not yours. I'll leave you to make all the arrangements. Let me know the minute you get the results." Fortis said with a look of dismay.

Without looking back, Stephen walked out the door, closing it behind him.

Fortis Green let out a gasp as he spoke under his breath.

"You'll be the death of me Stephen, but you're never wrong damn you."

Inspector Dunn left the Inspector and headed straight for his office.

"Ellis, I need to see you, now," he called out.

Sergeant Ellis ended a telephone conversation he was having and headed straight for Dunn's office.

"Close the door Raymond and take a seat."

"Hmm, should I be worried, Sir."

"Hmm, let's just say, the next few days won't be easy. We need to get Buckton to agree to a DNA test. As I know him personally, he's likely to refuse. That is why you are the one to pay him a visit. Knowing him as I do, he will ask to have his legal representative present. He will also make you sign an agreement to have all the paperwork destroyed and not kept on record."

"Can he do that?"

"In his position, he can do what the hell he likes. Just go along with anything he asks. Agree to all his demands. I want you to make an appointment for first thing tomorrow morning."

Inspector Dunn opened the top drawer of his desk and took out a well-thumbed personal address book. Flicking through, he stopped at the phone number of Clifford Buckton' chambers. He dialed the number and at the sound of his personal assistant, Dunn handed the receiver to Ellis.

"Sergeant Ray Ellis from Sydney Police Headquarters, I need to speak to Clifford Buckton," he said, in a brusque voice.

"No, it's not about one of his cases, it's a personal matter... yes, I'll hold.

After a lengthy silence, a familiar sounding man's voice resounded through the receiver, introducing himself as Clifford Buckton.

"It's Sergeant Ray Ellis, I visited your home with Inspector Stephen Dunn a few days ago."

"Ray, how are you, to what do I owe the pleasure?"

"I'm good thanks for asking. Look, I'm ringing in regards to the Laura Verwood case. I need to meet you at your home tomorrow morning to take a DNA test,"

Judge Buckton's tone transformed. "I can't see the point, however, if you must, I would prefer you come here to my office. If you could be here at nine sharp, I will make sure my legal representative is here with me."

"That's fine by me... your office at nine o'clock tomorrow morning, I'll see you then." Ellis ended the call and gave Dunn a sly wink as he handed the receiver back to him.

"Well done Raymond, I take it he didn't want you to go to his house?"

"Nope, I doubt very much he'd want his wife to witness anything about Laura Verwood."

"Phew, I think we should call it quits, we can continue with all this tomorrow. Do you fancy a drink?"

Skinner's band is playing in the pub at the Rocks tonight, you're welcome to join me.

"I think I'll give it a miss, I'm guessing I'd stand out like a sore thumb and you don't really want me hanging out with you," he said, managing a grin. "But thanks for the invite."

Ray shrugged his shoulders. "You said that, not me, I think you're wrong and you might be surprised and enjoy yourself. If you change your mind, you know where to find me," he offered.

Chapter 26

"Okay Sir, I'm off, wish me luck," Sergeant Ellis called out as he popped his head round the doorway to Dunn's office before setting out for The Honourable Chief Justice Clifford Buckton's Chambers.

"Just a word of advice Ray," Inspector Dunn called back. "Act responsibly, don't let your emotions run wild. This is not just your run of the mill person you're dealing with. He will be difficult and we want nothing to spoil our case at this point. We're treading on thin ice."

"I'll do my best, Sir," he frowned as he pulled back from the doorway and headed out of the office. Passing Detective Sally Hunter's desk on the way, he gave her a pleading look. She gave him a wide flat grin. "Break a leg," she whispered, trying to be jovial.

The Honourable Chief Justice Buckton's chambers were only a short walk from police headquarters. However, feeling apprehensive, about his meeting with the Judge, the few blocks seemed like a million miles. Ellis felt as though he was walking through treacle.

The security guard, standing in front of the building, instructed Ellis to take the elevator to the eighth floor. As he stepped from the elevator, the ultra-modern reception came as a surprise in such an old building. The colour scheme of pale grey walls with plush navy carpet and contrasting grey leather lounges in the waiting area was stunning. Taking up half of the room was a dark smoked glass reception desk where two efficient looking women, wearing smart navy suits were busy. Oblivious to everything, they were unaware Ellis had approached the desk.

After clearing his throat to attract their attention, the older of the two women raised her head with a look of surprise. "Oh, I'm sorry, I think you might be on the wrong floor," the lady said. "The solicitors and barristers are on the lower floors. This is the Judge's chambers."

Holding up his ID badge, Sergeant Ellis introduced himself. "You misunderstand, I'm Sergeant Ray Ellis from Sydney Police headquarters, I have an appointment with The Honourable Chief Justice Buckton at nine o'clock, I'm a tad early," he smiled.

"I appologise, Sergeant Ellis, I was not aware, Justice Buckton was scheduled for visitors this morning. I'll see if he is ready to see you."

Picking up the phone, the woman turned away to speak as though it would make a difference to him hearing. As he waited for her to confirm his appointment, Ellis scanned the room. Across one wall was a display of life-size portraits of both men and women, dressed in judge's robes and white wigs. The Honourable Chief Justice Buckton, took pride of place, resplendent in his official garb. Ellis gave a sardonic grin, knowing the circumstances why he was visiting this respected man.

The receptionist ended her conversation and replaced the receiver. "Apparently, he *is* expecting you, Sergeant Ellis," she said, sounding surprised, then pointed to two glass doors at the end of the reception.

"Go through those doors and follow the corridor to the end, you will see his office," she said, with a fake smile, then carried on with her work as though he'd never interrupted her.

The frosted glass doors were emblazoned with the Law Society gold shield with the words 'Omnium Jura Defend Imus'. As they slid open, Ellis made his way along a wide hallway where the decor transformed dramatically. The modern design of the reception was now gone and in its place was the original high, varnished wooden skirting's and door frames. The original wooden floor boards had a glass-like finish from years of polishing and the place smelled musty.

Portraits of the same theme, to those in reception stretched the length of the walls and on either side of the wide corridor stood six busts carved in marble on ornate plinths. Ellis could only presume were of predecessors. At the end of the long hallways, he reached a door with the name 'Honourable Chief Justice Clifford Buckton' sign written in gold leaf.

Taking a deep breath, he knocked twice on the door and waited with trepidation. When there was no response, Ellis found himself in an awkward situation. Had the Judge heard, but was taking his time to open the door and if he knocked again he'll be annoyed. Or had he not heard at all, and Ellis was standing like a goon. He threw caution to the wind, deciding to knock again. As he raised his fist ready to knock, the door swung open, held by a well-dressed man in a pinstriped navy suit.

"Good morning, Sergeant Ellis, please come in," he said as he stepped aside allowing Ellis to enter. The Judge's office looked exactly as Ellis expected with the Honourable Chief Justice Clifford Buckton seated in a high backed dark red leather chair, behind an enormous, older style desk. The thought passed through Ellis' mind, he resembled a king, sitting on his throne and could feel the hair on the back of his neck bristle knowing the truth about this holier-than-thou man.

Ellis was having the shits at all this pomp and ceremony when the man was capable of deceit and perhaps, even murder. Ellis snapped himself out of it, being concerned that how he felt might cloud his judgment.

As he looked beyond the Judge and out through the only window, the therapeutic view of Sydney Harbour, just beyond the Botanical gardens, made Ellis feel marginally better.

"Sergeant Ellis, meet my solicitor, Alan Henderson. I have asked him to attend this morning's interview, you understand, I hope."

The man in the pinstriped suit held out his hand and gave Ellis a limp handshake.

"Please sit, both of you" Buckton ordered as he pointed at two winged back chairs opposite him.

Alan Henderson spoke. "My client tells me you wish to take a DNA test to confirm the paternity of the two sons of Laura Verwood, is this correct?"

Sergeant Ellis pushed his hand into his pocket and pulled out a clear plastic vial containing cotton wool buds, placing it on the desk in front of him.

"Look, Ray, you don't mind if I call you that, do you?"

"Not at all,"

"It won't be necessary for you to take the test as Judge Buckton has agreed to make a full confession about being the father of the two children." The solicitor said as he nodded to Judge Buckton, giving him his cue to speak.

"Raymond, Inspector Dunn and I go back years. I've known Stephen Dunn for more years than I care to mention. Since you were a mere boy," he said, with a patronising tone.

Wondering where he was going with this, Ellis could feel himself becoming irritated by the man, sitting there on his throne, talking as though butter wouldn't melt in his mouth. In reality, he knew exactly what the man was capable of. If he could just do the DNA test and be on his way. Then he wouldn't be subjected all the crap the Judge was banging on about.

"I know how Stephen works, he has a different mindset to most other people." Buckton began. "He'll go on about having a 'hunch'. You must have heard him say that many times?" he said, raising his eyebrows. "But we know it's more than that. He has an uncanny knack of unearthing information and secrets that no one else can. That's what made him an Inspector. Are you aware he refused the offer of a promotion to Superintendent of the Sydney Police Headquarters?"

Sergeant Ellis nodded. "Yes, yes, I did know that"

"And not just once, he was offered several times and each time he refused, insisting an office job was not for him and he was right. His place is in the front line, solving crimes. It would have been such a waste of his great talent and ability to solve crimes."

Ellis gave a knowing grin. "Very perceptive of you Judge but I think you're getting off the subject. I didn't come here to talk about Inspector Dunn."

"I apologise, I'm digressing, however, there is a reason I'm saying all this." The judge leant towards an intercom on his desk and asked his secretary to serve morning coffee.

"Now where was I, Raymond?"

"Hopefully, you'll make your point and tell me everything we need to know, then I can head back to headquarters."

Justice Buckton rested his arms on the desk in front of him with his hands clasped together as though in prayer. His voice was low and precise.

"For twenty years I kept my relationship with Laura Verwood private, a secret, for her sake and mine. We met when she worked at the bank. I don't know why I asked her out, perhaps it was because she was funny, charming a breath of fresh air. I tried to give her up, so many times," he said, looking wistful. "But I couldn't, I was smitten by the woman. I know it all sounds cliché Sergeant Ellis, but I love my wife, I could never leave her, *never*. But I couldn't give up Laura either."

"The way I see it, you were enjoying the best of both worlds." Ellis snapped.

Before The Judge could respond to Ellis' remark, a knock on the door interrupted their conversation. Henderson hurried to open it, allowing a young woman to enter carrying a tray with three cups and saucers, placing one in front of each gentleman;

then left.. The interruption, giving everyone a chance to calm down.

Justice Buckton took a sip of coffee and placed the cup back in its saucer. "See it how you like Sergeant, that's not how it was," the Judge said self-importantly. Laura and I dated for about six months and then she dropped the bombshell, she announced she was expecting my baby. I was devastated, a baby with Laura was the last thing I needed. My wife had been trying to fall pregnant for five years and was going through hell, emotionally. How do you think I felt, making another woman pregnant?"

"I don't know, you tell me," Ellis replied, sounding a little harsh.

"An abortion was out of the question for both of us, I couldn't' let her kill a baby that my wife was so desperately wanting and Laura wouldn't hear of an abortion on moral grounds. So as you now know, Laura gave birth to a beautiful baby boy, she named Peter after her father who died tragically. Laura suffered post-natal depression and I'll admit our situation made things worse. Time and time again, she begged me to leave my wife, but I couldn't. Then Laura had a full-blown breakdown. I paid for the best clinic in Sydney and she agreed it would be best that baby Peter was adopted.

It was an emotional turmoil for both of us and we found solace in each other's misery. So much so, she fell pregnant again." The judge said lowering his voice.

Sergeant Ellis rolled his eyes. "That simple, eh?"

"That wasn't meant to sound so flippant. Trust me, Raymond, I'm being completely honest. Now this is where it becomes more complicated. When I heard the news of her second pregnancy, I had an ingenious idea. If I could persuade Laura to have the second baby adopted, I could arrange for Felicity and myself to adopt it. Yes, I cut through some red tape, but I did it for the right reasons."

It was a double sided sword. I hated seeing Felicity suffering month after month and I knew Laura couldn't handle the demands of a baby. She gave birth to a second son and insisted he too was to be called Peter before she handed him over to the agency. Out of respect, my wife and I kept the name."

"Did Laura Verwood know that it was you and your wife adopted her second child?"

The Judge bowed his head, not speaking for a few moments. "No, she had no idea we adopted Peter, there was no reason she should know. As I said, I did it for all the right reasons. A few weeks ago, Laura called me from New York, she was irate because she'd discovered my secret, that Peter was with me and my wife."

"I'm sorry, Judge Buckton but I can't for the life of me get my head round the cruel lies and deception you've lived for the past twenty years. How do you live with yourself, knowing your wife has absolutely no idea that the son she'd looked after all this time is your flesh and blood. A baby you conceived with your secret lover. For eighteen years, your wife has lived in complete oblivion you are the biological father of her adopted baby. You blatantly continued with your affair with the mother of the child." As Ellis continued, his voice intensified. "On top of all this, you kept it a secret from your lover that her baby, the baby she gave up for adoption, is being raised by you and your wife, the woman Laura begged you to leave."

"Don't you think I know that? There's no need for you to spell it out," said Buckton, raising his voice. Henderson glared at him, annoyed he was losing his temper.

Composing himself, the Judge continued. "Have you any idea how difficult it has been for me carrying this enormous burden for twenty years? You have no idea young man."

Ellis leaned forward. "Do you really expect me to sympathise? It's a burden you brought on yourself, you could have ended this twenty years ago. Did you honestly believe this would never get out? And do you realise the people who are going to be hurt when it does?"

"I'm not sure I like your attitude, Raymond."

"Why, because I'm telling home truths?" Ellis said, putting strength in his words.

"No, because you have no idea of the emotional upheaval I've been through, you have no right to judge other people and should keep your opinions to yourself."

"So, Your Honour... it's all about *you*... *your* emotional upheaval. Well, that's rich. I need to ask then where were you the night Laura Verwood fell from her balcony?"

Judge Buckton looked at Henderson, who shook his head and glared at him, intimating not to say another word on the subject. The judge held up his hand to Henderson in defiance.

"It's okay, Alan, I have known Stephen Dunn for years. He can be discreet if he needs to be." He turned to face Ellis. "I'd say you already know I was at Laura's apartment the night she died. We always see each other just before she leaves for America. Before you ask, yes, we had a romantic evening."

"Is that what you call it? We know she was sexually active just prior to her death. So that was you? Unless, of course, the DNA test proves otherwise" Ellis said bluntly.

"What are you implying? Laura was definitely not seeing anyone else, romantically." He replied indignantly.

"What time did you leave?"

"Let's see, I worked late here till about eight o'clock, then I took a cab to her place." The judge gave a small giggle before he continued. "We have a foolproof way for me entering and exiting her apartment without being seen. I left about ten thirty, I walked to the next block and caught a taxi back to my place."

"Tell me, did you know Laura Verwood intended to reveal your sordid affair to your wife? We have this on good authority I can assure you. So tell me, Your Honour, is that what happened, she threatened you and you got angry, then you pushed her over the railings, that would shut her up, wouldn't it? You then made a quick getaway. You said yourself you have a foolproof way of getting out of the apartment without being seen,"

"What are you talking about Sergeant," Henderson barked, jumping to his feet in outrage. "How dare you accuse the Judge? Your assumptions are utterly unfounded and ridiculous. He's offered you all the information you need. I think it's time for you to leave."

Ellis felt indignation at the solicitor's attitude, deciding he would not let this matter drop. Especially as all the evidence pointed at Judge Buckton being guilty.

Sergeant Ellis stood and placed both hands flat on the desk in front of him. "Sorry, Your Honour, but your telephone conversation with Miss Verwood was overheard. We know you argued and she threatened to tell your wife your secrets. There's no way you could allow that to happen? After all, you risked losing *everything*? So you needed to put a stop to her hysterics. We know you were the last person to visit her apartment and to see her alive and you had the motive."

Judge Buckton got to his feet and leant towards Sergeant Ellis. "Stop, stop, you're talking rubbish, I loved Laura, there's no way I could hurt her."

Henderson lunged towards Ellis and grabbed him by the shoulders. "Stop this, you have no right to make these accusations."

Ellis pushed his hands away in anger, his voice rising. "What did you do, eh? Did you lose your temper and drag the poor woman out onto the balcony, the balcony you knew she hated, which terrified her. Then you pushed her over the railings. Come on, Your Honour, admit it, you wanted her out of the way. Why not get it off your chest once and for all, release the burden you've carried around all these years?" Ellis said, now incensed.

The Chief Justice was feeling anxious. Reaching for the intercom, he called for security. Henderson tried to grab Ellis' arm to pacify him. "I suggest you leave right now Sergeant, you're not making things easy for yourself. This is not looking good for you."

Ellis yanked his arm away and faced the judge squarely. "I'm not going anywhere, I will, however, arrest you on suspicion of murder. Honourable Chief Justice Clifford Buckton, I'm arresting you for the possible murder of Laura Verwood. You do not have to say anything. But it may harm your defence if you do not mention when questioned, something which you rely on in court and anything you say can be given in evidence."

"Good God, do you know what you are saying, who you are dealing with?" The solicitor called out.

"I'll make sure you lose your job over this Sergeant Ellis. You have stepped over the line, this time, you're mad." The Judge said out loud.

Without knocking, two Security Officer's burst through the door.

The Judge got to his feet. "Take this man away and make sure you escort him off the premises," he demanded.

Taking an arm each, the security men, grabbed Ellis and escorted him out of the office. Yanking away from their grip, Ellis stormed through the door ahead of them.

Once they'd gone, Henderson closed the door and turned to see Justice Buckton with both hands gripping the arm of his chair, bent over as though in pain.

"Are you okay Your Honour?"

Without looking up, the Judge spoke in a low monotone voice. "The impudence of the man, I told him what he wanted to know. How dare he accuse me of murdering Laura, I loved that woman, she was what kept me going."

He clenched both fists and banged them down hard on the leather arm. "I didn't even have the luxury of attending her funeral to pay my last respects, for God's sake," He whimpered. "I have to mourn her death in secret." Straightening up, he turned to look at Alan Henderson. "I miss her Alan."

Henderson took out his mobile phone and pressed in a phone number.

"Inspector Dunn, Alan Henderson here, Chief Justice Buckton's solicitor, I'm sorry to be the bearer of bad news, there's been an incident here in the chambers and I think you should know."

Sergeant Ellis stood on the pavement feeling outraged by what had just taken place. Pulling his phone from his pocket, he called Inspector Dunn. Unbeknown to him, Inspector Dunn was now fully aware of what had transpired after Alan Henderson's call. As Ellis tried to speak, Inspector Dunn, stopped him mid-sentence and ordered him back to the office at once. Unable to get a word in edgewise, he gave up, allowing Inspector Dunn to rant. He was confused as to why Dunn was so angry with *him*. They had both agreed it was almost a foregone conclusion the Judge was responsible for Laura Verwood going over the rails of her balcony. And from what he'd heard, he was even more convinced. He'd never heard his boss so mad, now he was dreading facing him. The realisation he was now in deep shit, made Ellis feel unnerved, he would cop it big time when he got back to police headquarters.

Entering the main doors of the Command Centre, Julie Miller was standing by the elevator. Not feeling in the mood to talk to anyone and wanted to dodge out of sight, Ellis tried to slip past. She turned and smiled. "What's that look all about Ray, who's got your goat then?"

"Don't ask," he growled. They both stood in silence until Ellis couldn't contain himself any longer. He felt comfortable with Julie, he looked on her as a big sister and could always rely on her to say the right things or make him laugh.

Ellis banged his finger on the elevator button several times and tutted loudly. "I've just tried to arrest The Chief Justice Buckton at his chambers and was thrown out the building by two enormous Security Officer. Can you believe that?" he asked, dragging his fingers through his hair.

"Oh dear, d'you want to talk about it? Does Inspector Dunn know?" Julie asked.

"No I don't and yes he does, someone phoned ahead so he's waiting for me now, no doubt with a chopping axe," Ellis said gloomily looking down as he kicked an imaginary item with his foot, not speaking for a few moments. Without warning, he burst into life as he explained the reason for his actions.

"Well, he irritated me, the pompous shit. I listened to the man and couldn't cope with the fact he's up there all high and mighty, judging others. Just wait, though, he won't be so high and mighty when he's found guilty of murdering Laura Verwood. Once Dunn has sifted through all the evidence."

Julie listened patiently, waiting for him to finish telling her his story. She rested her hand on his forearm. "Ray, my advice to you is, be careful, you're letting your emotions get the better of you," she said, in a caring voice.

"I know, I know, I'm dreading facing Inspector Dunn, he's gonna haul me over the coals for sure. Especially as 'His Lordship' is a bloody old friend of his. This will not go down well."

"I don't think you need to worry about Inspector Dunn, from what I've gathered when I've spoken to him, he's indifferent towards the man… a criminal is a criminal as far as Dunn is concerned. You're right, though, he will have your proverbials for garters. The only thing I can advise is, just take the punishment like a man," she offered with a grimace. "Then I'll meet you for a drink after work and we can laugh about it. Or commiserate about you not having a job any longer," she giggled.

He looked at her doe-eyed with a forced smile. "Thanks, Julie, that's all I need to hear," he said as he punched her playfully on the arm. The lift jerked to a stop as it reached Ellis' floor. Stepping out, he turned back to give Julie a wink as the doors slid closed.

Ellis decided the best way to approach the situation he now found himself in was to face it full on. Barging through the doors of the incident room, he headed straight for Inspector Dunn's office. No one batted an eyelid as he marched through the main office as though on a mission. He knocked twice on the open door and entered without being asked. Inspector Dunn hastily ended his telephone conversation and placed his mobile phone on the desk in front of him.

"Close the door Raymond and take a seat, we need to talk," Dunn ordered, sounding offhand. In complete silence, moving as slowly as possible he closed a manila folder and placed it on top of a pile of folders at the side of his desk. Resting both arms on the desk in front of him, he expertly twirled a pen between his fingers.

Ellis slumped into the chair opposite Dunn brushed his hair back and he waited for the barrage of abuse he knew was coming.

After what seemed a lifetime, Inspector Dunn finally broke the silence as he spoke in a slow steady voice.

"Raymond, I've racked my brains wondering why on earth you took it on yourself to arrest Judge Buckton. All I asked you to do was to collect a DNA sample, *that's all*," Dunn said, suddenly raising his voice and banging both hands down on the desk in front of him. "How the hell did it go from that to an arrest? We still have a long way to go before we can lay charges on the man. My last words before you left were to *take it easy*. What's more, you have no authority to arrest a Judge."

"Can I at least explain what happened, Sir? Let me tell my version? I think I deserve to be heard." Ray said, trying hard not to raise his voice.

"Okay then, let me hear *your* version, tell me what happened in your own words and then we will discuss what needs to be done to salvage what we can from this debacle. As you can see, I'm *furious*; although let me warn you, nowhere near as annoyed as Superintendent Green, so be prepared for another bollicking. Let's hope he doesn't talk suspension," Dunn exclaimed. "I *cannot* afford to lose my main man at this stage of the game."

"All I can say, Sir, is he got to me. The man rubbed me up the wrong way from the moment I walked into his office, sitting there on his high horse, giving me this cock and bull story about how he loved both women equally. He prattled on how he couldn't give Laura Verwood up, but couldn't leave his wife either. He raved on about not wanting to hurt either of them. As far as I'm concerned, the evidence points to him being the one who threw Laura Verwood from the balcony and he gave me the impression he couldn't give a shit. I guess I snapped. I realise I let my emotions take over, which is not how we're trained."

Ellis nervously drummed his fingers rhythmically on the edge of the desk as he stared at the carpet, not speaking for a second; then sat bolt upright to resume his story.

"He relayed the whole story of how Laura had her first baby adopted and how he paid for an expensive clinic etc., etc., which we already know. He confirmed how he fixed it for him and his wife to adopt the second child and that Felicity had no idea he was the biological father. But the clincher is, Laura Verwood had no idea that the second baby she gave up for adoption, at his suggestion, was adopted by the Judge and his wife. The woman she begged him to leave for twenty years, so they could live happily ever after."

I'm sorry Sir, but I was infuriated when I heard those last words, how the man could be so false-hearted and, believing what he did was for all the right reasons. The supercilious shit." he mumbled the last words under his breath.

"It looks clear you've already beaten yourself up about what you've done. Although I can see your point, Raymond, I'm still not happy, but I think we better leave it there."

"Did you get round to taking a DNA swab?" Dunn asked.

"No, that was the first thing that set me off. The Solicitor, Alan Henderson refused to let me because he said, Judge Buckton would give a full confession."

Dunn's mobile phone buzzed in his pocket, interrupting their conversation. A text message from Superintendent Green lit up the screen. Dunn read it and groaned.

"Sorry Ray, I've been expecting this, we've been summoned. However, what I will do is, I'll speak to Superintendent Green first and give him all the information you've given me. You get us some good coffees and meet me in Green's office in about twenty minutes."

Sergeant Ellis rose to his feet. "I know you're both not happy with me, but in my defence, I was goaded by his holier-than-thou attitude. You would have done the same in my shoes. I keep thinking about the repercussion when this is all out in the open. The shit will really hit the fan when Lady Buckton finds out the truth. And God only knows the devastation it will cause for young Peter Buckton."

Without waiting for Dunn's response, Ellis stormed from the office.

Standing outside Green's office, Dunn checked to make sure his phone was turned off. *The last thing I want is to be disturbed in the next half hour.* He thought as he gave a knock and entered. "Fortis, we need to talk."

An hour later, after relaying Ellis' inexplicable outburst in Justice Buckton's Chambers and taking some time to placate him, Dunn gave a sigh of relief when Fortis began to calm down and agreed they needed to move quickly and interview him further.

"As you can see, Fortis, from the information we have, there *is* enough evidence to arrest Buckton, hence why Ellis thought he could. Buckton knowingly abused his official position and we have witnesses. The murder allegation is still very much a grey area at the moment; but if we question him further and put the thumb screws on, he might confess," Dunn scoffed.

A loud rap on the door made them both stop talking and turn to see Sergeant Ellis, carrying a cardboard tray holding three takeaway coffees. Placing them on the desk, he sat in the chair next to Dunn, giving a weak smile at the Superintendent.

"Okay, Ellis, Inspector Dunn has filled me in on what happened this morning and we've discussed it at long length. Personally, I could wring your neck for behaving so impulsively which could affect the case. Count yourself very lucky, I could have you suspended. However, Inspector Dunn has put up an extremely good case on your behalf. What the Judge admitted to you was remarkable and I have to admit I can see why it would be hard for you to swallow."

Dunn checked his watch before butting in. "Might I remind you, we need to make an arrest soon or we risk losing our credibility and our authority. However, we need to choose a time when he's most vulnerable when he hasn't got his sidekick solicitor to protect him."

A silence fell over the room while each one sipped their coffee while considering what Dunn had said.

Dunn sat up straight. "I've got it!" he blurted, banging his empty cardboard cup on the desk, sending froth over Ellis.

Superintendent Green and Sergeant Ellis both looked at him. "Go on," said Green.

"*The Honourable Chief Justice*, Clifford Buckton," he said, putting emphasis on his full title. "Is an avid golfer."

Green shrugged. "And you're telling us this, because?"

"I suggest we turn up at his next game and arrest him, while he's unaware and on his own."

"Brilliant, I like it," Green said eagerly.

Inspector Dunn glanced at his watch, "It's Tuesday today and as luck would have it, I know for a fact he'll be there this afternoon at two o'clock because he hounds me to join him."

"I suggest we bring along a reporter friend of mine. That way he can't wriggle out of anything, it will all be documented in the press." Green added.

Chapter 27

Looks like he's already here," Dunn announced as they parked in the almost empty car park of Sydney's oldest and most prestigious golf club at Rosebery. Dunn pointed to a black Mercedes parked a few bays up. "What about your man from the press?"

"See the blue MGF next to the Merc? That's *her*." Green replied. "I don't think she'd like being referred to as a man," Green said. "The name is Katrina Basenthwaite, she works for the Sydney Herald. Surely you've heard of her?"

"That's funny, when you said a reporter, I assumed it would be a man."

"I can assure you, this reporter is definitely not a man. Come to think about it, Stephen, you might like her, she's about your age and a tough nut like you, she could be your type," he remarked with a salacious grin.

"Not sure whether to be complimented or insulted at that. And since when have you thought of me as a tough nut?"

Fortis gave Stephen a sideways glance and shrugged his shoulders. "There's got to be someone out there that can put a smile on that miserable face of yours," he said as he opened the car door to climb out. Inspector Dunn grabbed his arm, pulling him back into the driver's seat.

"Have we decided how we're doing this? I don't think we should just barge in unannounced."

"I was just going over to say hello to Kat to let her know what we're doing. How about I go first and find out where he is, hopefully, he's still on the first hole, because it's a hike to the second one."

"No, I think we should walk in together, strength in numbers and all that."

"Okay Stephen, let's go."

As they approached the sports car, the door flung open wide. They stood and watched as an attractive brunette climbed out in an ungainly fashion, mumbling to herself.

"I've got to get rid of this fucking car! How am I supposed to get in and out without showing my knickers to the world," she cursed, not realising they were within earshot. Standing up and straightened her clothes she glanced over the top of the car to see Superintendent Green. "Fortis, darling, it's so good to see you again, it's been a while and who is this gorgeous creature?" she said boldly, nodding towards Inspector Dunn.

Fortis moved around the car to stand next to her and took her outstretched hand and pulled her towards him to place a friendly peck on her cheek. Keeping his arm around her shoulders, he swung her round so she was facing Inspector Dunn; who was not displeased at the way she looked. "Let me introduce you to Inspector Stephen Dunn, my oldest and best friend. Stephen, this colourful lady here is Katrina Basenthwaite from one of the biggest Sydney newspapers. Be careful what you say to her, she'll quote you and spread it all over Australia." He said with a smirk.

Katrina, tipped her head to one side. "You know me, always looking out for a good story, that's my job," she smiled before turning to Inspector Dunn, offering her hand for him to shake. "So good to meet you, Stephen. I've heard all about you and I can assure you, it's all good. Trust me, your secrets are safe with me. So, do you have any secrets you want to tell me?" she laughed out loud.

"You're incorrigible! And you'll be hard pushed to get anything out of this man, he's a dark horse."

"Hmm, I like a challenge," she said turning to Dunn. "We'll have to meet for drinks sometime."

"Okay, guys, we need to move, I'm hoping he's only at the first hole and hasn't batted off yet," Fortis said with a playful wink. Katrina opened the boot and took out a camera bag.

The three entered the foyer of the club that led into a large restaurant-cum-lounge which was deserted, making it easy for them to walk through without being stopped. French doors that stretched across the whole back wall, led out to a huge verandah with an expansive view of the golf green; as it disappeared into the distance. As they stepped out onto the verandah, Inspector Dunn breathed a sigh of relief to see Chief Justice Buckton was still at the first hole and alone. "There he is, let's go," he said out loud.

Walking across the well-manicured lawn as Katrina tried frantically to pull her camera from its case before they reached him. They watched as Justice Buckton took a perfect swing at the golf ball, sending it soaring into the sky then disappeared out of sight. He stood gazing into the air for a few seconds before turning to his golf buggy. A look of surprise spread over his face, seeing Inspector Dunn approaching him with two other people he didn't recognise.

"Hello there Stephen, at last, you've decided to join me? Except you're not appropriately dressed I'm afraid," The Judge called out. "Ah, you as well Superintendent Green," he added, after recognising the man standing next to Dunn. "How are you?"

Once the two men were up close to the Judge, Superintendent Green spoke in an authoritative tone. "We're not here to play golf, Your Honour and it's not a social meeting. We are here to arrest you in connection with the death of Laura Verwood. You do not have to say anything. But it may harm your defence if you do not mention when questioned, something which you rely on in court. Anything you do say can be given in evidence."

Justice Buckton threw down his golf club and pulled off his glove. "Here we go again… *for God's sake*… how do I get through to you lot?"

"I suggest you don't say a word, Cliff, this lady here is from the press," Dunn advised the Judge. "I suggest you have someone look after your golf equipment, we're taking you to police headquarters right now. There's a lot of loose ends we need to tie up."

Katrina clicked her camera and bombarded the Judge with questions while he was ushered towards the police car. He quickly telephoned his solicitor to meet him at the command centre.

“Was it your idea to bring the press along Stephen? I thought you and I were friends.”

“If you must know, it wasn’t my idea and don’t talk about being friends. I think it’s best we don’t speak, otherwise, I might say something I’ll regret.”

Buckton spent the long drive back to police headquarters in complete silence, staring through the window. Irritating Dunn with his repeated finger tapping. Green swung the car onto the driveway at headquarters, where a group of photographers and reporter s were already waiting.

“Looks like Miss Basenthwaite has informed her media friends already,” Dunn observed.

The crowd banged on the windows of the car, shouting out questions to the Judge, who had slunk down next to Inspector Dunn keeping his head down low.

Once inside the confines of the police headquarters, Justice Buckton was escorted to the interview room where his solicitor was waiting.

“Will you be sitting in on the interview, Fortis?” Dunn asked.

“No, I’ll leave that to you and Sergeant Ellis, I will be in the next room watching and listening. I hope to God, you’ve got the right man. If it looks like there’s any doubt, wrap it up and let him go, is that clear?”

“Yes, yes, I will. Rest assured, I will get answers one way or the other, did he push her or did she jump?”

“Maybe she jumped to get away from him.” Green offered.

They stepped from the lift to see Sergeant Ellis waiting to greet them, looking downcast.

Dunn stood next to him. "You okay, Ellis?"

"Yeah, why wouldn't I be? I was just miles away," he lied. He was concerned that if they discover Judge Buckton is not guilty of the death of Laura Verwood, he would be even more in the shit. "I'll be happy when this is over."

"Okay Ellis, let's find out if you're correct, in you go with Inspector Dunn. I'll be next door, watching on the TV screen."

Both detectives entered the interview room, followed by the duty sergeant. The Solicitor, Alan Henderson and the Judge were whispering to each other intently as Ellis and Dunn sat on the chairs on the other side of the desk. They stopped talking and Henderson leant forward and spoke to Inspector Dunn.

"I hope you know what you are doing Inspector, heads will roll when you realise what a huge mistake you are making."

"That's as it may be Mr Henderson, I suggest you sit quietly and let us get on with our job."

Dunn switched on the digital recorder and announced his name and that of Sergeant Ellis followed by the usual protocol required for interviewing a suspect.

"Your Honour, before we have any objections from either of you, I'm insisting the duty Sergeant is to take a DNA swab from you so we can confirm that you are the biological father of Peter Buckton and Peter Ashcott.

Alan Henderson whispered something in the Judge's ear. The Judge nodded to him in agreement.

"What you are saying is that now I've been arrested, I'm unable to object is that right?"

"Something like that," Dunn replied.

The two detectives waited in silence until the duty sergeant left the room.

"You've put me in a difficult situation, Dunn. When you realise you've made a terrible mistake, God knows what this will do to Felicity. She's not in the best health and she'll never forgive you. Come to think of it, I won't either. We go back a long way, I thought you knew me."

Dunn opened his mouth to speak wanting to retaliate. Then decided against it. This was not the time or the place for a personal matter. Instead, he stared at Buckton cold, hard expression, finding it disturbing he could turn it around so that someone else was the culprit. Taking a deep breath, Dunn opened the blue folder in front of him and flipped through the first few pages of the document inside. Taking out a single page, he began his questions. "Justice Buckton, you admitted to Sergeant Ellis that *you* are the biological father of Laura Verwood's two babies that she had adopted."

"That is correct."

"You also admitted that you kept the truth from Laura Verwood that it was, in fact, you and your wife who adopted the second child she gave birth to. You then raised the child with no knowledge, to him that he *was* adopted." Then added as a personal dig. "Or anyone else for that matter."

The Judge gave Dunn a blank stare. "That is correct."

"We have it on good authority you adopted the child by pulling a few strings. You used your position to jump the queue, so to speak."

The judge tilted his head to one side and frowned. "I suppose so. Understand, I did it for the best. It suited both women at the time and everyone was happy,"

"Everyone was *happy* you say? Is that what you thought? We all know how Laura Verwood suffered depression for years and even tried to take her own life on two occasions."

"*Yes* and *I* paid a lot of money so she could have the best treatment," The Judge baulked, intimating that that made everything right. "She was well looked after, that's one thing you can be assured of."

"During the twenty years of your affair, Miss Verwood begged you to leave your wife, you refused, knowing she was not of sound mind. You strung her along all those years, taunting her with lies and deception. You must have led her to believe that you'd leave your wife and set up home with her."

"I knew Laura was fragile, so said what she wanted to hear. There was no way I could leave my wife, but Laura was never to know that. I kept up the pretence, so she would never try to kill herself again. But it looks like I failed." He said, bowing his head.

"So you admit there was a possibility Laura could harm herself?"

"Of course, but while we were happy, I didn't think she'd try to harm herself again."

"You mean *you* were happy. Laura Verwood was not happy. Laura Verwood was a very unhappy lady, she'd lost both children she'd had with the man she loved desperately. She was forced to play second fiddle to a wife, always kept in the background. While the man she was in love with, lived the perfect family life with his wife and her child."

"She had no idea I had Peter. You're making it sound worse than it was."

"Tell me, how often did you visit Laura?"

"It wasn't easy, I have a very busy work schedule and my private life is also demanding…"

Dunn butted in impatiently. "*How* often did you meet up with Laura Verwood? Was it every week, once a month?"

"We always met on the same weekend, every month for years; which fitted in perfectly with my heavy commitments."

"Where did your wife think you were on those weekends?" Ellis asked.

"My wife understands the pressures of my work, therefore she understands when I take my weekend break away from everything and everyone. I have my own room at the Hydro Majestic in the Blue Mountains."

"How convenient for you," Ellis sneered, then had to bite his tongue so as not to blurt out something he would regret. The sheer arrogance of the man was riling him beyond belief. Trying to stay calm, he asked the question. "Are you able to tell us the last time you met up with Laura, before the night she died?

There was a brief silence as the Judge turned to stare out of the window next to him. By the look on his face, he remembered something unpleasant.

"Why do you ask?"

"We have it on very good authority that Laura phoned you from America, on her last trip about four weeks prior to her death and told you she'd found out that you had Peter, the son you persuaded her to have adopted. That you'd kept it from her that it was, in fact, you and Lady Buckton who adopted him. Justifiably, she was threatening to tell Lady Buckton everything.

"We met in a hotel in the city the day she got back from America. We talked for hours and yes, it got a little heated, she was angry. I wasn't able to pacify her and she left before we resolved things. I called her many times after that, but she kept asking me to do the impossible, to leave Felicity, or she would tell her everything."

You couldn't let that happen, could you? So you went to her apartment and confronted her. You argued and then pushed her over the balcony."

"No, you're wrong. I did go to her apartment because I knew she was leaving for America and I needed to settle things before she left. We never argued that night, we…" He paused.

"You what?"

Buckton coughed nervously. "We made love, if you must know. I loved that woman," The judge said, raising his voice. "How many more times do I have to tell you? Why do you keep banging on about it being me who pushed her over the balcony?"

"How do you explain that neighbours heard raised voices that night, one of which was a male?" Dunn lied, hoping to trick him.

As Justice Buckton said nothing, Inspector Dunn continued. "Were you really that naïve to think all this would stay hidden forever? You must've known the truth about Laura's second child would rear its ugly head one day?

"Yes, yes, I did. As I said earlier, the burden I've carried for eighteen years has been horrendous."

"Are you aware that both Peter's are best friends? They've both attended the same college for the past few years. Ironic, isn't it?"

A stunned look passed over the Judges' face.

"What? How can that be? They live under different circumstances. I know the first child was adopted by a very nice middle-class family, but there's no way they could afford Queens College."

"Well, that's true. However, unbeknown to you, Laura Verwood paid for Peter Ashcott's education."

The expression on Justice Buckton's face confirmed he had no idea what Dunn had revealed.

"They are both champion swimmers and have now gone into business together."

"What do you mean? What business? I'm afraid you are misinformed,"

Ellis interrupted before Dunn responded.

"They own a school for deep sea diving lessons and I can assure you this is true as I have dived with them on a few occasions."

The Judge jumped to his feet, sending his chair flying backwards, landing on the floor with a loud clatter.

"No, it can't be true, I will put a stop to it. I need to get out of here at once, I have to see my boy."

"Please sit down, you're not going anywhere till we're finished here," Dunn demanded as Ellis hurried to pick up the chair and entice the Judge to sit back down.

The solicitor shook his head. "Is this all necessary? Is my client to be charged with something or are we here just here for a chat?"

"Okay, let's talk about something else. Your client said he arrived at Laura Verwood's apartment at eight in the evening and left at around ten thirty. Is he still sticking to those times?"

Henderson gave the Judge a questioning look, prompting him to answer.

"Yes, that is correct, I have no reason to change my story," the Judge replied looking puzzled. "I caught a cab to Laura's when I left my chambers. Then when I left the apartment, I walked to the next block to hail a cab to take me home. This was always my routine on the rare occasions I visited her apartment."

Sergeant Ellis was finding it difficult to hide his annoyance. "You caught a *cab*? Are you sure about that? The reason I ask is, if you left at ten thirty in a cab, how do you explain your Mercedes being caught on a speed camera at ten thirteen on Darling road which is only a few minutes' drive from Laura Verwood's apartment?"

"That's impossible, as I said, I took a cab to Laura's apartment and then I took a cab home. I was definitely not driving my car that night. The reason I'm so sure is, I never drive at night. I have a chauffeur who drives me. Looks like your speed camera has got it wrong, Sergeant.

"So your chauffeur drove you to Laura's that night?"

"No, I went by *taxi*," Buckton snapped.

Removing a photograph from the folder in front of him, Dunn pushed it towards the Judge.

"This is the photo taken with our speed camera. As you can see, it is your car, the number plate is in full view and the time the photo was taken is printed at the bottom.

"This is impossible, it's a setup," he said looking bewildered. "As I told you already, I left around ten thirty, I know this because Laura was expecting a call from her producer in America and we had discussed the time difference between countries. We worked it out it would be about ten o'clock here in Australia when he rang. When I left Laura she was very much alive. We'd talked things through and she was excited about her trip. She mentioned something about taking a sleeping pill after the call from America, hoping to have a good night's sleep before the gruelling flight the next day." The Judge said, looking pitiful.

There was a short silence as Dunn glanced over Detective Jones's report regarding Miss Verwood's phone records.

"According to Laura's phone records, there were no calls made after ten thirty on her land line or mobile. However, a call *was* made from her landline to your home phone at nine forty-five pm." Dunn turned the list around allowing the Judge and his solicitor to have a better view, pointing to the entry with his pen. "Did you by any chance use Laura's landline while you were there? To phone your wife, perhaps?"

"No, I did not and I have no explanation why the record shows a call was made. Laura and I were in deep discussions or in bed throughout the whole time I was there. The only time we were not together is when I took a shower before I headed home, you know how it is?"

"Was that to get rid of any evidence, heaven forbid you should go home smelling of another woman's perfume." Ellis barked.

The Judge winced at the remark.

"Perhaps Laura phoned your wife while you were in the shower? After all, she was threatening to tell your wife everything, isn't that right." Ellis suggested. "I reckon there's only one way we can sort this out and that's to ask Lady Buckton to come in and tell us what she has to say."

The Judge's demeanour suddenly changed at the idea. He turned towards Henderson and whispered something in his ear. Henderson shook his head with a look of fear he would say something he might regret later.

Buckton sat up straight and spouted out in an angry manner. "All right, all right, I went by car. I got there about eight o'clock in the evening, we had dinner and a few glasses of wine and then we went to bed and made love, she's quite the demanding lady," he said with a forced smile. "Then we had a huge row, so I left just after ten. I felt bad, leaving, under those circumstances, knowing she was leaving the next day, so I drove back to the apartment."

Alan Henderson placed his hand on the Judge's arm to stop him from saying any more. The Judge pulled his arm away looking angry as he carried on talking.

"When I arrived back at the apartment, we made up and went out on the balcony, it seemed a romantic thing to do."

Listening intently, Dunn asked. "Did you unlock the doors to the balcony or just pull them open?"

"I turned the handles and pulled them open, what d'you think I did?" The Judge replied looking puzzled at the question. "Laura said she had taken extra sleeping tablets as she was upset by our row as she wanted to make sure she would sleep well. I walked back into the apartment and heard a scream when I turned round she was gone. All I could think was that a gust of wind must've swept her over the railings."

"So you say it was windy on the balcony?" Ellis asked.

"Yes, it was, that's right, it was windy" he replied sounding unsure.

Dunn and Ellis gave each other a sideways glance in disbelief. From the room next door, Superintendent Green gave a sigh of relief. Buckton had confessed at being there. It was all coming together and he had to admit once again, Dunn had been right all along.

"Tell me, when Laura fell, why didn't you call an ambulance or the police?" Dunn asked.

The judge looked at Dunn as though he was an idiot. "*It was eleven floors up*, for God's sake. I knew she couldn't have survived the fall so an ambulance would've been a waste of time and I couldn't call the police; I have my position to think of."

Sergeant Ellis was now shocked at the callous way the Judge was describing Laura Verwood's last moments. "What was Laura wearing, you must remember that? Was it a dress, a nightgown, did she have a cardigan or a coat on?" he asked.

The Judge paused for a moment. "I can't remember, I think it was a dress, yes, it was a dress with a cardigan thing over the top. It was chilly, so she was wearing a cardigan," The judge said as he demonstrated putting a cardigan on.

Once again Ellis and Dunn flashed each other sideways glances.

"So, after she fell, you left the apartment and drove straight home?" Ellis asked, sounding horrified.

"*Yes*, didn't I say that?" Buckton retorted.

Inspector Dunn held his hand up to halt Ellis, anticipating what he would say. "Can anyone confirm that?"

"Hmm, well, unfortunately, no, not really. When I arrived home, about midnight, Charles was in his quarters and so as not to disturb Felicity, I slept in the spare room that night."

"Can you repeat that loudly for the benefit of the recorder?"

The Judge repeated his last sentence slowly and with a hint of sarcasm.

"Right, that's enough," Henderson announced. "My client has said enough.

"You're right, Mr Henderson," Dunn said as he turned to the recorder. "For the benefit of the tape, the interview is terminated at sixteen fifty-five." Clicking the recorder off, Dunn looked directly at the Judge. "I need you to remain here until your wife arrives, Clifford. The officer will bring you a cup of tea, I'll be back in a while."

Dunn collected his paperwork and placed it back inside the folder. As he stood to leave, he tapped Ellis on the shoulder.

"Come with me Sergeant."

As Sergeant Ellis and Inspector Dunn left the interview room, Superintendent Green appeared from the connecting room.

"That's that then, he's confessed, well done Stephen,"

Inspector Dunn looked pensively at Superintendent Green. "Not quite,"

"What d'you mean, you've just got a confession from the man," Green baulked as he stared at him dumbfounded.

"Just trust me Fortis, leave it with me."

Opening his folder, Dunn took out the speed camera photo and handed it to Sergeant Ellis "Ask Jones to blow this photo up as large as he can. I need to know for sure it was *not* Buckton or his chauffeur driving."

Ellis made his way to the elevator, thankful he could have a breather from the interview wondering what Inspector Dunn knew that he didn't.

"Fortis, would you mind phoning Lady Buckton and ask her nicely to come on the pretence of collecting her husband. Don't mention anything about him being arrested, just that he's helping with our enquiries. I hope to God, she's not seen anything on the news."

"Why me?"

"Because she knows me, it might jeopardize things if she hears my voice."

The Superintendent headed back to his office to make the call, leaving Dunn alone to plan his line of attack and instruct the duty sergeant to inform him as soon as Mrs Buckton arrived. The sergeant agreed with a nod of his head as Inspector Dunn pressed the elevator button.

Circling Jones's computer, Lindsay, Jones and Ellis looked up as Inspector Dunn walked into the main office.

"What have you found Jones?"

"Wait till you see this Sir," Ellis called out. "It's definitely not Judge Buckton driving the Merc."

"Who is it then, let me see?"

The group parted, allowing Inspector Dunn to stand in front of the computer. Leaning forward, he securitized the image on the screen. Are you able to enlarge it any further?"

"Trouble is, Sir, it goes very grainy the larger I make it. It loses all clarity, watch."

The image became almost indefinable as Jones took the image to a higher level.

"I'd take a guess that that driver is a woman," Ellis called out.

"Only you would know that Ray," Jones replied. "Although I think you're right.

"Could it be Laura Verwood?"

"Nah, we know she didn't drive much so I hardly think she'd drive at night and anyway, she was a brunette. That person looks like a blonde" Ellis offered.

"What about Lady Buckton?" Ellis suggested. "She's blonde."

There was a short pause as all five men leaned towards the screen vying for space.

When the phone rang on Ellis' desk, Lindsay picked it up and listened for a moment. He placed his hand over the mouthpiece and called out to Inspector Dunn.

"Apparently, Lady Buckton has arrived and is at the front desk, Sir. Do you want her to be taken to the interview room where Judge Buckton is waiting, Sir?"

"Good grief no, tell the Sergeant to take her to the waiting room till I get there. In light of what we have just seen in the photo and the fact the Judge has just made up a complete phoney story about Laura Verwood's death, I do not want them alone together for a second so they can collude with each other.

"Did you get all that Sergeant," Lindsay smiled, then replaced the receiver.

Sergeant Ellis and Inspector Dunn returned to the interview room where the Judge and Henderson were waiting patiently. Discarded coffee mugs and a plate with a half-eaten biscuit, sat on the desk in front of them. Dunn ordered another chair to be brought to the interview room and for the dishes to be cleared away' as he and Sergeant Ellis sat down ready to continue the interview.

"Just letting you know Cliff, Felicity has just arrived. We will wait till she joins us here in the interview room before we begin. Buckton gave a blank look and said nothing. Two loud raps on the door made everyone turn. The desk sergeant entered, followed by Lady Buckton who looked puzzled. The sound of chairs, scraping on the wooden floorboards resonated around the room as everyone stood at the same time, to greet Lady Buckton. Her facial expression changed to one of delight at this gesture. Her eyes scanned the room till they fell upon her husband. No one objected as he stepped forward and took her hand and led her to the empty chair next to his.

Once seated, everyone followed suit and waited for Inspector Dunn to speak. Lady Buckton looked at Sergeant Ellis and then to Inspector Dunn, pleadingly.

"Stephen, what is this all about? Why are we here?"

"Thank you for coming in so promptly, Felicity, don't be alarmed," said Dunn, trying his best to keep her calm. "We have had Clifford here helping with our enquiries. And now I need to ask you a few questions to clear up a few matters," He said, pausing to look at Henderson, expecting an objection.

"You look so serious, Stephen… Am I allowed to call you Stephen here, or do I have to call you Inspector Dunn?" She smiled. "What has Clifford been telling you?"

"It's perfectly okay to call me Stephen. Before we discuss what Clifford has told me, I need to ask you something."

"Ask away, Stephen."

"You are familiar with the name Laura Verwood?"

A look of trepidation spread over Felicity Buckton's face at the mention of the name. Nervously twisting her wedding ring on her finger, she replied: "Yes, she is the biological mother of my son Peter."

"And you're well aware that Laura Verwood fell to her death almost two weeks ago."

Lady Buckton sighed before answering. "Yes, yes, I do," she stammered as she cast her eyes down at her hands nervously. "How awful, that poor, poor woman,"

"Now I want you to think back to the night she fell, do you remember getting a phone call around nine thirty? Take your time, there's no rush."

Justice Buckton banged both hands on the desk. "This is ludicrous, how could she possibly remember that?"

Inspector Dunn held his hand up towards the Judge. "Clifford, I suggest you refrain from any more outbursts, this is not helping." He turned to Lady Buckton. "Felicity, I'll ask you again, think hard, was there a call made to your landline."

"I'm trying to think, we get lots of calls, mostly for Clifford."

"I believe Clifford wasn't home that night, therefore, you would've answered this call."

Clifford Buckton stared at his wife as a feeling of dread swept through his whole being at what was about to be revealed to her. He felt sick to the pit of his stomach at how much he'd hurt the two most wonderful women in the world. He couldn't contain himself any longer.

"For God's sake Felicity, you may as well tell him, he already knows who phoned you, he needs you to say it for the sake of the tape," Buckton cried out.

Lady Buckton glared straight into her husband's face and without averting her eyes, she spoke in a slow fitful voice.

"You're correct, I answered a call… it was Laura Verwood… she sounded so angry and was saying there were things I should know about my husband," Mrs Buckton paused for a second. "She… she, she told me that the biological father of my son… our son, Peter… was Clifford, that Clifford was Peter's real father. I was confused as she was a little incoherent, I could just make out what she was saying. I was in shock. Then she said she'd been having an affair with my husband for twenty years and that Clifford and she were Peter's real parents, his biological parent."

Lady Buckton turned and looked straight at Inspector Dunn pleadingly. I thought at first, it was some joke Stephen. I thought it was some sick person who had a vendetta against Clifford because he'd found them guilty; someone who wanted to hurt us. How could this woman possibly think I'd believe her?"

"So you didn't believe her?" Ellis asked astounded.

Lady Buckton turned from Inspector Dunn and looked at Ellis before answering.

"Not… at first. Then she said something… something she could only know if she associated with Clifford." Lady Buckton said, turning back to look her husband straight in the eyes.

"What did she say to make you change your mind?" Ellis asked.

"She asked how I could possibly stay with a man who detested me, how he made fun of me behind my back. I really thought this was the ramblings of an evil mad woman until she said..." Suddenly, Lady Buckton stopped speaking as her eyes welled with tears. She quickly covered her face with both hands, as a heart-wrenching sob emanated from her lips. Inspector Dunn took out a neatly folded white handkerchief and reached over and handed it to her.

Justice Buckton lowered his eyes as he waited for her to compose herself and carry on with her story.

"She asked me what I thought he was doing on the last weekend of each month; that they'd been meeting up at their love nest in the Blue Mountains for twenty years. Then she said that Clifford was with her and they'd... they'd."

"Go on Felicity, what did she say?"

"That… they'd just had amazing sex." Felicity's head fell forward as she covered her face with the crumpled handkerchief and silently cried. The room fell silent while everyone waited for her crying to stop. She rested her hands on her lap. "I kept telling her she was lying, I knew Clifford was working late and he would never lie to me."

Sergeant Ellis coughed as he tried to hide a groan discharging from his throat, hearing what this poor woman was having to reveal.

"So what did you do?" Dunn asked.

"I slammed the phone down, I couldn't listen to her any longer. Then I phoned Clifford's office. I was put through to security, who informed me he'd left hours earlier to meet a client. That's when I realised that perhaps she was right. I asked for the address of the client."

"So you drove to the address they gave you, intending to confront him," Dunn asked.

Lady Buckton made eye contact with her husband once more. "Yes, I drove to the address in Balmain, an apartment block. One side of me knew this woman was lying, but one side of me couldn't help thinking all the evidence was there. What was I supposed to think?"

"So what time would that have been?"

"It was about ten o'clock because the news was on the radio. I parked across the street from the building giving me a perfect view of the main doors and the side garage entrance. Can you imagine how I felt when the garage roller doors opened to see my husband skulk out? He walked straight past me, he didn't even recognise his own beautiful shiny Mercedes… *Or his wife sitting in the driver's seat,*" she said loudly as she sobbed uncontrollably, her face contorting, making her very unattractive.

Inspector Dunn had a strong urge to give her a comforting hug. He couldn't imagine the emotional turmoil she must be going through.

Trying to speak between convulsive gasps, Lady Buckton continued. “I watched him hail a cab then he was gone. I would have confronted *him*, but it was Laura Verwood I wanted to talk to.”

Inspector Dunn glanced at Justice Buckton who was sitting in stunned silence. Buckton had no idea his wife had watched him leave the apartment that night.

“How did you know what apartment she lived in? You would have had to get through the main entrance doors which need a key or a code.” Ellis asked.

“My car is a little unreliable at the moment,” she fretted. So that’s the reason I was in Clifford’s Mercedes. I hate driving that car, it scares me. I don’t know what made me search the glove compartment. I found a remote door key and on the keyring was a large plastic card with the address painted in black. The remote allowed me to enter through the main doors of the apartments and work the elevator.

I knocked on Laura Verwood’s apartment and within minutes I could hear her calling out something like, ‘*You’re back again? What have you forgotten?*’ The door swung open wide and there she was. The woman my husband had been seeing for twenty years behind my back. I remember she had a look of sheer panic as she stood staring at me.”

The silence in the interview room was almost deafening as everyone focused on what Lady Buckton was about to say.

“What did she do then?”

“She said, ‘*Oh, it’s you!*’ which surprised me because we have never met.”

"So how did she know who you were?" Dunn asked before turning to the Judge. "Clifford, how did Laura Verwood know Felicity?"

Speaking In a croaky voice, Buckton replied. "Because Laura was fixated by my wife, she had seen her at functions or in newspaper articles. It wasn't difficult for anyone to check Felicity out, she's a socialite."

"So… Felicity, what happened then? Did you argue?"

"It was horrible, when Laura Verwood opened her apartment door, I heard a loud banging sound from inside the apartment. I thought someone else must've been there. She tried to close the door on me, but I pushed it open, then she ran into the lounge. The French doors were wide open and I remember the white curtains were blowing madly. Understand, I only wanted to talk to her." Lady Buckton pleaded, her voice shaking. "I wanted to ask her why she was being so cruel. But she began to act strange, talking in her throat like a demented woman with bulging eyes. I kept moving towards her, but she kept backing away while talking in this manic voice."

"She was saying terrible things, like I was a dried up old prune, how Clifford and she laughed at me when they were together. Then she said Clifford hated…" she stopped talking for a moment as she looked down at Detective Dunn's crumpled handkerchief on her lap. "You know,"

"What Felicity, what did she say?"

A heart-wrenching sound emanated from Lady Buckton as she forced out the next sentence.

"He hated having sex with me," she cried out, then covered her face with the hanky. It was all Inspector Dunn could do to stop himself from wrapping his arms around her, letting her know everything will be okay. But he knew that wasn't possible and it wasn't true. Everything would not be okay and the sad fact was, the lives of the Buckton's were shattered and about to change forever.

The Judge remained silent, not daring to utter a word.

Alan Henderson glared at Inspector Dunn. "You'll have to leave it there Inspector Dunn, Lady Buckton is very distressed."

Dunn knew he was right, but they were almost there. He held the palm of his hand towards Henderson. "Just two more minutes."

"Keep going Felicity, what happened after she said all those things, did you get mad? Did you push her out onto the balcony?"

"No, I didn't push her, she kept backing away from me. The balcony doors were wide open so she backed out through the doors and onto the balcony. Yes, I was angry, but I was hurt, devastated by what she was saying and how she was saying it."

Sergeant Ellis now asked a question. "She must have been freezing going out on the balcony. Do you recall what she was wearing that night?"

"It never occurred to me she'd be cold, that was the last thing on my mind. I do remember she *was* wearing a silk nightdress because she was having trouble holding it down as she stood close to the French doors."

Inspector Dunn and Ellis gave each other a triumphant smile. That was the correct answer, Laura Verwood was wearing a nightdress when she fell and not a dress and a cardigan as The Judge had described earlier.

Alan Henderson reached over to Lady Buckton and placed his hand on her arm. "Lady Buckton, you do not have to say another word."

Dunn half expected him to say that. "Just one more question, if you don't mind."

"Felicity, did *you* go out on the balcony? Did you follow her out?""

Lady Buckton looked directly at her husband.

"Please Lady Buckton, it is important, we need to know if you saw her fall or did you push her?" Dunn pleaded.

No one said a word, you could hear a pin drop. Ellis was just about to say something when Lady Buckton spoke.

"As I already said, she was saying dreadful things and I wanted her to stop, she kept backing away from me. I reached out to put my hand over her mouth to shut her up, it all happened so quickly, I remember there was a huge blast of wind. She seemed to trip backwards and then she was gone, I'll never forget her screams as long as I live" Lady Buckton said as she stared ahead as though in a trance.

"What did you do then?" Ellis asked.

She snapped herself out of it. "I panicked, I wanted to get out of there. All I could think was I needed to get home as quick as possible before anyone turned up. There was no one in the foyer so I was able to walk out without seeing anyone. When I got home, I thought Cliff would be waiting up for me, but the place was in darkness. As I walked along the hall to our bedroom I passed the spare room and heard snoring. I guessed Cliff must have come home and not wanting to disturb me, had decided to sleep there. It wouldn't have occurred to him I wasn't in bed at all.

"So he had no idea you'd gone out that evening?"

Lady Buckton nodded her head. "That's right."

Inspector Dunn leaned back in his chair and gave out a big sigh of relief thinking, at last, he had answers.

"Okay, that's it," Henderson jumped to his feet and announced. "Lady Buckton does not understand what she is saying, she's distraught, and you've goaded her till she's now talking hysterically. Her memory is clouded, she's in shock. It's obvious that Laura Verwood jumped of her own accord. The woman was of unsound mind. I would like the last part of Felicity's statement erased from the tape.

"*Please sit down, Mr* Henderson," Dunn scolded.

"Henderson is right, my wife *is* confused, I have already told you, it was me who was with Laura that evening. It was my fault she fell, but it was a tragic accident, nobody pushed her. How many more times do I have to tell you? My wife is the innocent one in all this."

Suddenly, without warning, Lady Buckton got to her feet and stood over her husband as though possessed. "You're right, you despicable man, it *was* all your fault, you've lied all this time, you've lied to me, to Peter and dare I say it, to that woman too," she screamed. "I've given you everything, you wouldn't be where you are today if it wasn't for me."

Henderson reached out to calm her down. Pushing his hand away, she continued to rant at Buckton whose head was bowed, unable to face her.

"All this time, you've known you are Peter's biological father and you never said a word. For eighteen… years… how could you?" Lifting her clenched fist in the air, she brought it down with force across his face almost knocking him off his chair.

Sergeant Ellis leapt towards Lady Buckton and grabbed her arm as she was about to take another swing. Coaxing her back to her chair, he looked at Buckton. "Tell me, have you known all along your wife was responsible for Laura falling?"

Buckton took a few minutes before answering as he regained his composure. "No, I didn't, not until you said my car was caught on the speed camera. Then I thought about what you said about a phone call being made to my home. I had a shower at Laura's apartment, that's when she must have rang Felicity, I put two and two together. I thought she must have jumped. I've been trying to end things for months and that night I tried to end our relationship. I told her it was over." The Judge looked sheepishly at his wife. "She begged me to make love one more time. I'm sorry Felicity, I'm so sorry my love," he cried out as tears streamed down his face.

A mixture of shock, hate and pain spread over Lady Buckton face as she slithered out of her chair onto the floor in a dead faint. Dunn reached over and quickly switched off the digital recorder as the solicitor and Ellis hurried to Lady Buckton's side to help her back onto her seat where she sat dazed and limp. The Duty sergeant dashed out of the room and returned with a glass of water. The Judge leant towards his wife and gripped her arm, which she threw off with force.

Inspector Dunn stood up and pushed his chair backwards with the back of his legs, fixing his eyes directly on Lady Buckton

"It's my duty to arrest you for your involvement in the suspicious death of Miss Laura Verwood. I'll arrange for the duty doctor to come and see you, as I think you might need a sedative."

"Stephen you can't arrest her," The Judge cried out, grabbing Dunn's sleeve in desperation. "Arrest me, it wasn't Felicity, I've confessed, what more do you need?"

"I'm sorry Cliff, your confession means nothing. There're too many inconsistencies. It was very gallant of you to protect your wife. Also ironic. However, we now have strong evidence that Felicity *was* involved." Dunn said as he pulled his arm from his grip. "We will leave you with your solicitor for a while so he can advise you what to do next."

The room cleared, leaving the Buckton's and Alan Henderson on their own. As Ellis and Dunn stood outside the interview room they were joined by Superintendent Green looking pleased.

"Okay, go on, say it, you know you're dying to,"

"Now, what could that be? D'you mean, *I told you so*?"

Ellis gave the Superintendent a winks. "He was right all along that there was foul play. You do realise, from now on, he'll be impossible to live with."

"Joking aside Stephen, well done," Green said, giving him a well-founded slap on the back.

"I'm just saddened that Lady Buckton got tangled up in all this after what her husband has done; and believe me, it will get very messy. A lot of stuff will come out. God only knows how their son Peter will handle what's about to be revealed to him."

"I'm stunned Lady Buckton was involved at all, she gave no sign whatsoever that day we visited their home. Not in my wildest dreams did I think there'd been a problem between them. Lady Buckton was the perfect hostess, serving tea and cake. I got the impression the Buckton's were the perfect couple. I actually really liked her" Ellis said.

"Maybe it's because I know them, but I noticed their body language and there was just something not right. Then I remembered something Felicity said. When she was talking about when they adopted the baby, she said Clifford was very thorough He'd had the mother checked out so well, it was like he knew her personally. There was a touch of sarcasm in her voice and mannerisms."

"I didn't pick up on anything and to think, it happened only days before we visited them."

"I guess she could shut it out of her mind, something to do with the English stiff upper lip perhaps," Dunn commented. "What I find weird, is he had no idea she'd visited Laura Verwood and she had no idea he was having an affair for years with Verwood. They both kept enormous secrets from each other makes you think doesn't it?"

"To stay single you mean?" Ellis added making them laugh.

"Changing the subject slightly," Dunn said, suddenly sounding serious. "We need to get the results of Buckton's DNA test, proving once and for all he is the biological father of the two boys. Then we had better go pay them a visit."

"We should go first thing tomorrow morning, they'll be at the dive school," Ellis advised.

"Expect the worst then," Superintendent Green said.

Chapter 28

Charles left the Command Centre with Judge Buckton slumped in the passenger seat next to him. As he drove through the slow moving evening traffic towards the Buckton's residence, the Judge broke into an emotional account of the events that had transpired over the last few hours. With the expertise of a psychologist Charles listened without interruption. In his twentieth year of employment with Judge Buckton, Charles was much more than his butler, he was his confidant and had shared the deep secret he'd been hiding in all that time.

"The next few hours talking to Peter will be unbearable. I'm not even sure what to say and how to tell him, it's all such a mess."

Only when the Judge took out a neatly folded white handkerchief and turned away to blow his nose, did Charles speak.

"The boy has a lot to take in, all you can do now, is for you to tell him the truth. Begin and the beginning. Honesty is your best policy from here on. No doubt he will react badly at first, but he's young, time will heal all wounds and he will come round when he sees things more clearly. I have every confidence in you and I'm sure it will work out in the end." Charles stopped talking as he executed the drive through the wrought iron gates and parked in front of the house.

"Thank you, Charles, I suggest you go to your quarters, lock your doors and turn your music up loud," he said with a forced smile.

As Judge Buckton entered the expansive foyer, he thought it strange the house was so quiet. Assuming Peter must be out for the evening he let out a sigh at the thought his talk with his son would have to be delayed. He burst into the formal lounge to find Peter sprawled across the sofa wearing the largest headphones he'd ever seen with his eyes closed, absorbed in whatever it was he was listening to; clearly unable to hear any other noise around him.

With caution, Buckton approached Peter and gently shook his leg causing him to sit bolt upright causing the headphones to fall off. "Shit dad, you gave me the fright of my life! I didn't hear you come in," he burst out.

"Clearly… I think you were in another world." The judge said as he gazed into Peter's eyes, thinking to himself what a good looking boy he was. He had always been extremely sensitive, and ironically, a bit of a mummy's boy. Peter moved over to one side of the sofa, allowing his father to sit next to him. The Judge placed his hand on Peter's shoulder in a fatherly gesture.

"Peter… I've got something to tell you… it's not very pleasant so you need to brace yourself."

"Goodness dad, this sounds serious, it's not mum, is it? Where is she? Where's mum, don't tell me something has happened to her?" he said, sounding anxious.

"Yes, it's about mum, but there's so much more I need to explain to you, please, just listen. You know I love you very much… you mean more to me than life itself. Everything I've ever done is for you Peter, you have to believe that…"

Knocking the hand off his shoulder, the boy butted in. "Dad, you're scaring me. What are you trying to say?"

Judge Buckton began the long explanation surrounding Laura Verwood. How he'd had an affair, resulting in her getting pregnant and giving birth to a baby boy; who was adopted at six weeks. He continued with his story, not leaving anything out. He told how Laura had given birth to another boy while Peter listened, not saying a word until Judge Buckton said the fateful words.

"Peter… Laura's second child is you. Mum and I adopted you. We both love you dearly."

Peter's hands shot up, covering his mouth as he rocked back and forth. A sudden wave of nausea surged through his body. Judge Buckton placed his hand on his son's shoulders once again, only to have it pushed away as Peter leapt to his feet and paced back and forth, without uttering a word.

"Peter… talk to me… say something,"

Peter stopped pacing, he turned to his father and stared hard. Judge Buckton stood up, his arms outstretched, pleading. "I'm so sorry you had to find out like this…"

Before he could finish his sentence, Peter pulled his arm back and with all his strength, took a swipe at his father, knocking them both off balance, falling onto the sofa.

Leaping to his feet, Peter rained blows down on his father's body "*How could you*? *How could you do that to mum? I hate* you," he screamed. Buckton managed to get to his feet and grab his son, wrapping his arms around him as tightly as he could to restrain him. Peter resisted for a while as he tried to free himself from his father's grip as he continued yelling at the top of his voice.

"Peter, Peter, listen to me, please listen to me."

Peter covered his ears with cupped hands. "I don't want to hear anything more you have to say. Where's mum? I want to see mum."

"I'll take you to see her tomorrow, please Peter, I need to tell you something else."

After much persuasion, Peter finally agreed to sit back on the sofa and listen while the Judge continued with his story, relaying the circumstances surrounding Laura Verwood's death. Peter sat motionless, listening to everything his father was saying without uttering a word. Suddenly, without warning, Peter jumped up and marched over to an ornate wooden cabinet with an assortment of framed family photos. One by one he picked them up and smash them to the floor. Blaspheming with each one.

Judge Buckton tried to stop him, but it was futile. He watched as Peter ripped the expensive oil painting of their family from the wall and slammed it across the back of a leather chair, splitting it in two. Judge Buckton slumped onto the sofa and watched helplessly while his son destroyed one expensive ornament after another.

Peter marched towards the door and yanked it open then turned to look at his father with hate in his eyes.

"Where you going Peter, don't leave, there's so much more to be said. Please don't leave."

"I'm not staying here, I don't want to see you again and I don't want to hear anything else you have to say." He bawled, before slamming the door as hard as he could.

By the time Judge Buckton made his way through the debris of broken ornaments into the hall, he heard the sound of an engine revving and the screech of wheels spinning on gravel. Flinging the front door open, all he could see was a huge cloud of dust billowing into the air as two red, rear lights disappeared into the distance.

Peter dragged the back of his hand across his tear soaked face, blinding him momentarily. As the car swerved, the sound of a horn blasting brought him to his senses, making him slow down. He wasn't sure where he was going, he wasn't sure if he wanted to see anyone. There was so much to take in, his head was buzzing from everything his father had told him. He pulled over to think things through. Suddenly he had the urge to talk to Ray, he would understand, he thought to himself.

Peter pulled out his mobile phone and dialed Ray's number and within seconds, Ray answered.

"Hi Ray, its Fish," he croaked.

"Are you okay buddy? You don't sound too good. D'you want to talk?"

"I don't know, I don't know what I want, it's all gone wrong Ray."

"I take it your dad has told you what's been going on?"

"Yes, yes, he told me everything… about his affair for twenty years behind mum's back… with the woman who fell from the balcony… the woman who is Asho's real mother. Turns out she's my mother too and dad is Asho's dad." A silence followed as though Fish had suddenly realised what that meant. "Asho and I are... *brothers*!" he exclaimed.

"And that's a good thing?"

"Yes, but it gets worse... much worse... mum caused the woman to fall... she's at the station. Because of dad, mum is in trouble... there's so much to take in, I don't know what to think anymore."

"Where are you now?"

"I dunno... on the highway somewhere, I don't know where I am, I've left home, I don't want to go back," he wailed.

"You're not driving are you?"

"No, I've pulled over, I feel sick."

"Fish, listen to me," Ellis started. "Go to Asho's house. You need to be with someone and it should be him."

"You're probably right, everything's so hideous. Mum's been locked up so I can't see her. I need to talk to her. She'll be all alone and in a mess. How could dad lie to her, to both of us, all these years?"

"Promise me you'll go straight to Asho's? I'll call and let him know you're on your way, he's not only your best friend... he's your brother, remember? You need each other more than ever now. I'll try and arrange for you to see your mum tomorrow, okay?

Swinging his car into the driveway of Mr and Mrs Ashcott, Fish braked too hard making a loud screeching sound. Switching off the engine he gripped the steering wheel and stared ahead into the darkness for a few moments, feeling apprehensive about facing anyone. The front door swung open and Asho appeared, hands on hips. "When you gonna learn how to drive that thing properly?" he called out, taking the two front steps in one leap and bounded towards Fish. "I think you've woken the whole neighbourhood."

As promised, Ray had called Asho, giving him the heads up he was on his way and in an extremely delicate state after hearing what had transpired that day, giving an abridged version of what Justice Buckton had divulged to Fish, regarding Laura Verwood. Leaving out the bit about being both their biological sons of Buckton, feeling that was up to Fish to tell him. Although it had come as a shock to Asho that Laura Verwood was his mother, he took the news well and was keen to talk everything through with Fish. Ray had warned him to tread carefully so in his infinite wisdom, Asho decided to treat Fish no differently than usual. He was thrilled to hear they were half-brothers, making sense as to how they looked alike and had similar interests.

Fish closed the car door and leant his back against it with his head bowed. He looked pale and drawn in the filtered light from the house. Asho stood in front of him feeling awkward, searching his brain for something to say.

"So… half-brothers eh?" He said, which all he could come up with.

Fish raised his head and stared at him for a moment. "Half-brothers?"

"Yeah! We have the same mothers… making us half-brothers."

"We have the same *father's*… my father is you're biological father... there's no half… we're full blown brothers. Dad's been having an affair for over twenty years and when mum found out…" he paused for a second. "She… she…" unable to continue, he covered his face with both hands and bent forward, his shoulders heaving as he silently sobbed.

"Come inside and we'll talk, mum and dad are out and Jenni's here."

Fish grabbed Asho's arm. "You realise I can never go back to that house… and I don't think I will ever be able to look at dad… I hate him."

"Our dad! Let's get inside."

Asho and Jenni listened in awed silence while Fish relayed everything his father had told him. Suddenly, Asho remembered they had a dive the next day and decided it would be the best therapy for all of them to go out on the boat.

"Are you going to be up for a trip out on the boat tomorrow?"

Fish gave a look that was a mixture of despair and anger. "I don't feel like going out on the boat tomorrow or ever again, I don't feel like doing *anything* anymore," he whimpered.

Jenni stretched over and patted his knee. "That's understandable Fish, you're in shock at the moment. We'll cancel the dive, that's not a problem. Except, I hate to tell you, we will need to drive to the shop so I can phone the people booked in. All the names and numbers are in my desk drawer."

"That's okay, we'll all go now, it shouldn't take too long and it's not that late," Asho said, jumping to his feet.

The drive to the dive shop was quick, with hardly any traffic to hold them up. Jenni unlocked the doors and headed inside. After switching on the lights she took the list out of the desk drawer, made herself comfortable and began making the calls. Asho grabbed Fish's arm and crossed the street to the marina where they both stood gazing out over the ocean watching the last remnants of sun as it set on the horizon.

"It will be a lovely sunny day tomorrow and according to the weather forecast, the conditions are going to be perfect for a dive. Why don't we go out on our own, just the two of us? We can have another search around to see if we can find anything."

"I know what you're doing Asho, but the answer is no. I'm not going out on the boat, not tomorrow, *not ever*." Fish's voice boomed.

"Can I take that as a maybe?" Said Asho hoping to humour him.

"Jesus Christ, Ash, my whole world has just come crashing down around me and all you can talk about is going out looking for your stupid fucking treasure. I can't believe you can even suggest it, you fuckwit. You're too stupid to understand what I'm going through. Let me spell it out, I… DON'T… WANT… TO… GO… ON… THE… BOAT.., GOT IT?" Fish said out loud as he swung his body around, kicked an empty drink carton out of his way and started to walk back to the shop.

After he'd walked a few steps, Asho shouted after him. "*You don't fool me…* you can insult me all you like, but I know you better than anyone, and I know you really want to go out, you love that boat and you love diving. Admit it, you're as keen as I am to find something out there"

Fish stopped dead in his tracks. He turned and slowly walked back towards Asho. “Ewan Wallace has already told us the area has been searched to death with no success. What makes you think *you* will find *anything*? Just leave it alone, why don’t you.” Fish snapped.

Asho’s mouth drooped at the corners. “Forget it then, I just thought going out on a dive might be therapeutic, it might help with the healing process,” he sniveled. Then a sudden thought struck hearing what Fish had just said. “Hang on a minute, what did you just say?”

“What part? That I don’t want to go out on the fucking boat?”

“No, the bit about Ewan Wallace saying the area has been searched to death! How would he know that? He said he was new to the area. Who loaded the search locality into the laptop that day we went out with the tow fish?”

“He did, I let him, seeing he was the expert with the equipment. Then I took over once he’d programmed it in.

“Hmm, let’s go to the cabin and check it out,” Asho suggested, pleased that Fish had momentarily stopped yelling at him.

They clambered onto the boat and headed for the cabin where Fish opened the laptop and fired it up. With their heads almost touching, they stared at the small screen.

Asho leaned forward and tapped the screen with his finger. “See, he marked out around the shipwreck. That’s not where I found the coin,”

“Why would he do that?” Fish asked.

“Good question. D’you think he set us up? If you remember, he wasn’t happy when we wanted to go back down, he tried to stop us.

"But, in his defence, that was for safety reasons."

"Or *was* it? Or was it to put us off the scent, stop us from searching elsewhere?"

"So what you're saying is that we should go back down on our own and check out the area where you found the coin?"

"Exactly. That's what we should do tomorrow, don't you agree," Asho said, sounding elated.

"You're right, we know how to use the equipment now. We don't need help from anyone and should keep it to ourselves what we're doing. With a bit of luck, we might find more coins," said Fish as he closed the laptop and stood up without speaking.

Asho ruffled Fish's hair with a stupid grin on his face. "That's what I wanted to hear… little bro."

Fish got to his feet as though about to start a bit of rough and tumble. But instead, threw his arms around Asho's shoulders in a strong man hug.

"It's okay Asho, I know I'll get through all this. I just thank God I have you."

The sound of a car horn made their heads snap round.

"We better go, looks like Jen is finished with her calls," Asho said, climbing over the rail of the boat.

Fish caught hold of Asho's sleeve. "I know by the way,"

Asho threw Fish a curious look. "You know what?"

"About you and Jenni. I saw you together the morning you got to the shop earlier than me. You were in a bit of a clinch," he laughed. "And before you say anything, I couldn't be happier. I just wonder why you kept it such a secret."

"I don't know either, it was Jenni's idea not to tell you just yet."

Asho wrapped his arm around Fish' neck. You've no idea how much it's been killing me. Come on then, we better let Jen know that you know that I know," they both laughed out loud.

At the Ashcott's house, Jenni place two cups of coffee and an open packet of biscuits on the coffee table in front of the boys and stepped back. "I'm off, I'm buggered and you two need some time together."

"Okay, see you tomorrow," said Asho with a flick of his hand.

Fish waited till she'd gone. "You don't have to put an act on now, haven't you told her?"

"It can wait, I have too many other things on my mind."

Fish rested his elbows on his knees. "It hurts, Asho like you wouldn't believe, it's all so bazaar and I don't know how I'll ever come to terms with it all, and mum causing someone to die. I desperately need to see her. Ray says he'll try and arrange it, and then I think I'll feel so much better."

Asho rested his hand on Fish's shoulder. "None of us can take the pain your feeling away, but we can try to make it hurt a little less. We're brothers, we're in this together."

Chapter 29

"I reckon today will be a perfect day, weather-wise," Asho remarked as he and Fish stood on the rear deck of their boat, staring towards the sun, rising over the horizon, evaluating the conditions.

Asho pulled his tracksuit top over his head, rolled it up and threw it to one side. "I'm already sweaty and it's still early. You've no idea how much I'm looking forward to this. I know I said only the two of us, but I couldn't leave Jen on her own."

Giving Asho a sly grin. "Yeah... there's no way you two could be separated. I'd have to put up with your miserable face all day," Fish scoffed. "That aside, what chance do we have things could go wrong today?"

"None at all, it will be perfect, and I've got a sneaky feeling we're going to strike gold today, I can feel it in my waters, little bro."

Fish did a drum roll on the chrome handrail with the flat of his hands. "Okay, let's get the hell out of here. And FYI, I'll punch your face in if you don't stop calling me that."

"What? Little bro? You mean calling you little bro?" Asho grinned as he reached over and wrapped an arm around Fish's neck as though about to put him in a half Nelson. Instead, he leaned into his ear. "We'll get through this together… okay?"

The loud, unforgiving sound of Jenni's voice made them turn. "It's okay you guys, don't worry about me. I'm just the dog's body around here," she shouted as she clambered on board hauling a large eski, containing their lunches. Asho grabbed it from her and plonked it down in the middle of the deck.

"You can fetch the other one Fish, that has all the drinks and there's no way I can lift it," she smiled.

"Is that everything? Are we ready to go?" Asho asked sounding happy.

"Hang on, I still have to collect some things from the workshop, give me a minute," Fish called out as he jumped down onto the aluminium walkway and hurried away.

As soon as he was out of earshot, Jenni gave Asho some words of advice. "Don't treat him with kid gloves Ash, but don't be too rough with him either."

"Trust me, Jen, I know how to handle him."

Panting for breath, Fish returned, carrying a large cardboard box. He climbed back on board and stowed it under one of the long bench seats.

"What've you got here?"

"Things we definitely need to go treasure hunting, there's the trenching spade and all our head strap torches, not to mention the hemp rope. You never know when you might need a bit of hemp rope," he smiled

"What would I do without you, little bro... mate, friend, pal," Asho grinned, not knowing what to call him. He was hoping the day's activities would keep Fish occupied. At least for one day, till everything settled.

"Okay, is that it? *Now* do we have everything?" Asho demanded, sounding irritated.

"All set. Unhitch the ropes and let's get out of here." Fish shouted as he pushed the ignition key into the slot ready to start the engine.

When Inspector Dunn pulled in front of the Marina security gate. Ellis could see the three on the boat. "Looks like they're leaving, quickly, blast your horn," he said as he leapt from the car and ran towards the gate, waving frantically.

Hearing the commotion, Asho looked up. "It's Ray," he said, turning to Jenni. "What on earth can he want now?"

"Not more bad news I hope. We've had enough of that to last us a lifetime, you better go let him in."

By the time Asho reached the gate, Inspector Dunn had joined Ellis. "Should we be worried, you both paying us a visit this morning? You're lucky, we were just about to leave on a little boat ride."

"That's good and no, you don't need to be worried," Ray replied. "We have some information you might like to hear, it shouldn't take too long. Can you spare a minute?"

"I suppose, follow me to the boat."

With little effort, Ray climbed on board the boat and stood next to Fish. "You okay, buddy?"

"I'm getting there," he replied with the saddest expression and a shrug of his shoulders.

Ray found it too hard to resist reaching forward and giving him a man-hug. "Not a bad idea taking the boat out today,

The sound of grunting made everyone turn to see an ungainly Inspector Dunn, clambering on board. "Humph, it's okay for you young ones," he remarked as he stood up straight and smoothed his trousers with the flat of his hand. He greeted the three friends with a nod, not being as familiar with them as Ellis. "Now then, is there somewhere for me to sit?" Dunn asked. This thing rocks a bit and I don't have sea legs like you lot," he added making everyone laugh seeing as the boat was quite still.

Asho pointed to the bench seats where they all found a seat. Sergeant Ellis began to convey the news.

"We felt you should know, we have the results from the DNA tests which confirms Laura Verwood and Chief Justice Clifford Buckton are the biological parents of you both; which means, there is no doubt whatsoever, you two are full brothers."

Fish and Asho gave each other beaming smiles followed with the three taking turns to hug one another, shouting with delight. Fish suddenly quietened as he sat back in his seat.

"So what happens now?"

"Well, we have more news. It turns out you're both the beneficiaries of Laura Verwood's inheritance. Laura had acquired a large collection of expensive antiques. However, her apartment is owned by… " He paused and looked at Fish before continuing. "By Justice Buckton."

"That would be right and I bet it's a luxury apartment. There's no doubt he would've made sure she had an expensive place for him to visit," Fish said, sounding bitter.

"I still can't believe they were never found out," Asho commented.

"Some people just know how to be discreet, I suppose," Ray offered.

Fish glanced at Ray but addressed Inspector Dunn, feeling he was more superior in this matter.

"What will happen to my mum?"

"Good question," Dunn began. "It's up to the courts now. We don't believe it was premeditated. We will examine the circumstances and Lady Buckton's position and sound character should be taken into consideration. Her punishment won't be severe if that is what's worrying you. I hear Ray is going to arrange a visit for you. With a bit of luck, she may even be allowed home sooner than you think."

"Oh, I do hope so," Jenni said, sounding hopeful. "That will really cheer you up, won't it Fish?"

"I can't speak for Asho, but I have no interest in any of Laura Verwood's inheritance. Until yesterday, I had no idea the woman existed, ironically, now she doesn't," he said, showing no feelings. "However, if my dad owns the apartment, it's only right I live there. In fact, we all can, what d'you say Ash?"

"I think we need to slow down, let's just wait and see what happens, there's lots of stuff needs to be sorted. But hold that thought, sounds good to me," he responded with an impish smile.

"I know you're a good friend of my parents, Inspector Dunn. This must be difficult for you." Fish said, sounding concerned.

"More than you can ever imagine, I hope the information we've given you is not too distressing."

"You are joking! I've just found out that my best friend is really my brother. That can't be bad."

"A Phoenix, rising from the ashes," Dunn added.

Fish smiled. "Whatever!" he replied, not really understanding. "What's more, it looks like I might have a new sister-in-law soon. Isn't that right Ash?"

Jenni threw Asho a deathly stare. "What? You told him?" she asked, sounding shocked.

Throwing his hands in the air, Fish answered for him. "He didn't have to Jen, I'd have to be an idiot or blind not to have known about you two. I can't believe you didn't want to tell me," he added with an exaggerated pout.

Asho gave Jenni a kiss on the cheek. "Well, it's all out in the open now so I can have a grope whenever I want," he laughed as he grabbed her bottom, making her yelp.

"It must be great being young," Dunn whispered to Ellis pensively.

"*Yes, it is, if you must know*," he replied with a grin. Changing the subject guys, weren't you taking divers out today?"

"Not any more, we cancelled today, Fish wasn't feeling up to it."

Ellis pointed to the equipment lying on the deck. "So how come your scuba gear is here?"

"The boys decided they'd have a relaxing day on their own with no responsibilities," Jenni said.

"We will have one last try at searching for that elusive gold, then we'll accept defeat," Fish added.

Ellis turned to Inspector Dunn. "What d'you say I go with them, Sir. Make sure they look after the detector? After all, its police property,"

After a brief silence, Dunn cast an eye around the boat with a grin. "Believe it or not, I've never experienced a treasure hunt. In fact, dare I admit, I've never been on a boat before," he grinned.

"Goodness, Sir, where have you been all your life?' Ellis asked, sounding stunned at the admission. "That's it then, we should both go out with them today and that'll give you a new experience to notch up," Ellis said, hoping he wasn't stepping over the line.

"All right, you've twisted my arm. Is that okay with you boys?" Dunn called out.

"Why not, if this is to be the last time, let's go in style. With half the police force with us, nothing can go wrong," Asho said.

"Bit of an exaggeration there," Dunn said, having no sense of humour.

The atmosphere was electric as Ray, Fish and Asho chatted amongst themselves while they loaded extra scuba gear on board. Inspector Dunn remained seated, as he made phone calls to his team, letting them know what he and Ellis were doing. Jenni fussed around making sure there were plenty beers and a good supply of food.

Fish checked the fuel and was about to give the thumbs up to Asho when he spotted him slip his arm around Jenni's waist and nuzzle into her neck. A pang of envy swept over him. They looked so good together, his concern now was that Asho would drift away as he spent more time with Jen; which was understandable. He shrugged the idea away, not wanting to think about losing anyone else in his life now.

Ash's loud, boisterous voice brought him back to earth as he overheard him chastising Jenni.

"For fuck's sake, Jen, we're only going out for one day, you've packed enough for a month."

"Nothing like being prepared and don't swear at me, you little shit," she replied as they both giggled.

Once the boat was ready to go, Fish gave the signal, "Painters away." He called out.

"Stop showing off," Asho shouted back, then turned to Ray. "It was something his Grandad taught him, he drives me mad with all his old nautical terms."

They moved gracefully out of the marina and into Botany Bay. As they cut through the calm waters of the Tasman Sea, Inspector Dunn leaned back in his seat, feeling relaxed for the first time in a long time. "I could get used to this," he thought out loud.

"It's something else, isn't it Sir,"

Dunn leaned towards Ellis' ear. "You can drop the Sir when we're away from the office Ray."

Ellis responded with a wink before putting on his Ray-Bans. Hearing Asho cursing at the computer system he headed to the steering station.

"Fish will have to look at this, it's not my area of expertise, that's for sure.

Pushing him out of the way, Ellis took over. "Let me show you," He said as he tapped on the keyboard. "So, what's your plan of action today then?"

Asho watched him in admiration. "Is there no end to your talents?" he frowned. "The plan today is to move away from the wreck and go further afield. We will make our search area much wider. I'm not sure what Wallace was playing at, keeping us hanging around the wreck the whole time. Then he had the cheek to say it had been searched hundreds of times and that we were wasting our time. I still thought it was a bit of a coincidence him turning up at the marina, which just happened to be the day we were mastering the tow fish.

"Fuck, I still have nightmares about that dive,"

"Why's that Ray?" Dunn called out. "What happened?"

Asho came to his aid. "That was the time I had trouble with my gas cylinder, wasn't it Ray?" Asho said, thinking quickly.

"Yes, yes, that's right, It was cylinder trouble," he responded with a look of relief.

Reaching the dive site, Fish switched off the engine. The only sound was the water, thumping against the sides of the hull. "It should be light on the seafloor with the reflection of the sun filtering through," Asho called out while he fastened them to the buoy. He then instructed Jenni on how to manoeuvre the boat by following the direction of the map displayed on the laptop. Jenni had an easy going personality and could keep up with the two boys in everything they tried. They both knew, they'd be lost without her with her calming influence. She had no trouble understanding everything Asho explained.

As Fish and Ellis slipped into their wetsuits, Asho decided Inspector Dunn should make himself useful. He led him to the rear of the boat, next to the dive platform.

"This is an easy job, but very important, I think you'll be able to manage it," he said sounding a little patronizing. Dunn took it in his stride, he was having too good a time.

"We will need you to keep a check on the tow fish cable. We don't want it getting snagged."

After securing the scuba tanks to his back, Asho headed for the dive platform and plunged into the calm sea, disappearing for a few seconds before surfacing. He signaled to Ray and Fish to lower the metal detector into the water, then guided it to the seabed. On reaching the white sandy bottom, he made sure the tow fish was aimed and ready to begin its search for gold. Heading back to the boat, Asho was captivated by the ever-changing colours of the sea, as it turned from deep navy to a light crystal blue as shards of sunlight pierced the surface. All he wanted to do was to relax and relish the moment.

Without warning, a strange sensation caught him off guard. He suddenly felt a strong surge of water from beneath. The water erupted with an almighty rush, forcing him upwards and rendering him powerless as his body tumbled over and over like a rag doll. After what seemed like an eternity, he finally stopped rolling. Stunned by what had occurred, he allowed his body to float while he regained his sense of direction. As his head bobbed above the water, his heart sank, he was way off course. The boat seemed a mere dot in the distance.

A wide curtain of water surged up and burst through the surface of the sea, making a direct hit to the boat, lifting it several metres into the air before crashing back down heavily. Taking the full brunt at the back of the boat, Inspector Dunn was thrown into the air and crashed down heavily. After skidding across the deck on all fours, Jenni's elbows and knees were badly grazed. Feeling no other pain, she was thankful there were no bones broken. Fish and Ray were standing at the scuba cage and had grabbed hold of the mesh and clung on for dear life.

"What the crap was that?" Fish called out.

"Buggered if I know. How is everyone, are you okay, Sir?" Ray shouted out, seeing Inspector Dunn, lying face down on the deck.

Dunn didn't answer. He rolled into a sitting position, his face contorted in pain. "No... I'm... I'm in fucking agony," he winced.

Jenni hobbled towards the cabin. "I'll get the first-aid kit, although I have no idea what we do for a broken arm," Jenni said, shrugging her shoulders.

"Just hurry, I'll sort it. Let's hope your kit has painkillers or a bottle of whiskey, something to deaden the pain," Ellis smiled.

Jenni reappeared with the medical case and unclipped the lid.

Without warning, she gasped out loud. "Oh my God, Asho... he's still down there."

With a look of horror, Fish raced to the back of the boat and stood on the dive platform scanning the water with his eyes. Jenni quickly joined him, trying hard to stay calm, as Ray skilfully placed Dunn's arm in a temporary splint and administered two painkillers.

"There he is, I can see his head bobbing in the water, about thirty metres away." Fish called out.

Asho had surfaced after being tossed helplessly through the water for what felt like an hour. Once he had his bearings, he could see the boat in the distance, shocked at how far he'd drifted. Still shaken, his legs felt like jelly and he found it difficult to swim. As he reached the dive platform, exhausted, Fish and Ray both reached down and hauled him out of the water.

"Geez, thanks for coming to get me, guys," Asho shouted as he clambered onto the deck, struggling to catch his breath. Jenni rushed to his side and tried to put her arms around him, but he pushed her away.

"Sorry mate, but we're all tied up to the towfish. Don't worry, we were keeping an eye on you, we wouldn't have let you drown out there." Ellis said, hoping to pacify him.

Asho got to his feet and began angrily pulling off his cylinder, throwing it to the ground with a clatter.

"We weren't exactly having a picnic here on the boat, Asho," Jenni said, sounding annoyed at his attitude. "It looks like Inspector Dunn's broken his arm and I'm battered and bruised," she continued as she swept her hand around the group. "Not to mention being scared half to death at whatever it was that almost keeled the boat over while you were down there."

"Okay, okay, guys, let's settle down, we're all in shock, but we're all alive," Ray called out. "We better pull the towfish up to make sure there's no damage.

Then we need to assess the situation. I think what we experienced there was an earth tremor or a small earthquake."

Fish and Ray set about dragging the detector to the surface, giving it a thorough checking over.

"Looks okay to me, nothing was broken, it looks intact."

"I've checked the laptop and they're still talking to each other, the picture on the screen hasn't altered."

"So what was it? Anyone any ideas, it came out of nowhere," Fish said.

"You're not going to believe this," Ray began. "After the earthquake disaster in Newcastle and being so close to home here in

Sydney, I became fascinated by the subject. I started reading up on it."

"Now how does that not surprise me," Asho said, rolling his eyes.

Frowning at him, Ray carried on. They are seismic waves, caused by a fracture on the ocean floor or a landslide causing a displacement of water."

"Maybe we should get out of here then," Inspector Dunn suggested. "That might be the first of many eruptions, I don't feel like being hurled across the boat again," he added, holding up his arm with the makeshift splinter.

"Or worse, smashed to a pulp and die," Jenni wailed.

"Well, I'm no expert, but I doubt there'll be another. It takes years to move two plates on a fault line."

Asho gave Ray an encouraging slap on the shoulder. "Well, in that case, let's get back down there."

"I'm game if you are," Ray flashed a look at his boss and by the expression on his face, wasn't happy.

"You must be mad, I think we should head back to dry land immediately."

With a look of dismay, Asho and Fish didn't dare speak as they waited for Ray's reply.

He gave Dunn an encouraging smile. "I'll be okay, we might as well have a quick look now we're here. Then when we get back we can have lunch."

"I can see you've got your mind set, you're incorrigible Raymond! You're a bad influence on these young ones."

Ray narrowed his eyes as he answered. "Hmm, I think you've got that the wrong way round." He laughed. The boys joined in, relieved it was sorted and they could be on their way. Asho sat on the edge of the dive platform and rolled backwards into the water, Fish followed a few seconds later. After checking to make sure Inspector Dunn was okay, Ellis jumped in the water to join the boys. Jenni released the rope from the mooring and made her way to the cabin and started up the engine. Following the directions on the laptop, she steered slowly along the lines.

As the three divers regrouped on the seabed, they were motionless, observing the damage caused by the small earthquake. A huge chunk of the continental shelf, directly in front of the shipwreck had fallen away, partially undermining the wreck which now teetered precariously. The crack that travelled from the edge of the continental shelf, in a massive semi-circle, behind the shipwreck and back to the shelf a hundred metres away had now widened.

When the towfish passed by, the three followed, hoping for a sign it had detected something. After fifty meters, they stopped and waited for Jenni to turn the boat and sweep back over the area. As it glided through the water along the edge of the continental shelf, zigzagging over the fracture where the wreck had been dislodged. The blue light burst into life, sending a message to the laptop.

"Whoohoo!" Jenni yelled from the steering station. "I hope that means they've found something."

On the seabed, the three divers swam towards the spot where the detector's light had flickered. While Asho and Fish set to, sifting through the fine sand and digging away the sedimentary rock, Ray continued on to where the piece had fallen away making a fresh rock face with many jagged ridges jutting out. Ray knew it was risky, but he felt confident nothing could go wrong. Inching his way down the steep rock face, he probed and poked as he descended. The deeper he swam the darker and murkier the water became making visibility poor. He wished he'd worn one of the headband torches Fish and Asho were wearing.

It occurred to him, he'd now lost his sense of direction. Without realising, he'd drifted away from the rock face and had no idea where he was. Stretching his arm out as far as he could, his fingertips touched a hard surface, a sense of relief spread through his body knowing he was back at the wall. Gripping a rocky ledge, he stayed still for a while, taking deep breaths to calm himself.

As Ray's eyes adjusted, he could see what looked like a white orb sitting on the ledge right in front of him. Curious that a rock could be so round, he reached out. Misjudging its close proximity, he knocked the orb with his hand causing it to roll forward, giving him a fright and making his hand shoot backwards as if getting an electric shock. His eyes almost popped out of his head as the creepy face of the skull, now almost touching his face, stared back at him through two empty black hollows; the wide set of teeth appearing to be grinning.

His automatic reaction was to swim backwards, to distance himself from the thing that had scared the shit out of him. With arms flailing in jerky circular movements, like broken helicopter blades, he wasn't going anywhere. *Fuck, I didn't expect that,* he thought, then chastised himself for over-reacting. After all, he'd seen worse things than an ancient old skull in his line of duty.

Out of morbid curiosity, he swam back and being careful this time, fossicked in the rubble around the skull.

Something grabbed his attention. Reaching further into the ledge, he could just make out the remains of a skeleton, curled up in the feotal position. Half buried in the midst of the pile of bones was a dark ornate square object. Moving the arm bones to one side, Ray brushed the silty sand away from the old box to reveal what looked like ancient hieroglyphics etched into it.

Ray now had a sudden urge to find the others and tell them what he'd found. The undermining of the shipwreck had unearthed what they'd been looking for. He was now uneasy about being in the dark, eerie depths of the ocean and was beginning to feel queasy and light headed.

As he was about to lift the box from the bony arms of the skeleton something moved out the corner of his eye. He turned to see a large black shadow moving towards him and could see two eyes peering through the dark murky water, moving closer and closer. *Shit, not again!* He thought as the memory of his last encounter with sharks came flooding back. Feeling a lump in his throat, he gulped hard, bracing himself.

Ewan Wallace warned him, when a shark appears, stand stock still. However, Ray's first instinct was to flee as fast as he could. Against all his better judgement, he decided to make a dash for it. Despite feeling weak, he swam back into the murky waters. Glancing back over his shoulder, the dark shape with two glaring eyes was now within feet. Somewhere in the recesses of his memory, he remembered something about punching a shark on the nose makes them flee. Ray lashed out with his fists hoping to connect with a nose. After being struck in the arm, he kicked out in desperation, making contact with what felt like flesh. To his horror, he felt a vice-like grip around his neck. With his weakening strength, his limp arms thrashed about while trying to turn and face the attacker that was scaring the shit out of him.

To his relief, he could see Asho's face. In his muddled state of mind and lack of clear vision, he'd mistaken him for a sea creature and what he thought were eyes were the lights from his torch headband. Asho lifted his hand up to his head and twirled his finger around in a circle, then pointed to Ray, indicating he'd gone mental. Ray responded by shrugging his shoulders in an exaggerated manner. As Asho pointed upwards with his thumb, Ray shook his head from side to side and gestured Asho to follow him.

When they reached the shelf he motioned Asho to take a look. Unable to see the expression on Asho's face with all his scuba gear he could tell by his actions the sight of the skull had given him a fright. His shock soon changed to curiosity as he leaned in for a closer look. The light from his torch made it easier to make out the well-preserved remains of a skeleton. From the position the bones were lying, Asho deduced that when the person was alive, they were endeavouring to protect the object. This intimated to him the contents must be precious. Feeling brave, he removed the object from the skeleton's clutches. As he lifted the skeletal arm, it fell apart in his hand. He held the bone towards Ray and shrugged his shoulders. With the arm removed, something caught Asho's eye. He tapped Ray on the shoulder and pointed eagerly at the rib cage. Just visible poking out of the sand and gravel was a large round object. Together they brushed around it to reveal what looked like a medallion attached to a heavy chain.

They turned to face each other and simultaneously raised their hands to high-five one another. Picking up the chain, Asho draped it around his neck, then carefully tried the lid of the box. Encrusted with barnacles and algae it was proving to be too difficult. They decided to wait till they got back on the boat to take a look. Asho's gut feeling was telling him, it was looking very promising. Asho conveyed his feeling of euphoria to Ray with animated hand gestures.

Ray tapped his wristwatch, then pointed upwards with his thumb. Asho made the okay signal. Grabbing the box, he tucked it under one arm and followed Ray to where Fish was waiting patiently. Asho held up the box and lifted the medallion around his neck towards Fish, who responded with the okay sign. The three made their way to the mooring rope when a sudden rumbling sound made them turn and look towards the shipwreck about a hundred metres away.

Together they watched in awe at the spectacular sight before them. As though watching a movie in slow motion, the section where the boat had rested for thousands of years, gave way and slid into the deep gorge. Within minutes the last remnants of the ancient Bireme disappeared, leaving a billowing mass of debris and sand that obscured their view.

Ray suddenly felt dizzy and struggled to breathe. With his last ounce of strength, he clawed at Fish who was standing closest, to warn him he was in trouble. Taking his arm, Fish dragged him upwards to where their heads could burst through the surface of the water. Fish yanked Ray's mouthpiece from his face, allowing him to take in deep breaths of fresh.

"What happened there," Ray asked as he pulled his goggles under his chin and swiped his hand through his wet hair while treading water.

"We forgot to keep an eye on our tanks, we've been down there quite some time."

Being so preoccupied with their discussions, they hadn't noticed the strange boat berthed next to theirs.

"Looks like you've had productive morning boys," an unfamiliar man's voice called out. The three turned to see a large silhouetted figure standing on the dive platform of their boat, hovering over them.

"Who the hell's that?" Asho called out.

Spitting out a mouthful of water, Fish shrugged his shoulders.

Realising something wasn't right, Asho whispered to the others that they should drop the box, we can dive for it later.

The voice boomed. "Don't even think about dropping what you have there, or it will be the last thing you ever do," the man threatened. He then turned and clicked his fingers at someone standing next to him. "You!" he commanded. "Take whatever it is they've got, and be quick about it!"

The three stared in disbelief when a familiar figure appeared at the edge of the dive platform. Dressed in black from head to foot, Ewan Wallace swung his body onto the ladder and lowered himself closer to the water. A rogue wave caught him by surprise, soaking his lower legs. Gripping the top rung with one hand, he stretched as far as he could towards Asho, indicating he wanted him to hand over whatever it was he was he had.

"Give it over, lads, I think you'll find that belongs to my boss here," Wallace demanded. Then his facial expression changed to one of concern as he lowered his voice and mouthed a warning. "Don't argue, he's not a nice person," he said with staring eyes and shaking his head from side to side.

"You can go get fucked," Asho called back. "There's no way I'm handing this over to you or anyone else, you can fuck off out of here and take your big ugly friend with you."

A third figure appeared out of nowhere, dressed identically to Wallace. To their horror, the man pointed a gun directly at them.

"You better show some respect, you little shit, and watch your language. Do exactly what you're fuckin told, then no one will get hurt," the man shouted, with a deadpan expression.

The sight of a weapon made Asho back off. He threw Fish and Ray a look of despair.

Ray spoke out the side of his mouth. "Looks like we've got no choice, I think this lot mean business."

With reluctance, Asho handed the box over to Wallace then one by one, they climbed onto the dive platform. With the gun pointed at them, they removed their scuba gear. The man pushed all three towards Inspector Dunn and Jenni who had watched in silence from the covered deck. Wallace handed the old blackened box to the big man who was now clearly visible. The balding man looked smart in a tailored navy suit and pale blue shirt with matching silk cravat and handkerchief.

"I think you'll find this here is what you've been looking for, Sir," Wallace said, sounding intimidated by the man.

"Open it!" Pullman demanded.

Wallace tried the box and found it impossible to open. Removing the army knife attached to his utility belt, he pushed the blade into the lock and twisted it causing the lock to flip open. As he lifted the lid, everyone gasped as its contents were revealed. The box was filled to the brim with ancient coins.

Pushing Wallace out of the way, Pullman demanded everyone to stand back as he dipped his hand into the contents scooping up a handful of coins. Raising them to his eyes, the gold coins glistened in the sun, sending a yellow glow across his face that had now taken on a look of pure evil.

"Nice work, boys, I must congratulate you on your tenacity to succeed, your persistence is outstanding. Perhaps you should come and work for me. Wagging his finger towards the two men, Wallace and McPherson. These two jokers here, couldn't find a beer in a brewery. Isn't that right?" he sneered.

"Well, I don't know about that, we... "Wallace began to speak, but was cut off mid-sentence. "*Silence,*" the big man bellowed. He pushed his face close to Asho, making him flinch at the acrid, overwhelming odour of cheap aftershave and bad breath. "I'll have you know, young man, we've been looking for these coins for some time," he growled.

Glancing down at Asho's chest, he noticed for the first time, the medallion hanging on a thick chain. Lifting it with the crook of his finger, he squinted both eyes for a closer inspection. "Hmm, very nice, looks like you've found me more than coins. Take it off and put it in the box." He growled.

"You won't get away with this, you do realise we have two police officers with us," Asho said, hoping to scare the obnoxious man.

"Tell someone who gives a damn!" the man replied with an air of authority. "Sorry to disappoint you all, I'm unable to stand around here chatting, I have an appointment with a gold smelter," he said, to the horror of everyone.

"You can't do that," Ellis said, raising his voice. "There's no way you can have the coins melted down, that would be sacrilege, not to mention illegal. Those coins are precious."

"Precisely! And worth much more melted down into pure gold ingots. Not stuck in some stuffy old museum. Besides, I don't remember asking your opinion. Do you know what I do to people who speak to me out of turn? Let me show you." Turning to the tall man standing next to him, he snatched the firearm from his hand. Raising it towards Sergeant Ellis' head he pressed the barrel into his temple. There was a deathly silence as Pullman bent down and pushed his face close to Ellis' ear and did nothing for a few seconds. Without warning, he leaned forward and yelled at the top of his voice. "BANG, you're dead." He threw his head back with a raucous laugh.

"You ought to think yourself, lucky young man, I'm in a good mood today, it would be such a pity to make a mess of such a handsome face," he said as he outlined Ellis' face with the barrel of the gun, stopping under his chin and flicking his head sharply to one side. Turning towards the group who were glued to the spot as they witnessed this madman's movements. He paced in front of Asho, Fish, and Dunn he tapped each one on the head with the barrel of the gun till he reached Jenni who was sitting on a bench seat. With a lecherous grin, he trailed the gun up her thigh, stopping at her groin.

"Hmm, I'm wondering if I should take this one with me. I could do with some fresh meat," he said with a salacious grin. "What d'you think boys? Should we take this one with us? You can have her after I'm finished," he said, pressing his face close to Jenni's ear. Jenni tilted her head away, her face contorted at the smell of his breath.

"Only joking, my dear, you look like you couldn't satisfy me anyway."

Ray grabbed Asho as he was about to lurch forward, and whispered in his ear. "Steady, they have a gun, don't antagonise him, that's what he wants."

Pullman ordered Wallace to take everyone's mobile phones, disable the radio and destroy the flares and for McPherson to immobilize the engine. Then, with a flourish of his arm, he called out. "Bon voyage, gentlemen… and lady." Doffing an imaginary hat as he backed his way to the rear of the dive boat where he turned and crawled ungainly across the short gangplank to his own boat. As his two sidekicks followed, Ellis grabbed Wallace's arm and spoke in a loud whisper.

"Why are you doing this Ewan? I thought you were a mate, the boys trusted you. You'll never convince me this is what you want, leaving us to drown," Ellis pleaded.

Wallace hung his head in shame, not wanting to look at him. "I can't talk, Sarge. The man's mad, you've no idea what he's capable of, and he'll shoot me if I don't do what he says." He said, yanking his arm from Ray's grip. "You won't drown… if you have your wits about you." He shrugged his shoulders before hurrying after McPherson, already on their boat, poised to start the engine.

Wallace untied their vessel as Pullman leaned over the boat rails and aimed his gun. The ear piercing sound of gunshots rang out as a volley of bullets hit the decking and sides of the boat. Wood and rubber matting shattered in the air, covering everyone in debris. Within seconds, water bubbled from the gaping holes and spread over the deck.

Pullman shouted from his boat. "Sorry everyone, but as they say at sea, you're scuppered." Letting out a raucous laugh.

Their engine suddenly roared into life and within seconds the hydrofoils lifted the boat high above the water as it sped off, disappearing into the distance.

As soon as they were out of sight, Ellis took charge. "Quick, we need to plug the holes and everyone put on a life jacket," Ellis yelled out as he grabbed a towel and rammed it into the gaping hole caused by the gunshots. Fish dashed to the steering station where his heart sank, seeing the radio smashed beyond repair. Turning the key in the ignition, the engine sputtered then died. After a few more attempts at turning the key, it was obvious they'd rendered the engine useless somehow.

"What the fuck have they done?" he hissed as he swung round to see the cover of the diesel engine compartment in two pieces lying next to the gaping hole. Lowering himself into the compartment, close to the engine, he felt the cold wet sensation of water on his feet. Seeing a bucket beside the engine and the lid missing from the fuel tank he knew at once the engine was now submerged in salty seawater.

"*Shit*… the bastards have stuffed the fuel," he yelled, before heading back to report to the others, who were now ankle deep in water. He could see Inspector Dunn, looking pale and exhausted, using only his good arm to bail the water out with a plastic container.

"This is impossible," Jenni said, incensed. "We will never get rid of all this water. As soon as we chuck it out, it's pouring back. We're gonna sink, for sure," she cried, as she straightened her body and wiped the moisture from her brow with the back of her forearm.

Inspector Dunn wasn't feeling too confident about their situation, but didn't want Jenni to know. "Bailing out is our only choice," Dunn said, trying to sound encouraging, as he worked through the pain barrier of his injured arm. "Just keep going Jenni, don't stop, that's all we can do," he said before turning his sights at Ellis. "Who in God's name were they?" We know the names of the sidekicks because the big man shouted them out. But who the hell is he? You seemed a little familiar with the shorter guy. Anything I should know about, Raymond?"

Ellis moved towards Inspector Dunn and sat down. "If you must know, we have crossed paths with the short guy, his name is Ewan Wallace. He's quite the expert on diving and he showed us the ropes with the tow fish. I thought there was something odd about him, how he appeared out of the blue at the marina; on the day, we went out with the metal detector. But we all agreed to let him dive with us so he could teach us what we needed to know. I was suspicious at first, but changed my mind about him. He turned out to be an okay bloke." Ellis was having a flashback of his near death experience. He hated to say it, but thanks to Ewan, and unbeknown to Dunn, he was still around to tell the tale.

"What Ray is not telling you, Inspector Dunn is the man conned us. He obviously lulled us into a false security with his 'Mr Nice Guy' act. And all the time he must've been sussing us out. We ignored Ray's warnings about him. I reckon they must have been watching us, they knew we were diving for treasure." Fish said.

Asho butted in. "Then a diver came out of nowhere and attacked me while on a dive a week ago. He'd sent Jen flying when he grabbed, what we think he assumed, was a coin she was holding; which was only a shell."

"Clearly the big guy is the mastermind behind all this and has hired those two thugs to help him search for the coins. I've bunged up the holes to stem the flow of water, but it won't hold for long." Ray announced, sounding worried. "Let's hope a boat will pass this way soon."

Fish plonked down heavily on a bench seat. "Even if they do, we have no way of telling them we're distressed. It's already getting dark and we don't have any lights either," he wailed.

"Hang on, we have torches, why didn't I think of that sooner?" Asho said with excitement as he jumped to his feet and waded through the deepening water to the steering station.

While searching for the torches, he knocked over the box of broken flares. To his delight, he noticed two were still intact. Picking up the two unbroken flares, he hugged them to his chest as he looked up to heaven and mouthed. "Thank you, God," with a grin from ear to ear, then raced back to the others.

"I've got the torches, but you're not going to believe what else I found. Two of the flares are okay, that little shit Wallace, wasn't as clever as he thought, he missed two." Asho sniggered.

Wallace's departing words flashed through Ellis mind and wondered what he meant. He'd sounded genuinely sorry. *"You won't drown if you have your wits about you,"* he'd said. Now Asho's found flares. "I think Wallace left them there on purpose. He wanted us to find them,"

"How can you think that? He's a crook, working with an even bigger crook, they want us dead!" Asho snapped.

"Or maybe Wallace is mixed up in something he can't get out of," said Ellis. "Anyway, we have flares, all we need now is for someone to come past.

Bailing out the water was proving futile, and one by one they gave up. Dunn's arm was hurting more than he was letting on. "You okay, Sir, you look exhausted," Ellis asked.

"All I want to do is lie down somewhere dry and close my eyes."

Fish had read somewhere that when people were suffering shock, you had to keep them talking. He sidled next to Dunn. "If we get out of this alive, Inspector Dunn, and those three are caught, will be able to keep the treasure?"

"Well, first, we *will* get out of this alive, stay positive about that. Second, they will be caught and hopefully, the treasure will be recovered before they destroy it." Dunn said with a feeble smile. "As for you keeping it, there's no simple answer to that."

"Shush," Asho yelled. "What's that noise?"

Everyone stopped talking to hear the faint sound of an engine.

"It's a chopper," Ellis yelled. "Quick, Asho, the flares, where are they?"

Pulling out the two flares from inside his life jacket Asho handed one to Ray. They both stood and waited. With the helicopter almost above them, at the same time, they removed the caps and struck the ends, sending an intense, bright red column of smoke and sparks skyward. The aura-like bright glow lit the sky, making the helicopter more visible as it hovered above the boat with a deafening sound. The swirling blasts of wind from the rotor blades whipped up the ocean, which pounded the small craft; causing it to list dangerously. While trying to keep their balance, everyone watched in awe as an officer in orange overalls lowered himself onto the deck.

The noise from the rotating blades drowned out the officer's instructions. Ray motioned for Inspector Dunn to be taken first and helped strap him into the hoist before he had a chance to argue. The remaining four, clung to the rails with the water now lapping around their knees. Jenni clung to Asho, fighting back tears, dreading being hauled hundreds of feet into the air, but fearing being left in the water to drown.

With everyone winched to safety, Ray waited alone for the officer to return. It was only a matter of seconds and the boat would be completely immersed in water. As Ray tread water, the officer lowered himself for the last time and fixed Ray to his hoist. As they swung metres in the air, the boat disappeared beneath the surface of the water.

With everyone safely on board the chopper, the pilot swooped around in a semi-circle and headed towards land.

"It's not the most comfortable mode of transport, but after what you lot have been through, I'd say you won't be too worried," said the Officer who'd winched them to safety as he handed everyone a thermal blanket.

Ellis wrapped the blanket around his shoulders. "You have no idea how relieved we were to see you," he said, his teeth chattering.

So, got yourselves in a bit of a mess down there. What the hell happened?"

There was a moment's pause as everyone looked at each other, wondering who should be the one to explain. All eyes fell on Sergeant Ellis. "It's a long story. We're just eternally grateful you happened to be flying past!" he said.

"Flying past? I don't think so. I got a call from an old Navy buddy saying there was a dive boat with five passengers, sinking. He was incoherent, but I was able to co-ordinate your position from his information. We've been searching for a while. There must be a hell of a current, cos you've been carried way off course. You're lucky, I was just thinking the bugger was having me on, we were ready to head back. He assured me you had flares, so that's what we were hoping to see."

Ray gave Asho a knowing glance. "Your buddy wouldn't, by any chance, be Ewan Wallace?"

"Yep, that's my mate. He's a bit of a joker, but he sounded genuinely concerned, I couldn't take the chance and ignore him."

Ray was convinced Wallace wanted to do the right thing by them. Deep down, there was a good bloke trying to get out. The more Ray thought about it, the more he felt the man was caught up in something and Pullman wasn't a man to mess with. Perhaps he had something over Ewan and his mate, forcing them to obey his every command, or else. "Did he say where he was phoning from by any chance?" Ellis asked

"Nope, all I got was something about having important business in the city and his boss was giving him a hard time so could not talk. He sounded agitated, but gave me the details of where you were and said five lives were in grave danger." The officer changed his position from kneeling to sitting with his legs outstretched and rubbed his knees vigorously to get the feeling back. "Wallace is not the brightest tool in the shed," tapping his forehead with his finger. "But I have to say he sounded serious. So, abracadabra! Here we are." placing the back of his hand at the side of his mouth he spoke in a lower voice. "Any excuse to take the beast out," he added as he held his index finger up and twirled it round.

Jenni turned to face Ray and Inspector Dunn with a look of revelation. "Fish and I went to a museum in the city, it has to be the same one. It had a fancy title, the Museum of pneumatics, I think."

"*Numismatics*," Fish called out. "The word is *numismatics, the study of coins*."

"Okay, know all," she said, sticking her tongue out at him. "Anyway, Ray, that's where we went."

"Do you remember who you talked to?" Dunn asked.

Fish and Jenni glanced at each other sheepishly. "Well, if you must know," Jenni began. "We didn't leave on good terms with the lady curator, whose name I forget. Fish sort of conned her into thinking he was studying metals so he could pump her for information about ancient coins without her realising. But she sussed him and chased us out of the building." they both now looked shamefaced.

"Let's be honest Jen, she's just a frustrated old cow," Fish said, defending himself. "She was okay when I was talking metals, but she changed her mood when I mentioned coins. She didn't like that one bit."

"Hmm, sounds suspicious, Ray," Dunn said. "If that's where those three are headed, there *must* be a connection."

"Is there any chance you can recall the layout of the museum? Is it a big place? Would it be easy to get around without getting lost?" Ellis bombarded Fish and Jenni with questions. "We may have to pay a visit to this museum tonight, as soon as we're off this chopper. If that's where they were heading, with luck they might still be there."

Asho tapped his wristwatch. "You do realise it's really late?"

"We don't have a choice if you want to see your precious coins again before they're melted down into blocks," Dunn remarked.

"As it happens, Ray, I do remember the place well and I know exactly where the curator's office is because we watched her come out of her door," Jenni replied.

"Jenni, are you able to do a sketch of the floor plan of the museum? I'm sure the officer here has a pen and paper tucked away somewhere," he grinned. "We need to know the route to the curator's office. I'm sure that's where they will be. Did you notice any emergency exits?"

"I did," Jenni called out. "I know for a fact there's one on the ground floor. When we were there I was bored. The thought crossed my mind, I could nip out, I don't think Fish would've noticed he was so engrossed in it all.

"What've you got in mind, Sir? I think your first port of call is the hospital and have that arm looked at and leave it to Special Response. They can swarm the building. Have you forgotten that big nob-head has a gun and held it to *my* head?" Ray said as he combed his fingers through his hair.

"No, I haven't forgotten. I will phone Superintendent Green when we get off this thing. It's too late to get a warrant, so instead, we'll take Green with us," he said with a wry grin.

Asho had listened intently to their conversation. "Inspector Dunn, would I be able to join you? After all, it's our boat they sank, and it's our treasure.

Fish raised his hand in the air. "That goes for me too Inspector Dunn."

"Hang on you two, settle down, this is not a game. These are dangerous people and this is a police matter. We have to have tactics put into place, one false move and someone could be injured, or worse... need I spell it out?"

"He's right, I want you three to go home for your own good. We will keep you well informed," Ray commanded.

The helicopter sounded louder as it swooped down and landed on an aluminium landing platform, floating on the river next to the Marine command centre. Happy to be back on terra firma, Inspector Dunn borrowed a mobile phone from one of the officers and made a call to Fortis.

Superintendent Green sounded very disgruntled as he answered. "I hope this is important Stephen, it's almost ten o'clock, and I was just heading to bed."

Hoping to and have his full cooperation, Dunn proceeded to explain the events of the previous five hours, relaying as many details concerning the events as they unfolded. He rattled off a list of requirements and ran past him a carefully thought out plan of attack. To Dunn's amazement, he met with no resistance.

"Where are you now Stephen?"

"We're at the Marine Command Centre in Balmain, which is where I need you to pick us up. There's somewhere I need you to take us and it can't wait. One more thing, I need dry clothes, we're the same size just bring me something of yours."

"They won't be designer labels, is that okay?" he snickered.

"I think I can slum it for one night. If we swing past Ellis' apartment, he can duck in and quickly change on the way. See you in half an hour."

◆◆◆

Asho had pleaded with Ray to let them go with them to the museum, but he wouldn't hear of it. He convinced them they needed to head home; then arranged an officer to take them to the marina where they'd left their vehicles. Asho and Fish were not convinced. They wanted to be there where the action was. After discussing it for a while they decided to head back into the city and be with Ray and Inspector Dunn. After all, it was their treasure. Jenni disagreed and begged the boys to leave it to the police, which fell on deaf ears. Asho was adamant that Jenni was to take his car and go home, while he and Fish drove to the museum.

Jenni sat in the car ready to drive away, livid at Asho's stubbornness. He leaned through the window and attempted to kiss her, but she pulled away. "Think about it Jen, this is all keeping Fish busy so he's not thinking about all that shit with his parents."

"Don't you dare use that as an excuse Ash, do you think I'm stupid? What I'm concerned about is, someone is going to get hurt and no doubt it will be you,"

"No one is going to get hurt," he said, then leaned forward and stole a kiss on her cheek. She turned and held her face up to his, allowing him to kiss her on the lips. "You bastard, Peter Ashcott, you always know how to get round me, you little shit. Be careful and leave all the dirty work to the officers in charge, don't be a hero and that goes for your little brother too," she smiled. That was the first time she'd referred to Fish as that and she liked it. The two vehicles pulled away from the marina and drove off in different directions.

◆◆◆

Inspector Dunn looked through the window of the Marine Command Centre to see a large black four-wheel-drive police patrol vehicle enter the car park. Clutching the thermal blanket with his good arm, he watched as Superintendent Green Stepped from the vehicle and headed towards him. Sergeant Ellis appeared at the same time after making sure Asho, Jenni and Fish were safely in a patrol car after taking some time to convince them they should head home.

Entering the reception, Green pointed at Dunn's bandaged arm in the makeshift sling with a surprised look. "What happened to you?"

"Don't worry about me, I'll explain later. First, did you bring what I asked?"

"I sure did, let's go."

All three headed out to the police vehicle. Green opened the rear door where a black metal ramming device lay in all its glory.

"That's good, what about the guns?"

Green opened the passenger door, took out a silver attaché case and laid it on the ground; flipping the lid open to reveal two handguns with shoulder holsters.

"I'll take one, Ray can have the other one, seeing as you're incapacitated," Green said with a deadpan expression.

"What about backup? Have you arranged for officers to meet us at the museum?" Dunn asked

"They're on their way there as we speak so I suggest we move." Green handed Dunn a large carrier bag. "I think these will fit, I've picked out the nearest I could find to match your colouring," Green mocked.

Within ten minutes, Dunn emerged from the building dressed in Fortis's clothes. He opened the front passenger door of the vehicle and climbed in.

"Goodness, it's like looking in a mirror," Green commented.

"Not funny, let's just go, we can discuss how we will tackle this on the way."

"Don't forget to call in at my place, I'm losing my credibility dressed in this dive suit in the middle of the city," Ellis called out from the back.

"That'll be the day," Dunn replied.

Although it was almost eleven at night, the City still buzzed with traffic and revellers. Fortis felt strangely exhilarated, memories of the old days were flooding back, when he and Stephen tracked down and arrested villains. There were many times when their lives were at risk, but they were a team, a great team.

Thirty minutes later, Green pulled behind a police patrol car parked a short distance from the museum. "Good, the boys are already here."

All five climbed from their vehicles. Green leaned into the back of his vehicle and pulled out two Kevlar vests and handed one to Ellis. He slipped it on and pushed his gun into its holster. According to the information Jenni had given them and the sketch she'd drawn, the emergency door led out the museum into the back lane. Green handed one of the officers a ramming device and for both to follow him.

◆◆◆

Arriving in the city, Fish parked his car a block away from the Old Bank Building deciding it was best to walk the last bit. Reaching the back lane of the building they could see Ellis and Dunn with a third person they didn't recognise, standing at the emergency exit, looking threatening in the semi-darkness. Keeping out of sight, they ducked behind a garbage dumpster to watch for a while.

◆◆◆

After only one attempt with the ramming device, the Officer was able to smash the door open. He stepped aside, allowing Ellis, Dunn and Green to enter into a large storeroom filled with boxes and old furniture. Seeing a door at the far side of the room, Ellis crept towards it. He turned the handle, opening it slightly. He could see the two men from the boat, standing at the far end of the corridor. As the tall man lifted his hand to his mouth, a red glow illuminated his face as he drew on a cigarette, confirming he was the man from the boat debacle.

Ellis pulled the door closed and spoke to Superintendent Green in a low voice. "Have your gun ready, Sir, they're out there. Looks like we've got them."

"Do you have names for these guys?" he whispered

"The shorter one is Ewan Wallace and the taller one we only know as McPherson."

"I'll go first… Ellis, you follow right behind me and Stephen, stay close to us."

With adrenaline pumping through his body, Ellis removed his gun from its shoulder holster and held it with both hands at chin level. Taking his position, he stood back as Green opened the door wide and stormed down the hallway towards the stunned men. With his gun held high, Ellis shadowed Green.

"Okay, you two, on the ground," Green yelled, sounding menacing. Sergeant Ellis moved to his side brandishing his gun as Inspector Dunn pulled out two pairs of handcuffs with his good hand. With a look of sheer panic and no regards to firearms being pointed at him, the taller man, known as McPherson, threw his cigarette at Green. Making a direct hit to his face. A spray of glowing sparks momentarily blinded him. He staggered in front of Sergeant Ellis making them lose precious seconds as the two men took off along the corridor.

As he passed a marble stand with a bust, perched precariously on top, McPherson reached out, bringing it down to the ground behind him where it smashed to pieces. Green stumbled into a parachute roll, giving the assailants more time to reach the fire exit next to the elevator. Wallace pushed the door open and disappeared into the stairwell, followed by McPherson, who turned to slam it shut. Throwing himself bodily against the door to stop him, Ellis jammed his foot in the gap.

Green was incensed at the indignity of being foiled by these thugs. He could see Ellis was struggling to open the door with McPherson on the other side. Using brute strength he ran at the door with his shoulder, making it fly open, sending McPherson skidding along the ground. Green rushed into the stairwell. As McPherson clambered to his feet, Green hurled himself through the air, rugby tackling him to the ground and held him down. "There's only one thing I despise more than a criminal... and that's a criminal who smokes." He cursed.

Ellis yanked McPherson's hands behind his back while Dunn clicked the cuffs on his wrists, with his good hand. "We've got him, Ray, you go after the other one," Dunn yelled.

Ellis took the concrete stairs, two at a time and reached the next floor in seconds. He opened the door and stepped gingerly into a large room filled with glass display cabinets. With his gun poised he felt a whack across the back of his neck, knocking him to the ground. The gun fell from his hand and spun over the floor. Ellis rubbed his neck and looked up just in time to see Wallace reach for the gun.

Without hesitation, Ellis lurched his body across the floor to grab it first. Wallace pressed his foot down hard on Ellis' hand to stop him. With his free hand, Ellis reached up and grabbed Wallace's lower leg, causing him to hurl backwards. His head bounced off a solid wooden display case as his short, stocky body crashed to the ground with a sickening thud. Ellis Jumped to his feet and rolled Wallace's comatose body onto his stomach. With his face squashed into the wooden floorboards, Wallace gave out a low moaning sound while his hands were cuffed behind his back.

Ellis leaned in close to his ear. "I know everything Wallace, you called the 'Marine Area Command' boys and you made sure a few flares were left intact. So I guess, I should thank you once again for saving my life. But what the fuck are you playing at getting involved in all this?" Ellis hissed as he rolled him over and making him sit.

Wallace grimaced, "Long story short, I ran up a big gambling debt, Pullman bailed me out but at a price. You know who he is, don't you?"

"No, I have no idea, tell me."

Before Wallace had a chance to reply the emergency door clattered open. Inspector Dunn barged through followed by Superintendent Green, shoving McPherson roughly in front of him; directing him to stand next to Wallace. Inspector Dunn approached the two men and looked from one to the other, his face contorted with anger.

"So where is he?" He said, into their faces. "Where's the big man? What's more, who is he, what's his name? I take it he's your boss."

Without answering the myriad of questions, Wallace pointed with his head towards a door along the hallway with a nameplate. Anticipating Dunn would want to know the name on the plate, Sergeant Ellis headed along the hall and returned within seconds.

"It says Caroline Hughes, Curator Sir."

Wallace coughed and spluttered before he spoke in a croaky voice. "If you *must* know, his name is Pullman, David Pullman. He's not a nice man and you wouldn't wanna be going in there just yet, believe me," he scowled.

"Now why would I believe anything you say?" Ellis snarled. The fact he'd said it, made Ellis want to charge into the office. He was now angry and not in the mood for stupid games. Plus everything hurt from his head to his feet.

Superintendent Green almost gagged after hearing the name Wallace had just announced. "Did you say, David Pullman?"

Wallace looked at Green with a vague expression before answering. "Yes, yes, his name is David Pullman."

Green looked at Dunn. "A word, please?" he said, nodding his head to one side. The two men moved out of earshot.

"David Pullman! Do you realise who that is? Vice tagged him The Baron before losing track of him when he slipped out of sight a few years ago. The man is an evil bastard, he was running a drug den and a brothel. He disappeared off the face of the earth two years ago after a sequence of drug related murders. Back in the day, if you got in his way, you ended up with concrete boots at the bottom of Sydney Harbour."

"Yes, yes. I remember, as soon as I heard the name. But I never ever met the man so had no idea who he was when we were out on the boat."

"This puts a different slant on things, the man is evil and will slay anyone who gets in his way."

"I can vouch for that," Dunn smirked.

Green removed his gun from its holster again. "Okay, so we

charge in and catch him unaware. With two guns aimed at him, we should manage to capture him easily. You better give Ellis the heads up."

As they returned to the group, Dunn steered Ellis to one side and gave him a quick rundown of the situation.

The expression on Ellis' face changed as he absorbed the information. "Okay, then let's get this over with before he gets wind of us being here," he announced as he turned to face the hallway.

"Steady on Ellis, you can't go in there alone. Remember, he's armed."

Superintendent Green shoved McPherson in the back. "We'll all go. Move it you two."

Dunn motioned Ellis to go ahead. As they positioned themselves outside the door Ellis held his gun at chin level and with one fell swoop, turned the handle and pushed the door hard making it slam open wide. Brandishing his gun Ellis stormed into the office. Following behind with his gun held high, Superintendent Green pushed the two men through the door.

All five men stood motionless, staring at the scene before them. The big man was standing sideways behind a large wooden desk, the lower half of his body hidden by the large box sitting on the desk in front of him. The expression on the man's face quickly changed from pleasure to shock as he turned to see the line of men, watching him. A red headed woman, kneeling in front of him, jumped to her feet and turned her back on the small crowd as Pullman hastily zipped up his trousers. "How dare you burst in here without knocking, this is outrageous," the man spluttered.

Still pointing his gun, Sergeant Ellis flashed his ID. "Sorry to interrupt you, Mr Pullman, I can see you were busy but you're in no position to question what we do." Ellis slipped his ID in his pocket and held the gun with both hands in front of him. "I'm not sure if you recall a meeting we had a short while ago when you took something that didn't belong to you."

Pullman was dumbstruck when he recognised the man standing in front of him wielding a gun. His eyes moved to Inspector Dunn. "This is impossible, it can't be, you two should be at the bottom of the ocean," he blurted out, as he wagged his finger from one to the other.

"Sorry, to disappoint, you Pullman but it seems we have a guardian angel watching over us, isn't that right Wallace?" Ellis said with a wicked grin. Wallace's eyes widened with fear at Sergeant Ellis's comment, even though Pullman appeared not to have understood.

"I thought I'd put a big enough hole in your boat."

"Well, you thought wrong, didn't you?" Inspector Dunn said.

Fish and Asho had watched the drama unfold from the shadows of the hallway. They'd followed behind the officers when they'd burst into the building. Everyone was oblivious to them being there. Fish could see the box sitting on the desk and had an overpowering need to get it back. Once he felt Ray had everything under control with his gun aimed at Pullman, he made his move. The coins were *their* property, and he had no intentions of losing them again.

Leaving Asho in the doorway Fish charged forward. He ducked and dived through the group of men, almost knocking Ellis over as he dashed towards the desk and attempted to snatch the box. "I think this belongs to me," he called out as everyone in the room stood in shocked silence.

Pullman saw his chance seeing Fish's bold entrance had caused a sudden diversion. He reached into his jacket and pulled out a small revolver. In retaliation, he grabbed Fish around his neck in a headlock and pressed the gun into the side of his head.

"That's what you think, boy, Pullman growled. "*Caroline*, fetch the box, and MOVE," Pullman screamed as he waved the gun around the room. "Now, out of my way. One move and I'll put a bullet through the kid's head."

Ellis and Dunn froze to the spot in shock. Not only at Pullman, pulling out a weapon, but at Fish, appearing out of nowhere. Everyone stepped aside as Ellis continued to aim at the big man.

"Give it up, Pullman, the place is surrounded, leave the lad," Ellis shouted.

Turning to face Ellis, Pullman spat out the words. "I don't know how you got off that boat, but by my reckoning, you should be all fish fodder by now. I should have shot you back there when I had the chance," he said as he shoved Ellis' head hard with the barrel. Ellis dodged sideways. Pullman returned the gun to Fish and swung his body like a rag doll as he scanned the room for Ms. Hughes. As she walked in front of him, holding the box, he shoved her hard through the doorway, then turned to face Ellis as he backed out waving his gun from one man to the other.

"Don't even think about coming after me or this boy gets it, DO YOU HEAR ME?"

Pullman backed into the hallway unaware anyone was there. As the adrenaline pumped through Asho's body, he lunged at the unsuspecting Pullman, sending him and Fish, crashing to the ground. The death curdling sound of a single gunshot rang out, followed by silence as everyone stared at the pile of bodies lying in a heap. Ellis rushed forwards, unable to see at first if anyone had endured a hit. Asho rolled over, taking Fish with him as he clung to his limp body. Ellis grabbed the weapon from Pullman's hand and gave it to Green.

The big man lay in a daze, speaking incoherently. He shoved Pullman roughly over onto his belly, grabbing another set of cuffs from Inspector Dunn and securing them behind his back. Pushing his own gun back in its holster, Ellis moved Asho away from Fish and dropped to his knees. Lifting Fish's head, he could see blood, pouring from a wound under his rib cage. Without saying a word not wanting to upset Asho, his first thoughts were that it didn't look good, he'd taken the bullet right near his heart. "Fish… stay awake," Ellis cried out, as he patted the side of his face.

Asho was hysterical, he pushed Ellis out of the Way and sat on the floor with his legs outstretched and held Fish's head close to his chest.

Sergeant Ellis stood up and looked towards Inspector Dunn, who was ending a call. Waving his phone in the air, he called out for all to hear. "The ambulance is on its way. Let's hope they're quick."

The two officers who were on guard at the front of the building burst through the fire exit doors after hearing gunshots while at their posts outside the building. "Anything we can do, Sir?" One of them asked.

Green dragged Pullman to his feet and pushed him towards the officers. "Yep, you can take these two," he scowled as he removed the box from the woman's grip and handed her to the other officer who placed the cuffs on her and led them out through the fire exit.

Superintendent Green pulled Dunn to one side. "That's got rid of those two perverts. Vice squad is going to be pleased to see that man. What d'you reckon her story is? I know she wasn't much of a looker... but geez, is she that desperate?"

"I'd say he's paying her," Dunn replied.

"You'd want to be paid big bucks to service that obnoxious turd," Green said as they both laughed under their breaths.

"I've phoned for another paddy wagon," Dunn announced.

Ellis sat on the floor next to Asho as he cradled Fish's limp body and rocked to and fro.

"The ambulance is on its way, buddy."

Asho wiped his eyes with the back of his free hand. "Bloody hay fever," he said, sniffing, then gave a nervous laugh.

Ray smiled as he reached over and patted his back. "Stay with it,"

To their surprise, a sound emitted from Fish's throat as he tried to speak. "I'm sorry Ash… that was stupid of me wasn't it?" he whispered.

"Don't talk now, save your strength. I have to say, it's getting to be a bit of a habit, taking you to the hospital, you've got me a nervous wreck," he said, trying desperately to make light of the horrible situation they were in, hoping to keep Fish's spirits up.

The paramedics calmly worked on Fish's limp body before placing him, semi-conscious, onto a stretcher and moving swiftly through the building and out into the lane. As the stretcher was carefully lifted into the ambulance, the shrill sound of a police siren could be heard drawing closer. Ellis stood next to a bedraggled Asho, his shirt spattered in blood. "Go with him, I'll talk to you tomorrow."

The police paddy wagon, with two officers, screeched into the lane and parked behind the ambulance. Superintendent Green beckoned the two officers to where he and Inspector Dunn were standing next to the two men.

"They're all yours," Dunn called out, as he and Green pushed McPherson and Wallace towards the officers to take away.

As they stood on the curbside watching the police vehicle disappear into the distance, Inspector Dunn turned to Ellis and gave a loud sigh. "What was it you said this morning about notching up another experience, Raymond?" I think I might just stick to my humdrum life."

Ellis grinned as he replied. "Where's your sense of adventure, Sir? These things are sent to try us."

Sounding concerned, Superintendent Green grabbed Dunn's good arm. "Stephen, you go too, you're not looking too good and that arm needs to be fixed up."

"I won't argue with you this time," he replied, under his breath.

"Well, that's a first," he smiled.

As Inspector Dunn was about to climb into the ambulance, he turned to Sergeant Ellis and placed a hand on his shoulder. "You see people in their true colours in times of adversity, Raymond. I certainly saw yours today. Well done."

"All in a day's work, Sir," he winked.

About the Author

Geoff is an emerging writer, his genre, crime thrillers and murder mysteries. After retiring from his own hectic business in the building industry and finding time on his hands; but not wanting to go down 'the Grey Nomad' rout, he decided to put pen to paper and unleash the ideas he had for his own stories, buzzing around in his head. While Geoff favors more action and mayhem, his wife, Lyn, whom he collaborated with, prefers romance. Marrying them together, they produced their first fiction novel, *Dark Gold*, under the pen name, Geoff Lynn; with three more stories in the pipeline.

Thirty five years ago Lyn and Geoff made up their minds to leave the UK and head to Australia. With their young family, they left the busy North London suburb, Muswell Hill; where bumping into a famous actor or musician while grocery shopping was a regular occurrence; and chose to settle in a quiet coastal town, close to the Hunter Valley of New South Wales, famous for its vineyards. That, together with owning their own travel agency, meant they could fulfill two of their many loves, travel and wine. Other things that make them happy are getting together with friends for good conversation and laughs over dinner. And with seven grandchildren, there's never a dull moment.